Having studied psychology and criminology at King's College, Cambridge, Ruth Newman loved the city so much that she stayed, and now works as a Web editor for the University's Judge Business School. *Twisted Wing* is her first novel.

Visit www.ruthnewman.net

Praise for *Twisted Wing*

'I absolutely loved it. It was so gripping, and I was both desperate and reluctant to get to the end. I found it scary, tantalizingly unpredictable and very, very hard to put down' Sophie Hannah

'A well-paced, rigorously researched and captivating crime novel' *Spectator*

'Intricate and gripping' *Woman & Home*

Twisted Wing

RUTH NEWMAN

POCKET
BOOKS

LONDON • SYDNEY • NEW YORK • TORONTO

First published in Great Britain by Long Barn Books, 2008
This edition published by Pocket Books UK, 2010
An imprint of Simon & Schuster UK Ltd
A CBS COMPANY

1 3 5 7 9 10 8 6 4 2

Simon & Schuster UK Ltd
1st Floor
222 Gray's Inn Road
London WC1X 8HB

Simon & Schuster Australia
Sydney

www.simonandschuster.co.uk

A CIP catalogue record for this book
is available from the British Library

ISBN 978-1-84739-248-0

Typeset by M Rules
Printed by CPI Cox & Wyman, Reading, Berkshire RG1 8EX

For my dad, David Newman: the smartest, funniest, stubbornest, most generous father a girl could ever want. You taught me to know myself, and to not care what anyone else might think. You gave me Woody Allen movies, serial killer books, carnation-eating in curry houses, vibrating leg syndrome, salad sandwiches, biting camels, atheism, Saturdays in old churches and mouldy hot cross buns. I can't tell you how much I love you.

Acknowledgments

I'd like to thank the following for all their help, feedback and advice on *Twisted Wing*: Mike Aitken Deakin, Raoul and Lorna Antelme, John Aspden, Gaia Banks, Julia Deakin, Adina Ezekiel, Vivien Green, Sharon Hicks, Susan Hill Wells, Tracey Horn, Sophie Janson, Grant Jerkins, Jane Kennerley, Linden Lawson, Sophie Legrand, Tim Loynes, Una McCormack, Charlie Middleton, Paul Miller, David Newman, Vanesther Rees, Susanna Sabbagh, Philip Stiles, Paul Taylor, Brett Van Toen, Sylvia Van Toen, Steve Woolfries, Vashti Zarach, all the Gurneys, and everyone at Simon & Schuster and Long Barn.

Twisted
Wing

Chapter One

Matthew Denison thought he was probably going to be sick. The last time he'd seen a murder victim was in the morgue during his medical degree, and back then he'd had to fight not to collapse in an embarrassed heap on the autopsy room floor. He was already sweating and feeling jumpy, and he wasn't even at the crime scene yet. What would he do if he saw the body and had to throw up?

Detective Chief Inspector Stephen Weathers glanced at him sideways as they drove along. 'Are you going to be all right, Matt? You know you don't have to come.'

Denison lowered the car window to get some air. 'We should take advantage of the fact I happened to be here.'

'This death . . . we don't know it's related,' Weathers said. He switched on the radio. Denison said nothing: they both knew that a murder at Ariel College was only going to mean one thing.

The DJ on the local Cambridge station was already talking about the murder, even though Weathers had only just got the call himself, even though it was late at night. Denison suddenly realized there were likely to be journalists at the college, and started to straighten his tie and run a shaky hand through his hair.

The familiar twin spires of Ariel's chapel appeared above

the rooftops of the houses and shops as they drew nearer. They rounded a corner and the chapel was revealed in all its Gothic glory. Denison blinked. It seemed to be glowing a shocking pink.

Even from the far end of the road they could see the cluster of vans and cars, men and women with microphones and cameras and clipboards. Blue lights flashed from the roofs of three panda cars, though the sirens were silent.

Weathers pulled up as close to Ariel's gatehouse as possible and they walked through the horde of reporters and a lightning storm of camera flashes. Denison kept his head down, but at one point he self-consciously readjusted his glasses, realizing with embarrassment that he was doing so in order to make it obvious he wasn't wearing handcuffs, just in case any of the reporters got the wrong idea about what he was doing with a CID officer. He had once written a paper on the contagiousness of paranoia; he wondered now if perhaps he was spending too much time with his patients.

A sergeant escorted them through a small door that was cut into the larger wooden gate of the gatehouse. On the other side they were greeted by the sight of hundreds of students in evening gowns and dinner jackets. The students were huddled in groups. Some sat on the lawn, despondent. Many of the girls wore their boyfriends' jackets over their glamorous dresses, and a few were wrapped up in police-issued blankets. They talked to each other in hushed voices, but there was no excitement in their tone. Their faces seemed pale despite their summer tans. One girl looked up at Denison, her eyes like smudges of soot in their sockets.

'It was their May Ball tonight,' the sergeant said quietly.

'That's why the chapel's lit up like a Christmas tree and there's a bouncy castle on the front lawn.'

'They know about the murder?' Weathers asked as they passed the students, who in the darkness looked like grey battlefield ghosts.

'They don't know who's been killed, but yes, they're aware there's been another murder.'

They walked under an archway, below the college library, and entered Carriwell Court. Gravel crunched under their feet. Chinese lanterns radiated colour into the shadows. There were more police here, but only two students – a boy and a girl – who were talking to officers on opposite sides of the courtyard.

Denison took a good lungful of the warm night air before following Weathers and the sergeant through a doorway and up the stone staircase. He could hear voices, and as they reached the top of the stairs he could smell something unpleasant: a strange coppery scent, combined with ammonia and the stench of vomit.

Denison paused at the top of the staircase, holding on tight to the wooden banister. Half an hour ago we were having a beer, he thought. What the fuck am I doing here?

Weathers turned back. 'You really don't have to do this, Matt,' he reiterated. 'If it's anything like the last two, it will stay in your brain for ever.'

Denison tried to shrug. His mouth was dry. 'I want to help.'

Weathers nodded. He said nothing more, but turned and let Denison follow him into a room bustling with people.

There was a young man in a dinner jacket, with blood and God knows what else on his hands and trousers. His white shirt was smeared with it. 'I was trying to put them back,' he kept saying to a WPC. 'I was just trying to put them back.'

In another corner a girl was curled up in the foetal position. She was bright red with the blood that covered her. At first glance Denison took her to be naked, then realized her bra and knickers were soaked through with the stuff. A paramedic was trying to shine a torch in her eyes. Denison instinctively went over to see if he could help. The girl was rocking to and fro, eyes unseeing, her pupils huge and black, ringed with only a thin line of iris. Her lips were moving but she made no sound.

'Is she hurt?' he asked the paramedic.

The paramedic shook his head. 'Not as far as I can tell. Not physically, at least. The blood doesn't seem to be hers.'

'Jesus Christ,' Denison heard Weathers say. He stood up, and as the paramedics and police officers and pathologists shifted position, he saw, between and beyond them, the body that lay spreadeagled on the floor in a pool of blood, torn open, intestines dragged out and over the floorboards.

Chapter Two

'She's completely withdrawn,' Denison said into his mobile.

DCI Weathers' voice sounded frustrated. 'What does that mean? She's still catatonic?' The girl they'd discovered at the murder scene had been unable to move, let alone communicate. Following a check-up at the local A&E, Denison had her transferred to the hospital ward of Coldhill, the London psychiatric institution where he worked. Weathers had been on the phone nearly every waking hour since, desperate to talk to the girl who had apparently witnessed the Cambridge Butcher's latest slaying.

'What she's exhibiting is severe psychomotor retardation, but I suppose the layman's term would be catatonia. I've prescribed antidepressants, but they tend to take a while to work. If she's like this too long there's a risk she'll die from malnutrition; we might need to resort to ECT.'

Denison was looking through the window into Olivia Corscadden's room, where the girl was tucked up into tight white sheets on a hospital bed. There was an IV in her arm providing her with enough liquid to prevent her becoming dehydrated, but the nurses had to feed her like a baby, mashing up the food and spooning it into her mouth. Half the food ended up on the paper napkin spread across her chest; half she seemed to be swallowing on autopilot, blank-eyed.

She was a pretty girl, Denison thought, even with the black eye and the split lip. Not for the first time he wondered what had provoked this extreme response. Had she really witnessed the murder? Had she herself fought off the killer?

Was the identity of the Cambridge Butcher locked away in that broken mind?

'Bloody hell, Matt, she's already been out of it for three days. How much longer are we talking?'

'It could be days, weeks or months,' replied Denison, and held the phone away from his ear for a moment in anticipation of his friend's response. When Weathers had stopped swearing, he said: 'Look, what the hell do you expect me to do? I can't snap my fingers and wake her up. You'll just have to be patient.'

'This is the last bloody thing we need,' said Weathers. 'We're about to release Hardcastle.'

'You're letting him go?' asked Denison, surprised. Nick Hardcastle claimed he had walked into June Okeweno's room to find her dead and Olivia nearly unconscious, but forensic analysis of the murder weapon had told a different story.

'Only on police bail. He's got to stay with his parents and report in on a regular basis.'

'But I thought his prints were on the knife?'

'They were. Unfortunately it turns out the knife came from the communal kitchen he shares with the others on that staircase. We found some partials from one of the other students on the bloody thing too.'

'And let me guess,' said Denison, 'the CPS said that meant you couldn't charge him?'

'Got it in one,' Weathers confirmed. 'So basically, until your Sleeping Beauty wakes up and gives us a statement, we're treading water. Look, if I can't convince you to inject her with a pint of adrenaline so I can interview her, maybe you can make yourself useful and come back to Cambridge. You see the papers today?'

'No, I've been here since four in the morning,' Denison answered. 'But the car's still in the garage, so if I catch the train I can grab some reading material at the station.'

'One or two journalists seem to think me being made SIO means the powers-that-be now accept it's a serial,' said Weathers.

'I guess it does,' said Denison. 'I hope you feel vindicated?'

A huffing sound came down the line. 'No. Just pissed off that the tabloids were right when my bosses were wrong. Call me when you get in.'

All the red tops in the King's Cross branch of WHSmith carried headlines about the murder: 'CLUELESS' was emblazoned on the *Sun*. 'TWO KILLERS?' posited the *Mirror*. 'COMA GIRL WITNESSED MURDER,' read the *Daily Star*. Denison bought them along with his regular paper and caught the 10.52 to Cambridge.

He got a seat by the window and opened the *Guardian*. On page three there was a longish article about the significance of Stephen Weathers being made Senior Investigative Officer on the case. The paper apparently had a source in the police, who claimed – accurately, Denison happened to know – that Weathers had lost favour among his superiors when he refused to back down on his assertion that one

killer was responsible for both the recent deaths of two
female students from the same Cambridge college. Another
officer had been put in charge of the second homicide investigation, leaving Weathers on the sidelines watching
potential leads and avenues of inquiry get missed by a man
who was determined to prove their bosses right that the
murders were unrelated.

And now a third student was dead; there could be no
doubt in anyone's mind that a serial killer was stalking the
grounds of Ariel College.

Denison folded away the paper and shook open the pages
of the *Daily Star*. The tabloid's story was focused on Olivia
Corscadden, the student currently lying in the hospital ward
of Denison's psychiatric unit. They erroneously reported
that she was in a coma, probably as a result of being
assaulted by the killer, and was in a critical condition. He
jumped a little when he saw his name – 'Dr Matthew
Denison was unavailable for comment.' He assumed his
personal assistant, Janey, had hung up on them.

Denison flipped the pages until he came across an edito-
rial on the case, which ended: 'Did the Butcher think he'd
killed her too? And if so, what was his reaction to the news
that she survived and can no doubt identify him? Could
Olivia Corscadden's life still be in danger?'

As he swapped the *Star* for the *Mirror*, Denison sensed he
was being watched. He lowered the paper and caught the
eye of a haughty-looking man with shiny brown brogues
and what Denison thought of as a public schoolboy haircut
(floppy, centre-parted, long enough just to brush the collar),
staring at him from a few seats away.

The man very slowly and deliberately shifted his gaze

down to the front page of the tabloid before glaring back up at Denison, and the psychiatrist experienced the same small lurch in his stomach he felt when he made a social faux pas – what if the man was a friend of one of the victims? He glanced around the carriage and realized at least half of his fellow passengers were in their late teens and early twenties; he could well be sharing a carriage with a load of Ariel College students. They wouldn't know he was involved in the investigation – to them he would just be a man who was entertaining himself with all the gory details of the latest murder, performing the reader's equivalent of rubbernecking at a car crash.

Denison tucked the tabloids under his briefcase and buried himself in the World News section of the *Guardian*. He was relieved when the train reached Cambridge station.

'Come to Ariel,' said Weathers when he called him. 'I've got to speak to the press in ten minutes, but there'll be a uniform keeping an eye out for you.'

Denison was not thrilled about the prospect of heading back to the murder site, not with the smell of blood and guts still so fresh in his memory. Ariel was such a beautiful college, an elaborate set of Gothic buildings that dated back to the 1400s, but since the murders he'd begun to think of it as a festering trap, the way an arachnophobe might think of a spider's web. Would it ever seem like just a college again, or would it for ever be a sinister place now, with the same connotations as Rillington Place or Cromwell Street? The houses of Christie and West had been torn down after their trials. That could hardly happen to Ariel College.

A gang of journalists had set up camp outside the college. As his taxi pulled up outside the gatehouse, Denison saw a young student emerge from its door and become immediately submerged by the reporters. The student fought his way through them to his bike, chained up in the cobbled area outside, unlocked it and hopped on. The reporters ignored his silence and kept throwing questions at him.

'Get out of the fucking way!' the student yelled, front wheel wobbling furiously as he tried to stay balanced without actually being able to move. He cycled over one photographer's foot and made his escape down Ariel Lane.

'Your turn,' said the taxi driver to Denison, giving him his change. Denison grimaced in response and got out of the cab.

The reporters recognized him straightaway.

'How's Olivia, Dr Denison?' one asked.

'Has she given a statement yet?' enquired another. 'Can she identify the Butcher?'

'No comment,' said Denison, looking through them for the PC who was meant to be guiding him through this melee. A young officer, sweltering in his full uniform, caught Denison's eye and finally realized who he was.

'Now then lads,' he said, reaching an arm through the crowd and grabbing Denison's elbow. 'Let the doctor through.'

'Where's Weathers?' Denison asked him once they'd broken free of the pack.

'He's just about to issue a statement,' said the PC. 'Heads up, here they come now.'

The door in the gate to Ariel opened and Weathers emerged, at six foot one unable to walk through without ducking. He strode up to the journalists and photographers, running a hand through hair that somewhat undermined his seniority by being a shade too dark; he was the only person Denison knew who was actually hoping for some grey hairs. Behind him followed his sergeant, and an older gentleman Denison didn't recognize. Glancing at each face before him as the reporters streamed in his direction, Weathers spotted Denison to his right and nodded to him.

'You and the DCI go way back, don't you, sir?' asked the PC.

'Twenty years back,' said Denison. 'We were at university together in Edinburgh.'

'What was he like as a student, sir?' asked the young constable with a smile at the corner of his mouth. 'Bit of a swot? Early nights before an exam and all that?'

Denison marvelled at the persona Weathers seemed to have created for his colleagues. From what Denison remembered, he had been the one asking Weathers to keep down the music as his housemate hosted yet another poker session, this time the night before their first final. What galled him most was that he and Weathers had achieved the same grade.

'That's right,' Denison fibbed to the constable. 'Would only drink at weekends, and went for a five-mile run every morning while the rest of us were having a lie-in.' That last bit was true, anyway.

As he watched his old friend address the crowd, he felt a strange sense of pride. He and Steve had known each other for nearly two decades now, but he could still remember those times at university when they'd got drunk together, slept on each other's floors, played practical jokes on their friends . . . Who would believe this serious, competent chief inspector who was running a major investigation was the same man who as a student had broken into the vice chancellor's office in the dead of night and released five ducks he'd kidnapped earlier from the local pond? Even now it made Denison laugh to imagine the vice chancellor's face when he'd arrived at work the next morning and discovered his new office mates.

'The 21-year-old male arrested yesterday in connection with the murder of June Okeweno at Ariel College on the seventeenth of June has now been bailed subject to further inquiries,' Weathers told the reporters, who reacted by trying to out-shout each other with questions. 'We'd like to reiterate our appeal to those who were present at the college's May Ball that night – if you saw anything or anyone suspicious, especially between the hours of eleven and one, please get in touch as a matter of urgency. I'm going to hand over now to Professor Raymond Whitley, who is in charge here at Ariel College. Professor . . .'

Some of the journalists tried to engage Weathers, especially when Whitley's statement turned out to be another plea to leave the college and its members alone, but Weathers just ignored them, smiling at Denison as he walked over. He had the kind of sardonic face that meant every smile inevitably looked as if he was preparing to take the mick.

'Hey there, Matt,' he said, shaking Denison's hand. 'Thanks for coming. You know Halloran.' Denison nodded at the sergeant, a potato-faced Manc with a receding hairline and old-school attitude. 'Let's get away from these pricks, eh?'

One step through the door in the wooden gate and they

were in the sudden hush of the main court. It was peaceful here, just the gentle gurgling of the fountain in the centre of the brilliant green lawn, and a couple of sparrows singing to each other from the lamp posts.

'We're doing run-throughs in Carriwell Court,' said Weathers, and Denison followed him down the same path they'd taken the night of the murder. The two of them had been putting the world to rights in the detective's local when the call had come in. Denison had known from the way his friend's face had flushed that the person on the other end of the line was informing him of another murder. If only Weathers' superiors had believed his serial killer theory, there might have been enough of a police presence in the college to have deterred the killer from this third murder.

Too late now.

They walked through the same archway as before and emerged into Carriwell Court, half of which was in the shade, the other half almost bleached white by the brightness of the sun. It seemed a different place in the day, with a set of gently curving stone steps leading to the library doors, and large tubs full of violets and cream-coloured pansies. In addition to the doors to the library, there were also entrances to three different staircases, each with a letter painted above them in black calligraphy: M, N and O. June Okeweno had lived and been murdered in a room on the top floor of the middle staircase, 'N'. From what Denison could remember of that night, each of the three floors on the staircase housed just two rooms, one on either side. June's room had been to the right; the room on the left was occupied by Nick Hardcastle.

Two students, Sinead Flynn and Leo Montegino, had called 999 to report the murder. They'd heard crying, and found Nick kneeling by June's corpse, Olivia in the corner of the room, beaten up and only semi-conscious.

Weathers shrugged off his jacket, laying it over one of the railings by the stone steps. He rolled up his shirt sleeves. 'So, where were we?' he said.

'Scenario number two of five,' Halloran replied.

'The killer, covered in blood, comes out through this door and . . . well? How does he escape being seen?'

Weathers' team used a technique of looking at all the possible ways a crime could have happened, and then using the location, witness statements and physical evidence to pick holes in each scenario until the most likely one emerged.

'Scenario one was that our victim was killed by one or both of the two people found in her room that night,' he explained to Denison. 'Scenario two is that they're innocent witnesses who found the body shortly after the murder. The victim was last seen about half an hour before her body was discovered, which only leaves a small window of opportunity for our killer.'

Weathers walked backwards, leaving a trail in the gravel. 'So,' he said, raising his voice as he moved away, 'we know there were at least four people in the courtyard at various points in that half hour. One of them was vomiting into that bush over there.' He pointed. 'Two of them were here, with their tongues so far down each other's throats that they probably wouldn't have noticed if the Prime Minister had popped by for a visit. Which leaves our Mr Godfrey Parrish. According to Sinead Flynn and Leo Montegino,

Parrish was sitting on the lowest step of the victim's stairs when they entered N staircase.'

'So either he saw the killer . . .' proposed Denison.

'. . . or he *is* the killer,' finished Weathers.

'Not necessarily,' protested Halloran, even though as a card-carrying, socialist Northerner he'd taken an instant dislike to the privileged and upper-class Parrish. 'The bathrooms in those rooms all have windows out into the street.'

'Or,' said Weathers, 'the killer could have hidden in one of the rooms halfway down the staircase, waited for Flynn, Montegino and Parrish to head up past him, and then come back down.'

'And then what?' said Halloran. 'He'd have been covered in blood.'

'What about that gate?' asked Denison, indicating the archway on the south side of the building. 'Doesn't that exit onto Richmond Lane?'

'Yeah, but it was locked that night,' Halloran pointed out. 'It was their May Ball, don't forget. All the entrances were locked apart from the main gatehouse.'

'Everyone inside the college grounds was checked,' said Weathers. 'Someone with blood on their clothes would have been spotted. So, could he have dumped them? And if so, where did he get fresh ones from?'

'He could have taken them from one of the other rooms on the staircase,' suggested Denison.

Halloran shook his head. 'The college's student laundry is in the basement, one staircase along. That's got to be the most likely place.'

They headed to M staircase and descended into a

basement that smelled of washing powder and fabric con-
ditioner. Despite being out of the sun the air was even hotter
down here, thanks to the tumble driers lining the far wall.
To the left of the drying machines were shelves packed to
bursting with abandoned clothes. A shirt, fallen from one of
the shelves, had draped itself suggestively across an ironing
board.

'Jesus H. Christ,' said Halloran. 'If they don't want 'em
any more, why don't they take them off to a charity shop so
some other poor bugger can make use of 'em?'

'They probably didn't mean to leave them here indefinitely,' said Denison, remembering his own year spent in
halls of residence. 'They probably just left them to dry in the
tumble driers and forgot to collect them. The next person
who needs a drier empties out the clothes and chucks them
on the shelf for their owner to get later. They'll probably
come back for them eventually.'

'Well, if our killer did come down here, he'd have had his
pick,' said Halloran grumpily, poking his toe at a punctured
box of Persil that lay on the floor.

'Yes, but not of dinner jackets,' said Weathers. 'Jack, I
want you to look again at the photos of the students from
that night. Look for anyone who seems underdressed.'

'Yes, boss,' said Halloran.

'And get forensics to check out the washing machines. I
know they didn't find any bloody clothes on the grounds,
but maybe the clever fucker stuck them in a Hotpoint.'

Back up in the courtyard Denison saw someone emerge
from N staircase. Both the police officers slowed to a stop,
at which point Denison recognized the tall and lean young
man as the boy they'd found trying to put June's intestines

back into her abdomen. He was carrying a sports bag and a rucksack, both stuffed to bursting, and behind him stood an older man and woman whom Denison assumed were his parents. The father was holding a suitcase.

Nick Hardcastle stopped dead in his tracks when he saw Weathers, anger making his skin flush red. 'Can't you just leave me alone?' he said. 'Isn't it bad enough that I'm going to have to leave through the back exit so my parents and I don't get mobbed by those fuckers outside?'

'Nicky,' whispered the woman with ash-blonde hair, clutching a handbag to her stomach as though it could shield her from all this unpleasantness.

Her son ignored her. 'Isn't it bad enough that, thanks to you lot, my friends think that I'm a bloody murderer?!'

Weathers raised his hands. 'We're not here for you, Nick. This is a crime scene, remember?'

Nick's mouth closed and he looked suddenly ashamed. 'Yes,' he said. 'I know. I was just picking up some of my stuff.'

Weathers shrugged. 'No problem,' he said. 'The SOCO boys were finished with your room. And let's face it, you could be living with your parents for quite a while.'

Nick smiled down at the floor, shaking his head and trying not to let Weathers get to him. When he looked up again he noticed Denison. 'You're the doctor,' he said. 'The one who's holding Olivia.'

Denison stepped out from behind Weathers and put out a hand for Nick to shake. The boy frowned at first, but set the sports bag down on the gravel and shook his hand.

'Matthew Denison. And I'm not "holding" Olivia so much as treating her.'

'Is she OK? The papers said she's in a coma, is that true?'

Denison heard Weathers behind him, clearing his throat.

'I'm afraid I can't tell you that without breaking all sorts of patient confidentiality regulations,' Denison told the young man. 'But let's just say don't believe everything you read in the papers.'

Nick looked relieved. 'Can I come and see her?'

Weathers laughed. 'You must be joking.'

'Next of kin only at the moment,' Denison said, more kindly. 'But we'll let you know if that changes.'

'If there's anything I can do to help . . .'

'It could be very useful for me to speak to you at some point,' said Denison, seeing an opening. 'Would you be prepared to have a chat?'

'Sure,' said Nick. He picked up the sports bag, dusty on the bottom now from the gravel. 'Whatever you need.' Without looking back to his parents, he walked out of the courtyard. They scuttled after him.

There was a silence in the courtyard for a moment, then Halloran said: 'I'm surprised you didn't offer him a hot toddy and a back rub.'

Weathers laughed. 'Don't take the piss, Jack. That promise of a chat could come in very handy.'

'Don't go thinking I'm going to do some covert interrogation work for you,' warned Denison. 'Olivia's my priority – if I've got questions for him they'll have to be about her, not about what he might have done with Amanda Montgomery's head.'

Weathers just laughed again. 'Come on, Matt,' he said, clapping him on the back. 'We've got work to do.'

*

Godfrey Parrish had a set of rooms in Audley Court, on J staircase. Each student's surname and first initial could be found painted in white on a strip of black over their door. Weathers knocked smartly on the outer door, which to Denison's surprise was pulled open a few seconds later by the young man who had been so disapproving of his reading material on the train from London.

'Chief Inspector,' he said, his face expressionless and voice flat. 'How wonderful to see you again.'

Five minutes later Parrish sat cross-legged in a Regency blue and white striped armchair, a window that overlooked the chapel casting summer light on him as he sipped Earl Grey tea from a china cup. He hadn't offered his guests anything to drink.

'No,' he said. 'Of course no one came past me while I was sitting there. Don't you think I would have mentioned that in my statement?'

'Maybe not, if the person in question wasn't someone you'd immediately think of as a potential suspect,' pointed out Weathers. 'A professor, maybe. Or a friend.'

'No,' Parrish said. 'The only people I saw were Sinead and Leo. They went up N staircase, but it was only a minute or two 'til I heard Sinead screaming and we went to investigate.'

'Could someone have been hiding somewhere along the staircase, maybe in a room or down a corridor? Someone who could have been waiting for you to join Sinead and Leo at the top of the stairs, then headed back down while the entrance was clear?'

Those thin shoulders gave a shrug. 'It's possible.'

'By the end of that evening, had you noticed anyone who

changed their clothes? Who maybe started off the night in
one outfit but ended it in another?'

Parrish's eyes didn't blink as he regarded Weathers over
the rim of his tea cup, taking another sip. 'No.'

Denison could tell Parrish's short responses were making
Weathers impatient.

'How long would you say you were sitting on that step
for, Mr Parrish?' asked Weathers, his London accent becoming more exaggerated. 'Alone, with no one to verify your
whereabouts?'

Parrish placed his cup in its saucer. 'I was never alone.
My date for the evening was only a few feet from me the
entire time I was sitting there.'

'So you say. But given her inebriated condition at the
time, she's hardly in a position to confirm that statement.'

Denison had questions of his own, and he wasn't going to
get far with Parrish if Weathers continued to antagonize
him like this.

'This is a Marieke, no?' he interrupted, standing up and
pointing to an original watercolour that hung on Parrish's
wall.

'Yes,' said Parrish, straightening up somewhat. Denison
could tell he'd taken him by surprise.

'It's beautiful,' he said. 'Must have set you back a few
bob.'

'It's an investment,' said Parrish, shrugging again. 'In a
few years' time her work will be fetching ten times as much.'

'So, your date that evening,' said Denison. 'The two of
you met in an art gallery?'

He and Parrish both laughed. 'No,' said Parrish. 'She's a
friend of a friend. She wouldn't know a Van Gogh from a

Vermeer.' He smiled to himself. 'I've never really gone for the intellectual type. Smart, yes, but museum-goers, no.'

'My girlfriend likes to tell people we met at an Ingmar Bergman retrospective,' said Denison.

'And you didn't?'

He shook his head. 'A Halloween showing of *The Exorcist*.'

Parrish burst out laughing and put his cup and saucer down on the antique occasional table in front of him. 'I didn't think people in your line of work went in for that kind of thing,' he said. 'Don't you get enough horror and gore in your day job?'

Denison sat down again, but this time in the seat next to Parrish rather than opposite him. He wanted the student's full attention, which meant taking Weathers out of his line of sight.

'It's the Ken Loach films I can't watch,' he told Parrish. 'The Shane Meadows films, even some of the Mike Leigh stuff. Too real, too grim. Give me a bit of escapism any day.'

Parrish nodded, glancing away at the floor.

'I expect you're looking forward to escaping, aren't you? What have you got planned after graduation?'

The young man ran a hand through his flop of hair. 'Father's got me a job at the bank lined up. Good old-fashioned nepotism.'

'Didn't you just get a First, though, Godfrey?'

'Yes . . . and?'

'Well, it's not just nepotism then. A First from Cambridge. I imagine any company would be honoured to have you.'

Parrish shifted in his seat uncomfortably. Flattery was obviously not something he sought out or even enjoyed. Denison tried another tack.

'You knew all three of the victims, didn't you, Godfrey?'

'Well, yes. The college is small enough that everyone in our year knows everyone else.'

'You were friends, though? With Amanda Montgomery, say?'

At that moment the sun went behind a cloud and the room was suddenly grey.

'Yes, we were friends,' said Godfrey quietly. 'As much as anyone could be friends with Amanda, anyway.'

'What do you mean?'

'Well, she was a bit of a narcissist. You know the type, I'm sure – everything had to revolve around her. She was a smart girl, but in a very calculating way. Had all the boys wrapped around her little finger, including me. Bit of a tease though, to be honest, as I think she was only interested in her bit of rough.'

'Her bit of rough?'

Godfrey chuckled. 'Rob McNorton, the rugger bugger from Fife. Not that he turned out to be quite what she had in mind.'

'No, I suppose not,' said Denison, who knew all about the Rob McNorton story.

'Listen, how's Olivia?' asked Godfrey, changing the subject. 'I understand she's at your hospital?'

'Yes,' said Denison. 'We're looking after her. Are you and she friends?'

Godfrey paused, watching Denison. 'Of sorts,' he said finally. Denison waited for him to elaborate. 'We're not close, but she's an intriguing girl. I've never met anyone quite like her. I think to start with she was quite intimidated by the whole Eton thing, especially with June Okeweno forever bleating on about what a git I was, but after a while she started to see me as a person rather than the posh caricature that I like to present. A sweet thing. Entirely wasted on Nick, of course, but there you go.'

'You don't think they're suited?' asked Denison.

'She's quite introspective,' Godfrey told him. 'She needed bringing out of herself, but I think one of the things Nick likes about her is that he gets to keep that side of her all to himself. Play explorer in an undiscovered country, if you like.'

'You don't sound as if you like him very much.'

Godfrey turned down the corners of his mouth. 'He's a good chap, actually. Brighter than he lets on.'

'You trust him?'

'Of course he does,' said a voice from behind them. 'We all do.'

Denison and Weathers turned round to face the young woman in the bedroom doorway, who had obviously been eavesdropping on their conversation.

'Paula, darling, would you like some tea?' Godfrey asked, amused. Denison had never met Paula Abercrombie, who by all accounts had been Amanda Montgomery's closest friend, but he recognized her immediately. She was wearing dark blue jeans that clung to her curves, and a little white vest that showed off her tan. Her glossy black hair flowed over her shoulders and she looked at Denison with eyes outlined in dark kohl.

'Nick's innocent,' she said in her throaty voice. 'If you're looking for someone to tell you otherwise, you've come to the wrong place.'

'You're friends?' asked Denison, which he noticed made Godfrey hide a chuckle.

'Nick's a good person. Godfrey here just doesn't get him. Nick went to a good school, but it was on a scholarship, and sometimes the scholarship kids can suffer a little bit from inferiority complexes.'

'When Nicky saw some photos of Paula's family estate, he got a bit freaked out, poor thing,' said Godfrey, raising his eyebrows, obviously entertained by the idea.

'Is that why the two of you split up?' asked Denison.

'They were never really going out,' laughed Godfrey.

'We were!' protested Paula. 'At least until Olivia started "bumping into" him at the bar and stuff.'

'Did you know Olivia well?' asked Denison.

Paula coughed up a laugh. 'Not as well as she knows me.'

'What does that mean?' Godfrey frowned.

'Oh come on, Godders, you must have noticed. She'd come in my room and scan the bookshelf, scroll through my iPod, check out my posters. Then a week later you'd be round at hers and the same music would be on the stereo, and a copy of the book you were reading would be by her bed.'

'Paula, you're delusional,' said Godfrey. 'All students have the same books, the same posters, the same music. It's an unwritten law. Don't you remember in the first year, when all you girls were reading the same Jackie Collins books? The "trash fiction lending library", that's what we used to call you.'

'Whatever,' said Paula. 'Some of us are trendsetters, and some of us are trend followers. Let's leave it at that.'

'Are you friends with Leo Montegino?' asked Denison.

'Yeah, good guy.'

'Sinead Flynn?'

'A bit of a cow every now and then, but generally a good girl.'

'June Okeweno?'

'You know those black people who reckon they're cooler than whites just because of the colour of their skin?' She waved a hand dismissively. 'She gave Leo a hard time, just because he wore his hair in dreads. Like that hairstyle is the preserve of our Afro–Caribbean population. It's not like he was trying to be black or anything.'

'Amanda Montgomery?'

Paula stared at him with eyes the colour of wet leaves. 'Amanda was the best. She was such a good laugh, that girl. We had so much fun.' She swallowed back tears. 'And here we are, three years later, and you still haven't arrested the bastard who killed her.' She was glaring at Weathers, who sat back in his chair and just looked at her.

'Paula?' said Denison gently. 'Paula, who do you think killed Amanda?'

She turned back to him, her thick jet hair swinging over her shoulder. 'Kesselich,' she said, hands on hips. 'Victor Kesselich.'

Chapter Three

Olivia Corscadden received electro-convulsive therapy, under anaesthetic, a week after arriving at Coldhill. Her treatments were scheduled on Mondays and Thursdays, and after a fortnight the nursing staff began to notice minor improvements; she would slowly chew on a piece of food, would react to noises and sudden movements, would brush off a fly if it landed on her bare arm. Twenty-nine days after being found covered in blood beside a corpse, Olivia asked a nurse where she was.

'No, you can't bloody interview her,' Denison said into his mobile as he strode down the corridor from his office to the medical ward. 'Steve, she's not going to be fit for that for quite a while. Of course I'll keep you informed. Yes, yes, I said.' He stood in front of one of the unit's set of nested doors – the staff called them airlocks – and waved at the security camera. The nurse on duty buzzed him through one set of doors, locked them behind him, and then opened the others. He nodded to her as he passed, still in conversation with Weathers.

'Apparently she's talking, but she's very confused. They've told her where she is, but it'll take a while to sink in.' He rolled his eyes, grimacing at something Weathers said. 'No, you're right, it's not every day you wake up in a loony bin. I'll call you later.'

Denison tucked away his phone in his inside jacket pocket, where the patients couldn't see it, and waited by the door to Olivia Corscadden's room while the nurse came round with her huge set of keys and unlocked it.

Olivia lay in bed, staring up at the ceiling. Her hair, in need of a wash, fell in curls across her starched white pillow. The IV was still in her arm, but Denison noticed a cup of water by her bed. The door closed behind him with a loud clunk, and very slowly Olivia turned her head until her gaze was fixed on him.

Her eyes, a strange shade of hazel that looked almost gold, seemed to Denison to be so searching that it would be impossible to lie to her without those eyes detecting the deceit. He felt as though there was an owl in the room with him rather than a young woman.

'My throat hurts,' she said, her voice hoarse.

'I'm not surprised. You haven't been talking or drinking much recently.' He walked over to her bed and indicated the cup of water. 'Would you like some? We'll probably have to elevate the bed first.'

She nodded, and he showed her how to press the switch which raised up the head of the bed so she didn't have to push herself up. Her fingertip turned white with the effort it took her just to hold the button down. He imagined her muscles had weakened somewhat during her month-long period of inactivity.

Olivia sipped the water, frowning at the pain of swallowing.

'Olivia, do you know where you are?'

She nodded. 'The nurses explained.'

'Do you know why?'

She shook her head, staring at him.

'What's the last thing you remember?' he asked her gently.

A sad smile crossed her face. 'I was at the May Ball, with Nick. We were dancing, going on the fairground rides.'

'And then?'

She frowned up at him. 'I don't remember. What happened? Why I am here?' She was growing increasingly distressed. 'Did he try to kill me?'

Denison used his voice to soothe and reassure her. It was a rule of his never to make physical contact with his patients, no matter how much they might want comfort. 'Did who try to kill you, Olivia?' he asked, keeping his voice low and relaxed.

'The Butcher,' she said, tears beginning to drop from her eyelashes.

'I'm afraid we don't know, Olivia. We were hoping you could tell us what happened.'

She sank back against the pillows, her grip on the cup loosening so it tilted down and spilled water over the blankets. Denison reached for it and set it down on the bedside table, then patted at the wet spot with some paper towels from a dispenser on the wall. Olivia was crying silently, biting her lip so as not to make any noise.

'It's OK,' he said. 'You're safe here. No one can get in without authorization.'

'I'm scared,' she whispered, looking up at him.

'You don't need to be,' he said. 'We're going to look after you. You're going to be OK.'

'Can I see my boyfriend?' she asked.

'That might not be appropriate right now,' Denison said. 'We'll have to see how you do.'

She turned away from him, curling up into a ball under the blankets. He watched her for a moment, thinking how small and vulnerable she seemed. The victimology of the Cambridge Butcher was clear – he liked strong, independent women. Was this what had saved her?

Denison's girlfriend, Cass, knew from the minute he arrived at the cinema that something was up.

'Bad day?' she asked, head tilted.

'You could say that,' he told her, rubbing his eyes under his spectacles.

'Well look, if you're not in the mood for gut-eating zombies we can skip the film.' She tucked her arm through his. 'Come on, let's go and get a cuppa somewhere.'

They were in a trendy part of London, and after a bit of exploring found a Moroccan tea house. Denison wanted to carry on searching out a branch of Caffè Nero, but Cass's eyes were twinkling.

'Don't knock it till you've tried it,' she said. They ended up perched on a red velvet chaise longue, sipping violet-flavoured tea while tinny Middle Eastern music played from a cheap set of speakers at the back of the cafe.

'So, tell me all about it,' she said, shifting closer to him, her thigh pleasantly warm against his own. 'Is it the Corscadden case?'

He nodded, sipping the tea and burning his tongue. 'She's conscious and alert.'

'That's great news!' said Cass, then saw his expression. 'No?'

'No, it's good. It's just she can't remember anything about what she saw in that room.'

'She's blanked it out?'

'Completely. Last thing she remembers is dancing with her boyfriend at the May Ball. I tried talking to her about it three times today – and frankly I shouldn't have tried a second time, let alone a third – and I think she genuinely can't remember that anything bad even happened. It's not just that she doesn't want to talk about it, or even think about it; she actually thinks June Okeweno is still alive.'

'But surely she's wondering what she's doing in a hospital?'

'She asked if she'd been attacked by the Cambridge Butcher, but I think any of those poor bastards at Ariel would think the same thing if they woke up in hospital and couldn't work out how they'd got there.'

'Was she concussed?' asked Cass.

'Nope. Never lost consciousness. No, I don't think this is anything organic. Psychiatrists used to see this a lot after the Second World War; Vietnam too, probably. The patient experiences something so horrific that their brain can't process it properly. It's a form of post-traumatic stress. Which means she's probably going to be suffering some pretty nasty nightmares and possibly even flashbacks in the next few weeks.'

'Oh, the poor thing,' said Cass. 'Have you told Steve yet?'

Denison sighed. 'No. He's going to throw a complete shit-fit.'

When they got home Denison went upstairs to make the call from his study, a small room with white walls covered in shelving for all those textbooks that wouldn't fit in his office. He could never bear to cull any of his book collection, fantasizing that someday he could afford a house big enough for a library. Lighting a cigarette to fortify himself, he dialled Weathers' number.

Weathers reacted with far less sympathy than Cass had shown.

'This fucking case!' he swore. 'Jesus Christ, can't *any-thing* go our way? How much time will it take for you to get her to remember?'

'I don't know – days, weeks, months?' said Denison, feeling a sense of déjà vu. He realized he'd said the same thing regarding how long it would take Olivia to 'wake up'. 'It could even be years. She might never remember what happened that night.'

'I want to talk to her.'

'That's *not* going to happen – you could cause her immense psychological harm if you just wade in demanding answers. She's my patient now; her mental health has to take priority.'

'The longer we leave this the greater chance that the Butcher is gonna kill someone else!' said Weathers forcefully.

Denison shook his head. 'It's not like I haven't asked her what happened,' he pointed out. 'She's not going to start remembering just because you're the one asking the questions! Christ, Steve, just trust me.'

He could hear heavy breathing as his friend made an effort to calm down. 'So what's your plan?' Weathers eventually asked.

'When she's feeling a bit better we can think about trying

to stimulate her memory with the same surroundings, smells, sounds and so on that she would have experienced that night,' said Denison.

'Right,' said Weathers dryly. 'I'll bring the pig, you bring the carving knife.'

'But in the meantime,' said Denison, ignoring him, 'we'll go down the talking therapy route. It's important that she gets to know and trust me, and likewise that I get to know her. I'll focus on her time at Ariel – that way we should find out quite a lot about young Mr Nick Hardcastle in the process. If she's repressing a memory of him murdering her friend, then her feelings towards him may be affected without her knowing why. It's something I should be able to pick up on.'

'Ask her about the Montgomery murder first,' said Weathers, and Denison was relieved to hear some enthusiasm in his voice. 'Hardcastle lived on the same floor as Montgomery, and remember it was his ex that provided his alibi. Corscadden can't have been happy that he was with Paula that night.'

'OK. But remember, I've got to take this slowly. I can't rush her, not at this stage. Look, can you set up a meeting between me and Nick?'

Weathers grunted. 'I'll see what I can do.'

Denison sat at his desk, tapping his pen on the polished surface. Olivia's first session was due to start, and he knew he had to tread carefully. She was still in a fragile state, and he couldn't risk her slipping back to her silent withdrawal. He had to find a way to learn what she knew without causing her further psychological trauma.

His intercom buzzed and he jumped to his feet. An orderly was sitting with Olivia in his waiting room.

'Thanks, Mike,' he said. 'We'll let you know when she's ready to be taken back to D wing.' He nodded to his PA and escorted Olivia into his consulting room.

The change in her took him aback. Her dark brown hair had been styled into a neat French plait, and someone had given her some mascara and blusher. She seemed composed, relaxed even.

'Thank you, doctor,' she said as he offered her a seat. A jacket hung over her arm, and she laid it on the armrest. She crossed her legs, folding her hands on her lap.

'So, how are you, Olivia?'

She nodded gravely. 'I'm well, thank you. How are you?'

'Fine, thank you,' he said, somewhat surprised. His patients didn't tend to enquire after his health.

His plan was to take his time in excavating the story of her time at Ariel College, getting her used to the level of detail he would need when he did talk to her about the night of the May Ball. In the process he hoped to find out more about this group of friends whose female members were being picked off one by one. Was the group being stalked by an outsider? Or did the threat come from within? Could Olivia really have been friends with someone so sadistic, and not had any hint of the monster hidden inside?

He decided to start with something innocuous.

'Tell me about Cambridge, Olivia. What do you like about it?'

She looked at him with suspicion, as though he was trying to catch her out. He returned her gaze, keeping his expression relaxed. Just having a chat, passing the time of day.

'It's pretty,' she said after a pause. 'Lots of nice buildings.' It was a child's response, obviously not what she really thought. He tried again.

'It must have been quite a change for you, growing up in London.'

She shrugged.

'What was your room like?'

'My room?' she repeated.

'Some student rooms are in the old parts of the college, with bad plumbing and draughts. Others are in newer parts, with en-suite bathrooms and all the mod cons.'

'I was in one of the hostels,' she said. 'By the Market Square.'

'And who were your neighbours?'

'I only had one,' she said. 'Sinead Flynn.'

'Irish?'

'How did you guess?' she asked, flashing a quick smile to sweeten the sarcasm.

'Did you get on?'

'Of course.'

'Who did you make friends with, during those first few weeks when you arrived at Cambridge?'

'Sinead,' she said. 'June.'

'June Okeweno?'

She nodded. 'We're from the same area of London, so we have a lot in common.'

He noted the present tense. 'You're still friends now?'

'Why wouldn't we be?'

He couldn't tell her the truth. 'Well, sometimes the

friends you make as a fresher aren't the same people you consider yourself close to later on in your degree.'

She nodded, smiling almost ruefully. 'I suppose you're right. I'm not as close to June now as I was when we were first years.'

'What changed?'

Something flickered in her eyes, but her expression didn't alter. She shrugged again. 'I guess we both did.'

'Who else were you friends with?'

'Danny . . .' she said. 'Godfrey . . .'

'Danny?'

'So you haven't met him, then?' she asked, one eyebrow raised in amusement. 'No, you'd remember him if you had. He's well over six feet tall, he's got limbs like a scarecrow and his hair's the exact same colour as Heinz tomato soup.'

He chuckled, wanting to encourage her. 'Who else?' he asked.

'Amanda,' she said, and that fleeting lightness was gone.

'Tell me about her,' he said quietly.

'The first time I saw her she was striding across the grass in Ariel's Great Court.' Olivia's eyes were focused somewhere in the distance, her mind somewhere in the past. 'You're not meant to walk on the grass, but everyone seemed to turn a blind eye to it when it was Amanda. It was windy, and her coat was flapping around her legs, her hair was whipped around her face like a halo on one of those Russian icons. She was laughing at how blustery it was. Then she strode on into the gatehouse, where we were all waiting for her, sheltered from the wind, and her hair fell back into place like she'd just come out of the hairdresser's.' Her eyes refocused and she smiled at him. 'When we got back to our rooms later that day, and I saw myself in the mirror, my hair looked like someone had chucked some balls of wool in a blender.'

'What about Nick?' he asked, and was interested to see immediate colour appear in her cheeks, a spark in her eyes. 'Do you remember the first time you saw him?'

She smiled to herself. 'On the river. He was punting.'

'In October?' said Denison. 'Wasn't it a bit chilly?'

She raised a shoulder. 'It was still a novelty back then. About twelve of them had piled into the one punt, seeing how many you could get in in one go, and it was so low in the water that a duck could have swum into it.'

'And where were you?'

'I was on the riverbank. It has the best view of the chapel. I used to go there when I needed to remind myself that I'd really made it out.'

'Out of what?'

'Dependence on other people,' she said. 'Of course, then I found Nick and suddenly I needed someone more than I'd ever needed anyone before. Ironic, really.' Her expression had softened to the point where those eyes, which he'd thought of as burnished gold, now seemed more the colour of warm honey. 'He was the one doing the punting, and even though he didn't know me, when he saw me there he steered over to me and said, "We may capsize at any moment, but if you're feeling brave, we're going for the record."'

'And you got in?'

'I got in,' she confirmed. 'Unfortunately next to Leo, who was only wearing a T-shirt, despite the fact it was only around five degrees, and he did have a bit of a body odour issue back then. So it wasn't the most romantic setting to meet your future partner! But Nick and I kept catching each other's eye, and he held my hand to help me out of the punt when we got back to Ariel, and . . . well, did you ever just know that something was going to happen?'

Denison nodded, thinking of his fingers bumping against Cass's as they both reached for the same packet of Maltesers at the cinema concession stand.

'So what did happen?' he asked.

She frowned, and he wondered if she was remembering what had caused the delay between that obvious first attraction and the two of them actually getting together.

'Nothing,' she said. 'We were friendly, but not even friends, really. I'd always chat to him when I saw him, but it seemed like he was always careful not to let it turn into anything. He'd never get drunk around me, for example, or be on his own with me somewhere private. I found out later that he'd been sleeping with someone else, so I suppose he just didn't want to complicate things . . .' She cleared her throat.

'Then one night in December it all changed. Sinead and I went to a party in Hicks Court, and Nick was there. He got me on my own, and we ended up chatting for hours. I kept waiting for him to make his usual excuses and go and speak to someone else, but every time he refreshed his drink he'd get one for me too, and when someone came over to speak to him he wouldn't let the conversation exclude me.

'Of course, everyone noticed. Rob McNorton was winking at him and I could see Amanda nudging her mate. I wanted to kiss him so badly, but not in front of everyone.

Eventually he said it was past his bedtime and he was going to hit the sack. When he left I was gutted. I wasn't in the mood to stay at the party, in fact I just wanted to go back to my room and get drunk, so I filled a pint glass with punch and took off.' She was smiling.

'That wasn't the end of the story, I take it?' asked Denison, smiling back.

'You could say that,' she laughed.

She took her pint glass and walked out the door, and there was Nick, hanging around in the corridor.

'Christ, I thought you were never going to follow me,' he laughed, and grabbed her hand, pulling her down the staircase.

They trotted down the steps, giggling as Olivia tried not to spill her drink, but nevertheless leaving spatters of punch behind them like the trail of a wounded animal. Outside they were instantly chilled. They half-ran, half-walked to a spot by the river that couldn't be seen from any nearby windows, Nick with his arm round Olivia's shoulders. He took the glass from her, setting it down on a nearby bench.

'Brrr,' he said, and they huddled together, looking up at the night sky.

'You can't see the stars this well in London,' she told him. 'Too much light pollution. I don't know half the constellations.'

Nick had both his arms round her, pulling her close. She felt his hands slide under her jumper to the warm skin of her waist and hips. She hooked her thumbs in the loops of his jeans. He nodded upwards, to the stars straight above them. 'That's Orion. He's got three stars in his belt. That's the Plough. Looks like a saucepan. That faint W is Cassiopeia.'

'What about that one?' Olivia indicated with her nose, having no hands free.

'That's the Great Chicken,' Nick told her with as straight a face as possible. 'The star in his beak is very bright.'

'Uh-huh. What about those over there?' She played along.

'Over there? Those are two separate constellations. The fifteen stars to the east are known as the Dancing Cheeses. The five further to the west are called the Dentures.'

'The Dentures? As in false teeth?'

'It's Latin for washerwomen.'

'Ah, thought it had to be Latin.'

He looked back down at her; both of them were smiling. Then the smiles faded as he stroked her back with his fingertips, and she pulled him closer. She felt some strands of his hair tickle her forehead as their tongues softly met and combined. His hands slipped out from under her jumper and slid downwards, cupping her bum, pulling her lower body closer to his. She could feel the hard bulge at his crotch. His mouth left hers, then he brushed heated kisses against her neck. She felt his breath on her skin; he was breathing hard. His collarbone was exposed above the neck of his jumper, and she kissed him there, gently stroking the hot skin over the bone with the edge of her teeth.

'My room's closer,' he said.

The way Olivia told it to Denison, it had just been a chaste kiss in the moonlight. He had to listen to so many rapists and sex offenders describing their crimes to him in minute details that almost any consensual sexual act seemed romantic in comparison, but he knew how embarrassed his patients often got when discussing sex. He couldn't expect them to be completely forthright, and so he let it pass.

For the next half an hour they talked about everything but Nick: about Olivia enjoying her independence at Cambridge, being away from home for the first time, about making new friends and the joy of exercising one's intelligence in an environment where it was actively encouraged rather than penalized. Denison gathered that Olivia had not had an easy time of it in her inner-city comprehensive, and made a note to dig up her school records and find out more.

Finally their time was up.

'Thank you, Olivia,' he said. 'I'm hoping that in our next session we can talk about what happened towards the end of Michaelmas term.'

'The Christmas dinner?' Olivia was trying to keep her face expressionless, but he heard the panic in her voice.

'Don't worry,' he said. 'We'll take it slowly.'

She closed her eyes briefly. 'When can I go home?'

'Not for a while yet, Olivia,' he told her gently. 'You've been very traumatized. We need to make sure you're OK.'

She stood up then, swinging on the jacket that had lain draped over the arm of her chair. He wondered if the jacket was hers, or if the nurses had found her some old clothing from their stash on E wing. He rose too as she offered him her hand. The handshake was firm, brisk; no hint of the anxiety he'd detected only a moment before.

'Thank you, doctor.' She swept out of the door.

He walked over to the chair at his desk, and sat down with a hefty sigh, pulling her file over to him. As well as the standard psychiatric notes the file also contained numerous copies of items from the police records of the murders, and he browsed through it yet again, still hoping to find that one piece of the puzzle that might give him the crucial insight into the two big questions: who, and, more interestingly for him, why?

His PA knocked on his door and breezed in. 'Dr Denison, there's a problem with—'

She stopped so rapidly that she rocked forward onto the balls of her feet. He looked up and realized she'd seen the photo at the top of the pile from the Amanda Montgomery crime scene. Despite her usual over-enthusiasm with the blusher, he saw the colour in her skin had drained away.

She couldn't tear her eyes from the picture. 'But . . . where's her head?'

He tucked the photos back in their envelope.

'It was never found,' he said.

Chapter Four

Weathers drove the unmarked police car down a country road, past a pub called The Three Pheasants, and then into a short, tree-lined driveway that ended in front of a detached house.

'Nice,' said Denison, looking at the Hardcastles' home.

'Apparently they're mortgaged up to the hilt,' said Weathers. 'Look, you're going to have to be careful here.'

'I know, I know,' said Denison, straightening his clothes as he got out of the car. 'No questions about the last murder.'

'Not if you want to interview him in his natural habitat, anyway—'

Weathers was prevented from saying any more by the appearance at the front door of Nick's parents. Geoff Hardcastle was fifty-ish, with glasses, a beard, and a small paunch that thrust out jauntily from under his red jumper. His wife, Valerie, was a few years younger, her blonde hair sprayed into place, wearing a tight pair of jeans that showed off her trim figure. She was playing nervously with the gold locket round her neck.

'Thanks for seeing me,' said Denison, introducing himself. Weathers stayed silent – he wasn't popular with the Hardcastles.

'I'll go and get Nick,' said Geoff, heading off up the stairs as Valerie went into the kitchen to make them coffee. Denison took the opportunity to look around the living room. It was impeccably clean and tidy, the books on the bookshelves in alphabetical order, each spine arranged flush with the edge of the shelf. Even the logs in the fireplace were assembled with care, no sign of soot or ash on the hearth.

Above the fireplace was a framed studio portrait featuring Valerie seated on a plush chair, legs crossed discreetly at the ankles, with Geoff and Nick standing on either side of her. Geoff had one hand on her shoulder and the other on Nick's. Nick, about fourteen years old in a smart school uniform with an emblem and Latin motto in gold stitching on the blazer pocket, was grinning at the camera. On another wall Denison found a much smaller photo, a candid shot of a six-year-old Nick at the beach, sand in his dark curls.

Denison and Weathers heard raised voices coming from upstairs, then the thump of feet on the staircase. Nick appeared, an expression of hostility appearing on his face when he saw Weathers.

'Didn't know you were coming too.'

Weathers grinned, did 'jazz hands'. 'Surprise!'

Valerie Hardcastle entered the room with a tray of coffee cups and a large cafetière. Denison could tell she felt more comfortable in the role of hostess, offering them milk and sugar, pouring out the coffee. The five of them sat on the sofa and armchairs, sipping from the cups in silence. Nick fidgeted, kept glancing up at Denison, and the psychiatrist knew he had questions for him.

After a few minutes Nick downed the rest of his coffee

and stood up abruptly. 'OK, let's do this in my room,' he said. 'You can bring your coffee up with you.'

Valerie and Geoff looked at each other, apparently uncertain about being taken out of the equation, but Nick ignored them and led the way up the stairs to his room.

It was the standard male student bedroom, with football and movie posters on the wall, sports trophies on the shelf, and clothes on the floor. Nick picked up the discarded T-shirts and boxer shorts and dumped them in the laundry basket.

'Does he have to be here?' he asked Denison, jerking his head towards Weathers.

'Under the circumstances, yes. You're still under caution.'

'Would you rather do this down the station?' asked Weathers. Denison shot him a warning look, and Weathers raised his hands as if to say: 'Fair enough, play it your way.' He retreated to the corner of the room where the desk stood and sat on its edge, folding his arms and pretending to focus all his attention out of the window.

Nick watched Weathers for a moment, then, deciding he was neutralized, turned back to Denison.

'How is she?' he asked. 'Is she OK? Why won't you let me see her?'

'She's improving,' hedged Denison. 'We hope there won't be any lasting ill-effects from the trauma she suffered, but it's too early for you to see her.'

'OK,' said Nick, searching his face. 'As long as she's all right.'

'Nick, do you mind if we sit down?'

The young man glanced around him, realizing there were limited places to sit, and – as Denison knew he would –

offered Denison the desk chair while he sat on the bed. This was to Denison's advantage; sitting on a chair carried more authority than sitting on a mattress, and better yet, the superior position had been freely given up. If Denison had chosen the seat himself he would have risked alienating Nick by asserting his authority. In addition the prompt had reminded Nick of his manners, hopefully taking some of the antagonism out of the situation.

'How long have you and Olivia been going out?' Denison asked him.

'About two and a half years,' said Nick.

'That's a long time,' said Denison. 'Especially at your age. How did the two of you meet?'

Nick smiled at the memory. 'It was my first day at Ariel. I bumped into her in the Porters' Lodge.'

'The Porters' Lodge?' repeated Denison, frowning. 'Not punting?'

'No,' said Nick. 'No, it was definitely the Porters' Lodge. Trust me.' He smiled to himself. 'They were teasing her about her name.'

'Her name?'

'Olivia's her middle name. Her first name is actually Cleopatra. She said her mum was a Liz Taylor fan.'

'So the two of you hit it off straightaway?'

Nick's blue eyes lost some of their focus. 'I fell in love with her the minute I saw her,' he said, and looked down at his hands. 'She was blushing, self-conscious. I just wanted to take care of her, to protect her. She was very uncomfortable at Ariel to begin with. She said she kept expecting someone to tap her on the shoulder and tell her there'd been a mistake. I told her everyone felt that way, but I don't think she believed me. I know about feeling like you don't belong, you see – I went to my school on a scholarship, and it took me a while to feel like I fitted in. After a few months though, I couldn't imagine being away from the place. I tried to tell her it would be the same with her and Ariel, and I was right. She soon made friends. Ariel became her home.'

'Can I ask you a personal question?' asked Denison.

Nick laughed. 'So that last one wasn't personal?'

'I appreciate your honesty. I know it's not easy, talking to a stranger like this.'

Nick shrugged. 'Ask whatever you want.'

'Thank you. If you fell in love with Olivia right away, I was wondering why you dated Paula Abercrombie first?'

Nick immediately looked embarrassed. He stood up and went to his wardrobe, rummaging around for a sweatshirt even though it wasn't anywhere near chilly. Denison knew it was just an excuse to hide his face for a few moments.

The young man pulled on a dark blue hoody that matched his eyes, and forced himself to look at Denison. 'It was just a bit of fun,' he said, his voice low. 'To be honest, my reaction to Olivia freaked me out at first. It's scary, when someone affects you that much. I was eighteen, in my first year at uni. I didn't want anything serious, and I knew if things started with Olivia they were going to be serious. So I kept my distance, and Paula's gorgeous, and she obviously fancied me too, and we flirted, and it was just . . . easy. She wasn't right for me, though. Too much of a prima donna, too demanding, too bossy. One of those girls who seems laid back and a laugh, then you go out with them and all of a sudden they're giving you a hard time if you stay out late drinking, or go to the cinema without them or something. After a few weeks of that I just thought what am I doing here? I know who I'm supposed to be with. And we split up – if you could call it that: we weren't exactly official – and I was free to get to know Olivia.'

'And did Olivia know about you and Paula?'

Nick's face darkened. 'No; at least, not until Amanda Montgomery filled her in. I didn't want Olivia thinking she was my second choice.'

Denison tilted his head. 'You think Amanda was deliberately trying to cause trouble?'

'I know you're not supposed to speak ill of the dead, but she was a cow. Not just because of the Paula thing, but in other ways. She played Godfrey and Rob off against each other. She knew the theatre crowd, could have encouraged Sinead with her acting ambitions, but instead she just made her feel like she was useless. She was a manipulative snob.'

'Well, it sounds as though a lot of people had reason to dislike her,' said Denison. 'Who do *you* think killed her?'

He saw something change in Nick's face, in his whole demeanour. It was only small, but it was almost as if a bristle of energy passed through him. And then he saw Nick hide it, his face hardening.

'You tell me,' Nick replied.

Denison stood at his window. Outside the magnolia trees were shedding their blossoms, coating the grass in a thick pale pink carpet. A magnolia petal, caught in the breeze, drifted past the window. He didn't see it; in his head he was back in that room at Ariel, a feeling of dread and horror in his gut as he crouched amongst the carnage. He knew it was just a memory, an illusion, but it seemed as if he could still smell the blood.

There was a knock on his office door. 'Olivia Corscadden's here, Dr Denison,' said his secretary. She sounded nervous.

'Thanks, Janey. Give me a minute.'

Denison picked up Olivia's file, which he had been going through again at his desk, and turned it upside down. Patients always seemed to have some curious desire to read their own files once they realized they existed. He sat down behind his desk, pressed the intercom button, and asked Janey to send in Miss Corscadden.

'Good afternoon, Olivia. Would you like to take a seat?'

Her hands were jammed into the pockets of the same grey jacket she'd worn to the previous session. A few strands of hair had escaped from her ponytail and were softly curling at her neck. Her eyes watched him as she took off her jacket and sat down.

'How have you been?'

She scratched her neck. 'Not good. I'm sorry if I sound hoarse. I have a sore throat.'

Denison had heard that before, from patients who didn't really want to be there. They used it as an excuse to keep their talking to a minimum.

'Would you like my secretary to get you a glass of water?' he asked.

Olivia shook her head. 'No thanks. She looks busy.'

'OK, so in our last session you were telling me about your first term at Ariel College. We spoke about some of your friends: your boyfriend, Nicholas Hardcastle; your neighbour, Sinead Flynn.' He looked up at her. 'The Irish girl,' he said with a smile, hoping to break the ice a bit, but she hardly reacted. 'June Okeweno and Danny Armstrong. Leo Montegino and Amanda Montgomery.'

'You've been doing your homework,' she said. 'I don't remember telling you their surnames.'

He shrugged. 'They were all involved, all interviewed by the police. Monday afternoon wasn't the first time I'd heard their names, Olivia.'

'Have *you* interviewed – sorry, "*spoken with*" – any of them?'

He looked down at his notes again, evasive. 'I've met with Nicholas. I have another appointment booked with him next week.'

When he looked up again, he was shocked at the change in her expression. Her face had opened up, her eyes hopeful. 'How is he?' she asked him.

Denison sat back in his seat. 'Well, not great,' he said. 'I can't really tell you much, I'm afraid.' Denison still hadn't filled her in on the events she couldn't remember – if he did, there was always the risk that it might affect any memories she later recovered, and could very well call their validity into question if she was required to give testimony in court. 'But I think it's safe to say that he's not doing too well. Frankly, the more you can tell me, the better.'

She dropped her gaze, but not before he'd seen the sudden tears in her eyes. Her hands were in her lap, and she twisted her silver ring round and round.

When he'd met Nick at his home and asked him how he and Olivia had met, Nick had told him a different story to Olivia. Denison was curious about whether this was just a mix-up over the timing of events, or if Olivia genuinely couldn't remember that encounter with the man who'd become her lover.

'I understand that Olivia is your middle name,' he said, 'and that you have quite an unusual first name?'

Her head drew back, almost like a small recoil. One moment she'd been softened by sadness, the next she was again suspicious and untrusting. 'What of it?' she asked.

'The porters teased you about it?'

She crossed her legs. 'Everyone teases me about it. That's why I don't tend to mention it to people.'

'Do you remember them teasing you about it?'

She shrugged. 'Not specifically, no.'

'You remember meeting Nick in the Porters' Lodge?'

The eyes had hardened back to gold. 'No one met there,' she said. 'We'd meet in the gatehouse.'

'What I mean is, are you sure that the first time you ever met Nick wasn't in the Porters' Lodge?'

'No,' she said, almost angry now. 'It was by the river.'

'You're sure?'

'It's not the sort of thing you forget,' she insisted.

Denison noted the discrepancy in their accounts and quickly changed the subject, wanting to build up Olivia's trust in him, not antagonize her.

'Tell me about the day before the Christmas dinner in your first year,' he said, 'if that's easier.' But it wasn't easier: that had been the day Olivia had found out that Nick's first conquest at Ariel had been college pin-up Paula Abercrombie. Her face went grey as she related their argument to Denison.

'I know I shouldn't have been so hurt,' she said. 'I mean, it's not like he cheated on me or anything. I really over-reacted.'

'Your reaction was completely understandable,' Denison reassured her. 'You felt a connection at your first meeting, and there was the promise of something. This was interrupted by what happened between him and Paula. If you'd been aware of it at the time it might not have been so painful, but the fact it was concealed from you made it seem like a bigger deal than it really was.'

She nodded, seeming to take comfort in his words. He took her back, to the afternoon before the Christmas dinner, when she and Amanda had met one of the college fellows for a supervision. It had been a disaster: Olivia was too upset by the argument with Nick to be able to concentrate, and Amanda had ended up answering all the fellow's questions on Olivia's behalf. At the end of the supervision he had looked at her tear-swollen eyes in obvious disdain and handed her a tissue. 'Next time you consider wasting an hour of my time, I would urge you instead to buy a box of these from the local chemist and stay in your room.'

Sinead was next door when she arrived back at the hostel, and made her wash her face and then hit the town for some retail therapy. Denison took her in detail through even the shopping trip. He wanted to know what shampoo she used in the shower that evening, how long it took her to do her make-up and blow dry her hair, what perfume she dabbed on her collarbone and wrists before she left for the dinner, until there was nothing left to talk about but the night itself.

'Do we have to?' she said, her voice small.

'You know we do, Olivia,' he said, keeping his own voice gentle. 'Tell me what happened that night. Tell me about the night Amanda Montgomery died.'

Chapter 5

A cold wind brushed across Olivia's cheek and flowed through the needles of the fir tree on the front lawn. The frosty grass under her feet crunched as she walked through the gatehouse and into Ariel's Great Court.

The chapel was lit up from the inside, the shards of stained ruby glass in its windows burning like embers in the darkness. Olivia could hear the organ scholar practising as she crossed the courtyard, the music haunting and melancholy, making the moths flit a little more uneasily around their lamp posts.

Amanda's rooms were in Hicks Court, a couple of floors above the dining hall and bar. 'Come in,' she called out when Olivia knocked. Olivia went in, smelling a soft, floral perfume. The room was decorated in white and cream, devoid of stuffed toys and posters. A framed print of John William Waterhouse's *La Belle Dame sans Merci* hung from the picture rail on the wall. Some scented candles burned on the windowsill, their flames reflected in the dark glass.

Amanda was sitting on her bed flipping through a book. 'Oh, it's you,' she said. She seemed distracted.

'You asked me to come and get you when dinner was about to start,' Olivia reminded her.

'Sit down,' said Amanda, throwing the book onto her bedside cabinet. 'I'll just get changed.'

She blew out the candles and pulled the curtains, then rummaged through her wardrobe. Olivia sat on the bed and looked away as Amanda stripped to some pretty, pastel-coloured underwear.

'Listen, I hope I did the right thing yesterday, telling you about Nick and Paula,' Amanda said, instilling her voice with sincerity. When Olivia didn't say anything, she carried on. 'It's just, well, *I'd* want to know if my boyfriend wasn't being, you know, completely upfront.'

'It's fine,' Olivia assured her, still averting her gaze. Amanda stepped into a chocolate brown silk dress that matched her eyes and pulled it up around her.

'Will you zip me up?'

She held her hair out of the way as Olivia got to her feet and zipped up the dress.

'If it makes you feel any better, he did a number on Paula too. You'd think she could get any guy she wanted, but Nick just humped 'n' dumped her.' Amanda spritzed herself from a large, square bottle of the same perfume Olivia had smelled when she came in the room, then vanished into the en-suite bathroom. 'Did you see Rob down there?' she called out to Olivia.

Olivia stood up and went to the doorway to the bathroom. Amanda was applying dark brown eyeliner. 'No,' Olivia said, 'but I didn't come through the bar.'

'I've been trying to call him all day, but the bastard's screening.' Olivia watched Amanda slick on some lipstick. She knew she was meant to be interested, to ask why the two of them had fallen out, but she didn't have the energy. She'd been screening calls too that day, not wanting to speak to Nick since finding out she wasn't the first girl he'd slept with since arriving at Ariel.

'I've liked you since the first time we met,' she'd said to him the night before, as they'd walked home from the pub where Amanda had 'accidentally' spilled the beans. 'From that very first day, and every day since, I've thought about you, wanted you. But did I even make an impression on you? Do you even remember meeting me? Here was I thinking it was the start of some big love affair, and there you were, straight off to Paula and ... doing what you did with her, and obviously not giving a shit about me until you finally got round to me.'

'Got round to you? Is that how you see it?'

'Well, how else am I supposed to see it? We could have got together weeks ago, but you obviously decided there were other girls you wanted to try first.'

'That's not how it was,' he'd tried to protest, but she'd turned on her heel and walked away, leaving him alone in the street.

She'd bought a new dress for this evening, wanting to make him regret choosing Paula before her. Amanda hadn't even commented on how she looked, even though it was obvious she'd made an effort.

Amanda stepped back from the mirror, checking all angles of her face. 'OK, ready to go.'

Olivia almost laughed. It had taken Amanda all of five minutes to get ready, and she would still be the most beautiful girl at the dinner that evening.

The pale stonework of the hall was glowing in the candlelight, a huge Christmas tree in the north-west

corner of the hall swamped in festive red and gold tinsel.
Twinkling fairy lights surrounded the leaded windows.
The long wooden tables were laden with plates, wine
decanters and silver cutlery, all stamped with the college
crest.

Olivia strode in, determined to make an entrance even
standing next to Amanda. Her dress was scarlet and
tight, with a long slit up to the top of her thigh, and her
lipstick was blood red. Heads turned as she and Amanda
went by.

Olivia immediately saw Nick out of the corner of her
eye, wearing his suit and a black tie, sitting next to Rob.
In addition to the countless voicemails, he'd come by her
room three times that day, and each time she'd stayed
silent, listening to him knock, listening to him give up
and walk away.

Amanda pulled her towards their own table, parallel to
Rob and Nick's. Rob was in a kilt – the McNorton family
tartan – which Olivia was pretty sure he wore to show
off his well-muscled rugby player thighs. He even had a
Scotland rugby shirt on under his dinner jacket.

'Hey there, Olivia,' he said as they walked past,
ignoring Amanda. Olivia smiled hello at him but refused
to make eye contact with Nick, although she caught his
hurt expression. She and Amanda sat next to Leo, who
had already pulled his cracker and put his paper hat on
over his dreads.

'Girls, you are looking absolutely stunning,' he said.

Olivia was determined at least to make it appear she
was having fun. 'Thanks, Leo,' she said. 'I'd like to say you
scrub up nicely too, but who can tell?' Leo refused to

conform to social expectations by dressing up for any occasion, and was in his tatty denim jacket and baggy jeans.

There was a hush then, as the master of the college stood up and said something in Latin. Everybody else rose too. Olivia didn't know if he'd told them to do so in Latin, or if it was just the unspoken rule that if a guy in a robe said something in a dead language, it meant you had to stand up. He congratulated them on a successful Michaelmas term, and wished them all a merry Christmas and a happy New Year, before reciting something else in Latin that she presumed was a prayer since afterwards some people said 'amen'.

As they sat down, the waiting staff appeared and distributed plates of artfully coiled slices of smoked salmon. The hall quickly filled with the sounds of conversation and cutlery making contact with plates. There was a flurry of cracker-pulling on Olivia's table.

'What do you call a fly with no wings?' read Leo from his slip of paper.

'A walk,' replied Amanda instantly. 'Are these crackers from 1984 or something?'

'"The price of wisdom is above rubies,"' quoted Olivia from her slip. 'Job, 28:18. Great punchline. Anyone would think the college swapped my joke for this in a vain attempt to get me to work harder.'

'Oh yeah, how did your supervision with Russell go?' June asked her, the light from the candles making her dark skin glimmer like polished wood.

'Don't ask,' warned Amanda, smiling to herself as she bit into a bread roll.

Godfrey had apparently overheard the biblical quote; he leaned over from the next table and fixed his foxish face in Olivia's direction. '"In much wisdom is much grief: and he that increaseth knowledge increaseth sorrow." Ecclesiastes, 1:18', he said with a grin.

'The benefits of a good Christian education', said June, rolling her eyes. But Olivia smiled at him.

'Thanks, Godfrey. I think I prefer Ecclesiastes to Job.' He winked at her, and then got back to the urgent business of refilling his wine glass.

Olivia felt eyes on her, and turned to see Nick staring at her. He was out of earshot, but still he opened his mouth as though he wanted to say something. Then he closed it and went to stand up. She saw Rob's arm reach up and pull him back down again. She looked away.

Between mouthfuls of smoked salmon Leo expounded on The Doors' 'Riders on the Storm', and how great it sounded if you'd taken some acid. As he told them about seeing colours dancing on the ceiling in time with the music, Olivia glanced back at Nick's table. He was now hidden on the other side of Rob, whose loud Scots laugh drifted down the hall. Olivia saw Amanda lift her head up and look over at Rob, but he had his back to her and was oblivious. I wonder how many of us are looking at people who aren't looking back, thought Olivia.

Halfway through the main course, Rob was already holding an empty bottle aloft and calling for more Chianti. Olivia's head was fuzzy and June was refusing to let her have any more wine, pouring her a glass of water instead. Leo had decided to convert to vegetarianism at some point between the first and second courses, and the waitress was looking to see if there was a spare veggie option in the kitchen. Bored with the wait, Leo had gone on walkabout and was currently sitting cross-legged on the table of some self-proclaimed eco-warriors, chatting with them earnestly about McDonald's effect on the rainforest.

'He's probably telling them about the time he spent with the Amazonian tribe, teaching them about Sartre and Descartes in return for some berries and barbecued tarantulas,' said June. 'Oh look, his risotto's arrived. Shall we tell him? Do we really want him to come back?'

Leo was very taken with his risotto, unlike Amanda, who only picked at hers before announcing she was going to mingle. This left her seat free for one of Leo's druggie friends to come over for a very serious chat with him about where they were going to buy their coke and speed now their favourite dealer had been sent down for trashing his college room and most of the windows in his staircase during one of his 48-hour binges. Olivia watched Amanda make another student move up so she could take a seat next to Paula. Paula's cello-shaped body was in a tight black dress to match her black hair, which as usual was loose around her shoulders to entice her prey. The only time she ever wore it up was when she was hungover and in no mood for ensnarements.

The two of them giggled, whispering in each other's ear. Their eyes were latched onto Nick as they conspired.

Dessert was next, and June welcomed the accompanying coffee a little too enthusiastically on Olivia's behalf, who had only just realized that her friend was trying to sober her up. Feeling rebellious, she refused to let June fill her cup, and poured herself a glass of red wine instead.

Olivia glanced back over to Nick's table and couldn't hide her expression upon seeing Paula now sitting next to him, body turned towards his, her hand on his arm. Something he said made her throw back her head and laugh, one hand flipping back her hair as she did so.

Godfrey saw Olivia's expression and was over in two seconds flat. He crossed his legs, careful not to crease the trousers of his elegant, bespoke suit. 'What's the story, morning glory?' he asked.

She laughed at him. 'Oasis fan now, are you?'

He pulled a face. 'Bunch of Mancunian yobs. The music scene's really gone downhill since Ralph Vaughan Williams died. But tell me about you and Nicky. What's happened to love's young dream?'

She blushed despite herself. 'Fuck off, Godfrey.'

'Does that mean you're available?'

'Even if I am, you're not. Didn't you get together with Eliza last week, despite your claim you "don't do Ariel women"?'

Only a couple of weeks ago, walking back from a showing of The Shining at Robinson College, Godfrey had told her: 'All you Ariel women are a classless bunch of whores. Amanda's about the only one of you I'd shag, and she must be a lesbian 'cause she's already turned me down. I'm saving myself for the fairer sex of Trinity. They're a much better breed.' Then Eliza, a little firecracker of a girl who had almost been expelled from her boarding school for sleeping with the gardener, had got him drunk and seduced him.

Godfrey took a big swallow of wine. 'Eliza's pissed, and when she's pissed, she's boring. She'll be passed out by the pool table in ten minutes. Anyway, I need a fresh victim to corrupt.' He casually draped a hand on her thigh. Olivia casually stood up.

'I need more drink,' she said, and walked out of the hall.

The bar was packed and noisy, the Stones' 'Paint it Black' thudding out of the jukebox in the corner. Surrounded by so many people and their energy, Olivia felt the fine hairs on the back of her neck tingling. It was nearly last orders, so instead of mere glasses of wine or port, whole bottles were purchased. The diners sprawled around the booths, sneaking fags and drinking. A drunken game of pool was going on at the far end of the bar, at the near end the Pogues' 'Fairytale of New York' was selected on the jukebox for the fifth time that night, and the students joined in raucously, shouting out lines about scumbags and maggots.

Olivia bought a bottle of wine and walked out of the glass doors into the courtyard, which was surrounded by college walls on three sides, and by an iron fence on the fourth. It was quieter out here – a few students sitting around on the benches smoking a discreet spliff, the fish in the pond wriggling away from Olivia as she approached, the reflection of the moon splintering off the surface of the water.

Too late she saw Amanda and Sinead, their backs to her, sitting on the posts by the side gate, murmuring in conversation.

'What the fuck was she playing at?' Amanda was

saying. 'In a place like this it's hard enough to be female – I'm sure half the crusty old fellows think women shouldn't have been allowed in in the first place. The last thing we need is them to think we're all pathetic bags of hormones. I'm surprised he didn't ask her if she had PMT. If she can't hack it she should just leave.'

Olivia felt some masochistic need to hear Amanda actually say her name, but her self-preservation instincts kicked in and she silently backed away. From the bar she heard voices singing about building dreams around other people.

She sat down on the ground outside the open bay windows of the north-east tower, hidden from view, and swigged from her bottle of wine. She didn't smoke, but at that moment she wanted a cigarette more than anything.

The windows opened onto the corridor that led to the toilets. Through an inebriated haze she recognized Rob's voice drifting through the window. What he was saying was mainly indistinct, but she caught some words: 'Amanda' was quite clear, and she also made out 'playing' and 'bastard'. And then there was Nick, too calm and reassuring in tone for her to hear any of what he was saying. Then another voice, someone joining them. This person's voice carried. 'Hello boys . . .' she said in a voice like molten chocolate. 'What are you two up to?'

The girl's voice belonged to Paula.

Rob said something guttural and Olivia heard a door as it was slammed open hard enough to hit the inner wall. Someone going into the toilets? Rob, Nick or Paula?

Not Paula. 'So, do you fancy a nightcap?' she was asking. Olivia could hear the smile in her voice, could almost imagine her lipsticked mouth next to the man's ear. She hoped that ear belonged to Rob and not Nick. Perhaps because she was drunk she found it almost amusing that Paula's voice carried so well, almost as if she thought she had more of a right to the soundwaves.

'"Avoid loud and aggressive persons, for they are vexations to the spirit,"' Olivia murmured to herself, quoting the *Desiderata*. She chuckled into the wine bottle.

She wanted to stand up, to confront the couple on the other side of the window, but knew if she suddenly appeared out of nowhere and it was Rob she caught with Paula, she was going to look like an idiot. Instead she took another gulp of wine, and moved away, heading back into the bar.

The noise hit her again like a tidal wave, subsuming her. No longer the Pogues but 'Hey Jude'. The students seemed to be competing on who could shout out the closing 'nahs' the loudest. Attempting to saunter, but not finding it easy in her red satin stilettos, she made her way over to the toilets, giving in to the temptation to find out who exactly Paula was trying to seduce.

Over the next few hours the bar would get quieter and quieter. The jukebox would switch itself off at seven past midnight on the dot, no matter how much money had been paid into it for songs that hadn't yet been played. One by one the students would smoke their last cigarette of the night, down their last drink. They'd lay down their pool cues and head for bed, either alone or in pairs. A few would have got lucky that night, the festive spirit and abundant alcohol making them both sentimental and horny. Eventually the bar would be empty. At around three in the morning a porter doing his rounds would come along and switch the lights off. The cleaners would arrive at seven, when it was still dark outside. They'd clear away the empty glasses and chuck away the empty crisp packets and kebab boxes. At eight the day-shift manager at the bar would arrive and get the coffee machine up and running, then start the dishwasher on its first set of grubby wine and pint glasses. The power cords on the vacuum cleaners would be sucked up back inside the machines, the cleaners heading upstairs to work on the floors where the students slept. And at half past eight that morning a cleaner called Tracey Webb would find the mutilated body of Amanda Montgomery.

Chapter Six

A constable was waiting for Detective Chief Inspector Stephen Weathers in the small car park in front of Ariel College. He waved the DCI over to a parking space.

The voice of the morning show DJ vanished abruptly as Weathers switched off the ignition and rummaged in the glove compartment for a tie. He had come from his girlfriend's flat, and they hadn't been going out long enough for him to have his own drawer there yet.

The constable waited patiently outside the car as Weathers knotted his tie and checked himself in the rear-view mirror, running a hand through his messy hair. He eased himself out of the car, still a bit stiff from a squash game the night before.

'It's a bad one, sir,' said the PC.

Weathers had known this from his first glance at the PC's face. The officer was sweating, despite the chilly wind. 'Alec, is it?' Weathers had only recently transferred in from the Met, and hadn't been at the Cambridge nick long enough to know everyone's names yet.

The constable nodded. 'PC Alec Liman, sir.'

'If you want to take a break, maybe grab some breakfast and a coffee at the cafe across the road for five minutes, that's fine with me.'

'No. No, thank you, sir, I'm fine.'

'You'd better take me to the body then.'

The college bar was crammed full of students, all of them anxious, all of them desperately trying to work out what was wrong. All they knew was that a crowd of police officers, college officials and porters were huddled in one of the student rooms, and that the whole corridor had been sealed off, the occupants of the other rooms taken elsewhere.

They looked up as he strode through with the uniformed PC Liman. They had seen enough detective stories on TV to know that the guy in the tie and leather jacket was probably the investigating officer.

Weathers glanced over them cursorily, though he hardly expected his intuition to identify the culprit on sight. They looked like the usual bunch of students – some in jeans, some in dresses, some in chinos. There were one or two self-consciously wacky figures with pink hair or nose rings; one guy sunken inside a hooded blue parka, like a tortoise. A girl by the bar chewed her gum at top speed, running a shaking hand through her blonde bob.

Then he was out of the bar and Constable Liman was leading him up the stairs to the victim's room on the first floor.

'The bedder found her, sir,' Liman told him.

'And what's a bedder when it's at home?'

'A cleaner, sir. The college hires them to clean the students' rooms.'

'Jesus, these little sods still have servants?'

'I don't think it's quite like that, sir.'

The corridor smelled of toast and fried eggs, and
Weathers' stomach rumbled. He and Liman ducked under
the crime-scene tape and approached the man waiting
outside Amanda's door. Detective Sergeant Jack Halloran
had managed to persuade the porters that there was
nothing more they could do, and had delegated a WPC to
make them each a cup of hot, sweet tea back at the
Porters' Lodge.

There was a small puddle of vomit just outside the
room. Weathers looked down at it, then up at Halloran,
an eyebrow raised.

'Don't look at me, sir,' said Halloran gruffly in his thick
Manchester accent. 'I've got a stomach of steel. It was a
porter. The skinny one with the big tash.'

'Sounds like we've had half the college staff trampling
over the crime scene,' said Weathers.

'That pretty much sums it up, yes, sir. The bedder – a
Miss Tracey Webb – found the body at around 8.30 a.m.'

'Where's Tracey Webb now?'

'She's with WDC Ames, in a room downstairs. Ames is
taking her statement.'

'And what happened after Webb found the body?'

'She legged it to the Porters' Lodge. The old bastards
couldn't take her word for it that there was a dead body
in the room; they had to come and see for themselves.
Hence the vomit. Finally they dialled 999, asked for an
ambulance for some strange reason – when you take a
look you'll see why the paramedics might not have
appreciated the call-out – and also for the boys in blue.
We got here at . . .' he looked at his notes, '08:56. By
that time the commotion had caused some interest, and

some students from nearby rooms – a Paula Abercrombie and a Nicholas Hardcastle – were also on the scene.'

'They see the body?' asked Weathers.

'Not sure. They're being interviewed as we speak. Took them down the nick to get a bit of privacy.'

'OK. Anything else?'

'Not yet. You wanna take a look?'

The view of the room was obstructed by the door to the bathroom. The first thing Weathers saw when he stepped into the bedroom was blood. There was arterial spray in an arc over one wall, and lower velocity drops on the adjacent wall. There was also a pool of the stuff spreading across the carpet towards him. And then he saw the body.

He ducked his head back round the corner and looked at Halloran.

'No, sir,' said Halloran, interpreting his expression. 'We haven't found her head yet.'

WDC Ames appeared at Weathers' shoulder, wrinkling her nose at the smell coming from the corpse.

'Morning, sir,' she said.

He grinned. 'Morning, Ames. Sleep well?'

'Like a baby, sir,' she replied, not looking him in the eye. 'I've just finished up with the bedder's statement. Not much to tell – she arrived at the usual time, said the occupant of the room, a Miss Amanda Montgomery, was usually up and about by the time she got to her room. Knocked, heard no response, let herself in, got the shock of her life.'

'Jack, can you get this girl's home address from the

college authorities and send some local boys round to break the news?' instructed Weathers.

'One thing, sir,' Ames said, tucking a blonde curl behind her ear. 'How do we know it's Amanda Montgomery? We're assuming that because the body's in her room, but the condition the body's in, it could be anyone.'

Weathers groaned. 'Good point. DNA'll take a while. I'll get the pathologist to check for moles, tattoos, distinguishing marks. But we'll have to get the DNA to be certain.'

'I'll get the lads to make sure her folks know the ID's not a hundred per cent,' said Halloran. 'And we'll get DNA samples off 'em. But first of all you want me to check this Amanda Montgomery isn't one of that lot hanging around downstairs? We're gonna look pretty daft if we're off informing her parents of her likely death when she's down in the bar having a cup of tea and a biccie.'

Weathers nodded. 'Thanks, Jack.'

Ames dropped her eyes to the floor, waiting for Halloran to leave them alone. Then she began to grin as she raised her head to look at Weathers. 'So you remembered to lock up after yourself?'

He nodded, smiling back at her. 'Posted the keys through the letterbox like you said.'

'See you later?'

He pulled a face. 'We'll see. Case like this we'll probably both be on the job till gone midnight.'

She hooked her finger round his for a moment and they smiled at each other, then were back to being police officers.

*

Victor Kesselich had the room next to Amanda Montgomery's and was one of the first to be interviewed. DS Halloran took him to one of the fellows' suites in Audley Court that the police had appropriated for on-site interviews. Kesselich was playing nervously with some loose strands from the sofa covering, pulling the threads out, and Halloran had to resist the urge to smack the young man's hand and tell him to stop destroying the furniture.

'So, you weren't at the party?' he asked for the tenth time.

'No!' Kesselich was sweating. 'I told you, I had an assignment to finish. I don't like the college food, and I don't like drinking.'

'A Russian who doesn't like vodka! You'd be the first I'd heard of,' guffawed Halloran.

'I'm not Russian; I'm Ukrainian,' said Kesselich through his teeth.

'And you were in your room the whole time, but no one can verify this, and you didn't hear anything from Amanda Montgomery's room?'

'Yes, yes and yes,' Kesselich said. 'I told you, I finished my assignment at around eleven p.m. and went straight to bed. I was exhausted. The jukebox was still going in the bar – you can hear it even two floors up – so I put in my earplugs. I didn't wake up until your officer knocked on my door this morning.'

Olivia's interview took place in the afternoon, in her own room at Church Hostel. The second it was over all she wanted to do was find Nick and tell him that they should forget their arguments, that none of it

was important. When she saw the scrum of
reporters outside Ariel's gatehouse she nearly
turned back, but they'd already seen her and surged
forward.

'Did you know the victim?' shouted one journalist as
Olivia forced her way through them.

'How do you feel about the murder?' called out
another.

She pushed past and made it through the gate to the
other side. Crossing the court on her way to the bar she
heard someone wailing, and looked across to the garden
where she and Nick had first kissed. Paula was marching
back and forth along the river path, her black hair loose
and tangled. Throwing her arms up in the air she was
screaming that it didn't make sense, that it wasn't fair.
Two other students were trying to reason with her, to get
her to calm down, but their ineffectiveness was obvious
even from a distance. Olivia watched for a moment, then
carried on her way.

The bar was crowded, but unusually quiet. She nodded
to a red-eyed Sinead; Leo wanted to know what she'd
been asked in the interview, but she didn't want to talk.
She headed up to Nick's room. She needed to know if he
was OK.

Rob McNorton drank tea laced with Drambuie and
listened to the radio. Every half hour there was another
report about the body found at Ariel College. They
mentioned no names, but he knew they were talking
about Amanda. The jingle that preceded the news was
beginning to make his hands twitch. The next time he

heard it he put down his mug, tea sloshing over
the brim, and switched off the radio. He needed fresh
air.

Coat in hand, he trudged down the corridor. The door
to a friend's room was open; as he passed he saw her
engaged in an argument with an older couple, one of
whom seemed to be wearing slippers.

'I've been told I can't leave until the police say it's OK,'
his friend was insisting. She looked past her parents at
him and they exchanged a glance of understanding. Every
Ariel student was in this together.

'Young lady, you will pack right now and come home
with us,' Rob heard her father say.

Once outside Gardener Hostel, in the car park, Rob
saw Godfrey's new girlfriend Eliza throw a suitcase into
the back of her hand-me-down BMW.

'You're leaving?' Rob asked, zipping up his coat against
the freezing wind.

'You bet. There's a killer on the loose, one who likes
cute girls with long blonde hair. Would you stay if you
were me?'

'Stop thinking you're the star of some horror film,
you idiot,' said Rob. 'It's not about you. It's about
Amanda.'

'Rob, I'm sorry about Amanda, I am,' she pouted. 'But if
you think I'm going to stick around waiting for
Leatherface or Freddy sodding Krueger to come and get
me, you are very much mistaken!' With a swing of her
Barbie-like hair she swooped into the driver's seat and
shot out of the car park, narrowly missing a guy on a bike
on his way in. The cyclist and Rob rolled their eyes at

each other, and Rob set his course for the pub. He was planning on getting very, very drunk.

Two police officers escorted Nick to the side entrance of Ariel College, where there were no reporters to bother him. One of the porters was manning the entrance. He patted Nick on the back and asked if he was OK. Nick didn't hear him. He walked slowly, unsteadily, down the path to the entrance to the corridor that lead to his staircase. There were a few students around and they watched him pass but knew they should leave him be. He almost had to pull himself up the stairs using the banisters, he felt so enervated. The smell of the corridor, normally so familiar, would be now for ever associated with the smell of blood. He stumbled over the carpet tiles, round the corner to his room, and there was Olivia, sitting on the floor outside it, leaning against his door. She stood up as soon as she saw him and he let himself fall into her arms.

Dr Matthew Denison – a Matthew Denison slightly more eager and less tarnished than the one who was to meet Olivia a few years later – walked into the incident room and waved at Weathers, who was at the other end of the room talking to a woman in smart grey trousers and a leather jacket. Weathers nodded at him, abruptly finished his conversation and strode over.

'Matt, thanks for coming. You eaten?'

'I was going to stop at the Little Chef on the motorway, but it was closed for refurbishment.'

'Let's do this in the canteen then.' Weathers nipped

into his office to pick up a file from his desk and headed off down the corridor. Denison followed him, worried about the apparent urgency of the situation; usually when they met up they spent at least an hour just playing catch-up on each other's lives. It was strange for Denison to see Weathers in work mode: serious and the opposite of talkative.

The canteen was in the quiet period between lunch and afternoon tea break. They grabbed some toast and coffee, and went to sit at the furthest table from the serving ladies.

'So, what's the story?' asked Denison, polishing his glasses on his tie. All Weathers had told him was that he was working on a murder case and he wanted Denison's input.

'It's a Cambridge student. A girl at Ariel College. Her body was found this morning by a college employee. The body's in a bad way and the crime scene's gonna be a nightmare to process. You know what university was like – probably half the college had been in that girl's room at some point. If she was killed by one of the other students, trace evidence is going to be next to useless, as the killer has probably already been in the room before, legitimately, and will just say, "Yeah, so my fingerprint's on the window, so what? I had tea in her room a week ago."' He paused to take a breath, then took a large bite of toast and a swig of coffee. 'That's if she was killed by someone she knew,' he said more quietly.

'You suspect otherwise?'

'It's just that – well, the crime scene reminded me of a photo I saw once. The body of Mary Kelly?'

Denison put down his coffee. 'Jesus, that bad?' Mary
Kelly had been the last, most savagely mutilated victim of
Jack the Ripper. 'You're thinking it's a serial?'

Weathers swallowed his toast, the knot of his Adam's
apple moving down his throat. 'Can't be. Not yet anyway.
If we had any more like this, we'd know about it. Could
be the first though. I don't know, you're the expert. That's
why I called you. I want you to take a look at the crime-
scene photos, tell me what you think.' He slid the file over
to Denison, who pushed his plate to one side, the toast
only half eaten.

For some reason, maybe because of Weathers'
reference to the 1888 photograph of Mary Kelly, Denison
expected the photos to be in black and white. Instead
they were in colour and he could see the red of the
blood, the yellow of exposed fat, the ivory colour of bone.

Amanda Montgomery's body was splayed out on her
bed, the sheets beneath her sodden with blood. She was
naked, her clothes in a ripped pile on the floor. So many
stab marks punctured her skin that she looked like she'd
been encased in an iron maiden. Long gouge marks ran
down her arms, thighs and calves. Worst of all, her head
had been hacked off, the skin and flesh jagged round the
neck.

'Do you have a cigarette?' asked Denison. His face was
grey.

'Are you going to throw up?' Weathers wanted to
know.

'Steve, just give me a fucking cigarette.'

Weathers handed him a Marlboro and a lighter.
Denison opened the nearest window and leaned out of it,

alternately inhaling fresh, cold air, and then nicotine-laced tobacco smoke.

'There's no smoking in the canteen,' said one of the serving ladies, scratching her hair underneath a nylon cap. Denison ignored her, so she turned to Weathers. 'He's not meant to smoke that in here,' she insisted.

Weathers stood up, gathering the photos back into the file. 'Come on, Matt,' he said, putting a hand on Denison's shoulder. 'Let's take a walk.'

Neither of them spoke as they walked round the perimeter of the large park opposite the police station. Finally, after taking another fag from Weathers, Denison asked: 'This is going to be making the headlines tonight, isn't it?'

Weathers nodded. 'It's gonna be big.'

'A nightmare for you.'

'I think so. Four hundred potential suspects. More than three quarters of whom were planning on going back to their home towns this weekend. So anything you can tell me will be a help.'

'You know I haven't done much profiling,' Denison felt he had to say. 'I mean, I've been at Coldhill for three years now, so I've done a lot of forensic work, but you're only the third officer who's ever asked me to help with an unsub.'

'Unsub?' repeated Weathers, one eyebrow raised.

'Sorry – it's short for unknown suspect. It's an FBI term.' Denison would probably have blushed if his blood weren't still pooled in the pit of his stomach. 'I s'pose I should stop rereading *Silence of the Lambs*.'

Weathers smiled. 'Don't worry, I know the FBI are

pioneers when it comes to profiling. Maybe in five years' time we'll have coppers who can do this stuff, and we won't have to rely on highbrow intellectuals like yourself.'

Denison huffed a laugh out through his nose. As they came back to the police station, Weathers handed the file over. 'So give me a ring when you've had a proper read-through, let me know what you think, and I'll get Sally on to the paperwork to make this all official.' The two men looked at each other, their exhalations turning white in the December air.

'Good luck, Steve,' said Denison. They shook hands and Denison got in his car and drove back to London. The news was already on the radio.

'So, what's the last thing you remember of the night of the Christmas party?' Denison asked Olivia.

She sounded far away as she told him: 'I remember coming out of hall, going to the bar and buying a bottle of wine. I think I went outside. The next thing I remember is waking up in my room, with my neighbour Sinead banging on the door.'

Denison looked at his notes from the couple of hours he'd spent with Nick, and frowned. 'Did you buy the wine before or after you came across Nick with Paula Abercrombie?'

Olivia matched his frown, focusing now. 'I don't know what you're talking about. I don't remember seeing Nick with Paula. What were they doing?'

'Just talking. But when I spoke to Nick about the night of Amanda's murder, he told me you were very angry with him that night. When you saw him with Paula you stormed off. He said you had half a bottle of wine in your hand.'

'I don't remember that. I must have been very drunk. Did he say if he followed me?'

Denison pushed his glasses up his nose. 'He tried. You threatened to hit him with the bottle.'

Olivia laughed despite herself. 'You're joking. That does-n't sound like me.'

'That's what Nick said. Anyway, the last he saw of you, you were walking towards your hostel. But no one saw you actually *in* the hostel.'

She shrugged. 'Everyone was at the party. I guess I was the first one back.'

'At half eleven at night?'

She shrugged again. 'Maybe there were some people back at the hostel, but they were probably in their rooms. I don't remember seeing anyone, but I don't remember how I got back to my room at all.'

He tried again. 'Can you remember what made you go from the courtyard to the corridor where you found Nick?'

She shook her head. 'I told you, I don't remember *seeing* Nick.'

'OK. So the next morning, you say Sinead woke you up?'

'Yeah. She was hammering on the door, shouting my name. I had something of a hangover and to be honest the only reason I managed to get up was to make her stop. I couldn't take any more banging.'

'And what did she say when you let her in?'

'She wanted to know if I was OK. Her eyes were red and I asked what was wrong. She said people were saying some-thing had happened to Amanda.'

'Did she say what?'

'Nobody really knew at that point. All we knew was there were lots of policemen around and no one had seen Amanda. Later on, in the bar – everyone had just gathered there – someone finally said what we were all thinking, that she was dead. And someone else – Danny I think – started talking about heart attacks and epileptic seizures. But Leo said why would half the Cambridgeshire police force turn up at a natural death?

'Then the police said they were trying to locate Amanda and we got really confused. Who was hurt, if it wasn't Amanda? Did they think Amanda had done something, was that why they were trying to find her? Some people tried to get the police to tell us what had happened, but they would-n't say anything. Later on in the morning this detective turned up with Professor Whitley, he's the master at Ariel, and they finally told us that a fellow student was dead. They read out a list of names of people they wanted to talk to and said the rest of us should go back to our rooms. No one should leave Cambridge without permission.'

'Was your name on the list?' asked Denison.

Olivia nodded. 'Yes. Mine, Leo's, Sinead's. Everyone who was sitting at her table the night before. They were already interviewing Nick, Paula and Godfrey. Also her neighbour on the left, Victor Kesselich, who was a bit of a loner. We didn't really know him, so of course he instantly became the prime suspect as far as the group was concerned.'

'Who did you think had killed Amanda?' Denison was watching her carefully.

'I suppose at first I assumed that it was someone from college, someone we probably knew. But when I heard what had been done to her, I remember thinking that no one I knew could do something like that, something so vicious. I thought then it must have been a stranger, some psycho who broke into the college.'

'Who interviewed you?'

'A female detective. I don't remember her name. She was blonde.'

'Do you remember what she asked you?'

'Yes. She wanted to know what Nick and I had been arguing about the night before the party. One of the older students at Ariel had overheard our row and had obviously said something to the police. I suppose he heard us mention Amanda.'

'Did you tell her the truth?'

'Yes.'

'You weren't embarrassed?'

'Yes, but I knew they'd have asked Nick the same things, so there wasn't any point being coy. He wouldn't have lied to them.'

'What else did they ask?'

'Did she have any enemies, anyone whom she'd upset?'

'Did you tell them about the tension between Amanda and Rob?'

Olivia looked awkward. 'Yes. I felt really guilty about it, especially with all the trouble he had afterwards. But I could just about imagine Rob losing his temper and lashing out – I didn't know then how horrifically she'd been killed, and I wasn't going to cover for him if he'd murdered some-one.'

But what if it had been Nick she'd suspected? he wondered. Would she still have gone to the police? Has she blocked out the murder of June Okeweno because she witnessed her friend being slaughtered, or because she witnessed her friend being slaughtered by someone she loved?

Olivia's gold eyes settled on him. Her head was tilted slightly to one side. It was almost as if she was scanning him. 'There's something you're not telling me,' she said.

He felt caught out. Was he that easy to read? 'You know, I was just thinking the same thing about you.'

She looked scared at that. Scared and a bit bewildered. 'I don't know what you want me to tell you.' He noticed that at some point she'd slipped her shoes off; now she pulled her stockinged feet up on the chair, hugging her knees. Some curls of hair that had come loose from her ponytail dropped in front of her face. She began to nibble her thumbnail.

He was looking at her, disturbed, when the buzzer went on his desk. He picked up his phone.

'Dr Denison, you've overrun by nearly twenty minutes,' said his PA.

He turned his back towards Olivia, lowering his voice. 'Janey, this is important. You can't just interrupt me—'

'You've got a meeting with the Administrative Committee in two minutes,' Janey reminded him icily.

He sighed. 'Fine. Thanks.'

Turning back to Olivia he was surprised to see she was sitting up straight in the chair, her shoes on her feet, her hair neat and tidy.

'That's my cue to leave, I take it,' she said pleasantly, and let him walk her to the door, where the orderly was waiting to take her back to her room.

Matthew Denison sat at his desk at the Coldhill psychiatric unit, with his phone to his ear, four pages of scrawled notes in front of him. Data from solved cases showed that certain types of people committed certain types of crimes. Using that knowledge, profilers could look at the details of a crime and extrapolate the likely traits of the perpetrator. More of an art than a science, it was a way of focusing in on the most likely suspects in a sea of people with means, opportunity, but no motive.

Denison scanned his notes to find a place to start, knowing Weathers was waiting on the other end of the line. 'I think you should be looking within the college for the killer. This isn't a guy who saw her that day and decided to break into the college and risk being noticed as an outsider by the other college members. This murder was high-risk even for a student who had a good excuse for being in that corridor.

'Did the killer go there with murder in mind, or something less severe? I would say murder. I think he brought the knife with him. His first act was to cut her throat, which would have caused death in a very short time. I'm not sure yet if he'd intended for her to die so quickly. It's possible it was necessary, considering how easily any screams would have been heard by Amanda's neighbours, and that he would rather have kept her alive to torture her if he'd had the opportunity. On the other hand, it almost seems as though the primary goal was the mutilation, considering how extensive it was. If what he's really interested in is cutting, dissecting, destroying, then it stands to reason he would kill the

victim as soon as possible to reach that goal more
quickly, without having constantly to subdue and
control the victim.

'I doubt you'll find any evidence of rape. This guy's
more likely to have ejaculated in his underwear as he cut
her up than to have interacted sexually with the body.
He'll have been covered in blood. He would've washed
himself in her bathroom.'

'We've got the crime-scene techs checking the
bathroom, the plugs, the drains,' interjected Weathers.

'Good. OK, so the killer is someone who sees Amanda
every day, and is obsessed by her. You're looking for a guy
who knew her, but who wasn't intimate with her, and
wasn't a good friend. It may not be a student – in fact,
considering the intricacy of the murder, it could well be
someone older: this is something this person has been
fantasizing about for a long time. It can take years to
develop a fantasy scenario as extreme as this.

'Steve, this man really hated her. And he didn't even
really know her. He projected something onto her, and my
guess is that it won't be long before he comes across
another girl whom he wants to punish. The girls at this
college need to be extremely careful.'

'What's our suspect gonna be like? How am I going to
be able to recognize him?'

'I can't give you a physical description, other than that
he's male, like ninety-nine per cent of this kind of killer.
This is just guesswork, but I would imagine he's
intelligent—'

'Unlike the other 399 students at this college in the
top university in the country,' interrupted Weathers.

'He's intelligent, but not diligent. He gets bored quickly. He'll have superficial friendships, but will never reveal his true personality to his friends. He bottles up his anger and frustrations, and then will suddenly snap. You might want to ask the students if they've noticed someone losing their temper in a way that seemed totally out of character. Among his possessions you'll probably find true crime books, and possibly medical textbooks. Ones with lots of gruesome photos that would appeal to his deviant and distorted sexuality. More of the same on his hard drive too.

'No doubt at some point early in his sexual history he'll have felt humiliated by a girl – maybe he couldn't sustain an erection, or perhaps he ejaculated too quickly. The girl he was with may have laughed at him, or gossiped about it, or maybe the humiliation was all in his head, but either way it's led to a hatred of women, and a need to dominate them. If he has a girlfriend, which I would say is unlikely, she'll be very submissive, very passive. Not someone who challenges either his ego or his intellect.'

'Considering I'm basically interviewing everyone who knew Amanda, can you recommend a way of interrogating this person that will make him want to talk?' asked Weathers.

'He won't talk. Not if you've just pulled him in for a routine chat. He'll only talk to you if he thinks you've got him bang to rights. And possibly not even then.'

'Great.'

'Oh, one more thing – he'll have kept the head. It's a trophy for him. I won't go into some of the disgusting things these guys have done with decapitated heads in other cases, but trust me, when you find him, her head – or skull – will be in his possession.'

'Something to look forward to,' said Weathers grimly. 'Listen, Matt, I really appreciate this. If we get anyone solid for a suspect, will you come up and advise us during the interrogation?'

'Sure, of course. Anything to help.'

They both hung up. Ames waited for Weathers to come back to the table to finish his curry, and when he didn't she sat next to him on the sofa and rubbed his back, stroked the side of his face. He took her hand and kissed it, looking distant.

'You need to eat,' she told him. 'Keep your strength up. You don't want me to beat you again next time we play squash, do you?'

Nick had agreed to meet with Denison again: 'Anything to help Olivia.' Each time Denison saw him he thought he looked worse. Nick's previously slightly curly mop of hair was now short, cropped close to his skull. There were dark smudges under his eyes and his skin was colourless.

'How are you doing, Nick?' Denison asked, trying to smile warmly.

Nick's dead eyes regarded him without expression.

'Nick, I talked to Olivia again yesterday. She told me she didn't remember confronting you and Paula Abercrombie at that Christmas party, or threatening you with a wine bottle.'

The young man shook his head. 'Well, that's Olivia for you. She'd forget her head if it wasn't screwed on.'

'She's a forgetful person?' asked Denison, remembering

the discrepancy between Nick and Olivia's accounts of the first time they'd met.

Nick rubbed his eyes. 'That's one way of putting it. The number of times I've told her something and then the next day she's forgotten it. Or I refer to a conversation we've had, or a night out, and she just looks at me blankly. Christ knows how she managed to pass her exams; she has a memory like a sieve.'

'What grade *did* she get?'

'A 2:2. Like I said, she was smart, but she was crap at revision.'

'She sounds . . . well, flaky.'

This made Nick uncomfortable. He crossed his arms. 'Just a bit ditzy every now and then, that's all. But I loved her. I *do* love her.'

'Do you ever find there are times when you're not sure where you stand with her?'

'I suppose that's true.' Nick ran his fingers through his short hair, roughing it up. 'One day she can be very affectionate, and then other days she can't bear me to touch her. Sometimes she's sweet and sometimes she knows just what to say to really wind me up.'

'Nick, I know we've covered this already, but I'd like you to go back over what happened after Olivia walked off that night.'

Nick sighed, then repeated the chain of events, his voice flat. 'I went back to the bar and had another drink. Paula had her hand on my leg. Amanda saw and winked at me. I took Paula's hand off and went to take a piss. When I got back to the bar Rob and Amanda were having one of those whispering arguments that you see but don't hear. He was holding onto her upper arm. She pulled away and ran upstairs. Rob didn't follow her. He kicked the pinball machine and left by the other door. I finished my drink and went to my room. Paula knocked on my door ten minutes later. She was wearing a dressing gown and just underwear underneath. She was pretty drunk and tried to kiss me. I couldn't get her to leave. She lay on my bed and eventually fell asleep. I slept on the floor, in my clothes. I woke up the next morning when I heard voices in Amanda's room and then someone throwing up in the corridor. The porters were there. I pushed past them and saw her body. My legs wouldn't keep me upright; I ended up on my arse on the floor, backing away into the corridor. The porters didn't let Paula past, but she saw from my face that it was bad. I remember the police turning up, but I don't know how long it took them to arrive.'

Denison had heard the tapes of Nick's interview, conducted less than an hour after the discovery of the body. The boy had been incoherent. Paula had proven a pretty useless alibi; she couldn't remember what time she'd arrived in Nick's room, or what time she'd passed out. And so Nick had been one of the prime suspects for the murder in those first few days.

'Did you think about who might have killed Amanda?'

Nick shook his head. 'I wasn't thinking much of anything.'

'You didn't think it could be Rob?'

'No. He couldn't do that,' he said. 'No one I know could do that.' But he was looking away as he said it.

Chapter Seven

Denison was alone in his study at home. Pictures of Amanda Montgomery were laid out on the desk in front of him. Not her crime-scene photos, or photos from her autopsy; pictures of her alive. Here she was as a kid, dressed as a cowboy, arm in arm with her older brother. In another photo she wore a bridesmaid's outfit and was looking embarrassed at having to pose for the camera. There was a clipping from her local newspaper – 'Williamsden girl heading for Cambridge' – with Amanda standing outside her school gates, smiling professionally. Denison's favourite was one taken in the summer before she left for Ariel. Amanda was wearing a white vest and baggy, paint-spattered trousers. There was even a streak of blue paint in her hair. She had been helping her parents repaint her baby brother's room. The brother, Tommy, was giggling in her arms.

Then there was the college's matriculation photo. Amanda was almost dead centre. Her expression was cool, almost haughty. Looking from this photo back to his favourite, Denison wondered if maybe Olivia was right in believing the Amanda who attended Ariel was merely a persona. He couldn't help thinking the real Amanda was the one who was beaming at the camera as her brother wriggled joyfully in her arms.

He heard the doorbell ring, packed away the photos and went downstairs.

'This is absolutely delicious,' said Weathers, forking another piece of lamb casserole into his mouth.

'Glad you like it,' said Cass, helping herself to some new potatoes. 'My aunt's recipe. I've been trying to teach Matt to cook, but it doesn't seem to be taking.'

Weathers laughed. 'Matt's culinary skills at college extended to bacon sandwiches and spaghetti pesto. Though not both at the same time, thank God.'

Denison ignored them, sipping from his glass of Medoc. He had to admit that despite the piss-taking it was nice to see Weathers in a social setting for once.

'You've done wonders with this place,' his friend told Cass. 'Not to denigrate Matt's interior design skills, but it just seems a lot cosier now.'

'Thank you,' she said, nudging Denison, who had complained originally about the number of cushions that had materialized since Cass moved in.

'So, how's Sally?' Denison asked, thinking Cass had been buttered up enough.

'Mrs Weathers? She's good, thanks.'

'Sally told me at the wedding that she categorically wasn't going to take your surname,' teased Cass.

'I'm working on her. She reckons it'll be too confusing for the average PC having to cope with two detectives called Weathers in CID. I've tried to convince her that having a surname like Weathers means you get cool nicknames like 'Stormy', but she's having none of it.'

'Shame she couldn't make it tonight,' said Denison.

'Tell you the truth, the investigation's been a bit dead in the water since we released Nick Hardcastle,' Weathers told him, not meeting his eye. 'Until we get some new evidence, there's not much for us to do, so the super's got her working on some drugs case in Cherry Hinton. At this very moment she's probably dressed like a druggie, trying to score heroin from a dealer in some dodgy pub there.'

Cass pulled a face. 'Aren't you worried about her?'

'No.' Weathers grinned, chewing happily. 'She can handle herself.'

Denison shifted uncomfortably in his seat, aware that there'd been a veiled dig in what Weathers was saying.

'I'm going as fast as I can,' he explained. 'We rush this and there's a chance she'll bury it even deeper.'

Weathers put down his knife and fork, raising his hands. 'I'm not having a go at you, Matt. Don't get your knickers in a twist.'

'So, how's Olivia doing?' asked Cass, trying to change the focus of the conversation. 'Has she been suffering those nightmares and flashbacks you were talking about?'

Denison paused in the middle of raising his wine glass to his mouth. 'No.' He frowned. 'Actually, as far as I'm aware she hasn't.'

'Well, that's good,' said Cass, topping up Weathers' glass.

'I thought you said traumatic amnesia was a symptom of post-traumatic stress disorder,' said Weathers, paying close attention to his friend. 'Wouldn't you expect to see the other symptoms if that's the case?'

'Yes,' Denison admitted, 'but PTSD is just one of the possible causes. There are others.'

'Like what?' Weathers could see his friend's mind whirring.

'Like habit,' said Denison, putting down his knife and fork.

'You going to tell me what's on that clever little mind of yours?' asked Weathers.

But Denison's eyes were squinting off into the middle distance, lost in thought. 'No,' he said eventually, snapping out of it. 'Not yet. Early days. Could be on completely the wrong track. Anyway, I'm sorry the investigation's stalled. But shouldn't you be exploring other avenues anyway?'

Weathers smiled. 'You don't think Nick's our guy?'

'If there's anything I've learned,' said Denison, 'it's that people with anti-social personality disorder don't go around wearing hats that say 'sociopath'. Does Nick seem like a nice, normal young man? Yes. Does that mean he can't be a serial killer? No. But what if he was telling the truth when he said he ran into that room to find June Okeweno dead and his girlfriend beaten bloody? That means the Cambridge Butcher is still out there and you're no closer to catching him than you were before.'

'Thanks for the vote of confidence,' said Weathers, spearing a potato.

There was a brief silence. Cass looked between the two men, wanting to make sure their relationship was going to survive this case. She knew how much Matt liked and admired his friend, and Lord knew he didn't have a whole host of close male friends he could confide in in the way he confided in Steve. She decided to change the subject.

'Think you and Sally are going to be able to find time for a holiday this summer?'

The taxi driver who picked up Nick and Olivia at Oxford train station was trying to make small talk with them as he drove to Nick's parents' house.

'So, you two are students then? Which university?' he asked.

There was a pause before Nick answered, 'Cambridge.'

'Blimey, really? You must be glad to get out of there. I'd have been on the first train back home. Did you know that girl?'

Nick and Olivia shook their heads in unison.

'Have the police got any leads, do you think? From what I've read they're pretty much sitting around scratching their arses.'

Nick looked down at the compartment in the driver's side door, where a copy of the *Mirror* jutted out proudly. In the three days following Amanda's murder the tabloids had earned themselves the collective hatred of Ariel's students for ever, first by publishing candid photos of Amanda in a bikini – apparently not even being murdered excused you from the tabloids' obsession with half-naked women – and then by paying an ex-boyfriend from school for his 'I was Amanda's first love' story.

'We haven't been following things that closely,' lied Nick, taking Olivia's hand and squeezing it. They sat in silence for the rest of the journey, till they neared the Hardcastles' house.

Olivia hung back as Nick's parents trotted out to meet them.

'Oh, Nicky, we're so glad you're home,' said his mother, giving him a tight hug.

'You should've called from the train station, silly, we

would've come and picked you up,' said his dad, putting Nick in a headlock and administering a gruff kiss to the top of his head.

'Mum, Dad,' said Nick, turning back to Olivia, his eyes shining, 'this is Olivia.' He was bathed in the glow of the porch light, tall in his long black overcoat. Olivia watched him, breathed in the scent of the winter fir trees, and smiled.

Nick's mum turned to her and crunched through the gravel. 'Hello, Olivia dear, I'm Valerie.' She kissed Olivia on both cheeks, her powdery perfume wafting up Olivia's nostrils. She was gripping Olivia's arms with her hands as she kissed her, and Olivia automatically responded by putting her own hand on Valerie's arm. She could feel the brittleness of it through the silky fabric of Valerie's beige blouse.

'You must be hungry,' Valerie said. 'Come on in. This is Geoff, by the way, Nick's dad.'

Geoff and Olivia eyed each other, both unsure whether to follow Valerie's lead with the Continental greeting. Olivia stepped forward and offered Geoff her hand, then leaned in for one of those kisses in which lips don't quite make contact with the cheek. Olivia didn't like kissing men whose whiskers she could feel prickling against her mouth.

Geoff manfully grabbed Olivia's suitcases and swung them indoors. Valerie and Olivia followed him and Nick into the house.

It was warm inside, a log fire burning in the grate. There were two large sofas and two armchairs in the spacious lounge. The TV was in the corner of the room, an apparent afterthought. On top of it sat a number of old copies of the *Times* and the *Guardian*, all open at the crossword page.

Valerie was watching her, appraising her as she appraised her surroundings. 'Can I get you a drink, Olivia? We have tea and coffee, or I could probably rustle up some cocoa if you'd prefer.'

'I'd love a cup of coffee, thanks,' said Olivia, following Valerie into the kitchen. Valerie filled the kettle and ladled ground coffee into a large cafetière. As they waited for the water to boil, Valerie leaned back against the kitchen counter, clicking her salmon pink nails on the surface.

'How was your journey?' she asked.

'The train was packed,' Olivia said. 'We were lucky to get seats really.' She was wishing she'd worn something other than jeans. She felt very scruffy next to Mrs Hardcastle.

'You should have come earlier,' said Valerie. 'It's always bad if you leave it too late, too close to Christmas.'

Olivia shrugged. 'We left as soon as the police said we could go.'

Valerie's lips pursed. 'Why on *earth* they kept you there I'll never know. Putting you at risk like that! As if any of you could have murdered that poor girl.'

'We didn't mind,' Olivia said, her voice quiet. 'We wanted to help, if we could.'

Geoff poked his head round the door. 'Where shall I put Olivia's cases, dear?' he asked.

'I've made up the guest room,' said Valerie.

Nick appeared at that moment. 'Mum, we'd prefer to stay in my room.'

'Nicholas, you only have a single bed. You'd be terribly cramped. I'm sure Olivia would rather have a bed to herself.'

Nick rolled his eyes. 'What do you think we've been sleeping in for the past month, a kingsize four-poster?!'

Valerie gave him a warning look.

'Well, we are adults. It's not like the old days, with porters patrolling the college hoping to catch you in flagrante with some young filly and get you sent down.'

'Don't be cheeky,' said Geoff. 'You'll get your jollies in secret, behind your parents' backs, the way me and your mother had to when we were young.'

Nick and Olivia spent the next few days relaxing at the Hardcastles' home, trying to avoid reading the papers or watching the news, talking a lot on the phone to other Ariellians. One evening Valerie and Geoff got dressed up to go to Geoff's Christmas work do, and Geoff asked Nick to drive them over to the venue so he could have a drink. Nick and Olivia stopped in a pub on the way back, until they suddenly remembered that the house was empty, drove home just over the speed limit and had energetic sex.

Afterwards, lying tucked up together under the duvet Olivia looked around his room, noting the medals on a hook on his wardrobe, and the two silver cups on the shelf over his desk.

'Hockey and cross-country running,' he explained. Olivia nodded, thinking that cross-country running at her school would have involved jogging through council estates and the local park, which was where the resident pissheads liked to hang out with their stock of Special

Brew. She started to get dressed, Nick kissing the side of her arm as she hooked up her bra.

There was a poster of Oxford United on the wall. 'Why didn't you apply to Oxford instead of Cambridge?' she asked him.

'Why didn't you apply to any universities in London?' he countered.

'How do you know I didn't?'

'You told me once. Other than Cambridge you applied to York, Edinburgh, Manchester and Cardiff. None of which are exactly close to London.'

'I suppose I wanted to move away,' she said. 'Be independent. Get away from home.'

'Well, ditto,' he explained.

'Why? What's wrong with your parents?' she asked.

'You have to ask?' His eyebrows were raised. She frowned at him and he pulled his duvet higher up towards his chin, like a shield. 'Look, Mum's a bit neurotic and Dad's a bit dull, but that's beside the point really. There aren't many of us who are that keen on sticking close to our parents. You haven't even rung yours since we got here.'

Olivia turned her back on him, doing up her shirt buttons. 'They'll cope,' she said and walked out of the room.

Three days after Christmas they got a phone call from Rob. 'Can I come and visit?' he asked. They met him in the local pub. Olivia hardly recognized him – he was pale, unshaven, eyes hidden from view beneath the brim of a baseball cap. He looked at them from within the shadow cast by the brim, not smiling. His brown eyes were dull, his gaze detached, unconnected.

'How are you doing?' asked Olivia, her voice concerned.

Rob pulled his pint closer. 'Not good. How about you two?'

Nick and Olivia looked at each other. 'We're kind of getting through it,' said Nick. 'It's weird being home.'

Rob nodded. 'I know what you mean. Not wanting to go back to Ariel, but not wanting to be away from everyone either.'

Olivia took a large gulp from her glass of wine. 'Everybody here wants to know what happened, but you only want to talk to friends, people who were there,' she said, looking down at the scratched wooden table. 'It feels like no one else is entitled to talk about it.'

'Fucking vultures,' said Rob. 'Have you been rung by the tabloids yet?'

Olivia began to shake her head, but was surprised by Nick's affirmation. 'I didn't tell Olivia,' he said. 'But yeah, we've had a few calls. The same guy rang three times. The first two times my mum told him I wasn't interested – when he called back again I told him to go fuck himself.'

'They got my home phone number somehow, and they've been ringing non-stop,' Rob said. 'I think some bastard at Ariel must have told them who Amanda was close to. They can't be ringing everyone in our year as many times as they've rung me.' He was hunched over his pint. 'I've had enough of it. I want to get back to Ariel, away from that fucking phone.'

'They'll be waiting for us there,' said Olivia. 'At least

when we're all away from college we're too spread out for them to harass us. In person anyway.'

Rob shrugged without looking at her. 'The college will make sure the reporters don't get in. They've got to increase security by about a thousand per cent if they want any of us to stick around.'

'Do you think anyone will drop out?' asked Nick.

Rob nodded. 'Suzy Marchmont has already. Jenny McEvoy is talking about intermitting. Godfrey reckons Eliza is considering emigrating to Australia to get away from the place.'

Olivia laughed despite herself. 'A bit drastic.'

'Apparently Eliza reckons she's in more danger than anyone else because she and Amanda were like peas in a pod. Silly bitch – it's like comparing gold and brass.'

'I hope you didn't share that thought with Godfrey,' said Nick.

Rob swallowed some beer and didn't answer. 'Have you been thinking about who might have done it?' he asked eventually.

Nick and Olivia looked at each other again. 'We couldn't think of anyone capable,' Nick said.

'Yeah? You ever met Victor Kesselich?'

Nick put down his drink. 'You can't think Victor did it.'

'Why not? He's weird enough. And he had a thing for Amanda.'

'Rob, half the college had a thing for Amanda.'

'The police were interviewing him for hours that morning.'

'The police interviewed me for hours too – do you think I could have done it? Jesus, they interviewed everyone on her floor. Just because Victor's a bit of a loner and keeps to himself, doesn't mean he's a psycho.'

'Nick, he's a freak. Have you ever been in his room? There's black candles, he's growing this cactus in this stupid fucking skull-shaped plant pot – he dyes his hair black. He's into all those dodgy thrash metal bands that shout about ripping people's heads off. Leo said he told his fortune once with a pack of Tarot cards.'

Nick took a quick breath as though he was about to tear a strip off Rob. Then he seemed to think better of it. Olivia noticed the muscles in the corners of his jaw knotting and unknotting.

'Rob, we can't jump to conclusions. We've got to let the police do their job. They'll get him sooner or later, they're bound to. We just need to keep our heads down and get on with it.' He reached for Olivia's hand under the table. She squeezed his back.

'You didn't see your parents, your family, at all over that Christmas break?' asked Denison, surprised.

Olivia was biting her fingernails again. 'No.' Today her clothes were long-sleeved and buttoned-up, hiding her body. Her hair was tied back into a severe ponytail, and she wore no make-up.

'Why not?'

She bit at the skin at the edge of her thumbnail. 'I wanted to be with Nick. I knew my parents couldn't understand what I was going through. We all wanted to be together, really.'

Denison nodded. 'That's a common reaction to such an event.' Olivia's eyes watched him over her curved hand, her fingers flexing as though she were holding notes on the neck of a violin. 'Why don't you tell me about your parents?'

He could see her freeze. Her face was immobile. Then she looked down, hiding her face from him. Her hands moved to her temples, the fingertips meeting in a V over her forehead to shield her eyes. 'Don't make me talk about them,' she said, her voice sounding hollow.

'Why don't you want to talk about them, Olivia?'

She didn't look up. He could only see the bottom half of her face. She swallowed. There was a long exhalation from her mouth, even and controlled. Her fingertips slid down to her temples, then she placed her hands on her knees. When she raised her head she was smiling, calm. 'What do you want to know?' she asked.

'Do you get on with them?'

She shrugged, still smiling. 'We argue a lot. Especially me and my dad. It's been better since I moved out. It was really quite bad when I was a teenager – hormones, you know. I thought they were overprotective and they thought I was a bit of a tearaway.'

'You were in trouble a lot?'

'I'm sure you've got my school record.' He had; Olivia had gone through a long phase where she spoke back to her teachers and got in fights with other pupils. 'Well, I was given a hard time by the other kids for getting good marks. For a while I tried to hide the fact I was smart. And I'd backchat to the teachers so the other girls would admire me. I soon realized it wasn't worth it. A mate of mine – not a good mate, but someone to hang out with at lunchtimes – got herself pregnant and had to leave school. Last time I saw her she was working the five to midnight shift in a chip shop. I knew I didn't want that kind of life for myself. I started doing my homework again, working hard, trying to ignore the silly little kids who thought doing well at school made you a nerd.' She smiled again, but it didn't really reach her eyes. 'I didn't always manage to make myself invisible.' Her school reports showed that from the age of fourteen she'd got straight As, but was often caught fighting in the playground.

Juvenile police records were meant to be sealed and rendered inaccessible once the child reached the age of sixteen, but a friend of Weathers' in the Met remembered Olivia and an incident that had happened when she was fifteen. A fight at the Amhurst Park council estate in Clapton had ended with Olivia getting a black eye and the other girl receiving a broken arm and a face that looked as though it had been scraped along the pavement. A local man had come across the girls in one of the tower block staircases and had called the police. Officers had determined that this other girl, also at Olivia's school, had been bullying her for months. Neither girl wanted to press charges, so the police told them both off and let it drop.

'Did you ever talk to your parents about what you were going through at school?'

She pulled a face. 'No. They weren't much better to be honest. Neither of them is very bright – that sounds pretty mean, doesn't it? But they're not. And they didn't really understand the value of an education. They were worried they'd have to pay to support me through university. They wanted me to stay and help out in the shop full-time.'

'Do you have any brothers or sisters?'

Her hands clenched on her knees, then relaxed. The calm

smile reappeared. 'Dr Denison, I'm sure you know this. Yes, I have two younger sisters. One brother.'

'You get on well with them?'

That shrug again. 'You know what siblings can be like. We got on OK as long as they didn't nick my stuff. The oldest is only sixteen now, so we're not really close enough in age to be mates.'

'Do your parents have a favourite?'

The smile widened. 'You could say that.' She refused to be drawn further.

'They must have been terrified for you when they heard about what had happened to Amanda Montgomery. Did they try to contact you?'

'They left a couple of messages on my mobile. I think they just wanted some inside gossip to tell the neighbours.' Olivia pulled the hairband from her ponytail and ran her fingers through her hair.

'Did you ring them from Nicholas's parents' house?'

'Yes. I rang them on Christmas Day. Just to wish them a merry Christmas. They wanted to talk about Amanda, but I kept changing the subject.' Suddenly there were tears in her eyes. 'My kid sister Jodie told me that the thing she'd asked Santa for was for me to be OK in Cambridge. That was a pretty nice present.'

After their session Denison walked Olivia back to D wing. An orderly collected her from him as Denison stayed to chat to the ward manager.

'Good night, Dr Denison,' Olivia said, smiling shyly over her shoulder as the orderly took her away. He raised a hand in farewell.

'Think you've got an admirer there, Matt,' said the ward

manager, amused. She was an attractive woman in her thirties who liked to flirt with him at office parties. Not that he'd ever tried to take it any further, not even when he was single.

'Don't be silly, Susan,' he said. 'More of a father figure perhaps.'

She snorted, playing with her fringe. 'You're not that old.'

'Old enough to be her dad.'

'Never stopped Hugh Hefner. Anyway, to what do we owe this unexpected visit?'

He nodded towards Olivia, on the other side of the glass now, who was sitting down to play a game of backgammon with another patient. 'Just wanted to find out how you thought she was doing.'

'Corscadden? Pretty well, in the circumstances. She's started to put on weight – you know she lost over a stone that first month? Seems to get on well with the other patients. Well, most of the time.'

'Any trouble?'

'You see Jean over there?' Susan indicated a woman with long grey hair who was reading a book in the corner of the room. 'She and Olivia were thick as thieves for a couple of days. Next thing I know Jean's crying, refusing to come out of her room, 'cause she says Olivia's blanking her. Olivia didn't even seem to know who I was talking about when I asked her about it.'

Denison nodded. 'Sounds consistent with what I've learned about her behaviour prior to the traumatic episode,' he said.

'Really? That's interesting.'

'It's *very* interesting. Look, I wanted to ask you – has she reported many nightmares since she's been here?'

Susan shrugged. 'No more than anyone. No more than me, at any rate. Come to think of it, that is a bit odd, isn't it?'

Denison nodded. 'I'd been expecting regular nightmares by this stage, possibly even flashbacks. Have you picked up on any triggers?'

Susan thought about it. 'Nothing that's provoked a major reaction, no. I don't think she likes men with stubble, if that helps at all?'

'Men with stubble? Really?'

'Yeah – wouldn't go near Lennie the other day, but was fine the next day once he'd had a shave. Could just be a coincidence of course. Unless that suspect in the Okeweno case had five o'clock shadow?'

'No,' said Denison. 'No, he was clean-shaven.'

'Maybe it's nothing then.' She prodded him in the ribs. 'Sounds like you've got a theory.'

'I have,' he said. 'It's a bit out there though.'

'Does that mean you're not sharing?'

'Not yet,' he said, smiling at her and putting his hands in his pockets. 'Night, Susan.'

'Night, Matt,' she said, buzzing him out of the doors.

Chapter Eight

Memorial for murdered Ariel student

A memorial was held yesterday for Ariel student Amanda Montgomery, who was found murdered at the college on the night of 9 December last year. The memorial service was open to all members of the university, as well as to friends and family of Amanda's from her home in Cornwall. Over three hundred people attended the service at Ariel chapel.

The murder, as yet unsolved, has sent shockwaves through the university and has led to a number of requests from students wishing to intermit. Already Ariel has received so many enquiries from its students regarding the possibility of transferring to another college that the college authorities have issued a letter to all its members stating that such transfers would not be possible. A source at Ariel's admissions office claims that, although the college has not yet officially offered places for the next academic year, they are already receiving application retractions from those A-level students they interviewed in Michaelmas term.

Following the memorial service Cambridgeshire Police 'added insult to injury', according to one Ariellian, by asking those present at the college on the night of the murder to submit to fingerprinting and DNA swabs. Those who refused will apparently soon be issued with a court order forcing them to comply. At the moment the police appear to have no major suspects, although their last official statement claimed they were 'investigating a number of promising leads'.

Very few details have been released about the manner in which Amanda Montgomery was killed. Inevitably this has led to immense speculation within the student community, and Ariel College in particular, as to how, why and by whom Amanda was murdered. Although the college has tightened up security and installed CCTV cameras around its grounds as well as in its various hostels, many Ariellians have taken to staying in one another's rooms in order to avoid being alone and at risk. Counselling services are being offered to the students.

– *Varsity* student newspaper,
14 January

Olivia and Nick stood in front of the door to Amanda's room, looking down at the dozens of bouquets and smattering of teddy bears propped up there.

'This doesn't seem real,' Olivia said, reading one of the cards from a bunch of lilies. Earlier Nick had watched a police officer wipe a swab along the inside of Olivia's cheek, feeling that same nausea he'd experienced back in December when his own prints and DNA had been taken. A number of the students had looked the same way as their unique identifiers were recorded, feelings of persecution written on their scared faces, guilt for nothing, bewilderment that anyone could think they might be the bad guy.

'Come on, let's get a drink,' he said, taking her hand. They walked down to the bar, ordering coffees from the glum barman.

'There's Rob,' Nick pointed out. Rob was down the other end of the bar, by the quiz machine. He and a rugby friend of his were standing, arms crossed, watching Victor Kesselich. Kesselich was sitting by himself in one of the booths, sipping a coffee and reading a book by Michel Foucault.

Olivia saw the way Rob was looking at Kesselich. 'Uh-oh,' she said.

'I'll go and say hi,' Nick said. 'Try to talk him out of any bright ideas he might be having.'

Nick went to head off Rob. Olivia glanced around the bar and immediately spotted her neighbour Sinead, whose distinctive curls were the colour of brand new copper coins. Sinead caught her eye and waved her over to one of the booths on the other side of the bar, where she was drinking tea with Leo and Danny.

Sinead gave Olivia a big hug. 'How have you been? Did you really spend the whole time at Nick's?'

'Yeah, I did,' said Olivia. Paula was nearby and Olivia thought her rival's ears had started vibrating at the sound of Nick's name. She took great pleasure in making sure Paula overheard that she'd spent Christmas with him, especially when Paula tossed her hair and stalked off.

'I spent the vacation in Mexico,' Leo told her. Olivia did a double take when she saw he was wearing a poncho. 'The mosquitoes there are serious bastards,' he said. 'And I spent most of Christmas Day throwing up after a dodgy burrito. Plus we only had a hammock to sleep in. But the people are so cool, so chilled out and laid-back, despite the fact the whole place is corrupt as shit.'

'Sounds like you had fun,' said Olivia.

'Man, it was wicked,' he confirmed, oblivious to the irony in her voice. 'We drove to the desert on New Year's Eve, tripped out and watched the sun rise.'

Danny Armstrong, who was too dedicated to rowing to ever stay up past eleven the night before an outing, didn't seem very impressed. 'I spent my New Year's Eve in a dodgy nightclub,' he said in his Scouse accent. 'It was called Neon Lites.' Olivia snorted into her coffee. 'I know,' Danny grimaced. 'Tell me about it. They played cheesy stuff all night – I never knew Wham had so many hits.'

'You should've come with us,' said Leo.

'Yeah, well we don't all have a few hundred quid to spend on flights to Latin America,' Olivia said sharply. Danny raised his eyebrows and Sinead looked at her, upset. 'Well, some of us have a hard time getting the train fare together to get back home,' Olivia said, defending her outburst.

Leo didn't seem too hurt. 'That's what overdrafts are for. Christ, my bank manager hates my guts, but I'd rather be a few grand in debt and have all these amazing experiences than miss out and be in the black.'

Olivia drank her coffee.

The mood in hall during dinner was subdued. There were no raised voices, no laughter. Olivia sat opposite Godfrey, who was wearing a black armband. Next to him sat Eliza, who had changed her mind about moving to Australia when Godfrey, fearful of losing his guaranteed daily shag, had presented her with a diamond necklace and let her know there was more where that came from.

'I've been having nightmares since it happened,' Eliza confided in Olivia. 'Sometimes I wake up with tears streaming down my face. It's always the same dream.' Godfrey rolled his eyes; he'd obviously heard the details before. 'I'm running down this really long corridor and there's something chasing me. I keep trying the doorhandles, but they're all locked. Finally I find a door that opens and I run in. And Amanda's there, in a white nightgown, and she's covered in blood and really pale, and she says, "The door won't close. That's how he got me." And I hear this noise and turn round to face the monster who's chasing me, and that's when I wake up.' Goosebumps were rising up on Eliza's forearms. Olivia reached over and squeezed her hand.

'That must be awful. What a horrible dream.'

Godfrey snorted. 'Not as horrible as my dream about Gordon Brown in a white nightgown.'

'Latent homosexuality,' Olivia coughed behind her hand.

He winked at her. 'Give me David Cameron any day.'

'Anyway,' Eliza said, 'who do you think did it?'

'I don't know!' laughed Olivia. 'You sound like you're asking me about an Agatha Christie novel.'

'You must have some ideas. Everyone's got their suspicions.'

'Really? Who's topping the poll at the moment?'

Eliza leaned forward conspiratorially. 'Victor Kesselich.' She sat back. 'Some other people reckon her and Rob were arguing a lot. Godfrey reckons it's Laurence.'

'Laurence Merner?' Olivia said, looking at Godfrey in surprise.

'Yes, Laurence Merner.' Godfrey seemed serious. Laurence was part of a group of highbrow intellectuals that discussed Kurosawa, Nietzsche and Sartre in rotation, and had a tendency towards designer spectacles and long overcoats. 'He and Amanda had a falling-out at the end of last term.'

'What about?'

'Something to do with a conversation about game shows. She said it had been her ambition when she was a kid to win *Mastermind*. And he said he thought she was more *Wheel of Fortune*.'

Olivia winced. 'That's a bit harsh. But why would he kill her?'

'Well, he obviously had a problem with her. He didn't even know her, but he was judgemental enough to suggest she was thick, or lower class, or whatever. Why would he dislike someone so much whom he'd rarely even spoken to?'

'I dunno, seems like a bit of a stretch to me,' said Olivia.

At that moment Victor Kesselich came into the hall, carrying a tray. He headed for an empty end of a table and sat alone, steadily eating his food.

Olivia had been in his shoes before. Ostracized, her solitariness observed and enjoyed by others. She could go over and sit by him, strike up a conversation, but she'd never even met him before. How would he react to some strange girl turning up and blathering at him? She finished her tortellini.

'It's DCI Weathers on the phone for you,' said Coldhill's receptionist.

'OK, put him through,' said Denison. It was the fifth of their weekly phone calls about the Montgomery murder.

'We got the fingerprints and DNA of nearly all the Ariel students,' said Weathers. 'Some arseholes refused to give them to us, but we'll get a warrant.'

'You suspicious about any of those who refused?' asked Denison.

'Nah, not really. They all seem to be civil rights types. Can't say I blame them too much. Not sure I'd want my DNA on record somewhere, not when I hadn't actually done anything.'

'No matches so far I take it?'

'Oh yeah, we've got matches. Problem is they're all people who had a good reason to be there. We had one bloody fingerprint – and I'm not swearing there, Matt, I'm talking about a fingerprint in blood on the wall – that proved the person it belonged to was there during or after the murder. Unfortunately it turned out to be Tracey Webb's.'

'Tracey Webb?'

'The cleaner. Must have left it there when she found the body.'

Denison sighed in frustration. 'Sorry, Steve.'

'Also the DNA came back from the blood we found in the pipes in her en-suite bathroom. It was definitely Amanda's. You were right, the killer must have showered her blood off after the murder.'

'Suggests he's calm enough to take the time to cover his tracks, rather than panicking and running out of there covered in blood.'

'Our pathologist says it probably took him at least

twenty minutes to do all the post-mortem mutilation. I guess he thought if anyone had heard her death throes and was coming to the rescue, they would have arrived by then. He must have reckoned he was in the clear if no one had beat the door down when he was cutting her head off, and therefore he had time to take a shower.'

'Backs up our view that we're dealing with an organized killer,' mused Denison. 'Although this level of mutilation is usually associated with a more disorganized type. A total nutter, in other words. He must be able to hide this warped side of himself pretty bloody well.'

'We did try asking the students if they knew of any total nutters around,' said Weathers. 'Most of them laughed and said, "What, apart from me?"'

'Hilarious,' said Denison. 'What about Amanda's bathroom? You find any hairs or anything else in the pipes?'

'Yeah. Most of them are probably hers. The others are gonna be a bit of a nightmare to sort out. You know the college hosts conferences over the vacations? Well, we reckon there's probably some hairs from the last guest in there. And apparently this lot with the en suites sometimes take pity on the others who have to share a communal bathroom and let them use their baths. So again, if our guy is a student, he could always claim Amanda let him use the shower in the past.'

Denison knew even identifying the owners of the hairs would be difficult. Without a bulb at the root of the hair, a unique match could not be made – forensics could only say that two hairs were similar, not identical.

'So, our forensics are worth shit,' Weathers admitted,

sounding strangely pleased with himself. 'But it's possible the killer isn't the maniacal genius we were worried about.'

'What do you mean?' asked Denison.

'He may have left a note in Amanda's room. A handwritten note.'

Nick had gone home for the weekend for his dad's fifty-third birthday. Olivia was crashing on the floor in Sinead's room, under her own duvet. Sinead had lit some candles and they were lying there, listening to Blue Öyster Cult's 'Don't Fear the Reaper', telling each other creepy urban legends.

'So they have this sign arranged, so if one of them gets lucky and pulls, then she puts a scarf around the outside doorknob, and then her roommate knows not to disturb her,' Sinead was saying, her pupils dilated by the candlelight. 'But one night one of them comes back from a long night studying in the college library, sees the scarf, but just wants to go to bed. There's no way she's making herself scarce for two hours; she's shattered. So she goes into the room, but she doesn't switch the light on, not wanting to disturb her roommate any more than she has to. Anyway, she goes to bed and tries to get to sleep despite the moans and grunts coming from the other bed. Eventually she drifts off. The next morning the sunlight coming through the curtains wakes her up, and she turns over to say good morning to her roommate. And the roommate's lying there in a pool of blood, her guts hanging out of her. And written on the mirror in blood are the words 'lucky for you that you didn't turn on the lights".'

'Sinead!' protested Olivia, tugging her duvet closer around her. 'That was a bit out of order.'

Sinead pulled a face at her. 'Your turn,' she said.

Olivia sat up. 'Nope, I'm too scared already. We're not going to be able to sleep if we keep this up.'

Sinead, huddled up in her bed, rubbed her skinny arms in an attempt to comfort herself. 'I know. I've needed the loo for the past thirty minutes, but I'm not going out there by myself!'

'Don't be silly,' said Olivia, laughing. 'The killer's not going to be lurking in the toilets.'

'How do you know? He could be anywhere!'

'Do you want me to go with you?' asked Olivia.

'Yes please!'

Giggling, wrapped in their duvets, the two girls inched their way out of Sinead's room and down the stairs towards the toilets on the floor below. The lights were bright in the corridors, which were deserted.

'What time is it?' whispered Sinead loudly.

'Ten past two in the morning,' Olivia whispered back, pointing at her watch.

They turned the corner and screamed as a figure appeared before them. The figure shrieked equally shrilly. It was Eliza. The three of them collapsed in a heap of hysterical laughter and relief. A bloke who did Chemistry poked his head round his door and looked at them in disgust. They laughed even louder, especially at his Homer Simpson underpants, and he tutted and went back into his room.

Sinead went to the loo, Olivia standing guard outside as Eliza asked what they were up to.

'Winding each other up, mainly,' said Olivia. 'You want to join us?'

'Yeah, why not? I'd better get Paula though. She's in my room. Godfrey says he's sick of being woken up by me freaking out after having one of my nightmares, so he's buggered off to his own room tonight, the selfish bastard.'

Olivia couldn't think of anyone she'd less want to spend a late-night gabbing session with than Paula, but she hadn't given herself an opt-out. She could go back to her own room, but the walls were so thin it basically meant she'd be listening to them gossiping all night anyway.

Back in Sinead's room Sinead lit more candles and made everyone hot chocolate. Paula arrived in a dark blue satin vest and shorts, her boobs perky despite the obvious lack of a bra. Eliza had on a pink pair of pyjamas and was wearing slippers that looked like fluffy white dogs.

'So, do you guys know any creepy stories?' asked Olivia. 'Sinead was just telling me that one about the girl whose roommate was murdered . . .' She tailed off in embarrassment.

Paula didn't seem to notice. 'Do you know the one about the old lady and the dog?'

'No,' said everyone, settling down eagerly.

The story was long and clichéd, and ended with: 'On top of the wardrobe is her dog, cut in little pieces. And the old lady thinks – if that's my dog, what's in the dog basket, licking my hand?'

'Ew!' said Eliza.

'That's a bit convoluted,' said Olivia. 'I don't think you

can technically call it an urban legend – it's obviously made up.'

'But the story about spiders growing in someone's beehive hairdo is believable, is it?' pointed out Paula.

'That actually happened to a friend of my aunt's,' protested Eliza.

Paula and Olivia looked at each other and burst out laughing.

'Hey, you know what we should do?' piped up Sinead. 'We should have a seance!'

'Don't we need a Ouija board for that?' asked Olivia.

'We can make one,' said Paula. 'Do you have any paper?'

Sinead hopped out of bed and got her blank notepad and a black felt tip pen. Paula wrote the alphabet on the pad and then the numbers zero to ten.

'I'm not sure this is a good idea, guys,' said Eliza. 'Seriously. I saw *The Exorcist* the other day and that's how the girl ended up possessed.'

'Don't be such a wuss,' said Paula, writing the words 'yes' and 'no' at the bottom of the page. 'Sinead, you got a glass?'

All of Sinead's were pint-sized neon-coloured plastic. Olivia nipped across to her room, where she had a small glass she'd 'borrowed' from Ariel canteen.

'Perfect,' said Paula.

'Guys, please, this is a really bad idea,' Eliza told them.

'Eliza, fuck off back to your room if you don't want to be here. If you want to stay, then shut up.' Paula laid the paper on the floor between them and they knelt in a circle round it, even a reluctant Eliza.

'OK, everyone, put your forefinger on the glass,' instructed Sinead. 'Don't push it though. Just rest your finger lightly on the top.' They did so. 'We want to speak to the spirit of Amanda Montgomery,' Sinead intoned. Olivia stifled a giggle. 'Amanda, are you there?'

Silence. 'Nothing's happening,' said Eliza. 'In the film the girl had a triangular pointy thing with wheels, not a glass.'

'Where the hell do you expect us to get something like that from?' said Paula. 'The Early Learning Centre?'

'We need something of Amanda's,' said Sinead. She looked around at her friends, their pupils large and liquid in the candlelight.

Paula sat back, taking her finger off the glass. She thought about it, then removed the chain around her neck. On it was a moonstone set in a silver ring. 'This was Amanda's ring,' she said. 'She left it in my bathroom the day before she died. Mrs Montgomery said I could keep it.'

She laid the ring down on the piece of paper and put her necklace back on. Everyone returned their fingertips to the glass.

'Amanda,' Sinead tried again, 'are you there?'

They all gasped as the glass juddered over to the word 'yes'. Eliza snatched her finger away.

'You guys are trying to freak me out!' she squeaked.

'Eliza, put your fucking finger back on that glass,' hissed Paula.

'Maybe it'll work without her,' said Sinead. 'Amanda, are you OK?'

'Of course she's not OK, she's dead!' said Paula.

'I just want to ask if she's happy wherever she is!'

The glass jerked across to the word 'no'. Sinead looked sick.

'Amanda, who killed you?' asked Paula. The glass didn't move. 'Was it Rob?' she asked. The glass stayed on the word 'no'. 'Was it Laurence Merner?' Again the glass wouldn't move. 'Was it Victor Kesselich?'

This time the glass shot over to the word 'yes'.

'Christ,' said Sinead. 'What the hell do we ask now?'

'One of you is moving the glass, aren't you?' asked Olivia. 'I don't believe in ghosts and I know you lot don't either. One of you is taking the piss.'

'Honestly, Liv, I'm not doing anything,' said Sinead.

'Me neither,' said Eliza, who was shaking.

'Then let's ask something that only Amanda would know the answer to.'

'Amanda, why did he kill you?' asked Sinead.

But there was no more movement. They tried for another ten minutes, but the glass remained motionless.

The next morning the story of their seance spread throughout the college, and soon Olivia was sick of people asking about it.

'It was a joke,' she told June. 'One of us was fucking about with the glass.'

'Which of them do you think it was?' June asked.

'I don't know. Not Sinead. Maybe Paula. The ring probably wasn't even Amanda's.'

'The ring?'

'Paula had a ring on a chain round her neck. She said it was Amanda's.'

'What did it look like?'

'Silver, with a moonstone.'

'Yeah, that was Amanda's. I remember her wearing it.'
June was drinking coffee and took a long sip. 'Olivia,' she
said thoughtfully, 'if I died, would you hold a seance for
me?'

Olivia frowned at her. 'Would you want me to?'

'No,' June said. 'No, I wouldn't.'

Matthew Denison looked again at his scribbles from
yesterday's conversation with DCI Stephen Weathers.
He'd written out in full the contents of the note the
police had found in Amanda Montgomery's room, tucked
into a book of Sylvia Plath poetry: 'I thought you were a
friend. Some fucking friend. I wouldn't wish you on my
worst enemy. You just pretend to offer sympathy and
understanding, but you're a cold-hearted bitch who
doesn't give a shit about anyone else. I don't want to
know you any more.'

The note was unsigned. Denison thought this was not
because the author wanted to remain anonymous, but
because the author assumed Amanda would know
immediately who had written it. Weathers' team were
currently checking the note for fingerprints and would
compare any found with the sets they'd gathered from
the students and staff of Ariel.

Nick and Olivia were in Olivia's room later that night,
when there was an urgent knock at the door. It was Rob,
looking mad, Paula by his side with a determined
expression on her face.

'Olivia, is it true about this seance?' he asked.

'Is what true?' she queried.

'Did Kesselich's name come up?'

'For Christ's sake, Rob, you're not taking that seriously, are you? It was a joke!'

'Just tell me, did the board say it was Kesselich?'

'Tell him, Olivia,' prompted Paula.

'No! Rob, what's wrong with you, it was a bloody Ouija board! Do you seriously think Amanda's spirit visited us and told us who killed her? Don't be so bloody ridiculous!'

'You're not denying it said Kesselich was responsible,' said Rob.

'No, because it doesn't mean anything. If the board had told us the Pope killed her, would you have believed that?'

'Right,' he said, two points of scarlet high in his cheeks. His hands were clenched into fists and he half walked, half ran down the stairs.

'For Christ's sake, Paula!' Olivia swore, pushing past her and running after Rob, Nick hot on her heels.

She caught up with him at the gatehouse and tried to pull on his arm, but he shook her off.

'Rob, calm down,' tried Nick, but Rob pushed him aside and kept walking.

Victor Kesselich was in the bar, sitting by himself as he had been all term. Rob strode over to him and, without warning, punched him in the face.

The bar was almost full and everyone turned and stared, shocked. All conversations stopped – all Olivia heard were some gasps, the sound of the Motown classic that was playing on the jukebox and the incongruous noise Rob's fists made when they hit Victor's body.

Nick got in between them and received a blow to the face for his trouble. Olivia saw Godfrey rush over and expected him to help, but instead he grabbed Nick and pushed him away against the bar. Victor, dazed, had slid to the floor. Rob kicked him in the stomach, his face contorted. Olivia moved forward to try to pull Rob off Victor and was surprised when three policemen appeared from behind her and wrenched Rob away. Two of them grappled with him, forcing him face-down onto the ground and holding him there until he stopped struggling; the other went to help Victor up and to a seat.

Olivia turned as a man walked past her in a black leather jacket. She recognized him as the CID officer who had walked by her in the bar on the morning they found Amanda.

Weathers sat down on the coffee table nearest Rob's head. 'Mr McNorton', he said. 'You calmed down yet?'

Rob nodded mutely.

'Let him up', Weathers told the officer who held Rob's arms behind his back. As Rob stood the policeman made sure he wasn't going anywhere. 'Mr McNorton, we'd like to have a chat at the station. Are you willing to accompany us?'

'Rob, you don't have to', said Godfrey. 'You only have to go if they arrest you.'

Weathers looked at Godfrey coldly. 'Mr Parrish, isn't it? I suggest you keep your nose out of it. We witnessed your reaction when Nicholas Hardcastle tried to intervene just now.' Nick was leaning against the bar, wiping blood from his mouth. 'Now, Mr McNorton, are you going to come for a chat?'

Rob shook his head. 'I don't need Godfrey to tell me my rights. You want a "chat", you arrest me.'

'Fair enough.' Weathers stood up. 'Robert McNorton, I am arresting you on suspicion of the murder of Amanda Montgomery.'

Chapter Nine

Rob became paler and paler as Weathers read him his rights. 'Okay, take him to the station,' said the DCI.

The policeman holding Rob steered him out of the door, every student in the bar turning their heads as one to follow his path. Weathers rotated round to look at Victor Kesselich. The officer who had helped him to a seat was radioing for an ambulance.

'You OK, Victor?' Weathers asked. Kesselich just looked at him. One of his eyes was already swelling up. 'PC Liman will go with you to Addenbrooke's, then we'll take your statement. It's up to you if you want to press charges.' Weathers turned to Nick. 'The same goes for you, Mr Hardcastle.' Nick, white-faced, just shook his head.

Weathers stood, glanced at Olivia briefly and then followed Rob out of the door. Olivia watched him through one of the windows as he strode down the path to the gatehouse, then went over to Nick. She gently touched his face with the palm of her hand.

'That was brave of you,' she said quietly.

'Didn't do much good though, did it?' Nick said, his voice thick.

In Nick's room a group of them sat and talked about Rob.

'You don't think Rob killed Amanda, do you?' Danny asked Nick and Olivia. They didn't answer him, but couldn't help looking at each other.

'What?' Sinead said, noticing the look.

'He was really pissed off with her that night,' Nick said heavily.

'Why?'

Nick shrugged.

'Seriously, Nick, why?' asked Danny, pushing his thick-rimmed glasses up the bridge of his nose.

'Rob didn't tell him,' said Olivia, who'd already had this conversation with Nick.

'He just said he'd confided in her and she'd thrown it in his face. It must've been something pretty personal, because he was really hurt, and because he wouldn't tell me what he'd told her.'

'I'm not surprised if he'd already had one person using it against him,' said Leo.

'But you can really see Rob being angry enough to kill her?' asked Danny.

There was a knock at the door. Nick, who was holding a cold can of 7Up against his sore cheek, went to see who it was.

'Nick, I came to apologize,' said Godfrey, hands in pockets. 'I wanted to see Kesselich get what he deserved and I confess I got a bit carried away.'

'I thought *your* chief suspect was Laurence Merner,'

said Olivia, appearing behind Nick with a deep frown on her face. 'Are you sure it's not just that you like to see a bit of blood?'

'Olivia, stay out of this', Godfrey said. 'I'm here to speak to Nick, not to you.'

Nick swung the door shut in his face.

'I'd like you to explain this to me.' Weathers slid a clear plastic bag across the interview room table. It contained the note they'd found in Amanda's room.

Rob looked down at it, his Adam's apple bobbing up and down. He picked up the note and Weathers saw tears on his eyelashes.

'You wrote this, didn't you, Rob?' he said softly.

Rob nodded, wiping the back of his hand against his eyes. 'I wish I hadn't. I wish I could take it back.'

'You want to tell me why you wrote this note?'

Rob shook his head violently, jaw clenched, fighting back tears. He crossed his arms, looking at the ceiling so the water wouldn't fall from his eyes.

'Rob, I don't know what Amanda did to upset you so much, but I've got to assume it was bad enough to give you a motive to murder her. If I'm wrong, now's your chance to explain.'

Rob wouldn't look at him. 'Can I tell you off the record?'

'I'm afraid not, Rob. We can try to keep it quiet if it's not relevant, but I'm afraid I can't promise that until I've heard what it is.'

Rob shook his head. 'Then no comment.'

'Rob, you're in danger of being charged with murder.

I strongly suggest you speak to me, tell me what Amanda did that made you write that note.'

Rob recrossed his arms. 'I want to speak to a solicitor,' was all he said.

The desk sergeant looked up as a nervous young man in a long black overcoat walked in. The sergeant could tell just by looking at him that he was a student. The man walked over to the desk, adjusted his Christian Dior spectacles and cleared his throat.

'I'd like to speak to whoever's in charge of the Montgomery investigation,' he said. 'My name's Laurence Merner.'

There was a knock on the door of the interview room.

'Enter,' said Weathers, annoyed by the interruption.

It was DS Halloran. 'Think we need a word, sir.' Outside the interview room Halloran nodded down the hallway to where Laurence Merner was standing out of earshot. 'Another Ariel student. Says he was with Rob McNorton on the night of the Montgomery murder. At least during the four hours the doc pinned down.'

'Twelve a.m. to four a.m? What were they doing?'

Halloran half-smirked. 'What do you think?'

Weathers raised his eyebrows. 'Are you serious?'

'According to this guy. Name of Laurence Merner. Apparently he and Mr McNorton have been having a fling for a few weeks now. That's what the hullabaloo with Amanda was about – this was McNorton's last-ditch effort to try to be a good little heterosexual. But – according to Mr Merner anyway – he couldn't get it up, and when he confessed to Amanda that he thought he might be gay, she ripped him to shreds.'

Weathers looked thoughtful. 'Gives him a good motive. Especially if he thought she was going to out him, which he's obviously terrified of.'

'Yeah, he's got a motive, but he's also got an alibi.'

'You think Merner's telling the truth?'

'I do. You can tell he's reluctant to admit to anything – even though he's out of the closet at Ariel, it sounds like his friends wouldn't approve of his relationship with Mr McNorton, what with McNorton being your standard rugger bugger homophobic closet case. So the fact he's willing to come forward despite this makes me think he's genuine.'

'Maybe he's in love with McNorton and is prepared to lie to protect him,' Weathers suggested.

'Could be,' Halloran said. 'Not the impression I get, like I say, but maybe you should interview him yourself. I could find out if he's got any neighbours to corroborate his story.'

Weathers nodded. 'OK, but be subtle. McNorton's obviously got real issues with people finding out he's gay and we should respect that.'

'Aye aye, sir,' Halloran agreed.

Olivia sat meekly on the chair, her hands folded on her lap. Again she was wearing no make-up, and had her hair pulled back. She seemed to be finding it hard to look him in the eye.

'Dr Denison?' she asked. 'I was wondering . . . have you seen Nicholas recently?'

'Olivia, we need to talk about other things now. Things in

the past. Last time we spoke you told me about spending Christmas at the Hardcastles' house.'

She smiled. 'Yes. Mrs Hardcastle gave me perfume. It wasn't really my kind of scent, a bit too spicy, but it was generous of her.'

'And you and Nick returned to Ariel in January?'

Her expression darkened. 'Yes. We were all in mourning. People left. Some of us tried to change college, but they wouldn't let us. We stayed in each other's rooms. We were all scared. There were reporters everywhere. They printed interviews with students who hardly knew Amanda. They took photos of Rob when he was arrested. His parents must have felt so ashamed.' She brightened. 'But it was fine, in the end. Laurence told the police about him and Rob, and they let him go.'

Denison had been right: the writer of the note and the murderer of Amanda Montgomery were not the same person. Although in some ways Rob fitted Denison's profile – despite being gay he'd tried to sleep with girls in the vain hope that he'd grow to like it, but it was never a fulfilling experience for him – in other ways he was a polar opposite to the offender Denison had outlined. Added to the alibi given by Laurence Merner, it was enough for the police to give up on him as a suspect.

'Were you surprised when you learned Rob was gay?' Denison asked Olivia.

Her eyes seemed to be seeing the past. 'It made sense. I could understand why he had been so upset with Amanda. It didn't change the way I felt about him though.'

'What do you mean?'

'I was angry with him for a while, for attacking Victor

Kesselich. But when I realized how much of his own anger was to do with his guilt for the way he behaved with Amanda and the fact she died before they could make peace with each other, I couldn't help wanting to be friends with him again. The fact Rob was homosexual didn't mean anything to me. I didn't care.'

Denison was noticing that Olivia's speech patterns had become different; more formal. He made a note and realized she was waiting for his next question.

'And then?' he prompted.

'Then what?' she asked.

'Rob was released at the end of January. And the next murder didn't occur for months. What was life like for you in the intervening period?'

Olivia shrugged carefully. 'I concentrated on my work in the main. The college put on a self-defence class that I went to. I didn't bother with the counsellor they offered though.' She smiled at him. 'No offence.'

'None taken. How were your studies going?'

'The end of year exams went well – I got a 2:1. Nick got a First.'

'And your love life – was that going well too?'

'Yes.' She smiled to herself. 'We had a very nice time on Valentine's Day. He left a red rose in my pigeonhole. In the evening we went to see *Interview with the Vampire* at Peterhouse and then had dinner at Venezia. We agreed to try to get neighbouring rooms in our second year.'

'So you left Ariel in July feeling quite positive – you'd got a 2:1, your relationship with Nick was going from strength to strength. How was it going home for the summer?'

Her face became grey again. 'Oh, you know. Not that

great. I didn't like being away from Nick, but I think his parents had had enough of me coming to stay.'

'You didn't like being home?'

'My friends weren't there. When you're used to having all your friends around you, it's tough when they're suddenly spread around the country.'

'What about your friends from school?'

Her eyes were sad. 'I didn't make many friends at school.'

'That was one of the reasons why you wanted to change schools?'

'That and I wanted to do well. My school wasn't a great school.'

'According to your school notes you didn't get the scholarship you needed to change schools. Was that because of the fighting?'

She clasped her hands together. 'I don't know.'

Denison was hard pressed to reconcile the girl sitting before him with the scrapping, insolent individual described in her school records.

'So you were happy to get back to Ariel in October? You weren't nervous or anxious about anything?'

'No, what was there to be anxious about? I couldn't wait to get back.'

'Despite the fact the killer had yet to be caught?' Denison couldn't resist asking.

Olivia frowned. 'Yes. Yes, I suppose I was anxious about that . . . I just tried not to think about it. It had been ten months after all. I guess we thought it was a one-off.'

'But it wasn't.'

'No. It wasn't.'

*

Denison walked from Cambridge train station to the market square, humming to himself. The sky was a baby blue, green leaves rustled on the trees that lined the road. His good mood even survived nearly colliding with a cyclist who preferred the safety of the pavement to risking the traffic on the roads.

He had arranged to meet Sinead Flynn in Starbucks. He walked in and she was there on one of the squashy armchairs, her russet hair pinned up in a messy topknot, sipping from a large mug. She smiled at him as he approached.

'Hello,' she said. 'I recognize you from that ITV programme you were in last year.' Denison had featured in a recent documentary on Coldhill Hospital.

'Can I get you another coffee?' he asked, noticing her mug was nearly empty.

'Thank you. I'll have a decaff skinny latte please.' He joined the long queue of tourists and students and eventually came back with two mugs.

'Thank you for meeting me,' Denison said, sipping his double espresso. 'I could do with your help.'

'You need to know about Liv?' she asked.

'Yes, I do. But I'm also interested in hearing your impressions of your fellow students at Ariel. The further we get into this investigation the more it seems the culprit is a member of your college. The more I can learn about the victims and their friends, the better I can understand the tensions and motives that may have played a part in the murders.'

Sinead went quiet then. 'You're sure?' she said finally.

'What, that an Ariellian is responsible? Yes, I'm afraid so.'

'In my psychology classes they said there is no underlying motive to serial killings,' she said. 'That apart from satisfying the killer's urges, they're essentially motiveless.'

'Well, yes, that's generally true,' said Denison, thinking he should have checked his notes more carefully. Psychology students were always a contrary bunch. 'But it's also generally true that serial murderers kill to assert dominance over their victims. They enjoy having power and control over another human being. Certain types of women may unwittingly provoke these killers by stirring up their feelings of inadequacy, making the killer feel the need to commit murder in order to countermand these feelings.'

Sinead nodded; she could understand this. 'Amanda was pretty good at that,' she admitted. 'Making you feel inadequate, I mean.'

'She made *you* feel this way?'

Sinead rolled her eyes. 'Well, yeah. I was dead keen on doing some acting when I first came to Cambridge, and when I found out she was into drama too, I thought we had something in common. I suggested we audition together and . . . well, turned out she already had a plum role lined up in a play a schoolfriend of hers was producing. My bit part in *The Crucible* didn't really measure up. I went to her opening night, did all the whooping at the end when she was taking her bow, and she repaid me by leaving my opening night in the interval.' Sinead laughed, shaking her head. 'That was our Amanda for you. Always knew how to put the boot in. She made Olivia feel shit too – you know, telling her about Nick and Paula. She couldn't resist adding a drop of poison to any happiness you might be feeling.' She sat up a bit straighter. 'Not that I hated her though, I don't want you to think that.

She wasn't a very nice person at heart, but she was fun to hang around with and great if you just wanted a gossip and a bit of a moan. You just learned not to tell her anything personal about yourself, anything you felt insecure about.'

'How upset was Nick that she'd dropped him in it with Olivia?'

Both of Sinead's hands were holding her mug. He thought he noticed her knuckles whiten as she gripped the mug tighter. 'I think you already know the answer to that.'

'You think he killed her, then?'

'Everyone knows you don't walk into a crime scene, or touch a dead body,' she pointed out. 'When June was murdered, Nick supposedly did both. He's not that stupid. When Leo and I walked in on him, he looked guilty.'

'Not all of your fellow Ariellians seem to agree.'

'Paula you mean? Well, she wouldn't. She's still got the bloody hots for him.'

'Were you friends with Nick before all this happened?'

'Sort of. I was friends with Liv and knew him through her really. Not sure I would've hung out with him otherwise. I remember when they first got together thinking he was maybe a bit straight-laced for her, but she was madly in love with him right from the get-go.'

'You expected Olivia to be drawn to men who were a bit less . . . vanilla?'

'Yes, I thought Olivia would go for someone a bit darker in spirit than Nick appeared to be. Apparently I was right.'

'What made you think Olivia wouldn't be happy with someone vanilla?'

Sinead sat back, resting her cup on her belly. 'Because she herself wasn't vanilla, I suppose.'

'Nick has told me that she could be a somewhat temperamental person; that her moods could change quite suddenly.'

'Probably a symptom of being in love. The impression I got was more that what you saw wasn't necessarily what was there.'

'You think she was hiding something?'

'Yes, partly . . . but also that she felt she had to be somebody that she wasn't. And sometimes you'd suddenly feel like you were seeing the real her, not the one who was being demure, or being conscientious about work, or being funny.'

They talked some more and the picture Sinead painted for him was of a girl who was more insecure than she looked, who seemed to need to be aware of others' opinions and beliefs before she'd express her own.

Denison had long ago finished his cup of coffee. He started to put away his notebook and pen.

'Has she told you much about her parents?' asked Sinead.

He looked up at her from his briefcase. 'What makes you ask that?'

'Just thinking about the time I went to visit her in London. She didn't know I was coming – I looked up her parents' shop in the *Yellow Pages*; I knew they lived above it. I thought it would be fun to surprise her.'

Sinead had decided she didn't like London much. Covent Garden was nice and she'd had a laugh both times she'd gone to the theatre, but the inner-city suburbs made her uncomfortable. They were too dirty for one – she hated litter – and from the bus window she'd seen a tower block with a mattress lying in its small children's playground and 'JONNY IS A COCKSUCKER' spray-painted on a low wall. On the bus she had nearly sat down on a big fat piece of chewing gum that someone had thoughtfully left on the seat. And the driver had just grunted when she'd asked him to let her know when they reached Dalston High Street.

She read a sign over the seat opposite that informed her that London Transport's employees had the right to do their jobs without fear of assault and that prosecutions would be pursued. Another sign told her: 'Graffiti is vandalism, vandalism is a crime.' Underneath it someone had written 'JM 4 MK' in green marker pen.

'Dalston,' the bus driver announced loudly. She met his eyes in the mirror that gave him a view of his passengers, said thank you and made her way to the exit, apparently annoying the people she was forced to squeeze past.

Dalston was loud and bustling. She scanned the shop fronts, seeing barbers and hairdressers, clothes shops and fast-food restaurants, but no Corscadden Retail. Looking at her address book for a street number she nearly walked into a woman with a pushchair coming in the other direction. 'Sorry,' she said, as the woman sucked her teeth and stalked past her.

A Mediterranean-looking guy with a black moustache in a shiny grey suit walked by her and made a kissy-kissy sound. She blushed and kept going. As she passed Ridley Road Market she was offered apples, lace underwear and Nike trainers by various stall-holders, all of which she declined.

'Do you know where Corscadden Retail is?' she asked the guy selling fruit.

'You mean Barry's place? You're nearly there, love, it's just down the road.'

The shop front was weathered and blue, the name painted in faded black. Through the window Sinead could see electronic equipment practically piled up to the ceiling. A door sensor beeped as she walked in. A few people were browsing, looking at price tags and twiddling knobs. Sinead saw a bargain bin filled with a large variety of basic-looking second-hand cameras and realized the shop's business was resale. This was a place people came to when they needed money more than they needed their television.

There was a skinny woman behind the counter, her bleached blonde hair pulled back in a scrunchie, an inch of dark roots visible at her scalp. She was wearing a lime-green vest top and on one bare arm Sinead could see a tattoo of what looked like the name Barry.

'Yes, love?' said the woman, sucking on a cigarette.

'I was wondering if Olivia was around,' said Sinead politely.

The woman narrowed her eyes, then laughed, which made her cough. A stream of fag smoke came out as she choked.

'Sorry, love,' she said in a croaky voice, thumping her chest as though to dislodge the tar deposits on her lungs. 'Didn't mean to laugh at ya.'

She took a step back to an open doorway behind her and yelled up the stairs: 'Cleo! Cleo, come down here!'

Sinead started to shake her head, thinking she'd made

a mistake, but the woman was busy stubbing out her cigarette. She could hear loud voices on the staircase, both with strong London accents.

'Keep your fucking nose out of it, you facety little bitch!' she heard a girl say.

'Piss off, Cleo, I don't give a shit about your poxy stuff!' she heard another girl retort as the sound of feet thudding down the steps got louder.

Olivia appeared at the foot of the stairs.

'Mum, you better tell Jodie—' She suddenly saw Sinead and stopped dead in her tracks.

Sinead tried to smile. 'Hi Olivia!'

'You must be a mate from college,' said Olivia's mum, lighting up another Benson & Hedges. 'No one round here calls her Olivia. What's the matter Cleo, you don't like your name no more?' She reached over and pinched Olivia's cheek, leaving white marks on her skin.

Olivia seemed speechless. Sinead felt intensely uncomfortable and couldn't think what to say.

'Ain't ya gonna introduce us?' prompted Olivia's mum.

Olivia reached up a hand and smoothed down her hair. Her curls were gelled and pulled back in a black scrunchie, and she wore no make-up. She had on a baggy T-shirt, black and white nylon tracksuit bottoms with a stripe up the side, and Reebok trainers. Sinead realized she'd never seen Olivia wearing anything like that before, not even in the self-defence class when they were dressed for exercise.

'Mum, this is Sindy. Sindy, this is my mum. She's called Shelley.' Olivia's accent seemed to have become hybridized. It was no longer the cockney Sinead had

just heard, nor the pleasant BBC voice Sinead was used
to.

'Pleased to meet ya,' said Shelley, transferring her fag
to her left hand and shaking Sinead's with her right.
Sinead couldn't help noticing the yellow nicotine stains
on her fingers.

To Sinead's relief, and to Olivia's too she suspected, a
customer came up at that point and started complaining
about a TV he'd bought the week before whose remote
control wasn't working.

'You tried changing the batteries, love?' Shelley was
asking as Olivia jerked her head to the door.

'Fancy a drink?' she asked, her voice almost back to
normal.

'Sure,' said Sinead. Olivia went back to the staircase and
returned with a small backpack. She jumped up and slid
over the counter, pulling Sinead by the elbow to the door.

A large, bear-like man walked into the shop. His
greying hair was shaved close to his scalp, a Ralph Lauren
T-shirt tight round his beer belly. His forearms were hairy
and tanned, and Sinead saw her second smudged tattoo
of the day. This one read 'Shelley'.

'Cleo!' he said in a warm, gravelly voice. 'Where you
off to, love?'

'Just going out,' Olivia said, not looking at him.

'I realize that, sweetheart, I was asking where to?'

'We're getting a drink.'

He noticed Sinead then, and looked her up and down.

'Who's your little mate, then?' He was grinning and his
expression was friendly, but Sinead didn't like the look in
his eyes, green-gold like Olivia's.

'Sindy. Look, Dad, Mum's having trouble with some bloke at the counter.' The cockney accent was back in full.

Olivia's dad looked down the shop at the argument going on between Shelley and the dissatisfied customer. 'Fuck me, not another one. All right then, piss off for a drink, but remember to get your mum some fags on the way back.'

Olivia sidestepped him, careful not to make physical contact, and Sinead left with her. Olivia strode down the street, Sinead having to work hard to keep up with her.

'Why did you come here?' asked Olivia, looking dead ahead.

'I'm sorry, I didn't realize . . . Do you want me to leave?'

'It's a bit late now.'

Olivia took her to a pub full of England supporters cheering on the team in the World Cup quarter-finals. They found a small table at the back, away from the giant TV screen.

Olivia bought their drinks – Sinead had her usual white wine, but was surprised to see Olivia drinking a half-pint of lager.

'Is this your local then?' asked Sinead after five minutes of awkward silence.

Olivia gulped down half her lager. 'Yeah,' she said finally, wiping her mouth. She refused to look at Sinead. 'Would you rather we find a wine bar?' she asked, her tone cold. 'Or one of those nice pubs with the big sofas and the laminate flooring?'

'No, this is fine,' Sinead said. 'Look, Liv, I'm really sorry. I thought it would be fun to surprise you.'

Olivia's gaze suddenly turned on Sinead, fierce and penetrating. 'You won't tell anyone about them, will you?'

'I won't if you don't want me to . . . But, Liv, no one would think any less of you. Blimey, the way that lot at Ariel are they'd probably think you were even cooler!'

Sinead noticed a corner of Olivia's lip curling ever so slightly and decided to stop trying to make her feel better.

'Look, I won't say anything, I promise.'

Olivia seemed to accept this and they drank in silence for a while. Eventually Sinead wanted to know if she could ask just one thing. 'Why did you introduce me as Sindy, not Sinead? No one calls me Sindy.'

'Trust me – the less they know, the better,' Olivia said.

The day after meeting Sinead Flynn, Denison took the train to Oxford to see Nick. On the way he reread the notes he'd written the day before, which sparked another flush of the adrenaline he'd felt as he listened to her account of visiting Olivia in London. What Sinead had told him seemed to fit so well with what he had come to suspect. Soon he'd be able to test his theory – and if he was right he'd have some real news for Weathers.

'Did you ever meet Olivia's parents?' was the first question he asked him once the small-talk was out of the way.

'No.' Nick frowned. 'She didn't want me to. I got the impression she was ashamed of them.' Weathers had told Denison that Olivia's dad had previous convictions for grievous bodily harm and burglary. Denison could understand why Olivia might be reluctant to introduce him to Nick.

'Did Sinead Flynn ever tell you about the time she visited Olivia in London?'

'No . . . I didn't know she had. Olivia never mentioned it. When was that?'

'The summer after your first year.'

Nick bit at a fingernail. 'Olivia wanted to stay with me and my parents again. But my mum said no. She thought we were getting too serious too soon. I'd made the mistake of telling her we'd got neighbouring rooms in Carriwell Court. "*What happens when the two of you split up?*"' he mimicked his mother's voice. '"*You'll be stuck next to the girl for the rest of the year!*" I wanted to go with Olivia, to stay with her if she couldn't stay with me, but like I said she didn't want me anywhere near them.'

'How was your relationship in the months following Amanda Montgomery's murder?' asked Denison.

'I suppose it made us closer if anything. A lot of couples at Ariel split up after it – whether that was because the girl-friends didn't trust the boyfriends, or the boyfriends were being too overprotective, I don't know. There were a lot of guys who wanted to do the Rag Blind Date that year, I know that much.'

'What was that, some kind of charity event?'

'Yeah – all the colleges take part. You fill out a form with your details, answer a few silly questions, pay some money and they match you with someone from another college to go out with on Valentine's Day. But it didn't happen that year. Not for Ariel anyway.' Nick looked tired. 'None of the girls from the other colleges wanted to risk going out on a date with a guy from Ariel. They didn't want anything to do with us.'

'You went out on your date with Olivia though.'

He smiled. 'Yeah, we saved up for a bit and splurged it all on champagne in Brown's.'

Denison frowned. 'Brown's? Are you sure?'

'Yeah. Why?'

Denison flipped back through his notes from his conversations with Olivia. 'She told me you went to see a film – *Interview with the Vampire* – and ate in a restaurant called Venezia.'

'That was the next year,' Nick said.

'Are you sure?'

'Sure I'm sure. Liv's always doing stuff like that.'

'Like what?'

'Getting things mixed up. Thinking something happened at a different time to when it did. Forgetting things. This one time we were meant to meet up in town and she didn't turn up. I was worried, what with the so-called Cambridge Butcher around, so I raced back to our rooms and there she was, having a cup of tea and watching telly. I went mad at her, really yelling, and she just did her usual thing of going blank at me.'

'Going blank?'

'Yeah, she'll sort of go into a bit of a zombie state for a minute and her eyes will go blank. Then she'll either apologize and be all sweetness and light, or she'll spit like a cobra and launch into you.'

Olivia was gazing at the vase of bright anemones on the coffee table.

'They're pretty, aren't they?' commented Denison, trying to get the conversation going.

'Yes,' she said in a mousy voice.

'Olivia, how are you feeling today?'

She shrugged minutely. 'OK.'

'You know, I saw Nick yesterday. He says to send his love.'

She smiled. Just a small smile, but it was there.

'It was strange though. He didn't seem to think you'd spent that Valentine's Day you were telling me about at the cinema. He thought you'd gone to Brown's Restaurant – you know, the big one on Trumpington Street?'

She shook her head. 'No, I don't think so.'

'He's right, though, Olivia. I checked and Peterhouse's film society was showing *Casablanca* as their Valentine movie that year. You must have gone the next year. Do you remember having dinner at Brown's?'

She shook her head again.

'He says the waiter brought you over a red rose. There was a heart-shaped balloon tied to your chair. You don't remember this?'

Again she shook her head. A single tear spilled down her cheek.

'Olivia, I saw Sinead Flynn three days ago, in Cambridge. She told me some interesting things.' He saw Olivia shrink into herself, almost as if she were trying to take up less space in the universe. 'Can you think what she might have told me?'

'No,' Olivia whispered.

'Do you remember Sinead coming to visit you in London?'

'She didn't!' Olivia's voice was sharp.

'She visited one summer – came and found you at your

parents' shop. You took her to a pub packed full of England supporters watching the World Cup.' Olivia was shaking her head vigorously, more tears coursing down her flushed cheeks. 'You told her not to tell anyone back in Cambridge about your parents. Why was that? Why did you tell everyone your name was Olivia when it's actually Cleo?'

Olivia's whole body was shaking. Then Denison saw the blankness that Nick had described. Olivia stiffened then sat back in the seat. Her eyes stared ahead, seeing nothing, like doll's eyes. He watched, fascinated, holding his breath.

It only lasted a few seconds and then a ripple ran through her and she blinked. Adjusting her focus, she looked up at Denison. 'I'm sorry, Dr Denison,' she said, her voice calm. She reached forward for a tissue from the box on the coffee table and wiped her tears away as though she was wiping off make-up before bed. 'What were you asking?'

'I was asking your name,' he lied, toes curling involuntarily inside his shoes.

'Well, well,' she said with a smile, 'I was wondering when you'd work it out. My name is Helen, Dr Denison. Good to meet you. Officially, that is.'

Chapter Ten

The crime scene wasn't far from DCI Weathers' flat. His heater had barely had time to warm up the car before he pulled up on Victoria Avenue, the road that bisected Midsummer Common and Jesus Green.

It was the morning after Bonfire Night. Every 5 November there was a fireworks display and funfair held on the common, attended by thousands of Cambridgeshire residents. There were still a few caravans and lorries from the fair parked up, the grass churned into mud. Over by some trees that lined Jesus Green, Weathers spotted the blue and white police cordon tape. On the other side of the stream that ran across the park a white tent was already set up: the kind they used to shelter corpses from the elements and prying eyes.

He headed in the direction of the tent, walking gingerly along the plank of wood that bridged the narrow stream, and went over to a man in a crime-scene unit body suit, white booties on his feet.

'Hey, doc, you got here quick.'

The pathologist shrugged. 'I was staying at my alma mater last night.' Dr Trevor Bracknell also taught the university's medical students and was on the faculty of Magdalene College.

'So, what can you tell me?'

Bracknell led him over to the tent, which was nestled behind an overhanging bramble bush, between a group of evergreens. Weathers felt pine needles scrape his scalp as he manoeuvred himself through the trees. Bracknell pulled back the tent flap to let them both in.

The girl had been propped up against a tree, hands in her lap, legs together and in front of her. Her face was covered in blood, her nose crushed, the skin stained green. There was a deep gash in her lip that revealed her left canine tooth right up to the gum, giving her a strange leering expression. Her tights were laddered, one leg torn and bunched around her ankle. There was no sign of her shoes.

Weathers dropped into a crouching position, getting a closer look. 'Well, at least she's still in one piece. Any idea how long she's been dead?'

'Between around seven p.m. last night and two a.m. this morning,' said Bracknell. Weathers looked at him, but Bracknell just shrugged. 'You know I can't give you an accurate time of death till we get her on the table.'

'Yeah yeah. I'm guessing head injury for cause of death.'

'Probably. Although who knows what we'll find when we strip her off back at the lab. Maybe a puncture wound from a syringe. Or an ice pick injury in the eardrum.' The pathologist was known for his subtle sarcasm.

Weathers wasn't going to let him get away with it. 'You've been watching *Midsomer Murders* again.' Bracknell snorted.

'Hey, guv.' It was DS Halloran, wrapped up in a blue ski jacket.

'Jack, what've you found?'

'A fucked-up crime scene, that's what. There's beer cans, fag butts and rubber johnnies all over the shop. We could get DNA from fifty different people just from this crap.'

'Looks like she might have been raped,' pointed out Weathers, nodding at the torn pair of tights. 'If she was, fingers crossed we'll get her killer's DNA. Any ID on her?'

Bracknell shook his head. 'Nothing in her pockets but some make-up and a hanky.'

'No sign of a handbag? Or shoes?'

'Nope.' Halloran shrugged. 'Robbery gone bad? Or a rapist nicking the bag and the designer shoes as a nice set of trophies?'

'If he was after the cash he'll have ditched the bag by now. It'd be around somewhere. Radio in a request to let us know if any purses or bags get found or handed in. And find out if anyone was reported missing in the last twelve hours.'

The girl in front of him tugged away the hairband and freed her curls. She shook them up with her hand and leaned back into the couch, tucking her feet under her.

'You don't allow smoking in here, right?' she asked with a relaxed smile.

Denison just looked at her. Then he started and felt automatically for the pack of cigarettes in his inner jacket pocket.

'We're not meant to, no,' he said. 'But I won't tell if you don't.' He brought out the pack and offered her one, then lit one for himself. Then he remembered to get the ashtray out from its hiding place in one of his lockable drawers. The canister of apple-scented air freshener too.

The girl took a deep lungful of smoke and exhaled with a sigh of pleasure. 'I haven't had one of these in ages. None of the others smoke. Not the ones getting an outing, anyway.'

Denison nearly choked on his cigarette. He tried to appear nonchalant. 'The others?' he said casually.

'Yes, the others.' The girl's eyes watched him through the smoke curling up from her cigarette. 'If you want to ask me questions, you'll have to be more direct. You're not going to fool me into opening up more than I mean to. So you may as well be straight with me.'

Denison sat forward in his chair and stubbed out his barely smoked cigarette.

'OK . . .' he said. 'When you say others, who are you talking about? Olivia?'

The girl nodded. 'She's one of them. The main one, I suppose. And I'm probably what you'd call the second in command, though it feels as though I'm the one steering the ship most of the time, if you know what I mean.'

'Who else is there, other than Olivia?'

'Let's see – there's Mary, she's the smart one. The one who got us into Cambridge. Often couldn't be arsed to turn up for supervisions, so Olivia had a few panics. And there's Kelly, who I think you've met. She's a little mouse, wouldn't say boo to a goose, etc. And Vanna, the one you'd want to make an appearance if you were about to be mugged. Christie's the youngest, she's just a toddler really. There's Jude. And there's me, Helen. I'm not the smartest, not the toughest, not the youngest. I suppose I'm the one keeping it all together, trying not to make things too difficult for Olivia. The poor cow doesn't know about us, you see. I try and make the transitions smooth, but I can't always control the others.' Helen tapped her cigarette against the rim of the ashtray, dislodging a centimetre of incinerated tobacco.

Denison was scribbling swift notes. In the centre, ringed, was the name Jude.

'How long have you all existed?' he asked.

Helen's eyes looked up to the ceiling, as though she was trying to remember. 'I'm not a hundred per cent sure, as I wasn't there right from the start. I think Kelly was first, then Mary, then Vanna. Christie came last. I think maybe Olivia was three when it started. Three or four.'

Three or four years old. Denison knew where he had to steer the conversation. Nearly all the literature on the subject – at least, all the literature that believed what he was currently encountering was a genuine disorder – agreed that its cause was rooted in severe, prolonged childhood abuse. He took a deep breath.

'Helen, can you tell me what prompted Olivia to—'

'Split into all of us? Well, I would imagine that would be being raped by that son of a bitch who calls himself her father.'

The abuse didn't start with rape, Helen told him. Olivia's father thought she had to be 'educated' first. There was no age at which she could not recall abuse of one kind or another. She was born into it.

Her father raped her for the first time when she was five. She closed her eyes and pretended she was Kelly. Poor imaginary friend Kelly tended to get the worst of it. It was Kelly who featured in the photos that Olivia's father took, and

Kelly who was eventually passed onto other men he'd found with the same savage tastes.

When Olivia was eight the other men started to pay visits in person. Her father was paid well – either in cash or in kind. If the men hurt her – beat her, or marked her – they had to pay extra. It was Vanna who fantasized about grabbing a kitchen knife and castrating the bastards. When Olivia couldn't concentrate at school – when she knew an 'uncle' was visiting that night, or on those mornings when her father had winked at her over breakfast, which was his signal that she must come home in her lunch break – Mary would come out and take over doing the schoolwork. Christie appeared when Olivia was thirteen and didn't have the strength to do anything other than curl up into a ball and cry. When she was Christie she could pretend she was too young to know that what was happening to her was wrong.

Olivia went through puberty at fourteen, and by fifteen, when she looked more like a woman than a girl, the other men stopped calling round. She had two younger sisters, Samantha and Jodie, and she waited for the men to start visiting them instead. It never happened. Her sisters remained unmolested.

Her father punished her for each man who lost interest in her. He punished her by waiting behind the door in her bedroom and punching her in the kidneys when she walked into the room. He punished her by making her eat what their cat Tintin had left in his litter tray. He punished her once by shaving all her hair off – they'd loved that at school the next Monday – and once by making her lie on the floor with her eyes shut, then kneeling on her chest until he heard a rib snap.

'The ribs do break surprisingly easily,' the doctor at Accident and Emergency told her parents, trying to suppress a yawn. 'I'd recommend,' he looked at his clipboard, 'Cleo avoids netball classes for a while. Or at least plays with less competitive classmates.'

Puberty didn't allow her to escape from her father's sexual predation. However the rapes didn't appear to turn him on as they had in the past; it seemed more as though he felt it was his duty, his only way of keeping her in line. The attacks were more random and often as casual as if he'd fancied a wank and decided it would be as quick and convenient to spill his seed in his daughter instead of into a tissue.

Once Vanna came to the surface and the girl who normally lay motionless beneath him turned into a spitting, feral animal. She scratched at him, his skin amassing under her fingernails. He slammed her head against the bed's headboard so hard she nearly passed out, and as she lay dazed on the pink bed sheet, he got a metal coat hanger from her wardrobe and punished her with it. None of Olivia's personalities had ever worked up the courage to find out if she could still have children.

Denison swallowed hard past the lump in his throat as he heard Helen tell Olivia's story. He fought to stay objective.

'What about your mother?' he asked.

Helen's cigarette had burned out a long time ago. He offered her another, which she accepted. 'She knew. The bitch knew. He'd tell her, "Cleo earned us another fifty quid tonight." And she'd say, "Work her harder – it's Jodie's birthday next week."'

'Did *you* ever . . . were you ever . . .'

'You're very coy for a forensic psychiatrist,' said Helen. 'I thought the idea was to appear unshockable.'

'To be honest I haven't come across anything like this before,' confessed Denison. He cleared his throat. 'Helen, were you ever raped?'

She nodded, looking at the lit end of the cigarette. 'I got my fair share of Olivia's visitors. Not the violent ones, though. I tended to come out with the ones who wanted to be seduced. The ones who thought kids secretly enjoyed being fucked by old men.'

Denison looked at the myriad questions he'd scrawled on his notepad. 'Can I ask if you have any idea why your sisters weren't subjected to the same abuse?'

Helen shrugged. 'Not a clue. Olivia's parents treated her like she just happened to live in the same house, for their entertainment and profit. They treated her sisters as though they were their only true children.'

'Does Olivia get on with her sisters?'

'There's inevitably some bitterness and jealousy there. Although I can't imagine she would truly be happier if Samantha and Jodie had suffered the same fate.'

Denison leaned back in his seat, straightening the seams of his jacket. 'It's quite unusual,' he began, 'for survivors of such severe abuse to be able to form normal, healthy sexual relationships. But Olivia and Nick seem to belie this. Can you explain?'

Helen brought the cigarette to her lips, hesitated, then took a drag on it. 'Sometimes it's me he's with,' she confessed. 'But you're right, it's normally Olivia. I'm not sure I can fully explain it. My guess is that she just doesn't remember ninety-nine per cent of the abuse. That's what we were there for. Olivia hates her parents, feels sick at the very idea of them, but I'm not sure she even knows why. Not consciously.

'There's also the fact it's Nick. The boy is just a fundamentally decent human being. We felt safe with him the moment we met him. We trusted him. We knew he'd never hurt us. He made us feel like we were normal.'

Helen's eyelashes were wet. She coughed and stubbed out the cigarette. 'I'm aware I'm taking up much more of your time today than usual, doctor.' She sat up, putting on her shoes. 'Do you have any more questions?'

He hadn't looked at his watch for over an hour, which meant his next patient was probably getting very impatient.

'Just one more for now. Who's Jude?'

Helen's face was serious. 'He wouldn't be happy if I told you about him,' she said, almost whispering. 'I'm sorry. He can come out whenever he likes, you see.' She paused at the door. 'And I wouldn't want him to hurt you.'

The girl's body, washed and naked, lay on the metal autopsy table. The surface was angled so that any fluids escaping from the corpse drained down through holes into containers underneath.

The victim was slim, with manicured hands and trimmed pubic hair. There was a Y incision running down her torso, exposing her organs.

Halloran tilted his head. 'Nice tits,' he commented, receiving a disdainful look from Dr Bracknell.

Although the girl's face had now been washed there was too much damage to tell if she had been pretty. Her nose was flattened, her eyes swollen shut. Teeth jutted through the ripped upper lip. The skin on her stomach was mottled with pink, oval-shaped bruises.

'So, what can you tell us?'

'Severe facial trauma, as you know. Fractured cheek bone, broken nose. Contusion on the forehead and an underlying fracture of the skull. Massive haemorrhage. Wouldn't have caused death straightaway though. When she dropped unconscious or semi-conscious to the ground, her attacker kicked her repeatedly in the stomach and chest. Those round bruises are from the toe of a shoe or boot. She had four broken ribs and a ruptured spleen. But the head injury is what eventually killed her.'

'And does our theory about the murder weapon pan out?'

'The wounds are consistent with her head being driven repeatedly into the trunk of a tree, yes. I've taken samples of the green stains on her face so you can compare them to the moss and lichen on that tree.' They had found blood and hair on the bark of a tree next to the pine that had left needles in Weathers' hair.

'Time of death?'

'There was tortellini and some kind of chocolate dessert in her stomach. It was only partially digested – if you can find out when she ate, just add one to two hours and you'll have your window.'

'And was she sexually assaulted?'

'It doesn't appear that she was,' said Bracknell, sounding as surprised as they were. 'I know her nylons were torn, but she was still wearing her underpants, and they weren't damaged in any way. There were no signs of vaginal or anal trauma, no fluid present and the swabs came up negative.'

'Age?' asked Weathers, already wondering if there was a connection between this murder and Amanda Montgomery's.

'Late teens, early twenties.'

He exchanged glances with Halloran. 'I'd better call Matthew Denison,' he said reluctantly, feeling a headache coming on.

'Matt, I think there's been another one.' Denison was in a jeweller's, looking for a present for his girlfriend's birthday. Deliberating whether to choose gold, platinum or silver, and whether Cass would be able to tell the difference between a diamond and a cubic zirconia, it took him a while to register Weathers' voice. When he did he almost dropped his mobile. 'Matt?' Weathers repeated.

'I'm here.'

Weathers sounded urgent. 'Can you get down here?'

'Sure. I'll be there as soon as I can.'

He drove too fast down the M11, tremors in his hands as he gripped the steering wheel. Weathers met him in the reception area at the police station. There were dark shadows under his eyes and Denison was willing to bet he hadn't seen a razor that morning. He shook Denison's hand.

'Thanks for coming, Matt. Come on, I'll take you to the incident room.'

They walked along the corridor, Denison's rubber-soled shoes squeaking on the linoleum. 'Was it bad?'

Weathers almost laughed. 'Yes, it was bad. Not as bad

as Amanda, but then I'm not sure that it's easy to top a murder like that.'

There were about ten plainclothes officers in the incident room, most of them on their phones or PCs. WDC Ames was in the process of tacking up photos of the crime scene to a whiteboard at the back of the room. She nodded hello to Denison.

He scanned the photos carefully, swallowing. 'Any idea what killed her?'

'We're thinking a psychopath,' said Ames. She saw Denison's face. 'Sorry, Matt, bad joke.'

'It looks as though her face was battered into one of these trees,' Weathers told him. 'That's where that green colour's from, the bark. There was also a lot of bruising on her chest and abdomen; apparently the killer gave her a good kicking when she was down on the ground.'

'If there was bruising, then she couldn't have died straightaway,' said Denison.

'No. She must have been there a while, dying with hundreds of people just feet away from her. I wonder if she was left for dead, or if the killer watched the life go out of her?'

Denison rubbed his face. 'I think he would have made sure she was dead before he left, as long as he felt safe enough hanging around. In the dark these trees must have given some cover. Although there must be a chance that some randy couples came back here for a bit of privacy?'

'We're appealing for witnesses, but judging by the number of empty bottles in the bins around the park, a

lot of them will still be in bed. You got any ideas popping
up yet, Matt?'

Denison looked again at the photo of the dead girl
propped up against the tree trunk. 'Just that it seems
that there's the same level of violence. Look at her face.
He wanted to obliterate her. But . . . it's different from
the Montgomery murder. It seems impromptu: he had no
weapon on him, so was forced to kill her with his bare
hands, in public. I'd be willing to bet that he knew her,
that she'd been winding him up for a while and that
something she said or did last night just made him snap.
This wasn't planned.'

'You think it's the same killer?'

Denison looked at him. 'Is there any connection
between her and Amanda?'

'You first.'

'You're testing me? Fine. Yes, it's the same killer. Same
inferiority complex, same rage, same hatred of women.
Christ help you if there are two psychopaths like that in
the same town. It has to be the same guy.'

Weathers nodded, sighing.

'Well? There's a connection, isn't there?'

'We only identified her an hour ago, but it turns out
this girl's from Ariel too. Same year as Amanda. Her
name's Eliza Fitzstanley.'

'Eliza, you're going to be frozen,' said Sinead, who was
wearing two jumpers and thermal underwear. 'Take a look
at yourself. It's not worth frostbite just to look glam.'

Eliza was wearing a silk blouse, a short skirt, tights,
Jimmy Choo boots and her favourite Armani raincoat.

'I'll be fine,' she said. 'I've got a little friend to keep me warm.' She half slid a small silver whisky flask out of her coat pocket and winked at her friends.

Sinead rolled her eyes. 'Well, don't blame me when your toes fall off in a week's time.'

Olivia laughed, wrapping a scarf round her neck. 'Are we going to get going?' she said. 'I want to go on the rides before the fireworks start.'

'Just you hold your horses, missy,' Sinead told her. 'It's your tardy boyfriend we're waiting on.' They sat and watched the freshers, who had yet to calm down and settle into Ariel life, frenziedly mingling with each other. One of them put on the Velvet Underground for the fifth time that evening.

Eliza stroked her knee-high shiny boots of leather as she lip-synched along with the song, seductively eyeing a first year who looked as though he wasn't sure whether to be turned on or terrified.

'Ignore her, she's a married woman,' called out Sinead. On cue Godfrey sauntered over, knelt on the floor and kissed the tip of Eliza's boot. As if that wasn't enough he then ran a tongue up the length of the boot and growled.

The first year's mouth dropped open and he shook his head before disappearing in the direction of the pinball machine.

'Godfrey, pull yourself together,' admonished Sinead. 'You're scaring the children.' It was the older students' God-given right to be patronizing about the freshers.

Nick turned up, a packet of sparklers in each pocket, and they headed off towards Midsummer Common.

The night was cold but clear, and as they got closer

to the fair they joined an ever-increasing group of
fellow fairgoers. A river of them flowed into the ocean
of students and townspeople that filled the park.
Giant mechanical rides sparkled with lights, the heavy
bass of their music making the ground vibrate. Olivia
heard whoops and screams from the riders. She
identified the scariest looking ride and dragged Nick
towards it.

The Tornado seemed to involve being strapped into a
carriage and hurtled in every direction at top speed. Nick
looked reluctant, but Olivia only got more excited as she
watched the faces of those already on the ride. She paid
for both of them. After three minutes of centrifugal force
Nick was hoarse from manly screaming and Olivia
wanted to go on again.

'No,' he insisted, and pulled her to the hotdog stand.

'So,' she said, munching on a hotdog with mustard,
'are things OK between you and Godfrey now?'

He shrugged. 'I suppose so. The guy's never going to be
my best man or anything, but I think he does regret
getting involved in that thing between Rob and Victor
Kesselich.'

'And you're not one to hold a grudge.'

He looked at her. Her eyes were bright, still excited by
the lights, motion and sound. 'No, I suppose I'm not.'

He was buying her a glowstick necklace that lit up her
face and neck in a UV blue when they saw Rob and
Laurence. Some uncomfortable nods of greeting passed
between them.

'You having fun?' Rob asked Olivia.

'Definitely. You?'

Rob nodded, looking at Laurence. Olivia saw him very subtly brush Laurence's hand with his own.

'That's a very stylish necklace,' said Laurence.

'Thanks,' she said, pretending to preen. 'It's Gucci you know.'

He laughed. 'I can tell. Well, you guys enjoy the fireworks.'

The pair walked off towards the huge bonfire whose flames were engulfing a large part of the night sky.

'I still can't get my head round that,' said Nick, watching them go.

'No. But it's good for Rob that it's out in the open.'

'I just don't see why he had to quit the rugby team. He's not even rowing any more. I mean, it's not like they're homophobes. They don't care if he's gay.'

'Yeah, but they're not exactly the rainbow brigade, are they? Maybe he just doesn't feel comfortable there any more.'

'So he's hanging round with the pseuds and intellectuals? I wouldn't have said that was his scene either.'

'But that's part of what college is about,' pointed out Olivia. 'Exploring a bit. Finding out what you like. Finding yourself.' She pulled a face. 'Now *I* sound like a pseud. Quick, find me something alcoholic to drink before I get any worse.'

They found the others in a pub at the corner of the common called the Fort St George, squashed onto the end of a bench outside. The pub was heaving with people and Olivia immediately gave up on the idea of venturing inside for a drink. The queue at the bar was six deep.

Instead she took a swig from Eliza's hip flask, passing it along to Godfrey.

'Aren't you cold?' Paula asked Eliza. Paula was wearing a very cute beanie and thick woollen overcoat, with her own pair of dark leather boots. Paula knew how to dress warmly yet stylishly.

'Will everyone please stop asking me that?' said Eliza, a small dart of annoyance wrinkling her neat forehead.

'Aren't you worried you're going to ruin your Jimmy Choos in this mud?'

'Paula, leave her alone,' drawled Godfrey, sucking on one of his expensive Italian cigarettes.

'You should dress more sensibly, like Olivia here,' Paula persisted.

Eliza crinkled her nose. 'I don't own sensible clothes.'

'Or sensible underwear,' added Godfrey. 'Which is why I love her.'

'Besides,' said Eliza, 'I've never set foot in Primark and I don't intend to start now. Harvey Nicks would never forgive me.'

'Godfrey, have you ever dated a girl who wasn't the daughter of a millionaire?' asked Olivia, tilting her head as though she was genuinely curious.

'I didn't know such girls existed.' Godfrey lit another cigarette from the remnants of his first.

'Godfrey, you're such an arse,' laughed Sinead.

'Did you know Godfrey's got the Union Jack pinned to his ceiling?' said Paula, her tone cutting. 'He's a real patriot. Red, white and blue. Queen and Country. With an emphasis on the *country*.'

'I like my girls to be able to lie back and think of

England; explained Godfrey, blowing smoke in Paula's face.

'Paula, why are you being such a bitch?' asked Eliza. Her cute little girl voice was gone – she just sounded hard and angry.

There was an awkward silence. Paula sat back and forced a smile. 'Ignore me, Eliza; she said. 'Must be PMT.'

The group made chit-chat for a bit and split up at the earliest opportunity; Paula and Sinead went to the toilets together and didn't come back. The remaining four waited for a while, looking at their watches.

'We were thinking of visiting Madame Rose; said Nick.

'I didn't realize there were brothels in Cambridge; said Godfrey.

'The psychic, you idiot. Shall we see you at the boathouse at half seven?' Ariel's boathouse on the other side of the river had great views of the fireworks.

'Sure, see you then.'

So Nick and Olivia escaped, relieved to be away from the bad atmosphere.

'Madame Rose?' she said when they were out of earshot.

'I thought it would be a laugh; Nick said. 'Go on, I'll pay.'

'I'm not a charity case you know; Olivia told him.

'I know, I know, don't get touchy. It's just it's my silly idea – no reason you should have to fork out for it. C'mon, she might tell us how many kids we're going to have.'

Madame Rose inhabited a caravan near the river path, painted with roses and various tarot cards. Her prices

were written in black marker on a board by her door. A
net curtain wafted in the cold air.

'You go first,' prodded Olivia.

Nick knocked on the caravan by the open door. An old
lady with dyed black hair, half an inch of grey roots
showing, appeared with a smile, fag in hand.

'Hello, love. You want a reading?'

'Please.'

'Both of you together or one at a time?'

'One at a time,' said Olivia. 'I'll wait out here – give you
some privacy.'

Madame Rose threw the cigarette onto the mud and
ushered Nick inside. She closed the door behind them.

Olivia leaned against a park bench that faced towards
the river and wrapped her arms around herself, trying to
keep warm. Some pissed guys walked past drinking beer,
and one with a shaved head and ripped jeans asked her if
she wanted to go on the ghost train with him. She told
him to bugger off and pulled her scarf tighter.

After five minutes Nick reappeared. He seemed flushed
as he nodded goodbye to Madame Rose. Olivia walked
over.

'What did she say?' she asked.

'Tell you later. Your turn.'

She looked over his shoulder to Madame Rose, who
crooked her finger and beckoned her in.

'OK. See you at the boathouse?'

'I can wait for you here.'

'No, go ahead, I won't be long.'

The caravan was warm after the chill November air,
but it stank of cigarette smoke and cat food. Madame

Rose indicated to Olivia to sit down on a spongy green chair. She sat opposite, across a scratched wooden table.

'Your lover has already paid,' she said, 'but he didn't tell me what reading you would like.' Olivia must have looked bemused, because she continued: 'Tarot? Tea leaves? Palmistry? My crystal ball?' She chuckled. 'I'm just joking about that last one.'

'Uh . . . tarot?'

'A good choice.' She removed a black silk scarf from a stack of large cards and handed them to Olivia to shuffle. Then Madame Rose took them back and dealt five cards face down.

'Just make sure I don't get the death card,' joked Olivia.

'No chance of that,' said Madame Rose. 'I usually remove it.' She saw Olivia raise an eyebrow. 'Well, it tends to freak out the non-believers, who never comprehend that it doesn't literally mean death, just an end to one thing and the beginning of something else.'

'That old line,' said Olivia.

'I can tell you're a cynic too.' Madame Rose was smiling. 'Well, it's up to you whether or not you believe the cards. They'll tell the same story whether you're a believer or not.'

She turned over the first card. It showed two trees with a rope slung between them and a man hanging upside down from the rope.

'The Hanged Man,' she said. 'You're being self-sacrificing. You're doing something you're uncomfortable with, to get something you want. These days they call it passive-aggressive behaviour. Better to be direct.' She turned over the second card. On its face were three large stones. Behind them was an indigo night sky and a large white moon whose glow was obscured by a black mask.

'The Moon,' said Madame Rose. 'This is the card of illusion. You are either deceiving someone, or someone is deceiving you. Things are hidden, obscured. Someone is living behind a mask.'

'Well, one of my friends may be a savage killer,' said Olivia. 'I'm guessing they're being pretty deceptive.'

Madame Rose pursed her lips and turned over card number three. A man sat on a throne, a golden crown on his head. His shoulders were broad, his face stern. 'The Emperor. This represents a strong and powerful man. A man who protects his kingdom.' She noticed Olivia clasp her hands together in her lap.

The fourth card depicted a man in white robes, standing on a mountain top with his arms raised to the sky. 'The Shaman,' Madame Rose told Olivia. 'This is a very spiritual card. It speaks of a person who is travelling a lonely road, but who is on the verge of revelation. This person is about to see the world in a different way to us mere mortals.' She reached for the fifth and last card.

The card showed a blindfolded woman, a sword in one hand, a pair of scales in the other. 'Judgement,' said Madame Rose. 'This card tells me you stand in judgement of yourself. But you need to forgive yourself.' She leaned forward, grasping Olivia's hands and squeezing them. 'Whatever happened you need to stop blaming yourself. It wasn't your fault.' She was surprised to see Olivia was struggling to hold back tears.

The vulnerable ones tended to be most generous with their tips but Madame Rose could tell from the girl's cheap coat and scuffed shoes that she'd be wasting her time trying to get any more money. She looked at her watch. 'OK, lovey, time's up.'

Olivia swiftly wiped her eyes with the end of her scarf. 'Thanks.' She scraped her chair back and made for the door. Hand on the doorknob, she paused and turned back. 'Just so I know what to expect – what did you tell my boyfriend? About us?'

Madame Rose pulled a fresh cigarette from her pack. 'I told him nothing good could ever come of your union,' she said, looking Olivia right in the eye. Then, fag in mouth, she bent her head to her cigarette lighter, sucking on the filter tip. Olivia stared at her. Then Madame Rose winked. 'Just kidding,' she drawled, expelling a long ripple of smoke. 'I told him you'd have three kids and would die in your beds at a ripe old age. Goodbye, Olivia.'

Without a word, Olivia left the caravan.

Olivia reached Ariel boathouse just as the fireworks started. 'Have you seen Nick?' she asked Sinead and Paula, both of whom were sipping mulled wine and gazing transfixed at the show.

'Nope,' they said, refusing to look away from the fountains of green cinders that illuminated the sky.

Aware she was missing the show Olivia hurriedly squeezed her way through the crowd to the doors of the boathouse, where three members of the boat club were charging a quid for home-cooked burgers. 'Guys, have you seen Nick Hardcastle?' she shouted over the pops of the rockets exploding. They shook their heads, focusing on the meat sizzling on the barbecue.

She felt a dig in her ribs and turned to find Nick behind her. Grinning, he grabbed her hand and pulled her right to the edge of the riverbank, where they had an unobstructed view of the fireworks. There were 'oohs' to accompany a silver shower of light, 'aahs' in appreciation of pink pollen exploding from golden petals of fire and a spontaneous round of applause for the finale – burst after burst of multi-coloured sparks shimmering across the black November night.

'Whooooooo!!! Whooooooo!!' Leo skipped past, a velvet jester's hat perched on his dreadlocks. He grabbed Olivia and spun her round. 'Whoa, man, wasn't that fantastic? These magic mushrooms are fucking great!'

She shoved him off. 'Leo, you're a wanker. Now go and be a wanker somewhere else.'

He flicked her the V sign and danced off in the direction of some of his stoner friends, who were buying burgers with all the trimmings. They at least seemed happy to see him.

'So, what did Madame Rose tell you, then?' Nick asked, squeezing Olivia's hand.

'Let's just say we'd better buy some shares in Mothercare,' she reported.

'Do either of you know where Eliza is?' It was Godfrey, looking worried.

'No, but I'm sure she's around somewhere. Have you tried the boathouse?'

'She's not there. I've been looking for her for the last twenty minutes. She said she was heading straight here.'

'Have you tried her mobile?'

'Of course I have. She's not answering it.'

'Godfrey, I'm sure she's fine,' Nick said, trying to reassure him.

'Yeah, she probably just bumped into someone on the way here,' Olivia added.

Godfrey looked at them both, eyes panicked.

'That's what I'm afraid of.'

Chapter Eleven

'It's called Dissociative Identity Disorder, or DID for short. Used to be known as Multiple Personality Disorder.'

Weathers just looked at him across the table. It was two years and eight months since their meeting at Cambridge police station, when Denison had first seen the photos of Amanda Montgomery's corpse. Weathers now had some grey hairs and a few more lines on his face. Denison's waist size had grown by nearly an inch, mainly thanks to Cass's home cooking.

'You're not kidding, are you?' Weathers finally said. He looked at Denison for another minute, then turned to grab the waitress. 'Do you serve spirits?' he asked her. 'I need a double shot of whisky.'

The waitress looked at Denison. 'And you, sir?'

'I'll stick with my mineral water thanks.'

Weathers waited for her to move out of earshot. 'You're trying to tell me she's schizo?'

Denison took a deep breath. 'Stephen, as an experienced police officer I know that you're aware it's a common misconception that schizophrenia and multiple personalities are the same condition.'

Weathers did know this. It was one of Denison's pet hates; he had been known to walk out of films in which psychologists blithely referred to a character with multiple personalities as a schizophrenic, swearing under his breath about Hollywood producers getting their facts straight. Weathers, at this precise moment, wanted to bait Denison, the bearer of some bloody bad news.

'So she'll never be able to testify,' said Weathers.

'People with mental illnesses still have a right to be heard in court,' argued Denison.

'She'd hardly make a credible witness.' Weathers let out a massive sigh. 'So, basically we're fucked.'

Denison wasn't about to contradict him. There was considerable controversy in the psychiatric community about whether DID was even a genuine condition, with some arguing that it was inadvertantly created during therapy sessions by well-meaning doctors who were searching for something that wasn't there. Although Denison himself believed DID was a real disorder – there were plenty of documented cases of patients who exhibited DID symptoms long before they went near a therapist's couch – he knew it wouldn't be hard for the defence to find a psychiatrist who would argue the opposite. He reluctantly explained as much to Weathers.

'It's hard to know what would make the CPS think she was a worse witness,' said Weathers. 'That she actually has multiple personalities, or that she can be persuaded to think she has?'

'Look on the bright side,' Denison tried to tell him. 'At least now there's a chance we'll be able to recover her memory of what happened the night June Okeweno was murdered.'

The waitress arrived with their drinks. Denison waited

until she was back out of hearing range before he resumed the conversation, speaking low and leaning in.

'The fact she can't remember probably means an alter was in charge during the traumatic episode.'

'You've lost me,' said Weathers, looking at Denison over the rim of his glass as he sipped his whisky.

'Alters are what we call the other personalities. They each tend to serve a specific function, so one might be the protector, one might be the child, one might be the risk-taker. Back when she was a kid Olivia starting creating these alters to protect herself psychologically from the abuse she was suffering—'

'What abuse?' asked Weathers.

Denison pulled his MP3 player out of his pocket and handed it over to Weathers. 'I think you'd better listen to this.'

The detective rolled his eyes, but he put the earpieces in and pressed play. After ten minutes the waitress brought their pizzas. Denison ate his slowly, watching Weathers' expression. Weathers didn't touch his. He did down his whisky in one go though, taking big gulps, then motioning for another.

The recording lasted fifty-two minutes. By the time it had finished Denison had eaten his pizza and half of Weathers', and was entrenched in the *Independent*. Weathers had drunk six shots of whisky and didn't look anything other than stone cold sober. He carefully laid the earpieces on the table and pushed the MP3 device back over to Denison.

'Jesus, no wonder she was in trouble most of her childhood,' he said, rubbing his stubble.

'And no wonder she wanted to get into that boarding school,' added Denison. 'Poor kid.'

'Was this what you twigged about that night I was round at yours for dinner?' asked Weathers. 'Something was making those gears in your brain start whirring.'

'People with Dissociative Identity Disorder are predisposed to dissociate in periods of even minor stress,' Denison explained. 'It explained why Olivia "forgot" June's murder – another personality would have taken over to shield her from what was happening.'

'So, if you can get that personality to speak to you, we should be able to find out what happened that night,' Weathers worked out.

'That's right. And that's my plan. The first thing I need to do is explain to Olivia that she has this condition.'

He paused then. 'OK . . .' prompted Weathers. 'Why do I think I'm not going to like the second thing?'

'I'm probably going to need to hypnotize her.'

'Isn't that a bit risky?' Weathers asked. 'False memory syndrome and all that?'

'Well, according to you she's never going to see the inside of the witness box anyway, and it's pretty clear from the literature that it's the best way of drawing out another alter. It's a shortcut right to them.'

'Just make sure you don't accidentally draw out Jude,' said Weathers, signalling to the waitress for their bill. 'He sounds like a scary fucker.' He finished his final drink. 'Hey, you sure *she* isn't the Cambridge Butcher?'

Denison considered this. 'Most people with DID know the difference between right and wrong; they understand the nature and quality of their actions. Their personalities aren't necessarily psychotic, there are just more of them.'

'Could there be one personality that doesn't know it's wrong to cut a girl's head off?'

Denison frowned. 'Yes, conceivably. A very young personality, or one that acts purely on instinct and is totally unsocialized. But a personality like that couldn't have got away with even one murder. It would have needed the help of the others to cover up the crime.'

'So, even if the homicidal personality got away with pleading insanity, I could get the others convicted of being accessories after the fact?'

Denison nearly answered, then saw the gleam in Weathers' eye and burst out laughing instead. The two of them laughed for quite a while, only stopping when the waitress brought over the bill.

When Eliza didn't turn up at the boathouse that night, Godfrey alone had gone looking for her. None of the others took her disappearance seriously, knowing what a flake she was. Probably she'd bumped into an old friend from her boarding school – half of them seemed to be at Cambridge – and was currently sipping cocktails with Jocasta or Bunty in some bar nearby. Godfrey searched for an hour, then set off back to Ariel to see if she was there. Not only was there no sign of her in her room or the bar, but there were notes and flyers in her pigeonhole, a sure indication that she hadn't been back. All the students checked their pigeonholes every time they went in or out of the college. He scrawled a message himself, letting her know he was looking for her.

He spent three hours searching Eliza's regular haunts, but when he returned to Ariel her pigeonhole was still unemptied. He knocked on Paula's door, waking her up. 'Not tonight, Godfrey,' she groaned, rubbing her eyes.

'Don't flatter yourself, I'm looking for Eliza,' he told her. She went to her bedside table and looked at her watch.

'Maybe we should call the police station,' she said. 'Ask to speak to DCI Weathers. He'll know whether to take this seriously or not.'

'Of course we should fucking take it seriously!'

She started dressing herself over the vest top and shorts she was wearing. 'Godfrey, Eliza's been known to stay up past her bedtime before now.'

'I just have this odd feeling. I think something's happened to her.'

Nick and Olivia were having lunch when his mobile rang, Paula's name appearing on the display.

'Hi Paula, what's up?'

She sounded funny. 'Nick, can you come to the police station? I'm here with Godfrey and I think something's wrong.'

'What do you mean?'

'I mean Eliza's still not turned up. And I think there's something the police aren't telling us. Nicky, I can't cope with this on my own, can you please come? We're at Parkside.'

He looked at his watch. 'Sure, I'll be there in ten minutes.'

Olivia insisted on coming with him. They cycled there, locking up their bikes outside the station. A man was standing outside the entrance, talking into his mobile phone. He stopped in the middle of his sentence when he saw Nick.

'Nick? Nick Hardcastle?'

Nick frowned at him. 'Do I know you?'

'What's going on, Nick? Do you know the victim?'

'What victim?' Nick's face was white.

The man pressed a button on his phone. He held it up by Nick's mouth. 'There was a body found today on Jesus Green,' he said, recording Nick's reaction. 'A girl, around twenty years old, blonde hair, medium height, slim build. Sound familiar, Nick? I don't suppose that fits the description of any of your friends?'

Olivia slapped the reporter hard, feeling the bristles of his cheek against the palm of her hand. 'Fuck you, you bastard. Just leave us the fuck alone!'

The reporter looked shocked, his cheek already starting to redden. He pointed through the large glass windows of the police station's reception area to the desk sergeant, who had seen everything.

'Chris, you saw that, right? Right?'

The desk sergeant just met his eyes through the glass and slowly shrugged. 'What?' he mouthed.

'That dirty fucker,' swore the reporter, jamming the phone back in his pocket, stalking over to his car and driving off.

The desk sergeant half winked at them as they walked in. 'You want to try to avoid actually hitting them,' he told Olivia under his breath. 'You don't wanna be done for assault. Just keep telling 'em "no comment". Drives them nuts.'

'Is Paula Abercrombie here?' asked Nick. 'Or Godfrey Parrish?'

The desk sergeant rubbed his moustache. 'Yeah. They're here. Come on, I'll buzz you through.'

He got a PC to lead them through the station to where Paula was sitting, her face puffy and eyes bloodshot. Her sleeves were pulled down around her fingertips, and she twisted a mug of tea round and round in her hands. When she saw Nick she stood up, her face crumpling, and ran to him. He wrapped her up in a hug as she sobbed.

Olivia stroked her hair. 'Shh,' she said. 'Shh. It'll be OK.'

'I think something's happened to Eliza, but they won't tell us. She never came back last night; Godfrey's spent hours trying to find her. They keep whispering to each other, looking really serious, and I'm sure she's dead and they're just not telling us!' She wiped her nose with her jumper sleeve.

'I think they found a body,' said Nick gently. 'I don't know for certain – there was a reporter outside and he said something, but you know what those bastards are like.'

'Oh God . . .' she said. 'Oh, Nicky, I was such a bitch to her last night. I didn't mean to be! If I'd known I wouldn't have been such a bitch . . .'

'Does it have to be you?' Godfrey was sitting in one of the interview rooms, Weathers opposite him.

Weathers looked at Sally next to him, then back to Godfrey. 'You have a problem with me because of what happened with your friend Rob McNorton and that fight in Ariel bar in January?'

Godfrey actually laughed, rubbing his eyes. He gazed at Weathers blearily. 'No, not because of that. Because you're in charge of the Butcher case. And frankly I don't want the guy in charge of that case being the same guy who's talking to me about my missing girlfriend. It's damn well freaking me out.'

Weathers sat back in his chair. 'I'm sorry, that's not why I'm here. I'm just a senior officer at this nick – I deal with serious crimes. We take the fact your girlfriend's missing seriously – doesn't mean we think her disappearance is linked to the Montgomery case.'

Godfrey looked at him. 'I want to believe you. I'm just not sure I do. Please just ask me your questions and let's get this over with.'

Weathers looked at his notes. 'Can you tell me what time Eliza went missing?'

'It was between seven and quarter past seven last night. At least, that was the last time I saw her.'

'And where did you see her last?'

'Midsummer Common. We were at the funfair.'

'Was anyone else with you?'

'Earlier on in the evening, yes. Nick Hardcastle, his girlfriend Olivia, Paula Abercrombie, Sinead Flynn. We were all having a drink at the Fort St George. Then we split up and Eliza and I went to have a go on one of the fairground stalls. We didn't win anything. I went to the portaloos and she wasn't there when I came out.'

'Can you describe Eliza to us?'

Godfrey hid his face in his hands. 'Oh God . . . she's

blonde, five foot five, she's a size eight. She has blue eyes.'

'What was she wearing?'

'A black skirt, black boots. A pink blouse and a black raincoat.'

'And one last question – do you know what she ate yesterday evening?'

Godfrey froze. He looked from Weathers to Ames disbelievingly. 'You've found her, haven't you?'

'Mr Parrish, we don't know.'

'But you've found a body – a body that fits the description? Otherwise you wouldn't be trying to match her fucking stomach contents!'

'Mr Parrish, if you could remember what she ate . . .'

'Pasta. She had pasta. And afterwards she had some *tarte au chocolat* for dessert. She only ate half of it. She said you didn't absorb any calories if you only ate some of your dessert.'

He looked at their faces and knew it was her.

Weathers was back in the station having accompanied the Fitzstanleys to the morgue to identify the body. Mr Bertram Fitzstanley had asked Weathers how the hell he was supposed to recognize if that beaten and distorted face belonged to his daughter, but his wife Lavinia had with growing agony mapped out the landmarks of her daughter's body: the mole by her navel, the scar on her knee, the left foot that was half a size smaller than the right.

'It's her,' she managed to say and then seemed to collapse in on herself.

Sally was waiting for him in the incident room.

'Crosby wants to see you, Steve.' He could tell from her expression that she was worried.

'What's up?'

She shook her head. 'I don't know for sure. But they've got MacIntyre in there.'

He knocked on the door.

'Enter!' intoned Superintendent Crosby. His office overlooked Parker's Piece and was light and airy. Crosby was the kind of guy who would have preferred a wood-panelled study though, and had brought in leather armchairs and paintings of fox hunts that jarred with the cheap carpet tiles and office blinds.

Opposite Crosby sat DCI Colin 'Mac' MacIntyre. MacIntyre had been a DCI on the Cambridge force for ten years and there was no hint of a promotion in the pipeline. The general consensus was that he'd gone as far up the ladder as he was ever going to – not that Mac agreed. Each summer he held a barbecue for his CID officers and when his house was politely admired, he'd tell them to wait for next year: 'When I make Super, we're going to get an extension on the south side of the house, and have a conservatory added on over this patio area.'

'Ah, Weathers, come in,' said Crosby. 'Take a seat.'

The only empty chair was noticeably angled towards the two occupied seats, making Weathers feel like he was facing an interview panel. He automatically straightened his tie.

Crosby clasped his hands together on the desktop. 'Weathers, I've called you in to talk about this Fitzstanley situation. We're aware that you've jumped to the conclusion that the case is linked to the killing of Amanda Montgomery and frankly this raises a number of concerns about whether you should be the investigating officer on this case. The Chief Superintendent feels, and I tend to agree, that it would be best for DCI MacIntyre to handle the Fitzstanley investigation.'

'Can I ask why?' snapped Weathers, leaning forward, muscles tensing. 'What exactly are your concerns?'

'It's far too early for you to be working on the assumption that the cases are linked. You're obviously very focused on the Montgomery case and I'm afraid that it's affecting your judgement on this one.'

'Sir, that's not true,' Weathers protested. 'Look, it could be a coincidence that the two girls were from the same year at the same college, but it would have to be a bloody big one. How many female students are murdered each year, on average? Maybe one, if that? So what the hell are the chances that two years in a row the unlucky student is a girl from Ariel?'

'Weathers, we're not ruling out the possibility that the cases are linked, but for heaven's sake, the girl's body was only found ten hours ago! You've already made conclusions about the killer, and inevitably you're going to ignore any other possibilities. We can't take the risk that you might be wrong and that the perpetrator will go free whilst you're hunting the Cambridge Butcher, or whatever the hell these bloody journos have called him!' Superintendent Crosby sat back in his chair with a hard sigh, aware that the vein that stuck out on his temple was beginning to pulse.

'Look,' he said in a calmer voice, 'what I'm trying to say is that we feel it would benefit both investigations if DCI MacIntyre were to take over the Fitzstanley case. I'm sure if the evidence did point towards the same perpetrator being responsible for both murders then DCI MacIntyre would be more than happy for the investigation to be turned back over to you. And frankly there's been little progress made on the Montgomery case, so it would perhaps be best if you were allowed to focus all your attention on solving that murder before you moved on to another case.'

Weathers had to literally bite on his tongue until the urge to swear had been battened down. 'Sir, with all due respect, if the cases *are* linked it's going to be much easier for me to identify the killer if half the evidence isn't hidden from me.'

'Weathers, don't be ridiculous!' said Crosby. 'The evidence will not be "hidden" from you – you will be allowed full access to everything MacIntyre turns up.'

Weathers swivelled to face MacIntyre. 'Mac, you must have read my preliminary report – what do you think?'

MacIntyre's suit was seven years old and about two sizes too small for him now. He twisted in it uncomfortably, pulling at his shirt collar, which was digging into his flabby neck. 'In my experience,' he said, clearly dying for a cigarette, 'these kinds of murders, in public areas, tend to be perpetrated by opportunistic criminal types – muggers, rapists, smackheads. I don't see any similarities between this murder and Amanda Montgomery's. Montgomery was murdered in her own room, probably by someone she knew, and there was significant post-mortem mutilation. You don't see that here – this girl was killed with a blunt weapon, not a blade. She was not mutilated. She was murdered in a park, not in her own home. It's nowhere near as violent as the Montgomery killing. You don't get these guys becoming calmer with each murder – they tend to escalate, to get worse.'

'How could it get worse than the Montgomery murder?' asked Weathers, trying to stay reasonable but his voice getting louder with every word. 'Do you not think that maybe the reason why Fitzstanley wasn't as mutilated as Montgomery was because a) he didn't have a knife on him and b) he didn't have the privacy he needed?'

'DCI Weathers, will you please lower your voice!' insisted Crosby. 'My decision is not open to discussion. DCI MacIntyre is now in charge of the Fitzstanley investigation.'

'There's a serial killer out there,' hissed Weathers, pointing out of the window in the direction of Ariel College. 'You can ignore him, you can pretend he's not there, but that won't stop him from killing another girl.'

'How dare you?' said Crosby. 'Believe you me, our utmost priority is for the murderers of these young women to be brought to justice. And if I hear you mention the words "serial killer" outside of this office, you'll be back in uniform so fast your head will spin.'

'You have to kill five to be officially called a serial killer,' Denison said over the phone.

'Why five?'

'You tell me.'

'So, if you only kill four people you're just a normal guy with a nasty temper?'

'Look, Steve, they're obviously worried that there'll be a huge panic if they admit there's someone out there bumping off Cambridge undergrads. You know that at their rank half the job is about politics and PR. What the hell would happen to the town if suddenly no tourists visited and no students applied to study there?'

'So you think they were right to take me off the case?'

'Of course not. Nothing should be more important than catching this guy. I'm just saying I can see their way of thinking.'

'Yeah, you were always good at that.'

'It's kind of my job.'

'I should have grabbed that book about Jack the Ripper, shown them the photo of Mary Kelly compared to the other victims. Then they would've seen what a difference some time and privacy can make to a depraved psycho who wants to know what a woman's insides look like.'

Denison sucked air in through his teeth. 'Hmm, might have backfired. Kelly was the last victim: your rival chief inspector could argue that she illustrated the killer's tendency to escalate that's missing from these murders.'

'Matt, how sure are you that it's the same killer?'

Denison paused. 'Ninety-five per cent.'

Weathers released a frustration-logged sigh. 'So what the hell do I do now?'

'Revisit your witnesses and suspects from Amanda's murder. Among other things ask them about Eliza. Or rather let them ask you, because they probably will. Especially the killer. If he's among your interviewees he's almost certain to want to find out if you're linking the murders.'

'You think of any way I can get MacIntyre to see sense?'

'All I can suggest is that you try to make friends with him. Say "no hard feelings". Let him have his own territory. Eventually he may relax enough that he'll be happy to keep you informed. In the meantime, try to find a member of his team who will report to you on what the investigation's turning up. You want to learn all you can about Eliza without pissing off MacIntyre. The more we know about her, the more we know why the killer selected her; and the more we know why he selected her, the more we know about him. Look especially for similarities between her and Amanda. Shared friends, shared personality traits, shared enemies.'

'Got it. Thanks, Matt.'

'Anytime. And Steve? Unless you get really lucky, he's going to kill again. And you can't feel guilty about it. You can't feel responsible. The blood's on their hands now.'

Chapter Twelve

Eliza had not been popular at Ariel. She had a way of offending people without meaning to, a skill which was second only to her ability to identify within moments the sore spots in someone's psyche, and prod at them with the curiosity of a child investigating the effect of salt on slug skin. But she was also one of the college 'personalities', someone whom everybody knew, or at least knew of. And she was one of theirs. There was a bond between the students of a particular college; even more so in Ariel, whose students' siege mentality had become well entrenched in the year since Amanda Montgomery's murder. The common consensus now – based on beliefs whose origins were long since forgotten – was that the killer of Amanda Montgomery was an outsider. A stranger, a psychopath like the mythical escapee from the lunatic asylum, had invaded their ivory tower, murdered and then slunk away with the darkness. It couldn't be one of them; the police had taken DNA swabs, hadn't they? And no one had subsequently been arrested. They didn't know that there was no incriminating DNA evidence found at the scene; that the swabs had been collected but never tested, purely as a way of noting who was suspiciously reluctant to submit a sample.

Victor Kesselich was a ghost now, rarely seen, nervous of everyone since he assumed they all believed he was a killer. Rob too was changed, but for that they blamed the police, who had come in, treated them all like criminals, arrested the wrong man and then ... nothing. What were they doing? Why hadn't they caught anyone yet? Why didn't the police ever tell them what was going on – didn't they realize that as fellow students of Amanda's they had the right to know? And then there were the journalists, the scum of the earth, who took their words and spun them to create whatever impression they wanted to give. They made Amanda the saintly innocent sacrifice, then, bored with that, turned her into the whore of Cambridge. Finally there were their families and friends back home, who worried about them but weren't here, weren't living it, like the mothers of Vietnam soldiers, sitting in cosy homes in Colorado and Pennsylvania, screwing up handkerchiefs as their sons sat in fox holes, always seconds away from murdering or being murdered. So what if, unlike those soldiers, they could leave any time they wanted? That would be quitting. That would be betraying the others. And what were the chances of the bogeyman coming back?

The students at Ariel wore black armbands. They may not have liked her, but she was one of theirs.

The police issued a statement. They were treating the death as murder, but there was no evidence to link it to the killing of Amanda Montgomery. The officer in charge was reported to be bringing in junkies and registered sex offenders for questioning.

Despite the reassurances that there was no madman stalking Ariel students, a number went home in the following weeks and didn't come back. Five more left during the Christmas break. Of the seventy students in Olivia's year at Ariel, two were dead, ten had intermitted and seven had dropped out or changed universities.

The Ariel admissions department had noticed a strange trend. They had expected a huge drop in applications, but found in fact there were only ten per cent fewer than before the murders. Closer analysis of the applicants revealed that nearly all of them were male, and that nearly all of them were well below Ariel's usual standard. Apparently the murders had indeed scared people off – all apart from those willing to take advantage of the inevitable decline in interest. The admissions tutor likened them to the men for hire who turned up in war-torn countries, willing to risk their lives for a fat pay cheque. 'Scavengers', he took to calling them, and took great pleasure in sending them rejection letters. Financially the college relied on having a certain number of students each year. A crisis meeting was called. Nearly all were agreed – they could not allow their standards to drop and so inevitably the numbers must. The college would have to tighten its purse strings and rely on generous alumni to see it through. The students knew none of this and were incensed when their rent was increased.

'So now we have to pay even more for the privilege of being sitting ducks for this psychopath', complained Sinead. 'Bunch of fucking wankers.'

The police didn't release Eliza's body for nearly a month. Her parents arranged to hold the funeral in her home town, Richmond, and so a group of Eliza's friends travelled down the night before and shared hotel rooms.

Olivia and Nick woke early and lay beside each other in silence for a while, both lost in the painting on the wall opposite of snow-frosted fir trees. Eventually Olivia propped herself up on one elbow and kissed the tip of Nick's nose.

'Happy anniversary, sweetheart,' she said. Her dark hair looked almost black as it slid down around her white shoulders.

'Happy anniversary, Liv,' he said back, and pulled her closer for a more intimate kiss.

They caught up with the others in the hotel dining room. Sinead and Paula were both eating grapefruit, but Godfrey's table mat was empty except for a cup of black coffee.

'Good morning,' everyone said mutedly.

'Morning,' Nick said, looking worriedly at Godfrey, who appeared to be ignoring their arrival and concentrating on his cup of coffee.

'Tea, coffee?' asked a waitress brightly.

'Two coffees, please,' Olivia requested, and they sat down at the end of the table.

Leo appeared at the dining-room doors in a baggy T-shirt and black jeans. 'Guys, you would not believe what I just heard.'

'Leo, what the fuck are you wearing?' snapped Godfrey.

'Chill, man, it's not what I'm wearing to the funeral. I've got a shirt upstairs.'

'Jesus Christ', said Godfrey, leaning back in his seat. 'Why the fuck are you even here?'

'Hey, Eliza was a good friend, OK?' Leo looked hurt.

'Yeah, right. She just pretended to like you so you'd give her free drugs, you scummy piece of shit. Couldn't you even be bothered to shave?'

'I'll shave later', Leo muttered. 'Jesus, it's a funeral not a fashion show.'

Godfrey slammed his cup down on the table, half of the remaining coffee sloshing onto the tablecloth. He strode out of the dining room, the door slamming against the wall as he shoved it open.

'Should I go after him?' asked Sinead.

'No.' Nick shook his head. 'Leave him.'

'I'm going to smarten up before we go, don't worry, guys', said Leo. 'I just got a phone call from Danny and it threw me, that's all. You're not going to believe this, but Suzy Marchmont's dead.'

Suzanne Marchmont was one of the students who had left Ariel after Amanda's murder. From what Olivia could remember she'd managed to get accepted at Sussex University as a late starter. She'd been friends with June, and Olivia recalled June telling her Suzy was very popular with the students at Sussex, who all wanted to know the gory details of the recent events at Ariel.

'That's terrible. How did she die?' asked Paula.

'A car accident. She drove into a tree.'

'Jesus', said Sinead.

'Are the police treating it as suspicious?' Paula asked.

'I don't know', said Leo. 'Why would they?'

'Well, maybe the Butcher was pissed off that she'd got

away, taken herself out of the picture. Maybe he wants us all to stay caged up in Ariel so he can pick us off whenever he feels like it.'

'Paula, you're getting carried away,' said Nick. 'The idea that the Butcher's running round punishing anyone who leaves Ariel – it's ridiculous.'

'You're not safe if you stay, or if you go . . .' whispered Leo.

'Leo, don't encourage her,' said Olivia, trying not to laugh.

'It's a completely different MO, for another thing,' said Sinead. 'You think the Butcher would drive her off the road when he could get her alone and slice her up? I don't think so.'

'Well, he didn't slice Eliza up, did he?' pointed out Paula. 'According to Godfrey the police told Eliza's parents she'd had her face smashed into a tree trunk.'

'We don't even know the Butcher killed Eliza,' said Nick.

'Oh, don't we?' said Paula, narrowing her eyes. 'Seriously, is there anyone sitting here who doesn't think the same fucker that killed Amanda killed Eliza?' She looked around the table.

No one argued with her.

There was a gang of photographers and journalists outside the church. Olivia remembered the desk sergeant's advice and managed not to punch any of them. Godfrey had already left the hotel by the time they were all ready to go, and she wondered if he'd headed here or back to Cambridge.

Inside the church, the altar laden with white lilies, she saw Weathers in a smart black suit, black shirt and tie. He was talking to a shorter man whose own black suit had been to the dry-cleaners a few too many times. The buttons were almost at popping-off point, his paunch straining against the fabric. She recognized him as the officer who had been put in charge of Eliza's case.

He saw her staring at him and nodded sympathetically. She didn't smile back. All he'd done was interrogate street people who weren't guilty of anything other than not having a home, and complained in the press about how hard the fairground workers were to track down for interviews. Olivia couldn't blame them for not coming forward – she knew they would make easy scapegoats.

The students at Ariel hadn't understood why Weathers hadn't been given Eliza's case too, until they'd seen some police officers in fancy uniforms with a few more white flourishes on their caps and epaulettes than your average bobby arrive at Ariel with the mayor for a meeting with the master of the college and his minions. Afterwards everyone seemed to be issuing statements about the certainty that there was no link between the murders.

'There is no reason to believe the tragic death of the student at Ariel College last year was anything other than an isolated incident, and we remain confident that the perpetrator will shortly be brought to justice,' the police said. 'Our statistics show that Cambridge is one of the safest university towns in the country, and we hope visitors will continue to come and enjoy the incredible architecture and warm atmosphere that can be found at Cambridge.'

She watched with interest as Eliza's father detached his wife from his arm and went over to the police officers. She was too far away to hear what was said, but she got the impression there were sharp words flying from Bertram Fitzstanley's lips. And they were flying specifically in DCI MacIntyre's direction. Weathers seemed to interject, almost physically to shield the shorter man, but then MacIntyre held up his hands in a conciliatory gesture and walked out of the church.

The service opened with a traditional prayer and hymn, then Eliza's best friend from school, Lucinda Franz-Hurst, read a poem about how Eliza was now the wind in the trees and the song of the lark.

'More like the quack of the duck', said Sinead under her breath, and Olivia had a hard time keeping a straight face. Sinead loved to try to crack her up in the most inappropriate places; in fact that was probably what made it so difficult not to laugh.

A young man in a white shirt pressed the play button on a portable stereo and Elton John's 'Tiny Dancer' filled the church, the tinny quality of the sound at odds with the building's impressive acoustics.

Another friend from school read a piece of nineteenth-century prose, written by a man to his soon-to-be widow, reassuring her that he was 'just around the corner'. Paula had run out of tissues and needed one of Olivia's.

Olivia finally spotted Godfrey. She had expected him to be sitting near Eliza's parents, but he was five rows back. As she tried to catch his eye, she saw him lift a silver hip flask to his lips and take a swig from it.

*

Denison shifted uncomfortably in his chair as Olivia was led in. She smiled at him and sat down.

'You look worried,' she said.

'There's something we have to talk about, and to be honest it's quite a big thing.'

'OK . . .' she said, frowning and sitting forward. 'It's not about Nick, is it?'

'No, it's about you. Olivia, do you remember our last conversation?'

'Sure, last week.'

'No. Olivia, we talked yesterday. Do you remember?'

Her eyes widened and she shook her head. 'Are you sure? I'm positive it was last Friday that I spoke to you.'

'I'm sure. Olivia, I'm going to read out some names to you. Can you let me know if they ring any bells? OK, firstly: Helen.'

She pulled a face. 'I knew a Helen who came over to my school as a foreign exchange student. That's about it.'

'How about Vanna?'

She shook her head. 'I'd remember someone with a name like that!'

'Christie?'

'Nope.'

'Mary.'

'One of the bar staff at Ariel was called Mary. Plus the music teacher at school. I think maybe one of my great-aunts too.'

'Kelly?'

She began to shake her head again, but then blushed. 'This is kind of embarrassing, but when I was a kid I had an imaginary friend called Kelly.'

'Really? How old were you?'

'Not very old. Three or four.'

'How long did your imaginary friendship last?'

Olivia frowned. 'Hmm. I'm not sure. This sounds a bit strange, I know, but I sometimes feel that she's still around. Like I hear her voice sometimes. I mean, I know it's just me, just my thoughts, but she pipes up like she can't help putting in her penny's worth.' She laughed awkwardly. Denison looked at the last name on his notepad.

'Jude?' he said.

Straightaway she shook her head no.

'Are you sure?'

'I'm positive,' she insisted. She was wringing her hands.

'Olivia, yesterday we talked about lapses of memory. Can you tell me a bit more about your experiences of this?'

She looked caught out, like she'd given away secrets to him unwittingly. 'Well . . . sometimes I meet people that I'm sure I've never met before, but they talk to me like they know me.' He nodded, reassuring her that it was OK, she could tell him.

She shrugged, as though that was everything.

'Have you ever had friends tell you about something you've said, and you can't remember the conversation?' he asked her.

She nodded, not looking at him.

'Have you ever come across an item of clothing in your wardrobe that you don't remember buying?'

She nodded again, and he noticed that her eyes were beginning to well up.

'Have you ever found yourself in a place with no recollection of how you got there?'

She looked at him then, and there were tears running down her cheeks. 'How did you know?' she whispered.

He kept his voice gentle. 'Tell me about what happened.'

'I woke up and I didn't know where I was. I didn't have any money on me. I had to walk back to college, asking directions the whole way. It took me two hours to get home.'

'What else, Olivia?' he asked softly.

She swallowed hard. 'Essays. There would be essays in my pigeonhole that my supervisors had marked. They had my name on them. I didn't remember writing them! Nick would ask me why I was reading the same book for a third time. Once . . .' She took a deep breath. 'Once, one time, at school, they said I'd bunked off for a week and gave me detention – I don't remember what I did, where I was instead!' She was shaking now, the panic pouring out of her like he'd gashed some deep wound into her skin and released all the doubt and confusion. 'When I was seventeen I went to sleep in December and when I woke up it was February! I missed seven weeks, I missed Christmas and New Year!' She stopped suddenly, letting out a shaky breath. 'I'm sorry. I didn't mean to raise my voice.'

'There's no need to apologize. I'm sorry that we need to talk about this. I realize it must be very traumatic for you. This is something you've successfully concealed from people for many years. You've coped extremely well with it. But, Olivia, it's time for you to let us help you. It doesn't have to be this way.'

She looked at him, wiping tears from her reddened face. Her eyes were full of anguish. 'Please, Dr Denison,' she said. 'Please, tell me what's wrong with me.'

He shifted in his seat. 'I believe you have what we call Dissociative Identity Disorder.' She looked blank. 'It used to be called Multiple Personality Disorder.'

'I'm a schizo?' she said disbelievingly.

He took a deep breath. 'No, you're not a schizo. Schizophrenia is an entirely different psychiatric condition.'

'But I am crazy?'

'Olivia, you have a serious condition. But we can help you. We can treat you.'

She shook her head. 'You're saying that when I'm not here, there's some other person in my skin? Someone that's not me? It's not just amnesia?'

'Olivia, it's not another person. It's still you. Just a very distinct aspect of you. So distinct that you have separate memories, different tastes, different ways of dealing with things.'

She was leaning back in her seat, as far away from him as possible. 'No. This can't be right. You must be wrong. It must be something else.'

He reluctantly pulled out his MP3 player. 'Would you like me to play you some of yesterday's session?'

She breathed in sharply. 'Yes. Play it.'

Denison had already selected a couple of minutes that didn't go into the abuse. What she was about to hear would be shocking enough. He pressed the play button and Helen's voice appeared, sounding tinny through the cheap machine's speaker.

'*If you want to ask me questions, you'll have to be more direct. You're not going to fool me into opening up more than I mean to. So you may as well be straight with me.*'

Olivia's hand flew to her mouth.

'*Okay . . .*' Denison heard himself say. He hated listening to his own voice, always surprised by how stuffy he sounded. '*When you say others, who are you talking about? Olivia?*'

'*She's one of them. The main one, I suppose. And I'm probably what you'd call the second in command, though it feels as though I'm the one steering the ship most of the time, if you know what I mean.*'

'*Who else is there, other than Olivia?*'

'*Let's see – there's Mary, she's the smart one. The one who got us into Cambridge. Often couldn't be arsed to turn up for supervisions, so Olivia had a few panics. And there's Kelly, who I think you've met. She's a little mouse, wouldn't say boo to a goose, etc. And Vanna, the one you'd want to make an appearance if you were about to be mugged. Christie's the youngest, she's just a toddler really. There's Jude. And there's me, Helen. I'm not the smartest, not the toughest, not the youngest. I suppose I'm the one keeping it all together, trying not to make things too difficult for Olivia. The poor cow doesn't know about us, you see. I try and make the transitions smooth, but I can't always control the others.*'

He depressed the stop button. Olivia's whole body had tensed up. She sat rigid on the couch, her eyes glazed over; curtains pulled shut over the windows to her soul. Her face was blank, all the muscles lax. Then, like turning up the colour on a television screen, personality flooded back into her face. She frowned at him.

'Are you trying to give us a fucking panic attack? Jesus H. Christ, doc, can't you be a little more sensitive with her?' The accent was strong, the voice hard.

'Vanna?' he guessed.

'Yeah.'

'I realize this must be tricky for Olivia, but I wanted to talk to her about her childhood. Helen told me that Olivia suffered a lot of abuse when she was a kid.'

Vanna snorted. 'She wasn't the only one.'

'What can you tell me about what happened?'

Vanna narrowed her eyes. 'What, so you can go and jerk off to it afterwards in your little office toilet? I don't fucking think so. It's none of your fucking business anyway.'

'Despite what you might think I don't get off on hearing about men abusing young girls. I can't help you if you close yourself off to me.'

She gave him the finger. 'I want to go now.'

'Vanna, we're only halfway through our session.'

She leapt to her feet. 'I don't care! Mary says you want to get rid of us – well, I'm not going anywhere, so fuck you!'

'Vanna, I don't want to get rid of you. That's not how it works. You'll all be integrated, you'll all exist together. You'll combine into one full person.'

She could hardly speak. 'You want to integrate me with *him*? With *him*? No fucking way. *No fucking way!*'

Chapter Thirteen

Snow fell in Cambridge just a few days a year on average, and was inevitably accompanied by hordes of eager photographers doing the rounds of the prettiest colleges. Snow-covered bikes were a particular favourite.

On this frosty day in mid-January, at the start of her penultimate term at Cambridge, Olivia was ensconced in Ariel bar with Paula and Sinead, sipping a cup of soup from the vending machine and trying not to think about her heating bill. Danny stomped through the doors, his boots encrusted with snow, and swung into the seat next to Olivia, handing her a copy of the local paper.

'"Elvis Lives!"' she read. '"The country's best Elvis impersonator hits Cambridge this month, appearing at the Corn Exchange on 14 January."'

'Not that bit!' Danny said, shaking off his coat. 'That bit.'

There was a photo of a middle-aged man, dressed smartly in a blazer and tie as though he might be ex-military, holding a pocket watch.

Mortimer Grady will be visiting the Spiritualist Church in Bailey Road this Wednesday for an evening of clairvoyance. Mr Grady is a well-known medium, and has performed over a thousand readings across the country since he began his spiritual career five years ago.

'I found I had a gift for this very late in life,' Mr Grady says. 'My wife died seven years ago and shortly after her death I felt her spirit visiting me. She told me where to find a ring of hers that I'd lost and was feeling bad about having mislaid. Lo and behold it was exactly where she said it would be. I took great comfort in knowing that her soul lived on, and so when I began to pick up other spirits too, I wanted to share that knowledge with their loved ones. It snowballed from there. I never expected to reach the kind of audiences that are now coming to my sessions.'

The session starts at 8 p.m. Admission is £4.50 to members, £8 to non-members.

Olivia put the paper down on the table, where it was immediately picked up by Paula, who reread the article.

'You're not suggesting we go?' Olivia asked Danny.

'Of course we should go,' said Paula. 'This could be our chance to find out what happened to Amanda and Eliza.'

Danny shrugged at Olivia. 'If the guy turns out to be a fraud, at least we'll get a laugh out of it.'

Olivia looked at Sinead. 'I won't tell Nick if you don't,' the redhead told her, and winked.

They cycled through the snow, feeble bike lights illuminating the flakes that drifted down from the black sky. The road proved too icy for Danny, six foot three and all gangly limbs, who was clumsy enough at the best of

times: he took the corner at Bailey Road far too quickly,
his bike skidding out from under him and sending him
flying into a couple of bin bags awaiting the dustbin
lorries. This, on top of the four glasses of brandy they'd
had prior to setting off, gave Olivia and Sinead the
giggles before they even got there.

The church, an unattractive concrete construction
built in the sixties, was nearly full when they arrived.
Olivia was surprised by the variety of people there,
expecting a more homogeneous crowd. The four found
themselves some plastic seats at the back – the pews
were already taken – and waited for Mortimer Grady to
appear. Sinead and Olivia still had the giggles, and Paula
and Danny, who was bruised but otherwise unhurt, sat
between them in an effort to calm them down.

With a scattered round of applause Mortimer Grady
was introduced. He was wearing the same outfit as in his
newspaper photo, even down to his tie. Olivia wondered
if this was because he was very particular about the
image he wanted to project, or if it was simply that he'd
only packed a couple of ties and one blazer for his visit to
Cambridge.

'I'm getting a woman, someone older. Her name begins
with an E. Emily . . . maybe Ethel.'

A woman stood up, clutching her handbag. 'I know an
Ethel.'

Grady looked at her kindly. 'Yes, dear. She was a
relative, someone very close to you. Your mother?'

The woman nodded emphatically.

'She says she's worried about you. That you're under a
lot of stress at the moment.' More nodding. 'She says not

to get anxious, that it will all work out in the end. She says don't worry about the money.' The woman's chin began to quiver. 'Yes, there's been a lot of tensions there. But the money is not important, according to this wonderful woman who's got my ear at the moment. What's that? Ethel says to buy that new coat you were looking at. That it really would suit you. Okay, okay, Ethel has to go now.' Grady clapped his hands together and looked at Ethel's daughter, tears running down her cheeks. 'All right?' She nodded and sat down.

For the next hour Olivia watched Mortimer Grady work the audience. She thought she saw how he did it. He began by being pretty vague about the name, until it was confirmed by someone in the audience. Then he looked at them, assessing from their age, appearance and companions what their relationship to the 'spirit' was likely to be. The messages were general enough to apply to most of the audience – who didn't worry about money? – and the more specific touches only came up at the end, when the audience member was ready to believe whatever he told them. 'New coat? Oh yes, the one I have now *is* a bit too light for this cold weather. How like Mum to be concerned about me keeping warm.' By nine o'clock Olivia felt ready to jump in during the break and take over the show.

In the interval they sipped squash from polystyrene cups and exchanged reviews. Danny and Olivia were convinced Mortimer Grady was a fraud. Paula thought he was incredible. Sinead was moved by the tears and grief of the audience members, and their happiness at the communications from beyond the grave.

'Has he seen us?' asked Olivia. 'I bet, if he's spotted us in the audience, he's going to bring up Amanda or Eliza. He'd know that would be the only reason for four students to be here.'

Sure enough, the first spirit that visited Grady when he resumed his performance was apparently a young woman, in a lot of pain. 'Her name has a lot of vowels in it, something like Andrea, or Emma. She was taken before her time.'

Olivia suddenly noticed Paula was standing up next to her, eyes welling with tears. 'Yes, I think it's our friend.'

Grady nodded. 'She says hello. She says to be careful, that there's a dark force near you. She wants to know if you've remembered what you talked about by the river.'

Paula looked confused. 'Mr Grady, can you tell me which friend you're speaking with?'

It was his turn to appear bewildered. 'Don't you know, dear?'

'The thing is, two of our friends are dead.' There were loud murmurs washing through the crowd. 'One was called Amanda, one was called Eliza. Which one is it?'

He turned his head to the empty space behind him, then back to the audience. 'She says her name is Amanda. She tells me Eliza is with her, but is too shy to talk.' Olivia heard a kind of croak and saw Danny's freckled hand clapped over his mouth, trying to stifle the laugh that had burst out of it.

Paula was nodding. 'Yes, Amanda, I do remember the talk by the river.' There were perhaps ten bridges over the River Cam in central Cambridge. The college was beside the river. Paula's favourite pub was on the bank of it. Olivia wondered how Paula knew which talk Amanda was referring to, as there must have been many.

'Am I right in thinking Amanda left this world in a violent way?' asked the medium.

Paula nodded, fingering the ring of Amanda's that hung on a chain round her neck. 'She was murdered.'

All the faces in the church were now turned towards them, people craning in their seats to gawk at the four. Being friends of the dead girl apparently made them minor celebrities.

Grady pressed his fingertips together. 'Yes, that must be the dark force she warns of. I take it her murderer was never caught?'

Paula shook her head and a tear dropped onto the church's carpeted floor. 'Can she tell me who killed her?'

Olivia shook her head. Grady had really left himself wide open to this one. He coughed, cupped a hand to his ear, leaned towards the empty space.

'I'm sorry, dear, I'm losing her. She's very faint. What, Amanda, what did you say?' He shook his head. 'I'm sorry, she's gone.'

'How convenient,' muttered Danny. Paula was still standing, waiting for something.

Grady looked as though he was scanning the crowd for his next target, when suddenly his head snapped back and his eyelids slammed shut. The crowd gasped, leaned forward.

A croaky whisper emanated from his throat: 'Twisted wing.'

A split second later and he was smiling and working

the room as though nothing had happened, back to his routine.

When they got back to college they hurried to the library and hunted in vain through the encyclopedia for the phrase 'twisted wing'. 'I don't know why you're bothering,' said Olivia, watching the others pull reference books from the shelves. 'It was just part of his schtick. It's probably completely meaningless.'

'I wouldn't bet on it,' said Danny triumphantly, who was logged into one of the library terminals. They gathered round him as he read from the webpage displayed on the computer screen. '"The Twisted Wing is a parasitic insect. It invades the body of another insect and is so successful at mimicking the flesh of its host that the host insect fails to realize it is gradually being consumed from the inside. Eventually all that is left of the host is its skin, and other insects will interact with this skin, unaware that it is being worn by the Twisted Wing."'

'Do you think that creepy man was trying to tell us something?' laughed Sinead uncomfortably. 'Let's go. I need a cigarette.'

It was sweltering in Denison's office. The bloody window wouldn't open more than a crack in case some desperate patient tried to escape out of it. Denison looked enviously at the park opposite, where a couple sat on a picnic blanket, enjoying the shade of a sycamore tree and eating ice creams.

He walked back to his seat, feeling sweat sticking his shirt to his skin as he leaned against the back of the chair.

'Olivia, last time we spoke it didn't really go as I'd

planned.' Denison believed honesty was the best policy in this case. 'Obviously the shock of learning what had been causing these fugue states over the years was too much for you. I'm afraid one of the other personalities, the alters, took over to protect you. Can you tell me what you remember?'

He was encouraged by her demeanour and appearance. Her clothes and her hair were clean and neat, and there was colour in her cheeks. She seemed stronger.

She spread her hands. 'I was here. Then I was back in my room, with a splitting headache. I remember you telling me about . . . my problem, and I remember you playing a tape of me speaking to you as one of my other personalities.' She was obviously having a hard time talking so matter-of-factly about her condition, and he admired her determination. 'That was it. I was on my bed and there was a puncture wound on my arm, so I worked out that I'd got . . . emotional . . .' she smiled at the understatement, 'and that I'd been sedated.'

He nodded. 'You didn't calm down when you got back to your ward, so they were forced to sedate you. Olivia, your alter personality Vanna came out. I began explaining to her about the recommended treatment for your condition, which is gradually to integrate the multiple personalities into one, whole person. This idea seemed to panic her greatly. Do you know of any reason why?'

Olivia frowned and shook her head. 'Doc, you know more about me than I do.'

He pressed her. 'Can you think why Vanna would be scared of one of the other personalities?'

'Oh my God,' she said. 'Do you think I killed them?'

He put down his pen and notepad, straightening his chair

so it faced her dead-on. 'The third murder, the last murder, happened two months ago now. We found you and Nicholas in the room with the body. You were both covered in blood. Nicholas was clothed, but you were near-naked and in a state of shock. Olivia, three days later you still hadn't said a word, hadn't even shown awareness of your surroundings. Two doctors assessed you – I was one of them – and we agreed that you should be held under Section 2 of the Mental Health Act. This allowed us to monitor your mental state for twenty-eight days. In fact it was thirty-one days before you were able to communicate fully with any of us, or to eat a meal by yourself, or even to make it to the bathroom on your own.' Olivia sat rigid, arms crossed. She seemed to not want to hear this. 'You appeared to have no memory of how you came to be here and why you couldn't leave.'

'If you could only hold me for twenty-eight days, why am I still here?' she demanded.

'After twenty-eight days a social worker can apply for a Section 3 order if it seems necessary. This allows us to keep you for another six months.'

'And is Nick here too?' He could see her hands trembling.

'No.' He readjusted his glasses. 'I'm afraid Nick was arrested for murder.'

Her eyes instantly flooded with tears. 'No . . .' she said, her voice shaking.

'He hasn't been charged, but he is on police bail while they investigate further.'

'But he didn't do it!' she cried.

'Olivia, he was covered in the girl's blood. His finger-prints were on the knife.'

'But what did he tell you?' she protested. 'He must have had an explanation, even if you didn't believe it!'

Denison shook his head. 'He says he found you there.'

'And the fingerprints?'

'Apparently the knife came from the communal kitchen on his staircase. But if someone held that knife after him, why aren't his prints smudged?'

'Doctor, he was framed, he has to have been. I *know* him, there's no way he could have killed them!'

'Olivia, I know you love him and want to help him. But the truth is, we just don't know for certain what happened in that room. I need you to tell me.'

'But I can't remember.'

'But maybe your alters can.'

'So ask them!'

'It's not that easy. You can't just get them to come out at will.' He paused. 'But there is a way.'

'Tell me.'

Olivia was surprised to see June when she answered the knock on her door. June happened to have the room neighbouring Nick's this year, but as they spent most of their time at Olivia's she usually only saw her at lectures.

'Hey there,' said June awkwardly. 'I was wondering if you were going to the Shakespeare seminar today.'

Olivia looked at her watch. 'Um, I was thinking about it. The dissertation writing's going well, so maybe I've got time. It's *Macbeth* today, yeah?'

'Or "the Scottish play", as Sinead insists on calling it,' said June, rolling her eyes. They both laughed.

'OK, let me just get my stuff.'

Olivia opened the door wider so June could come in and wait as she gathered her pens, notebooks and copy of the play. June looked around the room – she hadn't been inside it before – noting the framed photo of Nick and Olivia dressed up to the nines and posing with glasses of champagne in a sunny courtyard, the print of Van Gogh's *The Starry Night* and the poster of Louis Armstrong, his cheeks ballooning out round the mouthpiece of his trumpet.

'What happened to your Mr Blonde poster?' asked June. The *Reservoir Dogs* one-sheet had been Olivia's favourite poster back in their first year at Ariel.

'Oh, you know,' said Olivia casually. 'It's just a bit stereotypical, isn't it? Standard student: one Beatles album, one Tarantino poster, baggy jumpers and moaning about student loans.'

'You're above that now, yeah?' teased June.

Olivia stared at her, eventually deciding to smile. 'Yeah, I've evolved,' she said. 'OK, I've got everything.'

After the seminar they went for a cup of coffee in the bar at the Picturehouse Cinema. They spent ten minutes discussing the role of the unearthly – namely Banquo's ghost and the witches – in the downfall of Macbeth, and then June finally admitted why she'd sought out Olivia.

'Liv, I hope you don't take this the wrong way, but . . . is everything okay with you and Nick?'

Olivia put down her cup. 'What do you mean? Everything's fine.'

'OK . . . It's just the other night I heard Nick yelling, and I was worried because he sounded so mad.'

'So you're eavesdropping on us?'

'No! Of course not, Liv, he was just loud that's all. Look, are things really OK? There's nothing going on?'

'I don't know what you mean,' Olivia said, her face set. 'He was angry with me and he had good reason to be. I'd agreed to meet his mum at the station as he had an appointment with his director of studies, and I forgot. I'd have been mad too.'

'But he really lost it, Liv. I nearly came over I was so worried about you.'

'We were just arguing, June. It's what couples do.' She stood up and starting pulling on her jacket. 'If you had a relationship that lasted longer than two weeks, you might realize that you can go through major rows and it doesn't mean the end of the world.' She threw her bag over her shoulder and hurried down the stairs and out of the building.

The sky was a soft pink, the clouds full like laundry bags heavy with wet clothes. Olivia walked along the Backs and turned right through Ariel's back gates. The path that led over the river and into the college courtyards was lined on either side with late-flowering daffodils. A blackbird hopped down on the path in front of her, pecked up a crumb of bread and launched itself back into the evening air.

It was a quiet night in Ariel bar. The dinner crowd had eaten and moved on, either to pubs or to the library depending on how conscientious they were feeling. Only a few stragglers remained: a couple of first years cemented to the quiz machine who didn't seem to know the name of John Lennon's assassin, and four third years at the pool table, taking a break from their revision. Leo was one of them, Sinead another. Danny and Nick were the only members of the group actually playing pool. Leo and Sinead held cues, but were using them more to gesticulate with than to pot balls. As Olivia approached she saw Danny trying to tell Sinead it was her go, and rolling his eyes at Nick when Sinead completely ignored him. Nick nudged Danny, urging him to take Sinead's shot.

'I just find it hard to believe that an intelligent, liberal guy like yourself could be in favour of the death penalty,' Sinead was snapping at Leo.

Leo had grown his dreads out during the Lent vacation and now had short hair that he gelled up into cones. The hairstyle reminded Olivia of a photograph of magnified bacteria she'd seen once in one of Danny's textbooks.

'Well, why the hell should the state have to pay thousands and thousands of pounds to keep some fucker alive who's raped and killed someone?' argued Leo.

'For Christ's sake, Leo, do you *know* how much it costs to execute someone in America? Over a million dollars!'

'I had no idea their electricity was so expensive,' answered back a deadpan Leo. Danny suppressed a laugh. Nick gave Olivia a kiss and offered her a sip of his pint.

'It's the appeal process that costs all the money. Some of those poor guys are on Death Row for ten years or more and they don't call that "cruel and unusual punishment"?'

'So, if it's the appeals that make it so expensive, why don't they just take them round the back of the courthouse after the verdict and shoot them in the back of the head?'

'Jesus Christ!' exploded Sinead. 'Have you ever heard the phrase "miscarriage of justice"? Or do you think that only happens in fascist dictatorships?'

Leo shrugged. 'So maybe one in a couple of hundred is innocent. It's probably better that he bites the big one rather than one psychopath goes free.'

'Amen!' said a voice from the booth nearby. Olivia hadn't realized anyone was sitting there. She looked up and saw Godfrey, his feet on the table, raising his glass of what looked like whisky to toast Leo's sentiment.

'See, Godfrey agrees,' said Leo, as though that settled it. 'I bet you'd want the guy who killed Eliza to be executed, wouldn't you?'

'I'd throw the fucking switch myself,' said Godfrey with a sick grin, and downed the rest of his drink.

Sinead knew better than to argue an ethical point in the presence of someone who had such a good reason to take it personally, and retreated to the company of Danny and Nick.

Olivia went over to where Godfrey was sitting, partly hoping she could block his path to the bar and more booze. She slid round next to him, smelling the liquor on his breath and clothes. There was a bottle of Jack Daniels nestled against his hip. He pulled off the screw top and poured his glass full.

'Want some?' he said.

'No. Thanks.' Olivia picked at a stray thread on the seat's cushion cover. 'Godfrey, are you OK? I mean, I know that's a stupid question, but we're all worried about you. If you ever need anyone to talk to . . .' She trailed off, anxious that she was leading herself into a tongue-lashing. She was surprised when Godfrey eventually managed a small, rueful smile.

'Thank you, Olivia,' he said. 'But I wasn't brought up that way. Stiff upper lip and all that. I'll get through this. I'm just a bit surprised by how much I miss her, to be honest. I thought she was a pain in the arse about forty per cent of the time we were together.' He twisted the glass round on the table. 'You know how the Yanks are always talking about closure? Well, I think I know what they're getting at. I do feel as though I'm waiting. Waiting for them to catch the bastard. And what if they never do? Maybe I'll be stuck in this limbo state for ever.'

Olivia squeezed his hand. 'Maybe it'll be easier when we're not here any more. This place must hold a lot of memories for you.'

Godfrey grimaced. 'Yes. But at the same time how weird will we find it, being in an environment where we're not surrounded by people who understand? Here, we're pretty much all in the same boat. I'm not sure I'm going to be able to cope when I'm back in the real world, stuck with a bunch of innocents who don't know what it's like to have your friends ripped away from you.'

Olivia lay stretched out on the sofa in Denison's office. Her head rested on a pillow, her hands clasped over her stomach, her feet crossed at the ankles. Denison could tell from her posture that she was not relaxed. He himself sat a good five feet away, wanting to give her lots of personal space.

'Try to make yourself as comfortable as possible. Feel

free to really relax, to settle into the sofa cushions.' He was gratified to see her ankles untwine as she wriggled around and smoothed out her trousers and shirt.

'OK,' she said.

'I want you to close your eyes and let your legs and feet go limp. Relax your hands down by your sides. Let your shoulders sink back into the cushions.' His voice was reassuring, soothing. 'I want you to concentrate only on my voice. You may hear noises outside, or traffic, but these sounds will barely register with you. You will feel relaxed and calm throughout this session.

'I want you to imagine that you're on an island, lying on the beach. It's warm and sunny, and you can feel the sun on your skin. The skies are blue and you can hear the waves lapping on the shore and palm trees rustling in the breeze. You are enjoying the sensation of the rays of the sun, warming you. It's so peaceful, so relaxing. You don't have a care in the world.' He watched Olivia's breathing slow and deepen, her hands uncurl, her feet slump further apart.

'Deeper into the island, among a clearing in the trees, there's an old church. It's empty, and very quiet and still. You walk through the palm trees and into the church. You're aware of the smooth wooden floor beneath your feet. Sunlight is streaming through the stained glass windows and illuminating the inside of the church in the most brilliant blues, reds and greens. You can walk around, stepping into the different hues of light, noticing how each one makes you feel different when you're bathed in it.

'There's a heavy wooden door in the back of the church. You go through the door and find yourself at the top of a winding staircase. You begin to travel down this staircase.

And with every step you're feeling sleepier and sleepier. Your eyelids are getting heavier. Your limbs are so tired, so tired. You just want to lie down and go to sleep. With each step you're going deeper, deeper, deeper. Down and down and down.'

He paused. Like most people in a deep hypnotic trance Olivia appeared to be fast asleep.

'You've reached the bottom of the staircase. You are in a safe environment; nothing can hurt you here. When we discuss things that have happened in the past it will be like watching a film on a television set. You can pause the film, or stop it. You can scan forwards and backwards. You can turn the sound up or down, or even mute it. Now, can you tell me which of you I'm talking to?'

Olivia's eyes moved under her eyelids as though she was in a REM state of sleep.

'Kelly,' she said drowsily. The scared one, the one who took the majority of the abuse.

'Kelly, can you tell me about Olivia?'

Olivia's nose wrinkled. 'She's nice. I like her. She's not very observant, but then we protect her so she doesn't need to be, I s'pose.'

'Who else protects her?'

'Helen, mainly. Helen's the eldest, she's the grown-up. She usually knows what to do, what to say. I'm too shy. And Mary helps too. She's very clever, she likes to read books and learn things. She got us away from him.'

'And Vanna?'

'Vanna can be mean. She usually just makes things worse; she winds people up something chronic. But I'm glad she's around sometimes. When we're on the Tube and it's late. Or when some of the homeless guys are giving us lip because we won't give 'em money.'

'What about Jude?' Denison kept his voice calm and reassuring, but he could still see the instant tension in Olivia's muscles, the speeding-up of her breathing. 'Kelly, take a deep breath and let it out slowly, slowly . . . Kelly, you're safe here. There's a barrier around you, protecting you. It's like a forcefield, a bubble that no one can get into.'

'He's already in,' whispered Kelly. 'Don't wake him up.'

'I want to speak to him,' said Denison.

'No,' she hissed. Then her facial muscles rearranged themselves and her voice changed, became more assured and less accented. 'Doctor, please don't try to bring out Jude. It won't help. He's . . . incoherent.'

'Is that you, Helen?'

She nodded. 'I can tell you what you need to know.'

'Helen? Was it Jude? Did he kill these women?'

She ignored his question. 'What would you like us to show you on this little snuff movie we're watching? Amanda? Eliza?'

'Amanda,' he said eventually.

Helen let out a long, long breath. 'It was horrible, doc. Really bad. Are you sure you want to hear about it? Are you sure it'll help?'

'I'm sure,' he said, and steeled himself.

Chapter Fourteen

MacIntyre was having a plate of egg and chips outside the local pavement cafe, simultaneously chugging his way through the second of three fags he allowed himself during his lunch break. Weathers took a seat opposite him.

'Hey, Steve,' said MacIntyre, displaying a mouthful of egg yolk and fried bread.

'Hey, Mac. How are things going? Coffee, please,' Weathers said to the waitress. It was chilly and he pulled his coat tighter around him and huddled closer to the patio heater positioned near their table.

'Not good, not good.' MacIntyre speared his last four chips on his fork, stuffed them in his mouth and pushed the plate away with a sigh. He picked up his smouldering cigarette. 'You?'

Weathers shrugged. 'Depends if you're asking personally or professionally. Professionally my case is dead in the water. Personally things are great. You might have heard – Sally's making an honest man of me.'

MacIntyre managed a grin. 'That's great, Steve. Congratulations. You proposed on that dirty weekend you took a fortnight ago?'

'Oi, you're not allowed to call it a dirty weekend when you're with your fiancée. It's a romantic break.'

'Oh well, s'long as you get a few shags out of it, that's all that matters,' puffed out MacIntyre with a lungful of smoke. A few mental flashes in Weathers' mind streamed by with the smoke: Sally moaning in the big hotel tub, hair wet, bath bubbles slithering down her skin; Sally's tongue licking his earlobe in the gondola, the gondolier averting his eyes with a knowing Italian smile; Sally wrapped in the soft white bedsheets, snoring daintily.

The waitress brought Weathers' coffee.

'But the Montgomery case – you think that's it?' MacIntyre looked relieved he wasn't the only one whose inquiry had stalled.

'Well, we've investigated every angle. There was no meaningful forensic evidence. No witnesses. No one with a grudge that we can find. I'm pretty sure it's one of those little Ariellian fuckers, but they've closed ranks. They've got such an "us and them" mentality now that if they found out who'd done it they'd probably go vigilante and string up the bastard themselves.'

MacIntyre snorted and sucked his cigarette right up to the filter. 'Well, I've got too much fucking forensics. Do you know how many condoms we found in a twenty-square-foot area around the body?' He stubbed out the cigarette and lit another.

Weathers sipped his coffee. It was instant, but no worse than the crap that came out of the police station dispensing machine. 'But none of them had Fitzstanley's DNA?'

'Exactly. And Dr Bracknell reckons she wasn't raped.

But I've got about fifty cigarette butts and ten cans of soda and beer that might have DNA on them.'

'Might have?'

'Yeah. I was told I couldn't get all of them tested, just the ones that looked recent. Waste of resources, apparently. Anyway, we got DNA from five cigarette butts and two cans. DNA was female in three cases. We compared the four samples of male DNA to the swabs we took from some of the lowlifes we brought in for questioning, but no joy. I dunno, it was a long shot anyway. First of all I don't think the killer was smoking a fag or drinking a can of pop while he offed the girl, and second, even if we did match some DNA, all he has to say is, "Yeah, I was hanging around there the day before, threw my fag in the bushes, what of it?" Not exactly incriminating.'

'I'm beginning to see their point regarding the waste of resources,' admitted Weathers. 'So you thought any of the guys you brought in looked good for it?'

MacIntyre scowled, displaying his tobacco-yellowed teeth. 'Who knows? They'd all bump off their grannies if they reckoned they could make a few quid out of it. And some of these guys can really go off on one if they're high on the right stuff.'

'But where's your motive?' asked Weathers. 'I thought the hypothesis was that they were looking for money to score. If they were already high, why would they be looking for cash? These guys don't think more than ten minutes ahead.'

'Well, say they got high and they got horny. And they beat her up when she turned 'em down.'

'Guys like that – how would they lure her into an overgrown, secluded area? Would *you* follow them anywhere?'

MacIntyre laughed, smoke exploding from his nostrils. 'Sorry, Steve, I'm being rude. You want a fag?' He offered his pack of Dunhills.

Weathers shook his head. 'Nah, thanks. Trying to give up.'

MacIntyre nodded. 'Aren't we all. Anyways, I reckon they managed to "lure" her, as you put it, because she thought they were selling. Apparently Miss Fitzstanley was a bit of a coke fiend. Well, rape gone wrong is one theory anyway. The bag snatch is the other one – she fought a bit too hard to hang onto it, and got her face smashed in for her troubles.'

'But again, Mac, how come she was in the bushes, the trees?'

'Maybe she needed a pee.'

'A girl like that, going in the bushes? When there's about five pubs within walking distance?'

MacIntyre got up, throwing some money on the Formica table top. 'You still think it was someone who knew her, don't you?'

'Come on, Mac, it's the best explanation for how she ended up being killed where she was.'

'And the missing bag? The bag and the boots turned up five hours after the body, discovered in the Cam by a college boat crew. Cash was all that was missing.'

'An attempt to make it look like the motive was robbery. Mac, come on, you know it was personal.'

MacIntyre sat down again suddenly, his face intense. 'You know, Steve, you're losing your way here. Make up your mind, is it a serial killer or not? Serial killers don't know their victims, Steve, remember? It's not personal for them, remember?'

'That's not always true, Mac,' said Weathers, shaking his head. 'A number of Fred West's victims were people he knew. One was his daughter! John Wayne Gacy killed kids who worked for him. Ed Kemper killed his mother and her best friend.'

'I can see you've been reading up,' said MacIntyre. 'Well, don't let it go to your head. There's no glory in getting a serial killer. No glamour in it. We're just doing a job, and it should be just the same to you as nabbing a bloke who's bumped off his wife 'cause she shagged the milkman.'

Cigarette number three joined one and two in the foil ashtray and Weathers was left by himself, those around him wondering what he could have said to make his companion storm off in such a bad mood.

The riverbank that faced Ariel College was patchworked with bright towels of turquoise, hot pink, lime green and midnight blue. Most students sunbathed in shorts and vests, the more confident in bikinis or swimming trunks.

June and Danny were stretched out on neighbouring towels. Olivia and Nick threw their textbooks on the grass and sat down next to them.

'Hi there,' said June, who'd braided her hair tight against her head in an attempt to keep her scalp cool.

'Feels like I haven't seen you guys for ages. How's the revision coming along?'

'It would be easier if it rained once in a while,' said Nick. 'Geertz's *Interpretation of Cultures* is finding it hard to compete with this sunshine.'

'Tell me about it,' said June, stretching her arms up into the air, enjoying the warmth from the sun. 'I haven't looked at my Chaucer notes since Monday.'

Danny pulled his cricket hat down lower on his face. 'I think I'm burning,' he said sourly. June handed him his Superdrug factor 40 sunblock.

'Hey, have you two seen Leo?' she asked, grinning.

'Not recently, why?'

'He's around here somewhere. Check out his haircut.'

Ten minutes later a punt swanned down from the Mathematical Bridge, helmed by a smart-looking young man with a short back and sides and a white shirt. The punt and its pole were painted with the Ariel colours of purple and white, so the group looked more closely at the punter and his passengers.

'Oh my God, is that him?' said Nick.

The punt pulled up to the bank, and the guy standing at its rear removed his Armani sunglasses, grinning at them. With a respectable haircut and the classic white shirt he was wearing, Leo could suddenly pass for a City banker on his day off.

'Hey, guys,' he said. 'Beautiful day, isn't it?'

Godfrey was reclining on the punt cushions, an arm round a blonde girl, the other hand casually holding a large spliff. Olivia recognized his fellow passengers – three men with matching floppy hair and expensive shoes – as some of his Trinity College friends. 'We've just run out of Pimms,' Godfrey drawled. 'I don't suppose you lot have any alcohol on you, do you?'

'I've got a can of Special Brew you can buy off me for a fiver,' said June, deadpan.

Godfrey ignored her. 'Come on, Leo, punt us somewhere that serves alcohol, there's a good chap,' he said, but Leo had spotted Sinead further up the riverbank.

'Why don't you take over, you lazy fucker?' said Leo amiably, and handed Godfrey the punt pole. 'I'll catch up with you in Grantchester.' He jumped onto the grass and headed towards Sinead.

Godfrey inclined the pole towards one of his floppy-haired friends. 'Rupert,' he ordered, and Rupert took the pole and jumped up onto the platform at the end of the punt. He wedged the pole into the river bed and shoved hard. The punt drifted off again, Godfrey smiling at them beatifically as they disappeared into a throng of punts overrun with French and Spanish teenagers and their water pistols.

'Are you sure you don't want to join them, Liv?' asked June. 'I thought you and Godfrey were like that.' She held up two crossed fingers.

'Don't say it like that,' Nick told her with a frown. 'You don't know him, not really. He's changed a lot since Eliza died.'

'Yeah, you can tell,' said June, the image of Godfrey's hand caressing the blonde girl's lightly tanned shoulder fresh in her mind.

'June, you weren't the one staying up with him all night as he got drunk and read the poetry he'd written about her.' Nick sounded angry, but June wasn't backing down.

'He wrote poetry?' she laughed. 'Boy, I would have loved to have heard that.'

Nick stood up, grabbing his books. 'I'm going to the library,' he told Olivia, and walked off back down the riverbank. The others watched him go.

'What do you see in him?' asked June.

'Excuse me?' said Olivia, eyebrow arching.

'Well, come on, he's a nice little public school boy. I can't exactly see him strutting his stuff down Dalston High Street. He'd be terrified of being mugged by drug dealers.' Danny looked away, focusing on some tourists on the opposite side of the river, uncomfortable at the argument.

'What makes you think he's going anywhere near Dalston High Street?' she said, London accent surfacing somewhat as it always did near June, like she brought the old Olivia to the surface. 'I'm not going back there. Fuck that.'

'So where are you headed then, Miss Doolittle? Hampstead? Mayfair?'

'We might go and live in Oxford,' said Olivia. 'Or Brighton maybe, if Nick gets funding to do an MA.'

'And what are *you* doing after graduation?' asked June. 'Job-wise, I mean.'

Olivia shrugged. 'Dunno yet. I suppose I'll wait and see what grade I get.'

'So, basically your life's going to revolve around whatever Nick wants to do,' concluded June.

'You've always had a hard time understanding the

nature of commitment,' Olivia said with a bitter smile, rising to her feet in one fluid movement. She scooped up her books and went further down the riverbank to where Sinead was sitting with Leo, wearing a large floppy hat and a long-sleeved blouse. On her towel sat some Clinique factor 50 suntan lotion.

'It sucks being a redhead,' she told Olivia, squinting up at her. She saw Olivia's expression and frowned. 'You OK, sweetheart?' she asked.

'Fine. June's just being an arsehole about Nick again, that's all.'

Sinead pulled a bottle of Orangina out of her cooler bag and handed it to her. 'Drink up.'

They stretched out on the grass, sipping their drinks and absorbing the sun's rays. When it got to lunchtime Leo went and bought baguettes from the sandwich shop, having apparently forgotten his arrangement to meet Godfrey. They read Milton, Shakespeare, Dostoyevsky and Homer. When they got bored they read Zadie Smith, Salman Rushdie, Michael Marshall.

Lying on her front, propped up on her elbows and engrossed in *The Straw Men*, Olivia heard wolf-whistles and turned over. Paula was sashaying down the riverbank in a bright blue bikini and flimsy sarong. There were tiny brass bells sewn onto her silk thong sandals, so she jingled with every step, a musical accompaniment to the shimmying of her tanned cleavage.

She reached them and swept back her glossy black hair with her sunglasses. 'I've got something to show you,' she said, and turned round, tilting up one butt cheek. There was a large white bandage taped to it.

'I've told you before, Paula, these S&M sessions with other guys are going to have to stop if we're ever going to get together,' admonished Leo.

Paula ignored him, peeling back the bandage to reveal a butterfly etched into inflamed skin.

'You got a tattoo!' squealed Sinead. 'Oh my God!'

'Do you like it?' Paula asked. 'It hurt like fuck.'

'It's pretty,' said Olivia.

'It's gorgeous,' said Leo, who was finding it hard to keep from drooling. 'How much did it set you back?'

'Twenty quid, but that was a special offer.' Paula winked at Olivia.

'Why was it a special offer?' Olivia asked.

"Cause it was on her arse, eejit,' said Sinead. 'Where is this place, then?'

'Near that Oddbins opposite Parker's Piece. You going to get one too?'

'Maybe,' laughed Sinead. 'Depends what kind of designs they've got. I'd quite like something that celebrates my Irish heritage.'

'Like a shamrock!' joked Leo. 'Or maybe a little green leprechaun!'

'Fuck off!' Sinead giggled. She nudged Olivia. 'How about you, Liv? You up for it?'

'Do you think Nick would like it?' Olivia asked shyly.

'Ah, what do you care?' laughed Sinead. 'He's your boyfriend, not your da.'

'I think he'd like it,' said Leo. 'Tattoos are very sexy.'

'You could get his name in a heart,' suggested Sinead with mischief in her eye. 'Then he'd have to like it.'

*

'Olivia heard Amanda. Talking about her, in the courtyard.'

'This was the night Amanda died?'

'Yes. She was talking to Sinead Flynn, referring to that supervision where Olivia had made a fool of herself. Mary had done all the work, but she couldn't take over when the time came to pop up and discuss the topic. And Olivia panicked, and worse, did it in front of Amanda, who ended up complaining to Sinead that it gave all female students a bad reputation amongst the stuffier fellows, reinforcing the view that women weren't really cut out for Cambridge.'

'And this made Olivia angry?'

'No,' laughed the alter, Helen, who was still stretched out on Denison's sofa. 'No, it hurt her feelings. Made her feel inadequate. And that's what wakes up Jude.' She almost whispered the name. 'Olivia only lasted another five minutes, and then he took over. Nearly whacked Nick with an empty bottle of Rioja and ran off. Jude saw Amanda on her way back from the Porters' Lodge. I don't know why she'd gone there – maybe she was checking her pigeonhole for something. Anyway, he followed her into Hicks – the rooms above the bar – and knocked on her door. She opened it, not knowing she wasn't letting in Olivia, she was letting in a monster.

'He had a knife in his hand – I don't even know how it got there. Amanda didn't see it. She was tidying up the stuff on her bed, the lecture notes and books, so she could go to bed. I was trying to take over, Doc, I swear I was, but he's always too strong! He never retreats until he's done what he came out for, and I was trapped there behind him, forced to watch, to be there with him.' Helen's chin was shuddering, her jaw tight. 'She turned round and he just swiped at her.

There was blood – everywhere – spraying all over the walls. Her body fell back onto the bed. He cut through her dress with the knife and threw it behind him. Then he sat on her naked body and just kept stabbing her and stabbing her. He just wanted to see blood and to destroy. That's his obsession, to tear things apart.' Helen swallowed hard. 'Are you sure you want to hear this?'

Denison cleared his throat. 'I'm sorry, Helen,' he said. 'But I have to.'

She sighed. 'After the stabbing he'd lost some of the frenzy. He was clearer. That was when he cut her breasts and tore at her thighs.'

'Why?'

'To desexualize her. To make her repulsive.' She swallowed rapidly, her nostrils flaring as she breathed hard. Denison gave her a minute and eventually she continued. 'He stuck his knife into the wound in her neck and cut away all the skin and everything until there was just her spine connecting her head to her body, and then he stuck the knife in between her vertebrae and he . . . he . . .' Helen suddenly turned on her side and vomited onto the floor.

The cleaners had done their best, but there was still a faint odour of vomit under the strong scent of the carpet cleaner.

'Can't you open a bloody window, Matt?' asked Weathers who had driven down as soon as he'd got the call from Matt. Denison shook his head.

'They don't open. Someone might jump out.'

'Yeah, me.' Weathers was looking a bit green. 'She didn't tell you what she did with the head?'

Denison wiped his glasses on his tie. 'Says she managed

to break away from Jude at that point, and none of the
alters know what happened between then and waking up a
few hours later.'

Weathers looked at him, surprised by his flatness. 'Look,
Matt, you got a confession. You should be pleased.'

'Why?' Denison snapped, shoving his spectacles back on.
'Some poor kid that her dad passed around to paedophile
after paedophile, in between beating and raping her himself,
grows up to want to hurt people herself – well, that's pretty
bloody understandable if you ask me.'

'Right, so we let her go then? Say, OK, you killed three
people, but you had such a shit childhood that we'll forgive
you?!'

'Steve, don't be an arsehole. I'm just saying that at one
point she was a victim too. I don't take any pleasure in
helping you to lock her up.'

'Well, we've still a long way to go, partner. She needs to
repeat that confession to me, with her being damn clear she
knows her rights, for us to get a conviction. That's if you
agree she's capable of standing trial.'

'At this point, Steve, I'm not sure I *do* agree.'

'Matt, she's a fucking psychopath!'

'She's sick. She belongs in a medical facility and that
would be the outcome if she went to trial or not.'

'You don't know that. The jury might not be as gullible as
you.'

Denison looked shocked. 'You don't believe her?'

Weathers shifted in his seat. 'I don't know. It's a bit fucking space cadet for me, to be honest, Matt.'

'Do you believe she suffered the abuse she reported?'

Weathers looked extremely uncomfortable. He was

refusing to meet Matt's eye. 'Yeah. I do. We found child porn all over the place.'

'What do you mean?'

Weathers tugged at his tie. 'The Met raided the Corscaddens' shop and residence, on the pretext of searching for stolen property. They didn't find any hard copies of any kiddie porn, but there was one computer with around seven and a half thousand illegal images of children stored on the hard drive. He's going down for a long time.'

Denison was horrified. 'You just went ahead and did this without talking to me? Do you have any idea what you've done?'

Weathers finally looked at him. 'Yes, I've got a sadistic paedophile who's been abusing kids for over twenty years arrested. What the hell could be wrong with that?'

'You did it because of what Olivia told me. Not even Olivia, but one of her alters! That's not the same thing as her reporting abuse to the authorities, Steve! Christ, *she doesn't even know her parents abused her*. We should have told her first. You should have got her permission before you barged in. It's not fair on these kids for you to take control away from them!'

'She's not a kid, Matt, she's a grown woman. And what will the consequence be for her – that her parents might be mad and might never speak to her again? What a bloody shame that would be!'

'What about her kid sisters? You think they'll let her see them again?'

'The parents might not get much say in it. Mrs Corscadden was in enough of the photos that the kids are likely to end up in care.'

'Oh, well, that's great, isn't it? All's well that ends well.'

'You think it's better they're left in the care of a pair of perverts?'

'Olivia said he didn't touch the other kids.' Weathers was silent. Denison pressed him. 'Well? Did they find any photos with Olivia's sisters in them? Did they?'

Weathers shook his head. 'No.'

'But there were plenty with Olivia in them, I take it?'

'Yes,' said Weathers quietly, looking Matt dead in the eye. 'There were plenty. It doesn't excuse her, Matt.'

'I'm not trying to excuse her,' said Denison. 'I'm just able to have sympathy for her. Don't you have any compassion?'

Weathers stood up abruptly and walked to the window. He could see people strolling on the street outside the unit's fortified walls. Some were smiling, some even laughing. They didn't know how lucky they were. He thought if the general public could see what he'd seen, the world would grind to a halt.

'Plenty of kids are abused and don't turn into killers,' he said, his back to Denison. 'The majority of them. They survive it. They grow up and they're decent people, good people. Most of them would never pass on the hurt they experienced to another human being. You can't say she's not responsible for the murders. There is such a thing as free will.'

Denison shook his head. 'You don't understand. There's little point in free will if you've been warped to the point where you just don't care. Where inflicting pain and suffering is more important to you than whether society condemns you for it. You can know it's wrong because you've been told it's wrong, but you don't feel it. It's not their fault that they don't feel it.'

'You're saying Olivia lacks a conscience?' Weathers turned back from the window.

'*She* may have a conscience. The alter personality that killed those girls doesn't. He may even just be a bag of motor functions and homicidal mania.'

Olivia was wearing a black vest top that showed off her brand spanking new tattoo. Nick had seemed a bit disapproving about it at first, but when she'd told him the Chinese characters meant 'eternity', and that she'd intended it for him, he'd reddened and given her a big kiss.

It was Strawberry Fair day in Cambridge, which meant crusties, hippies, teenagers and students travelling in from far and wide to enjoy the town's mini Glastonbury. Midsummer Common was bursting with stalls, dance tents, blankets laden with silver jewellery and dogs on string leads. The enticing smell of burgers and salty chips wafted across the field.

Nick and Olivia strolled through the fair, stopping here and there for Olivia to look at earrings and colourful T-shirts, and Nick to check out knock-off CDs and an array of mini Venus flytraps and cacti.

'So, did you hear Leo's been going to those recruitment events?' Nick asked as Olivia bought a paperweight in the shape of a turtle.

'No!' she laughed. 'I thought his plan was to sponge off the state indefinitely. Unless of course he's just going to these things for the free food. Apparently their buffets are pretty good.'

'No, I think he genuinely is searching for a job. He's

realized drug-dealing at college is one thing, but it's a whole other ball game in the big bad world.'

'Scared of getting gunned down by the Yardies, is he?' chuckled Olivia. 'Yeah, I don't think they'd be too worried about having Leo for competition.'

'Have you thought any more about what you want to do?' asked Nick, trying to sound casual.

Olivia was sick of the question. 'Well, let's see, what does a degree in English literature qualify you for? Maybe I could earn money analysing the works of Shakespeare? Or writing essays about the effect of emancipation on twentieth-century literature?'

Nick avoided a man passed out drunk on the grass, a helium balloon in the shape of a Tasmanian Devil tied round his left ear. 'Don't be sarcastic. There are jobs like that in academia. Or you could write reviews for magazines or newspapers.'

'Or I could give up now and go and work in Burger King. Nick, to be honest, I'm not going to decide in the middle of Strawberry Fair what I'm going to do for the rest of my life, so why don't we see how I do in my exams and take it from there? OK?' She wrapped an arm round his waist and grinned up at him. 'OK?'

'OK.' He kissed her on the forehead. 'You want to get some noodles?'

'Sounds good to me. Then we'd better get back – I want to revise my Virginia Woolf before the exam tomorrow.'

'Just make sure she did kill Eliza,' Weathers had requested the day before. 'If MacIntyre was right and we've got another killer running around Cambridge, I'd rather know sooner than later.'

Denison had told his friend he was ninety-five per cent convinced that Eliza and Amanda had been murdered by the same person, yet as he began to hypnotize Olivia he was nervous she would go on to describe an uneventful night of fireworks and fairground rides, with no reference to Eliza's death.

First she told him about the visit to the fortune teller.

'All the cards seemed to be about my childhood,' she said, eyes shut, prostrate on the couch. 'She told me I was self-sacrificing and too subservient. She mentioned my father, how powerful he was. She said I needed to forgive myself.'

'What did you feel you needed to forgive yourself for?' Denison asked.

'For being such an ungrateful brat to my parents. For thinking I was better than them, that I could do better.'

Then she told him about the fireworks and the bonfire. 'Godfrey turned up and he was really worried. I don't think I'd ever seen him like that before. He's normally so sure of himself.'

'What was he worried about?'

'He couldn't find Eliza. She did have a tendency to go off on a whim and do her own thing without thinking to tell anyone, so we didn't really take it seriously at first. But Godfrey knew, somehow.'

'Thank you, Olivia. If it's OK I'd like to communicate with Helen now. Helen, I want you to come and talk to me. When you're ready, Helen, I want you to raise up your right hand so I can see that you're here.'

After a moment Olivia's right hand lifted up off the sofa cushion.

'Hello, Helen?'

'Hi, Dr Denison.'

'Helen, Olivia's just told me about Bonfire Night. Did you listen to her?'

Helen laughed. 'Yes, poor cow. Imagine feeling bad for the way she treated our parents! Those tarot cards completely freaked her out, but she didn't really have a clue why. The old lady struck a chord with the Emperor card. Our father, the ruler of his domain. And us, hung from a tree, like that woman in *King Kong*, the sacrificial offering. Then she took out the Shaman card – the person who saw things differently to "mere mortals". She was lucky Jude didn't make an appearance at that point and take a bow.' She paused. 'We took the Judgement card to mean that we shouldn't blame ourselves for what Jude had done.'

'And after that?'

'Olivia was panicking. Nearly everything the fortune teller told her went right over her head, but she still left that caravan like someone had lit a fire under her arse. It's not a good state for her to be in. It makes her vulnerable to us, to Jude. Especially because that mad old bint had told her nothing good could come of her union with Nick. That really set Olivia off.

'Kelly came out. She didn't know where she was, and it was noisy and there were loads of people around. Kelly doesn't like crowds. She just wanted to go back home, back to college. But she bumped into Eliza on Jesus Green.'

Denison sat up straighter. Olivia had reported the drink at the pub as being the last time she'd seen Eliza.

'What happened?' he asked.

'Eliza was drunk. She asked where Godfrey was and told Kelly she was looking forward to getting some action. Kelly didn't know what she was talking about. Eliza poked her in the ribs and asked her if she didn't think Godfrey looked hot in Prada. Kelly, poor child, said, "Where's Prada?", like it was a country he'd gone on holiday to. Eliza made the mistake of laughing her head off. That hyena sound she made caused Jude to come sprinting out of his dark little cave. He told her he had something to show her, and took her into the trees. He pointed out a tree trunk. She said she couldn't see anything. He told her to look closer, look closer. She was about half a foot from the trunk when he grabbed the back of her head and slammed her face into the bark. She made this funny sound, kind of a yelp. Her nose was bleeding. He still had his fist in her hair, and smashed her into the tree again. I think she was unconscious after that, because she didn't struggle. He bashed her into that tree trunk about five more times, then let her go. He kicked her when she was on the ground. Her face was just this mash of blood and skin and pulp.'

A tear appeared from under Helen's right eyelid, the side facing him, and dropped onto the sofa, darkening the fabric.

'And whose idea was it to take the boots and the handbag?' Denison asked when it appeared she had no more to tell him.

Helen's mouth twisted as she said: 'Mine. He made us help him again. It was me that suggested taking the bag and the boots. I thought maybe the police would think someone had killed her because they needed money.

'We didn't have blood on us, except on our hands. We wiped the blood off on her coat and left her there. We dropped the bag and boots in the river as we walked towards the boathouse, where we'd arranged to meet Nick. And on the way we let Olivia come back. She didn't even realize that she'd blanked out, not even when she found the extra money in her pocket.

'That Judgement card was wrong, wasn't it, Dr Denison? We're as bad as him, aren't we?'

Denison had a faraway expression in his eyes which his girlfriend Cass knew well. She called it his 'lost in La La Land' face. Her preferred method of bringing him back to the here and now was to plonk herself on his lap. He invariably jumped out of his skin, which gave her the giggles for a good five minutes.

But she knew he was having a hard time with the Olivia Corscadden case and took pity on him, joining him on the sofa rather than sitting on him. She picked up his hand, stroking his fingers, focusing especially on the bump on his middle finger caused by too much writing.

Denison sighed and reclined back. He rubbed his eyes under his spectacles.

'Hard day?' Cass asked.

'Horrible. You wouldn't believe it.'

'Try me.'

He shifted round to look at her. 'You wouldn't say that if you knew what I'd tell you.'

She stood up and went into the kitchen area, pulled the cork out of a bottle of Merlot and poured two glasses. She came back and handed one to him. Then she lit the three large scented candles on the coffee table and put on some soft piano music. He'd always thought Cass would make a good relaxation therapist.

'Try me,' she said again.

He couldn't tell her about the sessions. Sometimes he did confide in her about his work, certainly more than he should bearing in mind the confidentiality issues, but he knew he would feel awkward talking to her about Olivia. How could someone so self-assured, so comfortable in her own skin as Cass was, understand the psychology of a girl like Olivia?

'Is it Steve?' she asked, putting her bare feet in his lap and leaning her head against the sofa cushions.

'What do you mean?'

'Well, not only is it a huge case, but one of your oldest friends has put a lot of faith in you. I know you, Matt – I know you're worried that if you make a mistake it will reflect badly on him.'

He let out a sigh, taking a big mouthful of wine and sinking back into the sofa. 'I've been trying not to think about that side of it.'

'Well, he's old enough and ugly enough to take care of himself,' Cass said.

'I know, I know. As if trying to treat Olivia Corscadden weren't responsibility enough. Christ, Cass, today she found out the identity of the third victim. Some arsehole new on the ward decided to share the gossip with her.'

'She didn't know June Okeweno was dead?' frowned Cass.

'Part of her did,' Denison allowed, not wanting to elaborate. 'But let's just say a lot of what happened that night is still a big mystery to her. It wasn't the way she should have found out. I should have been the one to tell her.'

'How did she take it?'

'She was upset about June, and angry with me for holding the information back. Took a while to get her to understand why I wanted her to remember for herself that June had been the one who died that night.'

Cass rested her glass of wine on her lap. 'I don't know how you do what you do, Matt,' she said, one soothing hand stroking his arm. 'I don't know how you can bear all that misery.'

'It helps that I've got you to come home to,' he told her, lifting her hand and kissing the back of it, a lump in his throat. 'You take the darkness and filth away. You make me feel there's light and good in the world.'

She put down their drinks and pulled him close, enveloping him in her soft, cashmere-covered arms. He rested his head on her bosom and closed his eyes. The candles burned, flames reflected in the discarded wine glasses.

Each morning the finalists at Ariel gathered for breakfast in hall and shared the nightmares they'd been having.

This morning it was Danny's turn. 'So I dream it's after the exams, and I'm on holiday in the South of France, enjoying my freedom. I'm sunbathing, reading a book, drinking wine, eating bread and cheese. There's a swimming pool and I decide to have a dip, so I go to my room to get a towel. I pull it out of my bag, and with it falls a piece of paper. I take a look at it, recognizing it's my exam timetable. And then I see it. One last exam, scheduled for that morning. I thought I'd finished them all, thought I was done, and there's still one to go! And that's when I woke up.'

Leo looked around the table, pen poised to note down the scores. 'Six,' voted Paula.

'Seven,' voted Sinead. 'I liked the cruelty of the holiday setting.'

'Two,' said Godfrey. 'Lack of realism.'

'Six,' said Olivia. 'My dream about being arrested by the invigilators for stealing the pens from the exam room was more Kafka-esque.'

'No, a dream about your pens turning into bugs would have been Kafka-esque,' said Danny, poking out his tongue at Olivia.

'So, where's lover boy this morning?' asked June, who'd abstained from the vote.

Olivia noticed that the taste of her grapefruit juice and the sound of June's voice seemed to have a lot in common.

'He had his last exam yesterday,' she said. 'So I imagine he's probably lying face-down in a gutter somewhere. Either that, or sleeping it off in his room.'

'Lucky bastard,' said Paula. 'How dare he have this nightmare over with when I've still got four exams to go?'

'He did start a week before us,' pointed out Leo. 'That's a week's less revision.'

After her nightmare Olivia had taken to carrying a set of six pens into each exam, paranoid about borrowing one from the invigilators.

She found the exams tough. Over the past year the students would have covered a certain number of topics

for each paper. That those topics would come up in
the exam was not guaranteed, and there was always
the possibility of having to answer one question on a
subject you knew nothing about. Each time you turned
over the exam paper and saw the questions for the first
time, there was always that fear: would you know
enough?

Olivia found she knew enough to answer the necessary
number of questions, but only just. After her last exam
she felt strangely deflated. She knew she should be
ecstatic, ready to go out and celebrate. Yet she couldn't
escape the feeling that she had missed an opportunity;
that she should have tried harder.

'Everyone says it's anticlimactic,' reassured Sinead, who
still had two exams to go. 'You've worked really hard for
three years and it all comes down to a few exams. Of
course those exams don't feel like the climax of the
training your life's revolved around for thirty-six months.'

'Come on, let's go out and have cocktails,' said Paula,
who was already drunk and experiencing none of the
anticlimax Sinead was on about.

'Or maybe you're just sad this stage of your life is
coming to an end,' suggested Sinead. 'We've had some
tough times, Lord only knows, but we've also made
friendships that will last a lifetime. And think how good
it will feel to be free of this place. No more walking in
pairs after dark, regulation panic alarms in our pockets.
No more worrying that some psycho will break into your
room in the middle of the night and rip you to pieces.
We've got our whole lives ahead of us, Liv.'

*

Valerie Hardcastle always felt nervous when Nick left the house. She stood by the mock Tudor window that looked onto the driveway, pinching at her cotton handkerchief, waiting for him to get back.

Geoff put a soothing hand on her shoulder. 'Come on, Val, he'll be back soon. Why don't you go and sit in the conservatory and I'll make you a cup of tea.'

'He only went to the local shop,' she said. 'He should have been back by now.'

'Now don't be silly. You know it takes at least ten minutes to walk there. Come on, dear, how's he going to feel if he gets back and finds you watching for him like a hawk?'

She let herself be led to the conservatory, where the sun was warming up the black and white floor tiles.

'Now do you want Earl Grey or English Breakfast?' Geoff asked.

'Earl Grey, please.'

'Right you are.'

Valerie looked out at the garden, at the greenness of the lawn in the sunshine. A blackbird hopped across it, on the hunt for worms. It eyed her beadily, but when she leaned forward for a better look it flapped into the air and was gone. Her ears strained for the sound of the front door.

Last week she'd enlisted Nick to steer the trolley on her visit to the garden centre. Someone had recognized him: a large man with big sideburns and a ruddy face, who obviously had read the tabloids' lurid stories about the last murder at Ariel. The man had spat at Nick, the spittle sliding down Nick's denim jacket.

'You ought to be shot,' the man had said in a thick Oxfordshire accent. 'All I can say is it's a shame they got rid

of the death penalty.' It was the indignance that had angered
Valerie, the self-righteous bluster. How dare they judge her
son?

'Now look here,' Valerie had said, poking a well-
manicured finger in the man's face. Nick had grabbed her
arm.

'Leave it, Mum,' he had said. The red-faced man had
said his piece and turned for the door, his puffed-up wife
muttering a 'disgraceful' in their direction as she followed
him. Valerie's fists had clenched up so hard she'd broken
one of her fingernails. Geoff hadn't been there, hadn't seen
the viciousness in the man's eyes, and so couldn't understand why she didn't like Nick going out on his own. What
if someone else recognized him, someone who wanted to do
more than spit at him?

Geoff came back to the conservatory, a mug of tea in
each hand. That was when she heard the shouting coming
from the front of the house. She leapt up so quickly that she
knocked her tea out of Geoff's grasp, the mug shattering on
the floor tiles.

When she flung open the front door she saw Nick squar-
ing up to another young man, with ginger hair. A girl with
long, copper-coloured curls was in between them, trying to
stop Nick hitting the boy. It looked as though Nick had
already got in a punch or two – the boy's T-shirt was torn
and his left cheek was bright pink. An aerosol can lay in the
gravel, its top missing.

'Nick, I'm ringing the police!' Valerie called out in panic.

At the sound of her voice Nick stepped back and lowered
his fists. He didn't take his eyes off the boy though.

'Don't, Mum,' he said. 'They're just leaving.' Geoff

appeared and shouldered past her to stand next to Nick, but he didn't need the back-up – the pair seemed happy to go.

The boy strode off without saying anything. The girl made sure she was positioned between him and Nick, just in case either tried to continue their fight. At the gate she paused.

'Just tell the truth, Nick, for fuck's sake,' she said in an Irish accent. The pair walked to a car that was parked further down the road, and drove off. The boy flicked a V sign out of the window as they went past.

'Are you all right, Nicholas?' asked his mother.

'I'm fine.' Nick stalked past his father and grabbed the two carriers of shopping he'd dropped at the end of the driveway. On his way back into the house he bent down and picked up the aerosol can too.

'What on earth was that about?' asked Geoff, and then he saw the front of the house. They'd sprayed the word MURDERER in bright blue paint across the brickwork and the front door.

'Don't worry,' said Nick, refusing to look at them as he went inside. 'I'll clean it off.'

Chapter Fifteen

The results came out the same day as the Ariel May Ball. On their way to the hairdresser's Sinead, Paula and Olivia stopped at the Senate House and scanned the lists of names displayed in glass cases attached to the exterior wall of the building.

'Yes!' Paula said, punching Sinead in the arm. 'I got a First!'

'Congratulations!' said Sinead, giving her a kiss on the cheek. 'Looks like I got a 2:1. Too much bloody rehearsing, not enough revising.'

'Don't be silly, a 2:1's great,' said Paula. They both looked at Olivia, further down the wall. She shrugged.

'A Desmond.'

'All the best people get 2:2s,' said Danny, appearing at her side. He put an arm round her and squeezed her in solidarity.

'You got one too?' she asked.

'Yep. So much for that MSc place at Bristol.'

'I'm sorry.'

He shrugged. 'How did Nick do?'

'A 2:1. He's chuffed.'

'What about the rest of the English lot?'

Olivia swallowed the envy in the back of her throat

and rescanned the results as though she couldn't remember them.

'June and Leo both got Firsts.'

Paula tapped her watch. 'We're going to be late. Come on, Desmond.'

'You coming tonight?' Olivia asked Danny.

'Yep. See you there. Say congrats to Nick for me.'

'Sure.'

The hairdressers manipulated their hair into soft waves, curling and pinning until Olivia felt like she was about to star in a biblical epic. The hairstyles didn't exactly go with their casual clothes, and Nick laughed when he saw her with the posh hair but still in her Garfield T-shirt. She hated telling him she'd only got a 2:2.

He hugged her tightly. 'You just got too stressed during the exams. You know what you're like. It doesn't mean anything.'

'Apart from that I'm thick.'

'You're not thick! Your coursework was amazing. You're just not good at exams. Or at revising for that matter.' He'd made her laugh. He capitalized on it. 'At least you're not poor Laurence Merner. He got a Third.'

'You're kidding! What happened?'

'Who knows? Probably something to do with Rob dumping him last term. Apparently he didn't take it well.'

'How did Godfrey do?'

'Not sure, haven't heard. How about Leo?'

'He got a First,' she said, rolling her eyes. 'How the hell did he manage that? He's been stoned for the past three years.'

'And practically living in the library for the past three months. No one here is stupid, Olivia. You're talking about drawing distinctions between the smartest 21-year-olds in the country. Splitting one per cent into quarters. How much difference do you really think there is to quantify?'

'I wish I thought that was true,' she said quietly. 'But I suspect to the even smarter brains that are marking those exams, there's a world of difference.' She extracted herself and pulled her ballgown from the wardrobe. 'Fuck. Why can't they just give us IQ tests or something and base the results on that?'

Nick laughed. 'Because we're meant to have learned something, dumbass. The degree certificate proves you've had an education, not that your IQ's over 120. Hey, that dress is nice.'

'It's bad luck to see it before the ball,' Olivia said sarcastically. 'Go on, get lost. Come back at seven thirty.'

She took a long bath, ignoring the five people who knocked on the door, impatient for their turn. Her hair was carefully kept out of the hot water, but the steam made her wavy hair curl even more.

She sat in her towel at her desk and put on her make-up. Her lipstick was a gold-tinted nude colour that emphasized her tan. As she lined her eyes with kohl she mused on the extent to which the tan had been attained at the expense of her degree grade.

Her ballgown was made of bronze-coloured velvet, low cut, with a halterneck that exposed her smooth shoulders and newly healed tattoo. It fitted her perfectly. No one had any idea how much she'd paid for it.

Nick came for her and they left for the ball. In her room the kohl pencil lay on the desk, snapped in two.

It was a balmy June evening. The air was soft and warm, fragrant with the jasmine that bloomed in the main courtyard. Transformed for one night into glamorous beings, Ariel students wandered the grounds dressed in tuxedos and silk and satin dresses.

Chinese lanterns glowed in Carriwell Court. Fairy lights twinkled along the huge white marquee on the lawn by the chapel. A band played swing music on the main stage, and students who were already tipsy threw themselves about on the bouncy castle.

Nick handed Olivia a flute of champagne and they clinked glasses. 'To the end of an era,' he said, noticing that her knuckles were white.

'Did I say something?' he asked when she wouldn't meet his eye. She tried to smile.

'No, of course not. Come on, let's find Godfrey. I bet you a tenner he's wearing his white tux.'

Godfrey stole their casino chips, won at roulette and gave them a share of his winnings. The chips were valueless outside of the ball. He was already drunk and getting obnoxious, so they left him to it. Outside the sun was disappearing, leaving a smear of pink and orange on the horizon. They went on the Ferris wheel, laughing at the idea of enjoying an aerial view of Ariel. They ran into Sinead and Leo, and got the giggles trying to bump them on the dodgem cars.

'Come on, let's get some Archers and lemonade,' said Sinead, dragging them over to a stand set up expressly to serve schnapps. June was there, chatting to a friend of hers, her hair in long braids.

'You look fantastic,' said Olivia, admiring June's bright yellow dress.

'You too. Where did you get that amazing dress from?'

'Debenhams,' Olivia said brightly.

'Really?' June frowned. She slipped behind Olivia and pulled the label out from her dress, ignoring Olivia's protests. 'Jesus, Liv, that's a designer dress. I thought you were skint?'

Nick was now frowning too, knowing that Olivia got no money from her parents, and relied on student loans and her overdraft.

'I put it on my credit card,' she said.

'What credit card?' he asked. Everyone looked awkward at the shift in conversation.

'I don't fill you in on every aspect of my financial situation,' Olivia told him in a low voice, as Sinead tried to start up a new topic with Danny, pretending they were oblivious to the argument.

'The last thing you need is massive credit card debts,' said Nick. 'Why didn't you ask me? I'd have lent you the money.'

'I don't want your bloody money!' snapped Olivia.

'Fine!' He raised his hands in impatience. 'I'm going to look for Leo. See you later.' He stalked off in the direction of the marquee.

'Thanks, June,' said Olivia, voice twisted with sarcasm. 'That was great.' She turned her back and stepped up to the schnapps stand, asking the guy behind the counter for a double, straight up.

'I'm sorry!' said June. 'I didn't know Nick thought the dress was from a bargain bin.'

'Fuck you,' snapped Olivia, downing the schnapps and indicating for a refill.

'Olivia, for Christ's sake, he's not worth it!' cried June. 'I know how hard you're finding it, trying to make him happy. But there are some people that will never be happy, and he's one of them. You know what I'm talking about, *don't* you, Liv.'

Olivia didn't turn round. She was leaning on the schnapps counter, hands flat on the wet surface, shoulders hunched. The waiter watched her, feeling awkward. She took the glass of schnapps and snapped her head back, swallowing it in one.

'Again. Please.'

He poured her out another, not wanting to refuse and upset her further.

'Liv?' said June from outside the tent. Her dark skin was glowing in the setting sunlight.

Olivia swallowed her third double, back still turned to the others.

'OK, fine,' said June, her voice wobbly, turning on her heel and running off. Her friend gathered up the skirts of her dress and took off after her.

Sinead and Danny exchanged glances. 'I'll go and find Nick,' he said and headed towards the marquee. Taking a deep breath Sinead went and stood next to Olivia.

'Just a lemonade please,' she asked the nervous waiter, who was grateful for the chance to pretend to be completely distracted by this new task.

Sinead touched Olivia's shoulder. 'Liv? Don't be upset.

Nick's a nice guy, she just doesn't see it, that's all. She just wants you to be happy. Come on, let's find Nick and explain to him how much of a profit you can make from that dress on eBay tomorrow morning.'

The clock in the chapel chimed midnight. Leo and Sinead were slow-dancing to the string quartet on the back lawn. The white glow from the globes hung between the old iron lamp posts was making them both feel romantic. Sinead rested her head on Leo's shoulder and sighed happily, enjoying the smell of his aftershave. Leo slid his hands further down her back, liking the feel of her body under the satin gown.

'Shall we go somewhere more private?' he murmured in her ear.

She looked up at him, pretending to be shocked. 'Why, Mr Montegino! Oh, all right then. Just don't ever tell Paula. She gets upset when one of her admirers takes a time-out from making cow eyes at her.'

'I don't make cow eyes!' protested Leo, but Sinead just laughed and dragged him towards her room in Carriwell Court, picking up a half-consumed bottle of Veuve Clicquot on the way.

They passed a couple in the courtyard, tongues lodged deep down each other's throats, the guy's hand sneaking up the girl's leg to her stocking top. At the foot of the staircase Godfrey sat on a step, watching the amorous couple and sipping a glass of champagne.

'Having fun?' asked Leo, winking at him, glad someone would know he'd got lucky tonight.

'Not really,' said Godfrey in clipped tones. 'My date is

somewhat the worse for wear.' They followed his gaze
over to the girl he'd sat next to in the punt some weeks
before, who was vomiting into the shrubbery and seemed
to be missing a shoe. 'That's what I get for dating sixth-
formers. They just can't hold their liquor.'

Sinead patted him on the head as she stepped past.
'Get her some coffee. Maybe she'll sober up before her
curfew.'

Leo followed her up the stairs, feeling a twitch of
anticipation in his trousers as she reached up to her hair
and pulled out the clip, loosing the amber tresses down
her pale bare back. On the second floor Sinead took her
room key from its hiding place on the top of the
doorframe and smiled seductively at Leo as she slid it
into the lock. He leaned closer for a kiss of those sweet
rosy lips and then suddenly her fingers stopped him.

'Did you hear that?' she whispered.

'No,' he said, pulling her fingers out of the way, but she
stopped him again.

'Shh!' They both listened. Leo could faintly make out
the sound of sobbing. 'I think it's Liv,' she said.

Leo frowned. 'I thought her and Nick made up.'

'They did,' said Sinead, worried. 'I should go and see if
she's all right.'

'No, no,' Leo groaned, pinning her to her door. 'Stay
here. I'm sure she's fine.'

'Leo, get your groin off me. You can go in and wait if
you want, but I want to make sure she's OK.' Relenting,
he pushed himself off her, then followed her up to the
third floor, reasoning that if he left her and Olivia to it
they would probably be talking for hours.

The smell hit them first. A combination of bile and shit. Suddenly scared, Sinead and Leo slowed down. The sobbing sound was louder, but it was coming from June's room, not Nick's. Fighting the urge to tear down the stairs and run for the gates, they edged round the corner and stopped dead in the doorway to June's room.

Olivia, covered in blood and wearing nothing but a bra and knickers, was curled up on the carpet, tears streaming down her blood-streaked face. Next to her lay the body of June Okeweno, cut and split in a hundred places, exposed pink tissue contrasting sharply with her smooth brown skin.

Nick, still in his tuxedo, was kneeling over her, shoving her intestines back into her body.

It took very little now to get Olivia to go under. Denison found the beach visualization tended to do the trick on its own, and he could leave out that of the church and stained glass windows. She lay relaxed on the sofa, her cheeks flushed, her mouth slightly open. Denison thought she looked like a sleeping child.

'Hello, doc,' she said drowsily. 'It's Helen.'

'How are you, Helen?'

'Not good. I know you want to talk about June today.'

'That's right. I need you to tell me what happened that night.'

Helen sighed and was quiet for a long time. Denison started to wonder if perhaps she had actually fallen asleep; this wasn't unheard of during a session of hypnosis. It startled him when she suddenly spoke.

'She argued with us. Tried to drive Nick away. I actually

managed to control Jude, probably because she was quite sober at that stage in the evening. Things even calmed down. Mary was feeling a bit hard done by about the degree grade, so I was spending time trying to reassure her that she wasn't to blame if she hadn't managed to surface during all of the examinations. Maybe I should have been concentrating harder, shouldn't have let myself be distracted, but Olivia had gone back to Nick's room and been put to bed by him, and I thought it was safe. Then June came knocking at the door you see, and they began to argue. And Jude was there, waiting.

'He forced her back into her own room, closing the door behind them. She struggled with him, but you have to understand that Olivia is so much stronger, physically, when Jude's in charge. He killed June. And she suffered . . .' Helen suddenly burst into tears. 'She really suffered! The others didn't comprehend what was happening. It was over so quickly for them. But June had time to understand. That poor, poor girl.'

'Can you tell me what he did to her?' asked Denison, twisting his pen round in his fingers, hating putting her through this.

He took her guts out. And then he just stabbed and stabbed her and he wouldn't stop. I couldn't make him stop. Nick came running in and that's the last thing I remember. I don't know what happened after that. I don't know where we were during that time you say Olivia was catatonic.'

Denison rested his pen on his notepad. 'OK,' he said, 'let's get you out of this trance.'

Ten minutes later, refreshed and relaxed due to a post-hypnotic suggestion from Denison, Olivia sipped from a glass of water and looked at him.

'Olivia . . . do you remember anything from that day? Finding out your degree grade? Getting ready for the May Ball? The ball itself?'

She nodded. 'All of it.'

'You don't have any blank spots?'

She drank some more water. 'Maybe. There was a point when Danny was there and then he wasn't. I don't think I lost too much time though.'

Denison made a note. 'Do you remember going back to Nick's room?'

'Yes. I was quite drunk and drowsy. Nick thought he should put me to bed. He had to unzip my dress for me. I went straight to bed in my undies I was that tired.'

'And do you remember if he left then, or stayed in the room?'

She shook her head and took a long drink of water. 'I don't remember anything after that. It's like when you said I went to Brown's for Valentine's night, or took Sinead to the pub to watch the quarter-finals. I only know that Nick and I were in June's room because that's what you tell me.'

Denison, scribbling with his blue biro, suddenly found his pen had frozen on the page. 'What did you say?' The breath was stuck in his lungs.

'Don't be offended. I'm just pointing out that I'm taking what you tell me on faith. You could be lying to me. I just wouldn't know.'

Denison cleared his throat. 'I'm not lying to you, Olivia. I promise. Look, it's getting late. Let's wrap it up for today.'

*

'I think she's lying,' said Denison. He took off his glasses, rubbing them on his tie, and then put them back on, gazing at Weathers.

Weathers stared back. 'What happened?'

'People with DID have blank spots, fugue states which they wake up from with no memory of anything that's happened during that period. It's caused by one of their alter personalities coming to the fore. The main personality is oblivious to everything that goes on while the alter is in control.'

'OK,' said Weathers, impatient.

'That afternoon Sinead Flynn visited Olivia in London was supposedly during one of these fugue states. Olivia said she only knew they'd watched the quarter-finals in the pub because I'd told her so.'

Weathers looked at him, then raised his hands in the air, frustrated. 'And?'

'I only told Olivia they were showing the World Cup,' Denison said. He looked like he was about to throw up. 'How did she know it was a quarter-final match?'

'Matt, there could be another explanation for this,' Weathers said. 'If she had a general idea of what week Sinead Flynn visited her, she could have made an educated guess that it was during a quarter-final. Christ, are you sure you didn't tell her?'

'I've checked my tapes. All I said was it was a World Cup match. I don't think I even told her it was in June.'

Weathers tipped his head back and glared at the ceiling. 'So what the fuck's going on?'

'Maybe she's been malingering, faking all the symptoms of Dissociative Identity Disorder. OK, so she'd still have to be holed up in a secure unit until she can miraculously be cured, but it's got to be better than twenty to life in prison.'

'But why on earth fake multiple personality? From what you've told me it's not exactly guaranteed to get you a place in Coldhill rather than Holloway. Why wouldn't she fake something easier that everyone agrees exists, like paranoid schizophrenia?'

Denison shrugged. 'I don't know. Maybe she's scared of being put on anti-psychotic medication. Christ knows I wouldn't take it unless I absolutely had to. Plus there were no obvious signs of psychosis during her three years at Ariel, so how believable would it have been if she'd started declaring now that she was Napoleon and the CIA were trying to control her through her telly set?'

'Well, we need to be sure about this. How can we prove whether her multiple personalities are real or not?'

Denison almost laughed out loud. He loosened his tie, relaxing somewhat. 'You know what, if I could prove that then the condition wouldn't be so controversial. Most of the DID literature out there is about ascertaining whether or not the patients really do have distinct, separate personalities.'

'Great. So you're telling me there's no way we can prove that she has it or not?' Weathers scraped his chair back and went to glare out of the window.

'It's not like we can prove it with a blood test or something, no,' said Denison. 'But have you heard of Kenneth Bianchi?'

Weathers nodded. 'Yeah. One of the Hillside Stranglers in California back in the seventies.'

'Well, he blamed the murders on an alter personality.

What the prosecution managed to show was not that he was faking the other personality, but that he was faking being under hypnosis.'

Weathers' green eyes lit up. 'So, if we can show Corscadden isn't really going under then that suggests she's probably faking the whole thing? Matt, you're a genius.' He grabbed Denison's face and planted a smacker on his forehead. 'Let's do it.'

'Do you mind the video camera, Olivia?'

Olivia's eyes shifted from the camera lens to Denison unhappily. 'I suppose not, if you feel it's necessary.'

'I think it's appropriate for us to record this visually rather than simply audibly.' Denison felt bad about misleading her; it wasn't usually part of his job description. He left the camera on auto-focus, directed on her as she reclined on the couch.

They went through the full hypnotic induction: the beach, the church, the staircase. Olivia appeared to be in a deep hypnotic trance.

'Olivia,' said Denison, 'I want you to remain in this very relaxed state as you sit up and open your eyes.'

She smoothed her skirt over her thighs and sat up straight, back against the sofa cushions. Only when she was facing dead ahead did she open her eyes, which appeared glazed and unfocused.

'Olivia, I'm going to ask you some questions. Don't worry if you don't know the answer – just say you don't know, you won't have to guess. OK?'

'OK.'

'Can you tell me what the capital of England is?'

'London.'

'There are three colours in the American flag. What are these colours?'

'Red, white and blue.'

'Who was the first astronaut to walk on the moon?'

'Neil Armstrong.'

'The amethyst is a purply-blue gemstone. What colour is it when it's heated?'

A neat vertical crease appeared on her forehead. 'I don't know.'

'The amethyst turns yellow when heated. What was the name of Mickey Mouse's girlfriend in the Disney cartoons?'

The crease disappeared. 'Minnie.'

'That's very good, Olivia. Now, I'm going to come and sit next to you.' Denison took a seat at the opposite end of the sofa, careful not to invade her personal space. 'Olivia, please can you hold out your left hand?'

She moved the hand towards him, still looking ahead rather than at him. 'I'm going to draw a circle on the back of your hand with my finger,' he told her. 'When I've drawn the circle the skin inside it will become numb, and you won't be able to feel anything touching this area of skin. Do you understand?'

Olivia nodded. Denison used the tip of his forefinger to draw a circle, with a diameter of about two inches, on the back of her hand. 'Now I'm going to touch you in various places on your forearm and hand. If you're touched in a place where you feel it, I want you to say "yes". If you're touched in a place where you can't feel it, I want you to say "no". Do you understand?'

Olivia nodded again. 'OK, Olivia I want you to close

your eyes.' She shut them tight. Denison pressed her gently on her forearm.

'Yes,' she said. He touched her again, this time on her thumb. 'Yes.' He touched her within the imaginary circle. No response. He pushed with his finger on her elbow. 'Yes.' He tried again within the circle. Again, she said nothing.

'OK, Olivia, you can open your eyes again.' They blinked open. The afternoon sunlight was making her hair glow.

Denison stood up and drew the empty desk chair closer to the sofa, then sat back down on the couch. 'Janey, my PA, is sitting on that chair. Do you see her?'

Olivia nodded. 'Hello,' she said to the empty chair.

'Can you tell me what she's wearing?'

Olivia looked surprised. 'I don't understand. Can't you see her?'

'I just want to know what you see, Olivia.'

Her head tilted. 'A blue blouse. A black skirt.'

'Would you like to talk to her?'

Olivia looked embarrassed. 'I don't know what to say.'

'Why don't you ask her about her home life?'

The girl blinked. 'Uh . . . do you have a boyfriend?' After a moment she nodded.

'What did she say?' asked Denison.

'She said she did have until recently, but that they split up last month.'

Surprisingly close to the truth, but Denison wasn't here to assess Olivia's psychic abilities. He asked her to close her eyes, then stood up and went to the door, silently indicating for the real Janey to join them. Janey seemed almost as uncomfortable as Olivia, but dutifully walked into the room. Denison asked Olivia to open her eyes and Janey politely nodded hello to Olivia.

But Olivia, it seemed, couldn't see her. Her attention remained fixed on the imaginary Janey sitting in the chair.

'Olivia,' said Dr Denison. 'Look who's just come into the room. Look, it's Janey.'

Once he'd prompted her he watched Olivia's eyes flick from the seated imaginary Janey to the standing Janey and back in consternation. 'Doctor, what's happening?' she whispered. 'This is really freaky, I don't like it, please make it stop!'

'What's wrong, Olivia?' he urged.

'I think I'm hallucinating. Is she a twin? I can see two of them! How can she be in two places at the same time?'

'Olivia, please relax. It's OK to see two of them.' He turned to Janey. 'Thank you, Janey, you can get back to your desk.' Nonplussed, Janey left the room, closing the door behind her. Olivia visibly relaxed now that only the imaginary Janey was present. 'Olivia, Janey is getting off the chair and leaving. You don't see her any more.'

'Where did she go?' Olivia asked, concerned.

'Olivia, I want you to lie back on the couch again, and I'm going to bring you out of this trance. You're going to awake feeling completely refreshed and relaxed, but you won't remember anything that happened during the trance, do you understand?'

'Yes.' She was settling back into the sofa cushions, again making sure she was decently covered by her skirt. Denison reversed the stairs visualization, gradually bringing her back to full consciousness.

'. . . and one. You're now completely awake. How do you feel?'

Olivia pushed herself to a seated position. She ran her hands through her hair and smiled at Denison. 'Surprisingly good, thanks, Doc.'

'OK then, I just have a few questions to ask you. I apologize if some of these seem strange.'

She nodded a prompt for him to continue.

'There are three colours in the American flag. Which colours are they?'

'Blue, red, white.'

'What was the name of Mickey Mouse's girlfriend in the Disney cartoons?'

She smiled. 'Minnie.'

'Who was the first astronaut to walk on the moon?'

'Neil Armstrong.'

'The amethyst is a purply-blue gemstone. What colour is it when it's heated?'

Olivia laughed. 'You're kidding me. I studied English Lit, remember?'

'So you don't know?'

'Nope.'

'That's all right. Can you tell me what the capital of England is?'

'Thank God, an easy one! London, of course.'

Ten minutes later, with Olivia being escorted back to her room on the other side of the building, Denison was on the phone, a grim set to his mouth.

'Steve, it's Matt. I've got your proof.'

Chapter Sixteen

Olivia was in her room. She had changed into jeans and a T-shirt and was sitting on her bed reading a book, singing to herself under her breath. When she noticed Denison through the reinforced glass in the door, her face lit up and she got off the bed to come to him.

The orderly unlocked the door and Olivia's face went grey when she saw Weathers standing behind the doctor.

'What's he doing here?' she asked.

Weathers stepped forward, flanked by DS Jack Halloran and two uniformed police officers.

'Olivia Corscadden, I'm arresting you for the murders of Amanda Montgomery, Eliza Fitzstanley and June Okeweno. You do not have to say anything, but it may harm your defence if you do not mention when questioned something you later rely on in court. Anything you say may be given in evidence.' Olivia struggled as Halloran flipped her round and handcuffed her, pushing her against the wall.

'You don't have to be so rough,' complained Denison.

'Please, don't let them do this!' cried Olivia. 'Please, you've got to help me! Tell them about Jude! I didn't do it! I didn't do it!' Halloran jerked her out of the room and led her off down the hallway accompanied by the two uniforms. The other patients, all safely locked in their own rooms, heard her cries and began yelling themselves, banging against their doors, screaming just to join in.

At the end of the corridor Halloran dragged her through the doorway. She just had one more breath, one more chance to meet Denison's eyes. 'Matthew, help me!' she pleaded, and then she was out of sight.

Denison let out a long breath and the orderly next to him shook his head, not impressed with the turn of events.

Weathers was in Olivia's room, picking up a pair of her shoes.

'You'll need socks too,' said Denison, going into the room and rifling through Olivia's clothes. 'And a jumper.' He shoved them into Weathers' arms.

'Matt, don't feel sorry for her. She killed three girls.'

'There was no need for that ape to shove her around like that. She's still a human being.'

Weathers shrugged. 'Debatable. Look, don't worry about the rest of the clothes, I'll get them shipped out of here when the judge decides where to stick her for now.'

'Are you taking her back to Cambridge for interview?'

Weathers shook his head. 'Nope, we're using the nick at Newington Park. Chances are she'll be transferred to Holloway, so there's no point taking her out of London.'

'I want to be there. During the interview.'

Weathers nodded. 'Fine. I want you there too.' He tucked the socks into the shoes and set off down the corridor, turning round halfway to the door. 'I'll send a car for you in a couple of hours. Give her a chance to stew for a bit.' He spun back again, never stopping moving, and swept through the door.

Denison sat down on the bed. He'd set this all in motion

by signing a statement that said he believed there was no longer a justification for holding Olivia Corscadden under the Mental Health Act. He pictured her face as she was dragged back out into the real world, and felt awful guilt in the pit of his stomach.

There was a photo of Nick Blu-tacked to the wall by Olivia's bed. He was tousle-haired and smiling, standing with two friends in the gardens of his school, the impressive seventeenth-century building in the background. He seemed so happy, so relaxed. He wondered if Nicholas Hardcastle would ever look that carefree again.

Newington Park was in one of the rougher parts of East London. As the unmarked police car drove Denison through its streets, he witnessed one graffiti artist announcing his support of Arsenal on a tower block wall, one drunk bloke pissing against the side of a bus shelter, left hand clutching a Sainsbury's carrier bag, and one suspected drug deal outside a cafe-cum-social club. As usual the patch of pavement outside and opposite the police station was clean of both street scum and graffiti: an intended side effect of the newly refurbished reception area, in which brick had been replaced by bullet-proof glass that allowed the desk sergeant an unrestricted view of what was going on outside. It was now nearly nine in the evening and the setting sun was bouncing off the glass, illuminating the last streaks of pink cloud in the August sky.

The CID officer driving Denison swerved down a side street without indicating and turned into the parking area behind Newington Park police station. He'd hardly said two words to Denison on the trip from Coldhill. They went inside and the doctor was left hanging around in reception until DS Halloran turned up and grunted at him.

'How's she doing?' Denison asked as they made their way up the stairs to the first-floor CID area.

'Calmed down on the way over. She's got the sniffles now, but that's par for the course with the women. Never arrested a woman yet who didn't cry once she'd been stuck in the cells for an hour or two.'

'Has Steve – I mean, DCI Weathers – spoken to her yet?'

'Nope. Wanted you here first.'

'Has she asked for a solicitor?'

'No, lucky for us. She's been asking for you though. Obviously doesn't have a clue you were the one pulled the rug from under her, the dopey bitch. Come on, it's along here. The whole team's down from Cambridge.'

'Is WDC Ames around?'

'You mean Mrs Weathers?' Halloran winked. 'She will be later; she's in Balham at the moment, re-interviewing one of the Ariel lot, Danny Armstrong. Hardcastle didn't report it, but apparently Armstrong spray-painted graffiti on his house and had a bit of a punch up with him, so the guv's better half has gone to find out what set him off. Through here.'

Weathers was in the middle of the incident room, chatting with two men Denison didn't recognize, one in an ill-fitting suit and one in full uniform. Weathers looked across when Halloran opened the door and came straight over. 'Thanks for coming, Matt,' he said. 'This is Superintendent Walker – he's kindly letting us use Newington Park to hold Corscadden.' Denison shook the hand of the man in the black uniform with the silver buttons and ornate epaulettes. Weathers indicated the man in the baggy suit, who needed a shave and a haircut. 'And this is DCI Colin MacIntyre. He's been leading the Eliza Fitzstanley investigation.' Ah, thought Denison, the man who denied the existence of the Cambridge Butcher. He shook MacIntyre's hand.

'Well, good luck, Weathers,' said Superintendent Walker, striding away to more urgent police business. 'Keep me informed.'

'So what's the plan, Steve?' asked Denison.

'Yeah,' said MacIntyre. 'That's what I'd like to know.'

'The plan is we get her to confess that she faked the DID. And then we find out why. We were just bringing Mac up to date on the hypnotic logic tests you did on her. I'm not sure he's really got the picture.' Weathers raised a weary eyebrow.

'Well, what the fuck was up with that numb circle stuff?' protested MacIntyre, wiping his forehead with a hanky. 'You'd told her the skin would be numb, so of course she's not going to pipe up if you press her there. The girl got into Cambridge, so she's obviously not a retard.'

'There's a difference, though, between hypnotic logic and normal logic,' Denison tried to explain. 'You can't extrapolate from normal behaviour to behaviour under hypnosis. People simply don't respond in the same way.'

'But take the yellow amethyst stuff. You told her to forget everything that had happened during her trance, which would include what you told her about the amethyst turning yellow. Are you saying your hypnotic suggestions shouldn't work?'

'No, that's not how it works,' protested Denison.

'Forget it,' said Weathers. 'As long as Corscadden under-
stands, that's all that matters. Mac, for Christ's sake, just
keep your gob shut in the interview.'

The interview room was larger and better kitted out than
its counterpart in Cambridge's Parkside station, but like all
interview rooms it smelled of cheap cleaning products. The
window was high up in the wall so it could provide no dis-
tractions during an interrogation; even when standing, all
you could see was a faraway high-rise council flat block,
pinpricks of light beginning to shine from its windows as the
sun went off shift and handed over the job of lighting up the
city to millions of electric lightbulbs.

Along one inside wall of the room ran a large two-way
mirror, through which the occupants of the neighbouring
room could observe the interview. There was a desk and a
microphone in the observation room; the microphone could
be used to transmit information and suggestions to the interviewing officer via a small earpiece. Halloran and Denison
were installed in the observation room, the latter sitting at
the desk in front of the microphone. Denison had to press a
button in order for the microphone to transmit, and he was
worried about how much his fingertips were sweating.

'Testing, testing, 1-2-3,' he croaked into the mike.
Weathers, sitting in the interview room with his back to the
mirror, turned in his seat and gave him a thumbs-up and an
encouraging smile.

MacIntyre was pacing the room in his overly tight suit,
biting his pinkie fingernail.

'Look at that idiot,' said Halloran. 'Does he look like a
twat in that suit or what?'

'You think you should be in there instead?' asked Denison.

Halloran gave him a hard look. 'Course I do. If the twats in charge hadn't lost their nerve and tried to pass off Eliza's death as a one-off, drug-related murder, that arsehole wouldn't even be here. I should be in there with Steve. I know the cases back to front.'

'So why's MacIntyre here? They must accept by now that the deaths were all related.'

Halloran shrugged. 'They reckon he's the expert on the Fitzstanley case. Like I said – twats, the lot of 'em.'

The door to the interview room opened and the sudden movement made Denison, who was feeling very tense and nervous, jump a little in his chair. Olivia was led in by a uniformed WPC, who took her to her seat and then went to stand by the closed door.

Olivia's hair was still tied back in a ponytail, but long strands of it had escaped and were sticking to her tear-streaked face. Her eyes were red and a bit swollen. She looked very small in her grey cotton sweatshirt.

'Hello, Olivia,' said Weathers.

'Hello,' she said nervously.

'I'm going to switch the tape on now, OK?'

'OK.' She was barely audible.

Weathers pressed the record button on the video recording equipment and stated the date, time and people present. He then repeated to Olivia her rights, and she confirmed that she understood them. She still did not ask for a solicitor, and Halloran wheezed a sigh of relief.

'Olivia, you've been held at Coldhill psychiatric hospital for the past ten weeks, is that correct?'

She nodded. 'I believe so.'

'You believe so?'

'I can't remember all of it. I've been told I was catatonic for a while.'

'But since regaining consciousness you've been engaged in psychiatric sessions with Dr Matthew Denison, one of the men in charge of Coldhill?' She nodded again. 'And you've made some breakthroughs with Dr Denison?'

'He told me that I have this condition called Dissociative Identity Disorder.' She stumbled a bit over the name.

'Can you tell me about this disorder?'

Olivia shifted in her seat. 'It's basically multiple personalities. I . . . I didn't know I had it. But Dr Denison said sometimes when he spoke to me it wasn't me but someone else. This other personality apparently knew about the murders.' She started crying quietly. 'Knew that it was me that killed my friends.'

Halloran clenched his fist. Denison looked down at the fist and realized it was an expression of triumph at Olivia's first admission of guilt to the police.

'What did you tell Dr Denison about your friends' murders?'

'He said I told him that one of the other personalities, Jude, had been in control of my body and had killed them.'

'When you say them . . .'

'Amanda, Eliza and June.'

Denison realized that there was a limit to what Weathers could extract from Olivia in terms of a confession. The details about the murders had come from Helen and the other manufactured alters, and so all Olivia's admissions would be nothing but a parroting of information he'd passed back to her: she would never say to Weathers, 'I killed Amanda,' only, 'Dr Denison told me I'd said I killed Amanda.'

They could pretend to try to 'bring out' Helen, get her to confess on tape, but Denison doubted that hypnotizing – or even pretending to hypnotize – your suspect was considered acceptable practice by the Criminal Prosecution Service.

'How did Dr Denison manage to speak to these other personalities?'

'He hypnotized me.'

'They never came out voluntarily?'

She looked confused. 'I guess they must have done.'

'Could I speak to one of them now?' She just gazed at him, golden eyes blank. 'Could I speak to Helen?'

After a while she shrugged. 'I don't think it works like that.'

'You're not Helen,'

She twitched a smile. 'No.'

'Could I maybe speak to Mary then? Or Vanna?'

'I don't know how to switch to them, I'm sorry.'

'How about Jude?'

Olivia wrapped her arms round herself. 'It's not working. I don't think you can get them to come out just by saying their names.'

'How about if I make you mad? Will that bring them out? If I called you a stupid, stuck-up little tart, would that make Jude pop his head up?' A tear rolled down her face, alongside her nose and dripped off her lip onto one of her sleeves. 'I guess not. It's kind of convenient that he only pops up when you're on your own with someone and there aren't any police officers around, eh?'

Olivia's chin was quivering. 'Can I speak to Dr Denison?' she asked. Denison couldn't ignore the guilt he felt, watching her crying. He felt like he had betrayed her.

'No,' said Weathers. 'Tell me, why were you and your –
what did you call them, alters? – so happy to open up to Dr
Denison?'

'He made me feel safe,' said Olivia, staring down at the
desk. 'I trusted him.'

'Do you think he liked you?'

'I think he cared.'

'Did you think he was gullible?'

She looked up suddenly. 'No. What do you mean?'

'Well, you spun him this elaborate story about evil alter-
nate personalities and he swallowed it, didn't he? Happily
rubber-stamped your insanity defence.'

'I didn't lie to him.'

'Unfortunately for you, you slipped up. And he got suspicious. He started to think maybe you were just pretending
to be hypnotized. But the truth is you wanted to stay in
control, so you weren't going to let yourself go under. Have
you heard of "hypnotic logic"? No? Neither had I until a
few days ago. Turns out hypnotic logic is a bit warped.
Doesn't work in the same way as the logic we employ on a
day-to-day basis. That's what Dr Denison was up to today
in your session – testing whether you were really hypnotized
or not.'

Olivia had become very still. No tears, no fidgeting, no
nervous gestures. MacIntyre wheeled round a trolley on
castor wheels, on which a TV rested on top of a DVD
player. Weathers used the remote on the desk to switch on
the TV and pressed play. Olivia watched as an image of
herself appeared on the screen. Denison's voice, tinny and
off-camera, was asking her about astronauts, flags and
Disney cartoons. Weathers waited for Denison to tell her

that amethysts turn yellow when heated, then paused the recording.

'He asked you to forget that fact. And you did. The thing is, genuinely hypnotized people *do* remember the answer to the question when they're asked it again later; they simply won't be able to remember *how* they know it.'

Olivia just looked at him. 'I don't know what you want me to say. I didn't know the answer. I didn't remember. I still don't remember him telling me that!'

Weathers didn't respond except to press play on the remote. On the TV screen Denison appeared in the picture and sat at the other end of the sofa from Olivia. He reached over and drew a circle on the back of her hand. They watched as he tapped his finger at different places on her arm. Then they saw him, expression harsh, stand up and again move out of shot.

Weathers paused the recording again.

'He's told you the skin's numb in the circle, and he's also told you to say "no" if you are touched where you can't feel it. Since your eyes are closed, how are you going to know if you've been touched if you don't feel it? So you say nothing. But like I said, turns out hypnotic logic is a bit odd. Hypnotized subjects say "no" when they're touched inside the numb circle. Would you like to respond to that?'

Olivia shook her head mutely.

'Right, test number three.' Weathers pressed play. Olivia interacted with an invisible Janey, then with the real one. She appeared distressed. Weathers pressed stop and the screen went blue.

'So, induced hallucinations. Dr Denison asked you to imagine his PA, Janey, was sitting in the room with you, then he brought in the real Janey. You pretended you couldn't see the real Janey – how could you, when she was meant to be sitting on the chair in front of you, not standing by the door? But hypnotized subjects see both, and unlike you, they don't need someone to point out the real version to them. You know what else? Seeing both doesn't bother them. It's acceptable. You, however, freaked out. "Is she a twin?" "How can she be in two places at once?" According to Dr Denison that's the way someone would react if they were pretending to be hypnotized when actually they were completely conscious.' He sat back, his barrage nearly complete. 'So, Olivia . . . tell us why you felt the need to fake a hypnotic trance.'

Olivia just gazed at him. Her eyes were wet. He saw the tension flickering in her skin and sensed that she was barely holding it together. He just needed to give a tiny little push.

'Actually, don't bother. We already know why. You were scared. You knew that if you let Dr Denison actually genuinely hypnotize you, you wouldn't be able to keep up your pretence of having these other personalities. That he'd find out you'd been making it up all along.'

Just for a moment more her composure held. Then her face seemed to break. She covered her face with her hands and began to sob. It was a horrible, despairing sound.

Weathers leaned closer to her. His tone changed from haranguing to concerned, almost soothing. 'Olivia, you've been pretending for a very long time. I know it must be exhausting, trying to keep up this act. It's OK now, you can give it up. You can relax. No more having to fool Dr Denison. No more having to conjure up different voices and different body language and no more having to remember who knows what and who said what. Just tell us what really happened back then. Whatever it is, we'll understand.'

She shook her head, tears dropping from her eyes. 'I was just so ashamed. I didn't want Dr Denison to think badly of me. I wanted to give him something to blame it on, and I remembered these books Sinead was reading about DID when she did her abnormal psychology module . . .'

'So you constructed this whole story to gain Dr Denison's sympathy?' said Weathers. 'Nothing to do with an insanity defence then?' Halloran snorted at the sarcasm.

Olivia wiped her eyes with her sleeve. 'Either way I'm going to be locked up for the rest of my life, aren't I?' she said, almost defiantly. 'So what difference does it make to me whether I'm with criminals or psychos?'

'Olivia, you can't seriously be telling me that you made this whole thing up so Dr Denison would think less badly of you.'

She glared at Weathers with reddened eyes. 'It doesn't really matter what you think,' she said. 'As long as Matthew believes me.'

'You're on first-name terms, then?'

In the observation room Halloran nudged Denison, smirking. 'Remind me, doc, what do they call that, when the patient falls in love with their shrink? Transference, isn't it?'

'Is he here?' Olivia asked.

'Who?'

'Matthew,' she said. Denison felt his heart hike up in his chest, pained at the feeling he'd abandoned her.

Weathers shook his head. 'No,' he lied.

Even though his instinct was to go into the interview room and comfort her, Denison knew Weathers was right to lie. Olivia might censor herself if she thought he was listening to her confession. The truth had to come out.

'Olivia, maybe we can arrange for Dr Denison to come by and visit you. But first we need to get things straight here. You have to be honest with us, get this off your chest.'

Olivia was gazing down at the table, her hands clasped together. She nodded slowly. 'I know,' she said. 'I know.'

'Then you'll talk to us? Tell us the truth?'

She raised her head then and her face was strangely calm. 'I will.'

A PC brought drinks into the interview room. Olivia wrapped her fingers around the cup, the plastic heated by the hot tea, apparently taking comfort from the warmth.

'OK,' said Weathers. 'Let's start with what happened the night Amanda Montgomery died. Why did you kill her?'

'I don't know,' Olivia said hesitantly. She hid her mouth behind her teacup. 'I suppose I was angry with her for trying to spoil things for me and Nick.'

'How was she doing that?'

'He went out with Paula before me. I didn't know that and I think Amanda told me just to try to cause tension between Nick and me.'

'So why not Paula?'

'Pardon me?' She took a sip of tea.

'Why did you kill Amanda, not Paula? If I was jealous enough to kill someone, trust me, it would be the ex, not the person who told me about the ex.'

Olivia just shrugged, unable to explain herself. Sitting in

the observation room Denison leaned in even closer to the two-way mirror, frowning.

'So tell me how you killed her.'

Olivia mumbled something into her cup.

'For the purposes of the tape I'm afraid you're going to have to speak up, Olivia.'

'I said I killed her with a knife.'

'Did you bring it, or was it Amanda's?'

'I think it was hers. I don't really remember.'

'Were you arguing?'

'I was asking her why she was trying to split up me and Nick. She said I was just being paranoid. That's when I stabbed her.'

'Where?'

'Everywhere. When she stopped breathing I cut off her head.'

In the observation room Halloran was looking at Denison's frown.

'Why the face, doc?'

'Oh, it's just . . . it's probably nothing, but you see the way she's holding that cup so it covers part of her mouth? Well, her body language is suggesting she's lying.'

'Did you think she was lying when she told you about killing Amanda?'

'No.'

'Well, she's saying the same thing. If she wasn't lying then, why would she be lying now?'

'What did you do with the head?' Weathers was asking.

'Like I told Dr Denison, I don't remember. It's all very hazy.' She took a big gulp of her tea.

'You told Dr Denison that you couldn't remember

because Jude was the only alter present at the time. Now that you've admitted making Jude up, I was hoping your memory would improve.'

'It was like being in a trance when I killed them. This red mist just comes up and I hardly know what I'm doing. I don't remember what I did with Amanda's head. I haven't seen it since, so I must have gotten rid of it somewhere. Maybe the river, I don't know.'

Denison was shaking his head. 'This isn't right. She's being too vague.'

Halloran rolled his eyes. 'Christ, doc, you're not trying to tell me she's really a schizo?'

'No, no, I'm not saying that.' Denison was bewildered. 'I just don't understand why she's being so evasive.'

'Maybe she felt safe when she spoke to you, like the girl said. And now she knows she's in deep bloody shit. I wouldn't go too much into the gory details if I was her, not if I knew that the judge who'll sentence me will get to read this statement.'

Denison used the intercom for the first time. 'Steve, ask her about June. She was arguably closest to her, it should provoke more of a reaction.'

Weathers showed no sign to Olivia that someone was speaking to him via his earpiece. He leaned closer towards her.

'OK, let's leave Amanda for now. I want to talk about June.'

Olivia's face crumpled immediately and she lifted the cup to her face, resting her forehead on it as she cried. It was her only shield from her accusers. Once again Denison's heart went out to her.

'She was always on at me to leave Nick,' she sobbed. 'Telling me he was no good for me. I couldn't listen to it any more. I respected her opinion, that's why it hurt that she hated him so much. That night I'd just had enough. She'd already ruined my night by having a go at me at the ball, and then when I got back to Nick's room she turned up again and had another go! I just wanted her to leave me alone.'

'What happened, Olivia?' Weathers asked gently.

'I stabbed a knife into her stomach and cut it open. Her insides came out. I just kept stabbing her. Nick came running in and tried to stop me. He pulled the knife from my hand.'

Even from the observation room Denison could see the tension appear in Weathers' shoulders.

Very casually Weathers said: 'So most of the stab wounds were inflicted after you'd disembowelled her?'

'Shit,' said Halloran, his breath misting up the two-way mirror.

'What?' Denison wanted to know, but just got a harsh 'shush' in response.

Olivia seemed to have also picked up on Weathers' body language. 'I think so,' she said carefully. 'To be honest it's all a bit of a blur. Like I said, there's—'

'There's a red mist, yes, I know. But you have to remember whether June Okeweno's guts were hanging out of her body or not when you were repeatedly stabbing her.'

Olivia's fingers fluttered around the teacup. 'I think so.'

Weathers suddenly stood up, the legs of his chair scraping along the carpet tiles. 'Interview suspended at 22:15,' he said, pausing the tape. On the way out of the door he pointed at MacIntyre. 'Keep an eye on her.'

Denison and Halloran heard the door slam, then a few seconds later Weathers strode through to their room.

'She's lying,' said Halloran. Weathers nodded.

'What makes you say that?' said Denison.

Weathers' eyes turned his way. They looked very cold, like the river-frosted shards of green glass that wash up on the banks of the Thames.

'The pathologist told us that the multiple knife wounds occurred before the disembowelment. Most of them were defence wounds – June put up a hell of a fight. The gutting was what killed her, and none of the other wounds were post-mortem.'

'It could be that she genuinely got it wrong,' Denison said. 'She'd have been in a highly emotional state – could have affected her recall.'

'And you believe the same thing about Amanda Montgomery's head?' snorted Halloran. 'She just forgot what she did with a decapitated head? Jesus, I know women are always forgetting their car keys, but that really takes the cake.'

There was a knock on the door and Halloran went to open it. It was Ames, still in her overcoat and with a look of anticipation on her face.

Weathers ignored her, completely focused on Denison. 'Matt, what's she told you that only the killer would know?' he asked.

'Well, she knew the location of Amanda's injuries, that she'd been decapitated. That wasn't information that was available to the public.'

'Matt, Nick saw the body, remember? He could have told her what state it was in.'

'Eliza's boots and handbag,' said Denison, snapping his fingers. 'That wasn't public knowledge.'

'You're right,' said Weathers, shaking his head. 'But Olivia's mate Danny was one of the rowers in the boat that found them.'

'Christ, has she not told you anything that she couldn't have found out from one of her bloody friends?' complained Halloran, mouth open in disgust.

'I'll need to check my tapes,' said Denison.

'But why is she lying?' said Halloran. 'It doesn't make sense. Why on earth would she confess if she isn't guilty?'

'I think I might be able to answer that,' said Ames.

The statement was on official, headed police paper. Denison saw the name of the interviewee, printed in Ames' neat handwriting: 'Danny Armstrong.'

'He lives in south London now,' said Ames. 'Was a bit reluctant to speak to me – you know the Ariel lot have got that fucked-up code of silence thing going on . . .'

'What did he say?' asked Weathers, flipping through the statement.

'He repeated something June had told him a month or two before she was murdered. Apparently June, whose room of course neighboured Nick's, had overheard an argument between him and Olivia. Except according to her the yelling was all on Nick's side. Olivia sounded like she was trying to calm him down. There was a short silence and then the sound of a door slamming. June came out to see if everything was OK and saw Olivia running down the stairs to the shower room, clutching her arm. She found her holding it under the cold tap. There was a fresh burn mark on the underside of her arm. June told Danny it was the kind of mark a cigarette would make.'

Denison looked through the two-way mirror to Olivia, sitting in her chair with her shoulders slumped, like a broken doll.

'Did Olivia tell her what had happened?' asked Weathers.

'Nope – she told June to mind her own business. Danny reckons Olivia just avoided June completely after that.'

'I think we need to check Olivia's hospital records,' said Denison.

'I'll get on to Addenbrooke's,' said Ames, 'in case she went in for anything worse that a fag burn,' and left the room.

There was a long silence. The three men looked at each other, then over to Olivia, now sitting with her elbows on the table, palms together over her mouth and nose.

Denison sat down heavily. 'It was Nick. It was Nick all along. Christ, I can't believe I've been so stupid.'

'Hang on a minute,' protested Halloran. 'We find out her boyfriend knocked her about a bit and all of a sudden she's innocent and he must be the killer?'

'Do you know how rare female serial killers are?' said Denison. 'Especially ones who kill for pleasure, not for money?'

'Not that bloody rare!' said Halloran. 'What about Rose West? Or Myra Hindley?'

Denison shook his head with a pained smile. 'You've just made my point. They both killed in partnership with dominant men. I doubt either of them would have turned into serial killers if they'd found different lovers.'

'So you're saying Corscadden and Hardcastle were in it together?'

'I don't know. If she was actually involved in the murders, then how do we explain why she can't give us any of the details?' pointed out Denison. 'Why can't she tell us where Amanda's head is and why does she think June was stabbed *after* she was disembowelled?'

Weathers didn't look convinced. 'If she's not involved, why the hell is she covering for him? Not just covering, but taking all the blame?'

Denison tried to find a way to explain. 'Have you ever noticed the way some criminals can walk into a room and straightaway know who they can con, who they can shake down, who they can intimidate?'

Halloran nodded. 'Like lions with antelopes. They always go for the weak ones – easy pickings.'

'Well, some men can spot damaged women in the same way. They want someone they can dominate, someone they can completely control. They can tell which ones are vulnerable, which ones can be manipulated by the pretence of love and affection. Imagine being tortured, abused and despised your whole life, then imagine how it must feel when you finally find someone who loves you and takes care of you. He tells you he'd die for you, that you're the love of his life, that he couldn't live without you. Wouldn't you forgive him for delivering the occasional punch? Wouldn't you protect him, no matter what he's done?'

'Yeah, but faking a whole psychiatric condition?' said Halloran. 'Faking that la-la state she was in when we found her?'

'I don't believe she faked the catatonia. If she'd come into the room and seen what he was doing to June, that could have caused enough trauma to provoke the kind of withdrawal we witnessed.'

'And the whole multiple personalities thing? Why do that?'

'Maybe she was telling the truth about one thing,' spoke up Weathers. 'Maybe she really did begin to care enough about what Matt thought that she couldn't face taking the blame without at least having some excuse. Maybe all along she was trying to tell him "I didn't do it."'

Chapter Seventeen

Officially, Addenbrooke's Hospital's response to WDC Ames' query was: 'Sorry, can't reveal a patient's medical records without a court order.' Unofficially, Ames was mates with one of the sisters in A&E, who told her that Olivia Corscadden had come in with 'a broken finger here, a broken rib there – and the classic "I fell down the stairs" excuse.'

'But none of her friends seems to have been aware of any injuries,' Ames said to her friend.

'The broken finger was just after the term finished – she probably went home early so no one could notice the injury and ask what happened. And there's nothing we can do for broken ribs – people would have noticed she was in pain, but she wouldn't have been wearing any bandages.'

'If he did these things to her, she certainly didn't tell the staff at the hospital,' Ames reported back after her phone call.

'We need her to tell us the truth,' said Weathers. 'Matt, what do you suggest?'

'It won't be easy,' said Denison. 'Her strongest instinct is to protect him. You can try making her understand that nothing can excuse what he did, but I think in the end you'll have to use that protective urge against her – try to make her defend his actions.'

Weathers went back into the interview room with a

second cup of tea for Olivia, which he set in front of her, and a manila envelope, which he left unopened. He restarted the interview recording.

'Eliza Fitzstanley,' he said. 'Her wounds were nearly all blunt force trauma. All but one. She had a stab wound on her right buttock.' Olivia just looked at him, didn't react. 'Can you tell me why you stabbed her there?'

She cleared her throat. 'She fought back, we were struggling. I didn't stab her there deliberately.'

'What did you use to stab her?'

'A knife, you know.'

'What kind of knife? A penknife? A kitchen knife?'

'A penknife.'

'A penknife. And why didn't you use the penknife to kill her? Why just for this one small wound?'

She sipped at her tea. 'She knocked it out of my hand. It got hidden in the leaves.'

'So you left it there?'

'Yes.'

'So how come we didn't find it during our fingertip search of the area?'

Olivia shrugged. 'I don't know.'

Weathers opened the manila envelope and took out a 10 × 8 photograph. Olivia was pretending to be somewhat relaxed, but she watched him like a field mouse watches a sparrowhawk. He slid the photo over to her. A girl's naked body lay face-down on a mortuary slab. There were bruises on her back, but her bare buttocks were smooth and undamaged.

'That's Eliza, Olivia. Look – no stab marks. So, why did you tell me you'd stabbed her?'

Olivia's eyes moved rapidly over the photo; Denison recognized the external signs of her brain trying to construct some plausible explanation for her mistake.

'I thought I must have done,' she said. 'Like I said, I had a penknife, you said she was cut, I thought it must have been during the fight.'

'You didn't have a penknife, Olivia,' said Weathers with a sigh. 'We know Nicholas Hardcastle killed them and we know you're covering for him. What we can't work out is why. The man is a sadistic monster – what the fuck are you doing trying to protect him?'

'*I* killed them! *I* did it!' she cried, slamming her hand down on the table. 'For Christ's sake, I told you, it was me!'

'Olivia, I know you think he cares about you. But men like him are incapable of love. All their desires are focused on causing pain. How can you love someone like that?'

She shook her head. 'He's not like that. You're wrong. He does care about me. He does.'

Weathers tried for a further hour and twenty minutes, at which point he finally gave up and called an end to the interview. Olivia was returned to her cell.

'So what now?' said Ames.

'Now we have another little chat with Nicholas Hardcastle,' said Weathers.

They left Olivia and DCI MacIntyre at Newington Park police station and drove to Oxford. The traffic was light and they were there in a couple of hours. Ames had phoned ahead and arranged for them to borrow the facilities at one of Oxford's local nicks. By the time they arrived in the city it was two in the morning, and it was three a.m. before they pulled to a stop in the driveway of the Hardcastle house, flanked by a couple of Thames Valley Police's panda cars. Denison was instructed to wait in Weathers' car. Two of the uniformed officers scooted around the back of the house in case Nick tried to do a runner out of the back door. Weathers banged on the front door.

'Open up!' he shouted. 'Police!' A few seconds later a light went on in one of the upstairs windows. Weathers heard the clumping sound of someone coming down the staircase, and then the hallway light came on, silhouetting a short, broad figure.

Geoff Hardcastle, wearing a tartan dressing gown over his blue pyjamas, flung the door open. 'Do you have any bloody idea what time it is?'

'Where's Nicholas?' asked Weathers.

'This is unbelievable,' Geoff said, staring at him bleary-eyed. Valerie Hardcastle, her face cleansed of make-up many hours previously, appeared beside him in the doorway. She was wearing a cream satin dressing gown and hugging herself as though it were the middle of winter instead of one of the warmest nights of the year.

'He's not here,' said Valerie in a brittle voice. 'He's at his girlfriend's.'

Denison was waiting in the back seat of Weathers' car. Eventually Weathers, Halloran and Ames reappeared, crunching over the gravel to the car. They got in, slamming the doors, sitting in silence.

'Where is he?' asked Denison.

'You're not going to believe this,' said Halloran.

'What? Has he gone on the run?'

'Nope. He's staying at his girlfriend's place in Cambridge.'

'His girlfriend?' repeated Denison, bemused.

Weathers turned in his seat so he could look at his friend. He had a hard gleam in his eye that Denison couldn't decide was amusement or irritation. 'Paula Abercrombie.'

'Christ,' said Denison. 'How long has that been going on then?'

'God knows. As far as the mother's aware, only a couple of months. We're heading back to Cambridge – Paula's starting a masters there apparently and has found herself a nice little pad near the Grafton Centre.'

They stopped halfway to Cambridge at some twenty-four-hour services, and had bland coffee and stale croissants.

'Are you up for this?' Weathers asked Denison, as the psychiatrist yawned for the thirtieth time.

'I don't know. I can't say I feel at the top of my game.'

'Halloran?'

The older copper shrugged. 'I'm knackered. But so will that little toerag be. It's better to catch him off-guard.'

'Assuming his mother hasn't already rung to warn him,' said Denison.

'You think he'd answer his mobile at this time of night?' asked Ames.

'Who knows?'

'I've got men posted outside Paula's flat,' said Weathers. 'They haven't observed any signs of activity. Look, it's still the middle of the night. Let's get a few hours' sleep when we get to Cambridge and pick him up in the morning. If he's anything like I was at the age of twenty-one he's going to have a lie-in till midday. Especially as it's Sunday.'

Weathers and Ames were renting a terraced house on Holland Street, only a short walk from the river. The box room had a sofa bed in it. Ames got some bedlinen from the airing cupboard and made the bed up for Denison.

'There's some spare toothbrushes in the medicine cabinet,' she told him. 'Still in their packets. Nothing but the best service in the Weathers household. Anything else you want? A glass of water or something?'

'Maybe a vodka,' joked Denison, throwing his jacket on the bedspread. She kissed him goodnight and left him and her husband to it.

Denison admired the feminine touches in the room – the framed photographs of the couple on the wall, the Swiss cheese plant in the corner, the bowl of pot-pourri on the bedside cabinet. 'This is all very domesticated.'

'Just wait till we buy our own place,' laughed Weathers. 'Sally will have me down at Ikea and Homebase every other weekend. She's already decided what bathroom suite she wants and we don't even own a house yet.'

Denison nodded with a smile. 'Cass is the same. A month after she moved in my bedroom and living room had both been redecorated, and she was trying to talk me into buying a new three-piece suite.'

'So things are going well with you two?' asked Weathers.

'Yeah, really well.'

'Do you ever talk to her about work?'

'You mean my highly confidential psychiatric sessions? As a rule, no.'

'"As a rule"? That means "sometimes".' Weathers was grinning, so Denison knew he wasn't censuring him.

'Maybe. When I've had a really rough day it helps if she knows why I'm in such a foul mood.'

'You ever talk to her about Olivia Corscadden?'

'Not the details,' said Denison. 'You don't have to worry about that.'

'Does she know how you feel about Olivia?'

Denison frowned at Weathers, who just looked back at him seriously.

'What do you mean?'

'Come on, Matt, it's obvious you've got a – well, let's say . . . a soft spot for her.'

Denison started yanking at his tie knot. 'Well, excuse me for having sympathy for a girl who was put through hell by her parents, and then had the misfortune of finding herself a boyfriend who not only beat her but also killed her bloody friends.' He refused to look at Weathers as he pulled off his tie.

'Yeah, but it's not just that, is it, Matt? I mean, you felt sorry for her even when you thought she was guilty of the murders.'

'Do you know how rare it is for sociopaths to have had happy, normal childhoods?' snapped Denison. 'They're not generally born that way you know. Christ, it's a good job her father's in prison now, because if he wasn't I'd have been severely tempted to pay him a visit with my cricket bat.'

Weathers' eyes flickered, which Denison picked up on immediately.

'What?' he said. 'Steve, what is it?'

Weathers pulled a face. 'He's not in prison. He got bail.'

'What the fuck happened? You said his computer was full of child pornography!'

'It was. But he wasn't in any of the photos, not even the ones of Olivia. He's claiming that the computer was part of a batch he was selling on as second-hand, and that it wasn't his personal PC. Since it was one of about thirty-five that we seized his lawyer managed to argue that proving it was his was a matter for trial.'

'But there were photos of his daughter on the bloody thing! Isn't that evidence enough that it was his bloody computer?'

'As far as the court is concerned there are photos of a pre-pubescent girl whom *we say* bears a strong resemblance to his daughter. I didn't have a statement from Olivia, did I? If she won't make a complaint against him and assert that those photos are of her, then there's not a lot more the Met can do.'

'Oh, for Christ's . . .' Denison sat down on the bed, his head in his hands.

'I'm sorry, Matt. But Barry's far too smart to do anything before his court date, not now he knows we're onto him.' Weathers saw how upset Denison was. 'Matt, if you hadn't told us about Olivia, then we wouldn't even know that he was someone who needed watching.'

Denison looked up at his friend. 'Steve, she doesn't even know he was arrested. How's she going to feel when she finds out about all this?'

Weathers crossed his arms. 'He doesn't know that she told us about him. As far as he's concerned we were interested in the handling of stolen goods, and just came across the child pornography.'

'I hope you're right. Christ, at least tell me you got plenty of evidence for the fencing case?'

'Enough that he's definitely going to go down, at least for eighteen months.'

'That's all?'

Weathers shrugged. 'You want me to put the word out when he's in there that he's a ponce, then I can do. That way he may never come out.'

'You want the other cons to do your job for you?'

Weathers smiled, but there was no amusement behind it. 'I'm going to bed now. Sleep tight, Matt.'

Denison felt as though he had only just closed his eyes before suddenly there was light filling the room and Weathers was standing over him with a hot cup of coffee. Having brought no clean clothes with him Denison was forced to wear the same crumpled suit and shirt he'd sweated in the day before. It was only 7.30 in the morning, but already it felt like it would be a scorcher.

He went down to the kitchen, where Weathers handed him a plate of toast. Weathers had showered, his dark hair wet and slicked back. He was wearing a black suit and white shirt. Denison envied their freshness.

'So, I don't get a shower then?' he griped.

'I thought you'd rather have the sleep. Eat up, we're leaving in five minutes.'

They pulled up on Sturton Street in front of Halloran's car. Although just a few roads away from one of Cambridge's busiest shopping centres, it was a quiet, suburban road. Neighbouring a little park, Paula's place was a small Victorian terraced house in which only the front door separated the living room from the pavement outside.

Halloran got out of his car and scooted into the back seat of Weathers'. Denison couldn't tell if Halloran had enjoyed the benefit of a shower – he had too little hair to assess whether or not it had just been washed, and he was already starting to sweat, little droplets sprinkled over his forehead.

'The fellas say the house has been quiet since they arrived last night,' Halloran told them.

'Let's do it then,' said Weathers.

Again they left Denison in the car and strode to the house, two other men getting out of a car further down the street and joining them. One of these clambered over the wooden door that led to the house's compact back garden.

The front door was painted bright red. Weathers grabbed the cast-iron door knocker and slammed it down hard.

'Police, open up!' he shouted through the wood, and kept hammering on the door with the knocker. A woman with a buggy who was walking down the street towards them took one look and hastily crossed the road. Some kids playing basketball in the park stopped and watched, the one with the ball tucking it under his elbow.

It was a minute and a half before the door opened. Paula Abercrombie stood there in a pair of grey cotton shorts and a snug white T-shirt. Halloran could tell she wasn't wearing a bra and smiled at her broadly. Her long dark hair was mussed up, and apart from some remnants of mascara she was largely make-up free, but he thought she still looked like she belonged on the cover of *Playboy*.

'Go get Nicholas out of bed for us, sweetheart,' he said with a wink.

Nick appeared behind her in a pair of tracksuit bottoms and a T-shirt. 'Oh Christ, not you lot again,' he said.

'That's right, us lot,' said Weathers. 'Something's come up that we'd like to discuss with you down at the station.'

From the little room on the other side of a two-way mirror, Denison looked at Nick, sitting upright in the interview room chair, arms folded defiantly, and noticed the dark smudges were gone from under his eyes. He'd put on some weight – the skinniness replaced with lean muscles. He appeared fit and healthy. His hair had grown an inch or so and was beginning to curl.

Weathers had noticed the changes too. 'Seems like going out with Paula Abercrombie is agreeing with you,' he said to Nick.

Nick nodded, uncomfortable. 'I suppose so.'

'I'm guessing Olivia doesn't know?' Weathers prodded.

'How could she?' Nick said. 'You haven't let me contact her.'

'Would have been handy for you though, wouldn't it? Let you get your stories straight?'

Nick shook his head in disbelief. 'Jesus, what exactly is so strange about wanting to see your girlfriend?'

'Nothing. She didn't say much to start with though, so it would have been a bit of a dull visit for you. It was four weeks before she did anything but look at the TV and dribble.'

Denison could see Nick was trying not to rise to the bait. 'Look, Olivia and I had been having problems for a while before all this happened. Nothing I ever said or did was good enough for her. I'd get her flowers, take her out for dinner, buy her little surprise presents. She'd say thank you, but she never really seemed to mean it. Sometimes I'd touch her and she'd jerk away like my fingers were on fire or something. So yes, to be honest, some time apart has made me realize that things weren't working and couldn't be fixed.'

'And Paula? Did she help you come to this decision?'

'She's the only one who's been there for me. Thanks to you all my other friends seem to think I'm guilty. She stood by me and we just got close again, that's all. Look, I feel bad about Olivia, I do, but I don't pretend to be a saint.' He ran a hand through his hair and then leaned forward on the table, towards Weathers. 'There's something I should tell you. I should have told you at the time, but I didn't want Olivia to find out. When most guys cheat on their girlfriends they don't end up having to lie to the bloody police about it.'

'Go on,' Weathers said shortly.

'The night Amanda was killed, you know I said I slept on the floor and Paula slept on the bed? Well, that wasn't true. We shared a bed.'

'You had sex?'

Nick rolled his eyes. 'Yes, if that's relevant. Look, the important thing is that she's a very light sleeper, even when drunk – she can tell you she would have woken up if I'd left the room at any point that night.'

'And it's just a coincidence that a few weeks after the two of you got together, she suddenly provided you with an alibi,' said Weathers.

'That's right,' snapped Nick.

'Have you hit her yet?' Weathers asked.

'What?'

'It's a simple enough question: have you hit her yet? Punched her? Slapped her? Kicked her?'

Nick's lip curled. 'You've got to be kidding. I don't hit women.'

'No, just torture and kill them, eh?'

'For Christ's sake, how many times do I have to tell you, I didn't do it! I could never, ever do anything like that. I've never hurt anyone in my life, I've never even gotten into a fight.'

'That's funny, because we've got statements from people alleging that you used to assault Olivia Corscadden.'

'You're a fucking liar,' said Nick. 'No one told you that. I bet Olivia's never said that, has she? *Has she?*'

'She's told us many things,' said Weathers. 'She's told us she was responsible for the murders.'

Nick almost laughed. 'I don't believe you.'

'It's true. She can't get the facts right, but she's very enthusiastic about confessing.'

He shook his head. 'You're joking. You have to be joking.'

'I'm afraid not. She says she decapitated Amanda Montgomery, smashed Eliza Fitzstanley's skull against a tree and gutted June Okeweno like a fish.'

'But . . .' Denison watched Nick's face change, saw him look within himself, analysing something internally. It reminded him of watching an opponent decide on a chess move. Nick began to nod, apparently having made a choice.

'Then there's something else I have to tell you. Christ, I can't believe I'm doing this.'

'What?' said Weathers sceptically.

'My fingerprints were on the knife that killed June because . . . because I took it out of Olivia's hand.'

Chapter Eighteen

'That little shit,' said Denison under his breath in the next-door room.

Weathers was regarding Nick with disdain. 'You're saying Olivia had the knife and you took it off her, is that right?'

'I'm afraid so. Look, I didn't want to get Olivia into trouble, that's why I didn't say anything. I didn't think she'd actually killed June, just that she'd come across the body and didn't know what she was doing. But now you've told me that she's confessed, well, maybe I was wrong.' He gazed at them, eyes cornflower blue.

'I don't believe you,' piped up Halloran for the first time. 'We've just told you that your girlfriend of three years has confessed to a series of murders, and your reaction – rather than telling the truth and setting her free, in more ways than one – is to dump her in it even deeper? You, my friend, are possibly the evillest scrote I've ever had the misfortune to meet.'

Nick sat back in his seat, eyes darkening, crossing his arms again.

'I want my solicitor,' he said.

*

Paula was fully made up – eyeshadow, lipstick, the works – by the time she came in to give her statement about the night of Amanda's murder. She focused her attentions on the attractive DCI Weathers, ignoring Halloran, who now had sweat patches under each arm and down the centre of his back.

'We had sex,' she admitted. 'Nick didn't want Olivia to find out, so he asked me to pretend he'd slept on the floor.'

'How long were you guys asleep for before you got woken by the commotion outside?'

'I don't know – maybe seven or eight hours.'

'And you don't think it's feasible that in that time Nick could have got up whilst you were fast asleep, killed Amanda and come back to bed?'

'No. I'm a very light sleeper.'

'Even when you've had quite a lot to drink?'

She laughed throatily. 'Especially when I've had quite a lot to drink. I'm up every five minutes to use the bathroom.'

'And did Nick wake you up at all that night?'

'Yes, when he used the toilet. But he was only out of bed for a few minutes. He didn't leave – I would have heard the door.'

Halloran needed to click his fingers to draw her attention to him. 'Over here, love. Look, if you two have got nothing to hide, will you give us permission to search your house?'

She shrugged. 'Whatever. Just don't steal my sodding knickers.'

'Do you believe her?' asked Denison.

Weathers shrugged. 'I don't know. If she's in a relation-ship with Nick now it wouldn't be unusual for her to cover for him, especially if she thought he was innocent. What about you – do you believe her?'

Denison stubbed out his cigarette. 'I think if she's finally sunk her hooks into Nick the last thing she'd want is Olivia getting out.' He looked out over Parker's Piece, busy with people having lunch, playing cricket, reading books and generally enjoying the sunshine. 'So what now?'

'I can't stall any longer. I should have charged both Olivia and Nick with murder the day we found them in June's room. It's been over two months and we still don't know for certain what happened that night.'

'You're charging Olivia too?'

'I'm *only* charging Olivia. I don't have any more on Nick than I had back then. He's now got an alibi for the first murder and he's prepared to say in court that he found Olivia holding the knife at the third. If Olivia doesn't agree to testify then we're gonna have to focus the prosecution on her.'

At first Denison thought he was joking, but then he began to understand. 'So basically you're going to blackmail her into testifying against him?' he asked in disbelief.

Weathers took a cigarette from Denison's packet and lit it. He didn't reply, but as far as Denison was concerned he didn't need to.

'For fuck's sake, Stephen, you can't put her through that!'

'She's my only witness. If she doesn't testify we've got fuck all. I understand she's had a rough time of it, but that's not my problem. She can't let him get away with it just because she's scared, or in love, or whatever the fuck it is she feels for him. If you don't want to see her go down for this then I suggest you try to talk her into it.'

'You fucking arsehole,' said Denison, furious. 'I can't believe you're doing this.'

Weathers ignored him, sucking on his cigarette. He seemed to be watching a group of kids playing football in the September sunshine on the other side of the park. Denison waited, but when Weathers opened his mouth all that came out of it was cigarette smoke. Shaking his head in frustration Denison walked away.

Olivia was in her cell at Holloway Prison. She had one of the lower bunks, the one closest to the toilet bowl, and though she sat as far away from it as possible, she could still smell it. The youngest of her cellmates never bothered to flush it if she'd only taken a piss.

She was reading Tolkien's *The Fellowship of the Ring*. Not a book she would have chosen herself, but Dr Denison had brought it for her along with her clothes from Coldhill. She suspected he'd picked it for its length, knowing she was a fast reader.

Her cellmate Laticia poked her head in. 'Didn't you hear them call your name, Olivia? You've got a visitor today, you lucky bitch.'

Only Laticia would dare call her a lucky bitch. Olivia hadn't had to prove herself when she arrived; everyone knew what she was in for and steered clear of her. For the first few days Laticia too had avoided her, only joining her in the cell when she had to. Now she'd got to know her Laticia had relaxed a bit, and even started to tease her.

Olivia put a bookmark in her novel, left the cell and clanked down the metal stairs to the lower level. She joined the group of women waiting to be taken to the visiting area. Gritting her teeth as a guard ran her hands over her in a body search – she hated being touched without consent – she tried to work out who was going to be waiting for her on the other side of the door. Godfrey had visited once or twice, as had Leo. She hoped it was Nick, but she thought it was probably Dr Denison.

It was neither. It was her mum, Shelley, jigging eighteen-month-old Barry Junior on her hip. Olivia's steps faltered. The guard nudged her forward.

'Go and say hi to your ma, Corscadden.'

Olivia slowly walked over and lowered herself down onto the chair. She looked at her mum. Shelley was wearing a skimpy vest that showed off her tattoos and greying bra straps, and a pair of stonewashed blue jeans that hung off her thin hips. Barry Junior was looking plump and discontent, more irritated by the jigging than soothed.

'How are you doing, Mum?' Olivia asked.

Shelley sat down opposite her. 'You're looking good, Cleo, love. The prison food must be agreeing with you. Your dad used to hate it, but then he's got more of a taste for the finer things in life than you, ain't he?' Barry Junior took a handful of Shelley's lank, bleached hair and began to suck on it.

'Why are you here, Mum?'

'Well, that's nice, ain't it? I dragged myself here on the bloody bus, and you know how much Junior here hates public transport.'

'Why didn't Dad drive you?'

'He couldn't trust himself, love. See, he's just about spitting. You fucked him up good and proper, you little tart.'

'What are you talking about? I haven't done nothing to Dad.'

Shelley pointed a witchy finger at her. 'Don't you lie, you cunt. You told them about the photos. They arrested him! How the fuck am I meant to bring up three kids with your dad in prison? These are your sisters' and baby brother's lives you're fucking with, Cleo.' Her mouth was twisted in disgust, her nicotine-stained, crooked teeth bared. 'Tell them you lied. I mean it, Cleo. We know people in here. We just say the word and they'll fuck you up so bad you'll be avoiding mirrors for the rest of your life.'

Shelley glared at her for a few seconds more, just to really get her point across, then stood up and walked off, saying loudly to the guard: 'I don't want to talk to that little cow any more. Open the fucking door and let me out.'

When Denison arrived at Holloway two days later he was surprised when Olivia initially refused to see him.

'Tell her I have some information about Nick Hardcastle,' he said.

They took him to an interview room. It was small and windowless, with a solid metal door and a guard outside at all times. Olivia was led in and handcuffed to the metal table that was fixed to the centre of the floor.

'That's not necessary,' protested Denison.

'It's not up for discussion,' the guard told him. 'Yell if she starts trying to kill you.' The guard left them alone.

Denison sat down opposite Olivia. 'Are you allowed to smoke in here?'

She shrugged, looking at him gravely.

'You want one?'

She nodded. He got out his pack of Marlboros and she lit one up then sat back in her chair. Olivia looked at the hand that was cuffed to the table and laid it down, palm up, on the metal surface, as though she were reading her own fortune. She was wearing a short-sleeved T-shirt. Denison saw for the first time the small, round scars on the inside of her elbow and upper arms. There were maybe ten in total. Olivia saw him looking and swiftly turned her arms so the undersides weren't showing.

'When was the first time Nick Hardcastle burned you with a cigarette?' asked Denison gently.

Olivia took a deep drag on her Marlboro. 'You said you had news.'

'I'm afraid it might be quite painful for you to hear this, Olivia, but he told us that he'd lied about the night Amanda Montgomery was murdered. He said that he and Paula had had sex that night.'

Olivia looked like she'd been punched in the stomach. She coughed out cigarette smoke. 'No. He's just saying that because he needs an alibi.'

'Olivia, when we arrested him, he was with Paula.'

'So?'

'You don't understand. He was with her – in her house, in her bed. They're going out.'

She gazed at him, sudden tears dropping onto the metal table. 'No. He wouldn't. He loves me.'

Denison put his hand over hers. 'If he loves you why did he tell us that he found you in June's room with the knife in your hand?'

She couldn't stop shaking her head. 'No. You're lying. You're lying.'

'Olivia, I've never lied to you.'

'You betrayed me! I thought I could trust you, but you've told the police everything!'

'It's my job. You knew what we discussed wasn't just between the two of us. I was assessing you for them.'

'What's that got to do with what my dad did to me?' she cried. 'You told the police, didn't you? Didn't you? You had no right to do that without my permission.'

'You're right,' he said, trying to calm her down. 'You're right, I'm sorry. I didn't know that the person I told was going to arrest him. Olivia, listen, how did you know that your father's paedophilia was known to the police? I've been assured that your father had no clue that you were involved. They didn't even arrest him for that – they made out that they were after him for handling stolen property.'

'Well, their sodding smokescreen obviously didn't bloody work!' she snapped. 'Because I had my mum in here two days ago, telling me I'd better keep my bloody mouth shut.'

'Olivia, if she threatened you she's committed a criminal offence. You can't let her get away with that.'

Olivia wiped away her tears and put out her cigarette, dragging the burning curls of tobacco across the metal table until they were extinguished. 'You don't understand. My family have got mates here. A few hundred quid would be all it took.'

'Then you can't stay here. Look, Olivia, please make a statement. Tell us what really happened. If you don't Weathers will prosecute you, and then you'll be in here for life.'

'You want me to say it was Nick, don't you? You want me to blame this on the only person who's ever loved me.'

'He doesn't love you. Why would he blame it all on you if he loved you? Look how hard you tried to convince us that you were solely responsible for the deaths, to protect him. And all the while he was out free, getting closer and closer to Paula.'

He'd brought the crime scene photographs with him, hidden from the guards in a copy of the *British Journal of Psychiatry*. He knew he was going to have to hurt her now, to be cruel, and steeled himself for the task. He pushed the first photo in front of her.

'Look at Eliza's face, Olivia, or what's left of it.' Olivia gasped and covered her mouth with her hand, looking quickly away. 'Would you recognize her? Would you look at that bloody, mashed-up pulp of a face and say "that's Eliza, no doubt about it"? No, neither could her parents. They recognized her by the mole on her stomach and a scar she had on her knee. But they still had to look at that shattered face, Olivia. It's not like it could be covered up. They got to see that. Tell me, why are you looking so shocked? You did this, didn't you?'

Olivia was gazing fixedly upwards, tears welling in her eyes.

Denison slapped another photograph in front of her. 'Olivia, look at the photograph.' He clasped her chin and pulled her head down towards the table. 'Olivia, *look at it.*'

She looked. Her hands were gripping the table as she tried to push away from what she was seeing.

'That's what's left of Amanda Montgomery. You may not have liked her much, but did she deserve that? The police had to formally identify her from her DNA, because as you know the person who killed her cut her head off and mutilated her body so badly that not even her own mother could tell if it was her or not.'

'My God . . .' said Olivia.

He positioned another photograph on the table beside the one of Amanda's body. 'Look at the photo. You owe them that much.'

'Please, don't make me,' she whispered. 'I'm sorry, I'm sorry.'

'June Okeweno. She knew he was hurting you. She tried sympathy, she tried being blunt, but she couldn't get through to you. This is what he does to people who care about you, who try to shield you from him. He stabbed her over seventeen times, Olivia.'

She picked up the photo and cried, holding it to her chest.

'You need to explain something to me,' Denison told her, spitting the words out like pebbles. 'You need to explain why you find it so hard to look at these bodies, when you're supposedly the one who caused the injuries? Why are you so horrified, Olivia? Did he tell you that it was quick and painless? Did he tell you they didn't suffer? Didn't you realize how much pleasure he took in it?'

'Oh God,' she sobbed. 'Oh God . . . I didn't know, I swear I didn't know. I'm so sorry. I had no idea he'd hurt them all so much.'

Denison closed his eyes in relief. 'Oh, Olivia,' he said finally. 'Why did you protect him? Why did you say you'd done it?'

She was trying to control her crying, but was too upset. 'It was my fault! He did it for me. They were trying to split us up. Amanda wanted him to get back together with Paula.

Eliza reckoned I wasn't good enough for him. June thought I was *too* good for him. It was my fault. He was just so scared that they'd push me away from him. It was my fault. He did it for me. It was my fault.'

Denison set the fourth and final photograph in front of her. It was a photo of Olivia herself, taken the night of June's murder. She was covered in blood, so much so that her white underwear was almost completely stained red. There were bruises all over her arms and torso, and a welt under her right eye. Her lip was split. Although her gaze was towards the camera it was obvious that there was no consciousness behind the gaze. Her pupils were huge and black, eyes completely vacant. She looked almost as dead as June.

'It wasn't your fault,' said Denison softly. 'Look what he did to you. That man didn't love you. He didn't kill those women because he thought they were a threat to your relationship, although he may have used that as an excuse. Olivia, those murders were sadistic and unmotivated. Some men find pleasure in causing pain and death. Nicholas is one of those men. He would have killed them whether you two were a couple or not.'

'I wish I could believe that,' she said, wiping the tears from her face. 'I can't cope with all this guilt.'

He was scared to ask: 'Did he make you take part?'

She shook her head. 'No. I didn't even know until I found him killing June.'

'You mean you weren't there? He didn't bring you along?'

'No, of course not!' she said, surprised. 'If I'd known I would have tried to stop him.'

He felt like kissing her. She hadn't been an accomplice, a willing partner. She hadn't helped, was wrong to feel this guilt. Excited he pressed her for more information. 'But you witnessed June's murder?'

'I was in the bathroom,' she said, 'cleaning myself up – Nick hadn't been happy that I'd argued with him in front of other people. I thought he was in the bedroom. But when I came out he wasn't there, and I heard screaming from her bedroom. Not very loudly, more sort of . . . gasping. I went across the staircase to see if she was OK, but her door was locked. I could hear her through the door, saying "no, don't, no". I banged on the door, yelling her name, yelling Nick's name.'

'You thought he was inside with her?'

'I thought he was around. I thought he would hear me and come and help.' A half-sob, half-laugh escaped her mouth and she covered it with her free hand. 'But then I heard this . . . groan. It sounded like her soul was coming out of her or something. And then it was quiet. And the door opened and it was Nick who opened the door, from the inside. He had blood all down the front of his shirt and trousers and there was a knife in his right hand. I looked down and June was on the floor.' Olivia fell silent, trying to recover her composure.

'Some part of me knew she was dead. But another part of me was trying to convince myself that they were just playing some crazy trick on me with fake blood or something. I sat down next to her and I shook her, and told her to stop being silly, that she was scaring me. I gradually realized that I could see inside her body. Literally, I mean. And that there was no way even the best horror film make-up artist could fake that.

That's when I just lost it. I honestly don't remember anything after that. Not the police showing up, not being taken to Coldhill.' She shook her head. 'It wasn't her being dead that I couldn't accept. It was that if she was dead, then Nick must have been the one who killed her.'

'What did Nick do when you were shaking June's body? Did he say anything to you?'

She nodded, swallowing hard. 'He said, "What are you getting so upset for? She was trying to take you away from me. Look, I know she's in a mess, but we can clean her up if you really want to." Then he picked up one of the things that was coming out of her stomach and he started trying to fit it back in.' Olivia covered her face with her hands and began to sob again.

'It's OK,' Denison reassured her. 'It's OK. It's over now. But Olivia, you have to say at the trial what you saw and tell them why you tried to take the blame.'

'They'll want to know why I lied?' she asked.

'Nick's defence will say that you're the one responsible and that the confession was genuine. We'll have to tell them about what Nick did to you and why you were psychologically susceptible to being controlled by him, even after you were removed from his company.'

'You think that he liked me because I was a victim,' she said, her voice hoarse.

'I'm afraid so. I'm sorry, Olivia. But all the studies show that girls who are abused by their parents are far more likely to end up with a partner who also abuses them.'

She stood up then, still anchored to the table by her cuffs. 'I'm sorry, Matthew. I can't help you. Even if I could bring myself to testify against Nick I can't have you or anyone else say in court what my parents did to me. They'd have me killed before I even got back to my cell.'

Paula hated Nick's new bedsit. It was on the third floor above a takeaway pizza place in the Elephant and Castle, and whenever she stayed there she was kept awake till two in the morning by late-night revellers hankering after extra anchovies and garlic bread.

'The cold water tap still won't turn off,' she complained as she left the bathroom. 'And there's mould all over the wall underneath the sink.'

She saw Nick roll his eyes. 'I told you, Paula, I can't afford anything better than this.'

'Why did you come here then? Why didn't you stay with your parents, or come and live with me in Cambridge like I suggested?'

'It's too soon, Paula. We've only been going out a few months.'

'But we've known each other for years. Doesn't that count?'

'I don't want to be in Cambridge.' He was getting angry now. 'There are too many people there who know me, or at least recognize me. Here in London no one knows me. Or maybe it's just no one cares.'

She didn't want him to be mad for the rest of the evening. He'd not been happy since his rearrest a few weeks previously and she couldn't cope with his moodiness too much longer. When was he going to snap out of it?

Paula went over and sat next to him on the camp bed. She stroked the hair at the nape of his neck, letting a strand of it curl around her finger. 'It's OK, babe,' she said. 'It'll all die down soon. I promise. Then maybe things can get back to normal.' He wouldn't look at her – his eyes were focused out of the window, the irises an icy blue. 'Look, how about I cook us some dinner? I don't know about you, but I'm starving.'

He didn't react, so she got to her feet and went into the tiny kitchen, which was separated from the bed/living room by a beaded curtain. There wasn't much in Nick's cupboards, just some tins of beans and sweetcorn and some dried pasta. She pulled open the ancient fridge, whose handle tended to come off if you tugged too hard, and found only hardened cheese and half a pint of milk.

'Healthy,' she said to herself. At this rate they'd be eating pasta with a sauce of baked beans and cheddar rind.

She had to yank hard to open the freezer door. A thick layer of ice grew round the sides of the compartment, taking up at least a quarter of the available space. There was a packet of crinkle-cut chips and a box of potato waffles at the front of the freezer, but Paula and carbohydrates were not currently on speaking terms. She pulled them out to see what was behind and found a carrier bag wedged in the back.

Paula yanked on the handles, which were tied together in a knot, and pulled the bag towards her. Whatever was in it was pretty heavy; she was hoping it was maybe a chicken or a leg of lamb. As she moved it towards her her brain automatically began to process the shapes and patterns it saw, trying to assemble them into a form it recognized. What was that bone that was straining against the flimsy plastic of the bag – the joint at the end of a chicken leg? What were the two slightly darker streaks that she could see above the bone? And the pinkish smear underneath it?

With trembling hands Paula stretched the plastic at the side of the protruding bone, tearing a hole in it.

An eye stared out at her from the bag.

She jumped back, slamming the freezer door shut, and heard a swish of beads as Nick walked through the curtain into the kitchen.

He looked at her curiously. 'You all right?'

She swallowed hard and nodded. 'I think I saw a cockroach,' she stammered.

'Where, in the fridge?' He went to open the compartment door.

'No, no,' she said. 'On the wall, behind the fridge.'

'Great, another thing to ring the bloody landlord about.' He glanced at the wall and turned back to her. 'I can't see anything. Were you looking in the freezer for something to eat?'

She wasn't sure if he'd seen her close the freezer door. If he had, and she denied it, he would become suspicious, but she also knew she wasn't ready to admit – not even to herself – what she'd found.

'Actually, I fancy some takeaway pizza,' she said, trying to smile at him.

'Pizza?' he said. 'Really? I thought you were never eating pizza again.'

'That pepperoni smells really good though,' she told him. 'What do you say?'

'OK,' he agreed, though he was frowning. 'I'll just put my shoes on.'

'No, don't worry,' she said, going through to the other

room and pulling on her coat. 'My treat. I'll be back in a minute.'

She was out of the door and halfway down the first flight of stairs when he appeared in the doorway and called out her name. It took her only half a second to consider carrying on and another half a second to realize he could easily catch her up. She stopped, gathered together some composure and turned back to look up at him with a smile and enquiring expression.

'You forgot your handbag,' Nick said. He held up the small pink bag.

'Oh,' she said and slowly came back up the stairs. He searched her face, trying to read her. When she was still four steps away from him she stretched up and took her bag. 'Won't be long,' she said, then turned on her heel and trotted down the stairs as fast as she could. When she reached the front door she broke into a run.

'Phone call for you, sir. Sorry, I know you're off-duty, but she said it was urgent. A Paula Abercrombie.'

'Put her through,' said Weathers into his mobile. Sally, sitting across from him in the Chinese restaurant, raised her eyebrows. He waved at her to carry on eating her prawn crackers, thinking how pretty his wife looked bathed in the light from the red lantern that hung over their table.

'Weathers speaking,' he said.

'I found a head,' a woman's voice whispered. 'I found a head in his freezer.'

'Paula?' he asked. Quavering and scared, the voice didn't sound like hers.

'I think . . . I think it must be . . . Amanda's.'

'Tell me where you are.'

'London. South London. Elephant and Castle. Near the high street.'

'What's the address, Paula?' Weathers asked urgently.

'I can't remember. I can't think.' There was a pause. He could hear gasping sounds, like she was trying to breathe, or maybe trying not to cry. 'It's over a pizza place. Tony's Pizzas. It's on the third floor. Look for Tony's in the phone book.'

'Paula, are you there? Are you in his flat?'

'No. But he'll realize I'm gone soon. He'll know why. You have to come quickly. Please, come quickly.'

'This is nothing but harassment,' Nick said when they arrived at his door with the search warrant.

'You should have told us your new address, Nicky,' said Halloran, wheezing a bit from the three flights of stairs. 'Naughty boy.' Weathers' request for round-the-clock surveillance of Nick had been denied due to lack of budget, much to his frustration.

'Ring your solicitor if you want,' said Weathers. 'Just don't touch anything other than the phone.' Halloran went straight into the kitchen.

As Weathers watched him Nick rang Bird-Sewell's answering service. Then he tried Paula again on her mobile. He'd been ringing her ever since she'd failed to return with the pizzas, but she wasn't picking up and there had been no sign of her when he'd looked for her downstairs.

He noticed all the black and white panda cars on the street below and saw Paula beside one of them, talking to a police officer, looking up towards his flat.

'Jesus H. Christ,' they heard Halloran say from the kitchen. He appeared in the doorway, his usually ruddy face now looking grey and bloodless. 'Boss, you'd better get the SOCO boys in here.'

Glancing at the uniformed officers to make sure they were blocking Nick's exit, Weathers went past Halloran and looked in the open freezer compartment, at the carrier bag covered with frost that lay inside. There was a tear in it. Weathers put a gloved fingertip into the tear and used it as a peephole.

He saw an eye and dark eyelashes white with tiny particles of ice. He saw a nose and part of a lightly freckled cheek.

'Well?' he heard Sally say. She was rooted in the doorway. 'Was Paula telling the truth?'

Weathers just looked at her, the expression on his face answering her question. 'Arrest him,' he said.

'It's in very good condition,' said Dr Trevor Bracknell, touching the decapitated head of Amanda Montgomery with some strange implement. 'You say you found it in a freezer?'

Weathers nodded. 'The freezer compartment of a fridge-freezer, wedged behind a stack of waffles and a bag of oven chips.' He couldn't tear his eyes away from Amanda's head. Her blonde hair, wet from the melted frost, was draped over the top of the autopsy table. Her brown eyes had lost much of their colour and were glazed over with a whitish-blue tinge. Weathers knew she had been beautiful, but it was hard to believe now.

'The facial muscles sag,' Bracknell said, as if reading his

mind. 'Eyelids droop at the sides. Mouth loses its shape.' He leaned down and investigated her eyes more closely. 'There's very little decomposition. I'd hazard a guess that the head has been more or less permanently frozen since her death, give or take a day or two.'

'So she might not have gone straight in the freezer?'

'It was cold around the period of her death. If the head was kept outside it could have been there for a few days. If it started out in one freezer but was recently transferred to another, then it may have only been out a day in this heat before it achieved the same degree of decomposition. Tests will tell us more, whether the head was thawed out then refrozen or not.'

'We know for certain it hasn't been in the same place for the last three years,' Weathers told him. 'Hardcastle has only been renting that place for a month or so.'

'Found it on Hardcastle, did you?' said Bracknell, getting out his scalpel. 'Shame. I had a tenner on Godfrey Parrish.'

'You're looking at at least three years for perverting the course of justice,' Olivia's solicitor, Adina Kennedy, told her, 'and even though Dr Denison here is willing to give evidence on your behalf, you could well get more. Testify against him and there's a very good chance the judge will be more lenient.'

Olivia, hugging herself, looked from her solicitor to Denison. 'I just can't risk it. I told you what my parents can do. You know what they're capable of.'

Kennedy leaned forward. 'Maybe you don't have to explain everything. Look, it's the sexual aspect to the abuse that they're so afraid of you making public, is that right?'

Olivia nodded. 'So, would they be so concerned about the physical abuse, the psychological abuse? Would they care so much if people knew that?'

Olivia laughed a hard laugh. 'No. All their mates beat the living shit out of their kids. It's just my dad being a kiddie molester and child pornographer that they don't want getting out. They're afraid some vigilantes will burn the house down and string my dad up by his balls from the nearest lamp post.'

Kennedy looked at Denison. 'What do you think?' she said.

'It's risky,' he said, pulling a face. 'If they don't realize the full extent of the abuse they may not accept why Olivia was so willing to cover for Nicholas.'

'It's not as risky as my parents opening the *Sun* and reading the headline "My Childhood Hell, by the girlfriend of the Cambridge Butcher",' said Olivia.

'She's got a fair point,' Kennedy said to Denison.

'What about protective custody?' he suggested. 'There must be special prison wards for inmates who are at risk from the rest of the prisoners.'

'That's right,' said Olivia, frowning. 'A woman was found shanked in one of them just a few weeks ago.'

'Shanked?' he asked.

'Stabbed,' explained Adina Kennedy.

He raised his hands in defeat. 'OK, OK. So we don't mention the sexual abuse. The non-sexual violence and psychological abuse is probably explanation enough for why Nick was able to manipulate her to such an extent.'

Olivia still sometimes seemed vulnerable to the mention of Nick's name, even though she had finally accepted that he had never loved her, that he was incapable of it. Denison had made her understand that Nick was driven to murder by anger, by hate, not by love for her. Sometimes, though, he'd notice a flicker of pain pass across her face when she heard his name, and he would worry that she would be unable to go through with it.

'I feel like Judas,' she had told him in one session. 'Kissing him, then sending him on to his death.'

'Trust me,' he'd said, 'Nicholas Hardcastle is about as far from Christ as it's possible to get.'

Chapter Nineteen

Christmas came and Denison spent it with Cass and her family for the first time. The Storrs did it in style: log fires, real spruce trees, silk ribbons on presents, the lot. Late on Christmas night the family were tipsy and playing Pictionary, teasing each other with familiar anecdotes that had been exaggerated and elaborated on over the years. Perched by the window Denison looked on. He felt detached but content, watching over the happy family like some kind of benevolent spirit. But then as he sipped his eggnog his thoughts turned to Olivia, spending Christmas in Holloway Prison, and his warm mood turned cold.

It was another five months before the Old Bailey opened its doors to hear the case of the Crown versus Nicholas Hardcastle. The night before Denison was due at court it rained, and the next morning the May sunshine was reflecting off the puddles on the pavement as he walked along the street in his newly polished black shoes.

Once in the foyer Denison had to pass through a security unit that stopped more than one person entering the building at a time. The light turned green and he was moved on to guards who searched him and then towards a metal detector.

'Put any keys or change in the container,' another guard

told him. The detector remained silent as Denison passed through it. Finally he was given a laminated pass that needed to be clipped to the front of his suit.

Denison usually found he enjoyed testifying in court. In the past it had got him out of Coldhill for the day, let him show off his Paul Smith suit. He wasn't nervous about addressing a large number of people and was confident enough not to get rattled by the barristers' questions. This was a bit different though; this was court number one at the Old Bailey, with all the spectator seats taken and reporters recording your every word, every gesture. Court artists would sketch his likeness for the paper that he, along with a few million other people, would be reading the next morning over breakfast.

He was also nervous about not letting Olivia down. Over seven months now he'd been waiting for this day to arrive; waiting for the opportunity to tell the world the truth about Nick Hardcastle and his relationship with Olivia Corscadden. People needed to understand that she couldn't have prevented any of the murders; that she hadn't known that a monster hid under the skin of the man she loved. They needed to pity her, to understand that she was a victim too. He knew she got hate mail, knew she was despised by the other prisoners at Holloway. He couldn't imagine how tough these past months must have been for her; in limbo, needing to give evidence before the court could decide what her own fate should be. When her photo appeared in the press it was never the photo taken the night of June's murder, with her dilated pupils and bruises. They always used the photograph of her and Nick together, smiling as though they shared a secret.

As a witness himself he hadn't been allowed to sit in on the previous days of the trial in case it affected the testimony he gave. He'd seen people arrive though.

Nick was escorted in from the court cells. Like Olivia he had also spent over half a year on remand now, and he'd lost weight. He only had three suits, which he wore in rotation. They all looked slightly too large for him. His barrister was being very specific about the colour of the shirts and ties that Nick wore, apparently having researched which appealed most to the jury. His parents sat in the gallery every day, rigid and highly strung.

Paula came too, but as she was also a witness she couldn't sit in the courtroom either. Sometimes Denison would see her in the canteen, drinking cup after cup of hot chocolate, staring fixedly at a newspaper although he could tell she wasn't reading it.

Lavinia Fitzstanley came every day. Word had it that she was staying at the Dorchester. Her husband Bertram could only put off one business arrangement in seven or so, so he was rarely present; most days she was escorted by a dapper silver-haired gentleman with a lion-headed cane. Lucinda Franz-Hurst, Eliza's best friend from school, would arrive each morning and exit her taxi as though she were arriving at a red-carpet premiere instead of a trial. Denison was surprised she hadn't done a twirl for the TV cameras yet.

June's mother Claudette had been given compassionate leave from work so she could attend. She had a photo of June that she held in her hand each day as she listened to the testimony. Claudette felt that no matter how horrible the testimony got it was her duty to bear witness to her daughter's pain and suffering.

Amanda's parents, Julia and David Montgomery, wore black and had fresh white roses in their lapels every day. David Montgomery hadn't shaved since the start of the trial and each morning his suit looked more and more crumpled. Julia Montgomery appeared remarkably composed, even when the journalists pushed microphones in her face and chased her and her husband down the street. Her expression never changed during the trial; she didn't even shed a tear when she heard Tracey Webb describe finding Amanda's body, or when Weathers told the court that Amanda's head had been recovered from the freezer in Nicholas Hardcastle's bedsit. One day though June's mother went to use the downstairs toilets and found Julia in there, sobbing her heart out. Claudette took her in her arms, told her that it wouldn't be long before they'd be seeing Nick Hardcastle locked up for the rest of his life and gently wiped the mascara tracks off her cheeks with a tissue.

Denison's testimony went well. He could tell that the jury, initially hostile to his belief that Nick had manipulated and abused Olivia, were now feeling a large measure of sympathy for her. Nick's barrister would argue against it, but Denison hoped that during Olivia's testimony the jury would get to see her X-rays and the burn marks on her arms. That they would see the photograph of what Nick had done to her on the night of June's murder. All this relied, of course, on Olivia taking the stand and giving evidence against the man she had regarded as the love of her life.

Denison would have been even more nervous about

Olivia changing her mind about doing this if he'd seen her in her cell the night before she was due to testify, reading and rereading a letter that Nick had sent her that first summer they were apart.

> One day I want to take you to where I went to
> school. Introduce you to all my teachers. You'd
> especially like Mr Jenkins, he's mad as a hatter.
> The school grounds are what I really want to show
> you though – the gardens are amazing, there's even a
> little grotto. You can go into the woods at the end of
> the grounds and there are statues right there, among
> the trees. And the gazebo's great – we used to sit out
> there in the summer, lounging around reading books
> and sneaking a crafty fag or two. There are tennis
> courts too – I'm sure they'd let us play a game if we
> asked nicely.
>
> I can't stand not seeing you. I keep dreaming about
> you. Imagining your dark hair on my pillow, your lips
> on my skin. I'm going crazy here on my own. Let me
> come to London. I'm worried about you and I don't
> like thinking of you stuck there. No one ever answers
> the phone when I ring. Why won't you let me see you?
> Are you upset about my stupid bloody parents? You
> can't listen to what anyone says, Liv – we belong
> together. You and me, for ever. I promise I'll never
> let you go.

Godfrey was taking the day off from his City job to go and listen to Olivia's testimony. Sinead stayed over on his sofa bed the night before and they both woke up early. Godfrey ground some coffee beans and made them an espresso each to accompany their bagels. Neither of them was hungry and neither spoke much.

Later, as Godfrey brushed his teeth, he looked at his reflection in the bathroom mirror and thought about Eliza. Thought about the way she flicked her hair over her shoulder. Her painted toenails, usually a pretty shade of pink. Her tan lines. The way she covered her mouth when she giggled. The time she'd mispronounced 'bourgeois' so it rhymed with 'gorgeous' and had hit him when he'd laughed.

He'd been spared having to identify her, but often had dreams where he was back by the river on that Bonfire Night, endlessly searching as the fireworks exploded above his head. In one dream he actually found her body, not beaten to death, but drowned, floating face-up in the Cam, the coloured light from the fireworks reflecting in her blank eyes. He remembered that she'd had nightmares of her own, dreams in which the killer of Amanda was now chasing her. And he'd made fun of her, told her to stop being so melodramatic. He'd been the one who'd persuaded her to stay in Cambridge.

Sinead wasn't remembering dead people. Godfrey's flat looked out over the Thames and she was watching the tourist boats chugging through the grey water, thinking about the email she'd received the day before. Leo had forwarded it to her from some friends of theirs from college who had just had a baby – conceived, they thought, during their finals. 'Thought you might like to see the most recent photos of the baby. She's growing really fast and it won't be long before Paul starts teaching her the Periodic Table. He's already convinced that she knows the alphabet thanks to the animal frieze in her room (Ee is for Elephant).' The attached photos were of the baby – June Charlotte Zarach – looking bewildered in one and gurgling in another, eyes a dark blue and hair a marmalade orange. She was wearing a yellow romper suit embroidered with ducklings. Sinead wondered if she'd ever have kids herself and if she did, whether she'd call them Amanda or Eliza.

They arrived early at the Old Bailey. The trial wouldn't be recommencing till ten at the earliest. Godfrey was smoking a cigarette outside, ignoring the one or two members of the press who recognized him and tried for a soundbite. Sinead nudged him to get his attention and he turned round to see that Paula Abercrombie was walking towards them.

Paula noticed them too and he saw her falter in her step. Then she put her head down and carried on.

'Going to pretend you don't know us?' called out Sinead as she came near. 'Too ashamed to say hello?'

Paula stopped abruptly, took a sharp breath and rounded on Sinead. 'What are you trying to say?' she snapped. 'I've got nothing to be ashamed of!'

'Apart from the fact you were shagging a bloody murderer!' pointed out Sinead.

Paula shook her head. 'So he conned me, all right? Is that what you want to hear? It's not like I knew he was the killer.'

'Oh, don't be so naive,' said Godfrey, stubbing out his cigarette on the wall of the building. 'What did you *think* he was doing in June's room that night? Reading her a bedtime story?'

Paula nearly slapped him – only the presence of the

nearby photographers stopped her. Instead she put one foot in front of the other and walked away, angry and trying not to cry.

Olivia had been woken up at 5.30 that morning by the night nurse, who took her to a holding room and gave her breakfast: a runny boiled egg, two slices of toast with the corners curling up, cornflakes with just a half an inch of milk at the bottom of the bowl and a cup of weak tea. She ate the food slowly and steadily, then sat, hands clasped in her lap, waiting for the officers who were going to accompany her.

Olivia was driven to Newington Park police station sandwiched between two of them. They transferred her into police custody and she was taken to the same cell that she'd stayed in the night of her arrest. She sat on the hard bench, smoothing down her skirt. Remand prisoners at Holloway were only allowed three sets of clothing, but her solicitor had wanted her to wear a suit at the trial and had bought her a beige jacket and skirt from Jigsaw that she was wearing with a white shirt and brown heels. Her hair was partly drawn back in a clasp.

The letter from Nick was in her inside jacket pocket, over her heart. The notepaper was warm with her body heat. She twisted the ring on her right hand. It was made of silver and amber. Nick had bought it for her as a second anniversary present; he'd said the pale stone reminded him of her eyes.

Olivia couldn't stop the tremor in her hands. She was beginning to wish she'd taken the advice of her cellmates and requested a tranquillizer from the nurse at breakfast.

She just wanted the day to be finished with. The only thing she was looking forward to was seeing Nick again. It had been nearly a year since she'd last seen his face, last looked into his eyes.

The cell door clanked open and her solicitor appeared. Adina Kennedy gave her a big smile and a hug.

'You look very smart, Olivia,' she said. 'Are you nervous? Do you have butterflies?'

'Butterflies?' said Olivia, hand over her stomach. 'More like bats.'

Adina laughed. 'Look, it's been going well. Dr Denison did you proud yesterday. I bet half of those jurors went straight home and donated that month's salary to the NSPCC.'

Olivia's smile disappeared. 'What do you mean? How much did he slag off my parents? Did he mention the abuse?'

Adina put a hand on Olivia's arm. 'I'm sorry, Olivia, I didn't mean to worry you. Don't fret, Matthew didn't mention the sexual aspect of the abuse. He told the jury about the physical and psychological abuse, and about how that made you a perfect target for someone like Hardcastle. But the majority of his testimony was focused on explaining battered wife syndrome: why you didn't leave Nick, why you still loved him, why you were willing to sacrifice yourself for him.'

Olivia sat down on the bench. 'Did you see any of this morning's papers?'

Adina nodded. 'There was obviously coverage of the trial. "Psychiatrist tells jury why girlfriend covered for Hardcastle", that kind of thing.'

'Did he go into detail about my confessions?' asked Olivia, turning the ring round and round on her finger.

'Only that you'd confessed to the three murders, but that the facts of the murders didn't corroborate your account.'

The police were out in force outside the Old Bailey that morning, but it didn't stop the van carrying Olivia being pelted with eggs and even rocks by angry protestors.

'The usual rent-a-mob,' said Adina, grimacing. 'I wish they'd get a bloody life.'

The police van pulled to a stop around the back of the court house and one of the officers offered Olivia a blanket. Olivia looked at her gravely and shook her head.

They drew back the door and she was hit with a wave of jeers and insults. Careful not to meet anyone's eye she allowed the officers to escort her into the building, and counted herself lucky that she hadn't got egg on her suit.

They searched her, then took her down to the court cells in the basement. The cells were dark and gloomy, but at least she had one to herself. That was probably what she missed most about her previous life – having some time and space to herself. Some privacy, some peace. Silence didn't exist at Holloway. Even at night the other prisoners would have shouted-out conversations across the cells, and those mentally disturbed women who had so far escaped the attentions of the prison doctors and were yet to be sent to the 'Muppet' wing would scream and yell and bang their beds and mugs and heads against the doors of their cells. Olivia hadn't slept for more than a few hours at a time for months.

It was eleven o'clock before the call came for her. They

took her up the stairs, chatting to each other about barbe-cues and summer holiday plans. Adina Kennedy was waiting in the side room that led to the witness stand.

'I'm not sure I can do this,' Olivia blurted out. Adina, looking panicked, grabbed her by the arm and took her to one side.

'I'm afraid you have to,' she said. 'Three girls are dead because of that man and you're the best witness the prose-cution has. If he goes free because of some misguided loyalty on your part, all that guilt will be on your head.' Adina saw that Olivia was shaking, and her tone softened. 'Look, Olivia, all you have to do is tell the truth,' she said. 'Think of what he did to your friends. Think of their parents, their little brothers and sisters.'

'Miss Olivia Corscadden,' said the guard. Adina gave Olivia a quick hug and then Olivia was taken through the door and was suddenly in the courtroom.

The room was large, old, wood-panelled. It was also packed to capacity and every single person was looking at her. Including Nick.

He sat in the dock, flanked by two police officers. He seemed tired and yet his eyes were still a warm, vibrant blue. He gazed at her and they just looked at each other in silence. The moment seemed to stretch on and on. Eventually he smiled. She had to fight not to smile back.

'Can you give your full name for the court?'

She took a breath. 'Cleopatra Olivia Corscadden.'

The clerk came up to the witness stand. 'Please place your hand on the Bible and repeat after me: I swear by Almighty God that the evidence I shall give will be the truth, the whole truth and nothing but the truth.'

She repeated the oath.

'You may have your seat.'

She sat on the chair, stealing a sideways glance at the judge seated beside her in red robes and a white wig. He was wearing half-moon glasses and seemed stern.

The lawyer for the prosecution got to his feet. He too had on a white wig, but his robes were black. He began by asking Olivia how she was. Then he asked her to describe the history of her relationship with Nick.

Denison watched from the back of the courtroom. Hesitantly at first Olivia described the first time Nick had ever hit her, then the second, then the third, till the point where the abuse was a regular occurrence. She talked about how he had gradually detached her from anyone who disliked him, until the only people she ever socialized with were ones he approved of. And she told the barrister that her plans for the future had all revolved around Nick: where *he* wanted to move to, what *he* wanted to do.

Finally the prosecution brought this line of questioning to a close and then embarked on the next stage of the case: Olivia as a witness to June Okeweno's murder.

Danny Armstrong had already testified to the argument that had occurred between Olivia and June at the Ariel May Ball, and had admitted that he'd told Nick the details when he'd found him a few minutes later in one of the music tents.

'Nick was angry,' Olivia agreed. 'He was upset with June because he knew that she was trying to get me to leave him. And he was angry with me because I'd bought myself an expensive dress that I couldn't really afford and argued with him about it in front of other people.'

'What happened when the two of you were alone in Mr Hardcastle's room?' asked the prosecution lawyer.

'Well, he basically beat me up,' she said, blushing.

'Can you be more specific?'

'He punched me in the face a few times, dragged me around the room by my hair and hit me in the stomach.'

The prosecution wanted the jury to see the photo of Olivia that had been taken the night of June's murder. The defence argued that there was no proof, just Olivia's word, that it was Nick who had caused those cuts and bruises. The judge agreed that it could be entered into evidence, but that no inference of guilt could be made.

'What happened then?' continued the prosecution.

'When he finished I went into the bathroom. I had some antiseptic lotion and some cotton wool, and I cleaned up the cuts. When I came out of the bathroom Nick wasn't in the room any more. I heard a noise coming from outside the door and I went to see what it was. I thought it was coming from June's room – I could hear her through the door. She was saying "no, don't". I tried to open the door, but it was locked.'

'What did you do? Did you call for help?'

'I called out Nick's name.'

'Because you thought he was the one hurting June?'

'No,' she admitted. 'I called to him so he would come and help. I was banging and banging on the door, hearing these horrible sounds. And then eventually the door opened.'

'And who was it who opened the door?'

Olivia opened her mouth, but no sound came out. She closed it. Olivia looked at Nick. Her eyes were swimming with tears and her lower lip was shaking. Denison held his breath, his pulse suddenly pounding.

'Olivia? Who opened the door?'

She closed her eyes and two heavy tears dropped down her cheeks. She turned back to the barrister.

'It was Nick. Nicholas Hardcastle.'

Denison was waiting for her as she left the courtroom. He stood there and she ran into his arms, bursting into immediate tears.

'It's OK, it's OK,' he said, stroking her hair. 'It's over now. He'll never hurt you again, I promise.'

Denison was there on the last three days of the trial too, when Nicholas gave evidence in his own defence. As far as Denison could tell by their body language the jury had been decided on the day when they heard Paula Abercrombie testify on her discovery of Amanda Montgomery's head in Nick's freezer. He watched them as Nick swore on the Bible to tell the truth and could tell they were sceptical before he even uttered a word. When Nick explained away the head by saying it had been 'planted' by the plumber the letting agency had sent to fix some problems in the flat, one of them even laughed. As had been predicted the defence suggested that the true culprit was Olivia, though they could offer no evidence for this.

'So tell me, Mr Hardcastle, how did Miss Corscadden manage to spirit Amanda Montgomery's head into your freezer? Are you suggesting the plumber was actually Miss Corscadden in disguise?' No one does sarcasm quite like barristers, thought Denison. This time the whole court laughed.

Weathers and Denison bumped into each other outside the courtroom on the day the jury retired to consider its verdict and exchanged clipped 'hellos'. They had hardly spoken since that day in Cambridge when Weathers had been prepared to charge Olivia with murder if she refused to testify against her boyfriend. Denison had seen a side to his friend then that he didn't like; he'd been angry with him for a long time.

'I was going to get a quick pint over the road if you fancy coming,' Weathers said casually. Denison thought about it.

'OK,' he capitulated.

The pint ended up becoming four pints and then a curry in Soho.

'So, do you reckon we've got him?' asked Weathers, pushing away his plate of rice and bright red chicken. He sipped at his Cobra beer.

Denison nodded. 'I think so. Jurors number four and eight might be a bit soft on him, but most of them are ready to find him guilty.'

'I thought my heart was going to stop when Olivia suddenly froze in the witness stand,' admitted Weathers. 'Bloody Hardcastle was making cow eyes at her and I could tell she was wilting. I never asked you – how did you manage to get her to testify?'

Denison shifted in his seat, unable to admit to Weathers that he'd shown Olivia the crime scene photos. He shouldn't have let anyone involved with the case see them, let alone the person charged with the crimes.

'I managed to convince her that the murders didn't happen just because Nick lost his temper,' he hedged. 'There was a level of psychosis involved that couldn't be justified by anything as noble as defending your star-crossed love.'

'That's probably the most romantic thing you've ever said to me,' said Weathers with a grin.

Denison raised his glass. 'To stopping a serial killer before he reached the magic number five,' he toasted.

'And to your book – bestseller or bust,' said Weathers, clinking glasses with his friend.

'I didn't know you knew about that,' said Denison, a bit embarrassed.

'Your replacement at Coldhill told me. How are you going to get round the confidentiality issues?'

'Apparently it's pretty straightforward as long as I don't give away details of ongoing cases and change people's names if I'm discussing their psychiatric sessions.' Denison nibbled on his peshwari naan.

'You going to discuss this case?'

Denison looked at him over the bread. 'To be honest that's the bit the publishers are interested in. I mean, they approached me, not the other way around. The Cambridge Butcher case will be the first chapter.'

'And you'll discuss your sessions with Olivia?'

'To some extent. Obviously it would be a breach of her trust if I mentioned the abuse without her permission. I'll have to tread carefully.'

'And if Nick's found not guilty? Can you still publish the book?'

Denison considered. 'Paul Britton discussed the original Rachel Nickell investigation in his book even after the judge had thrown that prosecution out of court, so I guess so.'

'Fingers crossed though, yeah?'

They shared a suddenly serious look. 'Fingers crossed,' agreed Denison.

*

The jury returned with their verdict after fifteen hours of deliberation.

'Would the jury foreman please stand?' instructed the clerk. 'Mr Foreman, will you please confine yourself to answering my first question simply yes or no? Members of the jury, have you reached verdicts on all counts upon which all of you are agreed?'

'Yes,' said the jury foreman.

'Members of the jury, on count one, do you find the defendant, Nicholas Hardcastle, guilty or not guilty of murder?'

'Guilty,' said the foreman.

All colour bleached out of Nick's skin, like a photograph that has been left out in the sun too long.

'Members of the jury, on count two, do you find the defendant, Nicholas Hardcastle, guilty or not guilty of murder?'

'Guilty,' said the foreman.

'Yes!' hissed Eliza's best friend. Nick's mum collapsed against her husband, who hugged her tightly and stared at Nick with watery eyes, wishing he could defend him from the people who were about to take him away.

'Members of the jury, on count three, do you find the defendant, Nicholas Hardcastle, guilty or not guilty of murder?'

'Guilty,' said the foreman.

'And is that the verdict of you all?'

'It is.'

Claudette Okeweno and Julia Montgomery smiled at each other, and then hugged, tears streaming down both their faces.

Godfrey, who had the electronic BBC ticker-tape delivering up-to-the-minute news to his PC desktop at work, scanned it for the hundredth time that hour and finally saw what he had been waiting for. 'Yes!' he said under his breath, hitting the desk with his fist. He texted the news to Sinead, who sent it on to Rob McNorton, who had already received it from Leo.

Denison had no doubt that back in the 1950s the judge would have been placing a square of black cloth over his wig at this point, ready to deliver a death sentence. Nick withered further under the older man's stare.

'Nicholas Hardcastle, stand up. You have been found guilty of the murders of Amanda Montgomery, Eliza Fitzstanley and June Okeweno.

'There is no doubt in my mind that these are the most barbaric crimes over which I have ever had the misfortune to preside at trial. These three women were young, brilliant and beautiful. I cannot conceive that they would not have had admirable and productive adult lives if you had not seen fit to nip that promise in the bud. I have no option but to sentence you to the fullest extent of the law: on all three counts you will go to prison for life. It is my profound regret that I can sentence you to no harsher punishment. I recommend to those people who may in the future have the unenviable task of considering you for parole that they remember the faces of Amanda, Eliza and June, and decide in their wisdom that they can never risk setting you free.' He motioned to the guards. 'Take him down.'

It was only twenty minutes or so before the news filtered through to the prisoners at Holloway. Laticia came running

over to the TV room, where Olivia was watching a kids'
programme on the battered screen.

'They found him guilty, Olivia!' she said, shaking her
friend. 'He went down for about a hundred years or something!'

Olivia looked at Laticia's beaming face and nodded.

'It's all right to be happy, you know,' said Laticia. 'He
can't hurt you now. You don't have to be miserable about
it.'

'I'm not miserable,' Olivia said. 'Honest.'

'Give us a smile then.'

Olivia smiled.

'God this place is grim,' said Denison, who was on his sev-
enth visit to Holloway. Olivia shrugged, smiling at him.

'It could be worse.'

'How?' he protested.

'I could be in a Thai prison,' she said. 'Or a Turkish one.
I've seen *Midnight Express* you know. This isn't so bad.'

'Is it different?' he asked. 'Now that you're not a remand
prisoner?'

She shook her head. 'Not so different. There are fewer
privileges, but on the plus side I've got my own telly now.'

'It must be difficult though. Being locked up with murderers and drug dealers, when your crime was nothing more
than trying to protect the man you loved.'

She frowned. 'Don't romanticize this. You should know
better. During the time when I was trying to convince you
that I was to blame, Nick could have killed someone else. I
thank the Lord every day that he didn't. Look, Matthew, I
deserve to be here. Some days I think I should have been

given a longer sentence. No, don't shake your head. Adina said I could have got more than three years for perverting the course of justice. I was lucky, we both know it.'

For a while neither of them spoke. Finally Denison rummaged in his briefcase and brought out a multi-pack of cigarettes.

'Well, that should keep me going till I get parole,' said Olivia with a grin. The months she had spent on remand counted towards time served; in a fortnight's time she'd be eligible for parole. 'But you can't give them to me here. You have to leave them with reception; they'll pass them on. Thank you.'

'I'm not sure if the number you smoke a day has gone up, but by my calculations they should last a month or so. They wouldn't let me bring more than 200.'

'Thank you,' she said again. 'I'll try and ration them out. Just a couple more weeks to go, hopefully. They should last that long. By the way, what's the latest news on the book?'

'There was a bit of a bidding war for the serialization rights. Three major papers were interested. My publishers are thrilled.'

She nodded. 'I'm not surprised – money *and* free publicity. Have you thought of a name yet?'

Denison smiled. 'Actually I have. *Twisted Wing*. What do you think? Seems to sum up the sociopath's ability to integrate with others very aptly.'

She smiled back. 'Don't be surprised though if a certain spiritualist tries to claim a share of the royalties.'

Her hair had grown during her time in prison and the curls were now more like waves. She saw him looking at the dark locks and ran a hand through them, self-conscious.

'I need to ask you something,' she said.

'Fire away.'

'When I get out of here . . . not when I'm still on licence, but when I've served the whole sentence and I'm really free . . . could I see you?'

Denison looked for the last time into her burnished gold irises. 'Of course,' he said.

SEVEN MONTHS LATER

Chapter Twenty

Matthew Denison was sitting at the desk in his study. The stereo was on, playing Radio 4, and he was looking at a blank Word document on his computer screen. This chapter of his new book was meant to focus solely on Nicholas Hardcastle's background and character. His childhood, his sexual proclivities, how he'd ended up a monster of a human being. It was a hard chapter to write, as Nick's parents were of course refusing to have any contact with him. He'd even driven to Oxford, hoping that a personal visit might convince them to talk, but there was a 'for sale' sign outside and they hadn't opened the door. Weathers had later told him that they'd been forced to sell the house to pay Nick's legal bills.

Denison's first book was due to be published in three months' time and condensed versions of each chapter were already appearing in the *Mail on Sunday*. The newspapers' bidding war for the serialization rights had prompted his publishers to ask him for a book based solely on the Cambridge Butcher case, even before *Twisted Wing* had been published. He'd taken a sabbatical to write book number one and couldn't take off any more time to write book number two. Given a choice between continuing at Coldhill and all the money and celebrity he'd get from continuing his publishing career, he had handed in his notice before Nick's trial had even finished. Cass told him to check his bank balance every time he wondered if he'd made the right choice.

Procrastinating, Denison rifled again through the photos taken at Nick's bedsit the day they'd discovered Amanda Montgomery's head. The pictures of the carrier bag and its gruesome contents he put aside quickly, but he paused at the photo of the chocolate assortment tin that Ames had found in Nick's cupboard during the subsequent search.

The main photo showed a variety of batteries, all different sizes; a watch; about ten two pence pieces and fifteen one pence pieces; a gold signet ring that had previously belonged to someone who was no doubt a few years older than Nick; and a badge that was obviously meant to have pride of place on a school blazer.

Another photo showed the badge in close-up. There was a Latin motto in gold stitching, a shield portraying a bird perched on a globe and the name of the institution: 'The Rowe School'.

Denison tapped his forefinger on the photo. Why did the name of the school ring a bell? He gratefully switched away from the Word program and opened his browser. He went straight to Google and typed in 'rowe school'. The first search result was for the school itself. He clicked on the link and skimmed through the pages, but it said nothing that enlightened him.

After the fifteenth or so search result the school's name was mentioned in conjunction with Nick, as being the place he'd received his secondary education. Denison didn't envy them that association. He doubted it helped with admissions.

Deciding he wasn't going to find the answer on the web, Denison reluctantly switched back to the blank document on his screen and inwardly hoorayed when the phone rang.

'Matthew Denison speaking.'

'Oh, thank God!' said a frantic female voice. 'I've been trying to reach you for the last three days!'

'Who is this?' he asked.

'Sinead Flynn. Look, I'm sorry to ring you at home – I've been trying your number at Coldhill but they said you didn't work there any more and wouldn't give me your personal number. I had to snoop it from the Internet.'

'My home number's on the Internet?' he replied in panic.

'Everything's on the Internet,' she said impatiently. 'I have to talk to you about Olivia. I'm not sure what's going on, but I know something's not right. She could have faked it you see! She could have faked it.' Sinead was speaking too quickly.

'Calm down,' Denison urged. 'You're not making much sense. What could Olivia have faked?'

'The Dissociative Identity Disorder; the multiple person-alities. We covered it in my psychology class. I told her about it and she was so interested that I lent her my notes.'

'Sinead, it's OK. We know she faked the DID. That's how we got her to admit that she was covering for Nick.'

'*You don't understand*,' Sinead said urgently. 'I just fin-ished reading your article in the *Mail on* bloody *Sunday* – I *know* that you caught her out. But I'm trying to tell you that she knew about Kenneth Bianchi. She knew that he faked it and they caught him out with hypnotic logic. She'd read Martin Orne's bloody article on the tests they used to prove he was malingering! That's what I'm trying to tell you,

Dr Denison – you think you caught her out, but she could have passed your tests if she'd wanted to!'

'I need to speak to Olivia,' Denison said as soon as Weathers answered the phone.

'Whoa, hold your horses, Matt,' said Weathers. 'What's going on?'

'I've just had Sinead Flynn on the phone. She seems to think that Olivia was aware of the existence of hypnotic logic and knew how to behave in those tests so that we'd think she was really hypnotized. So why didn't she? Why did she let us think we'd tripped her up?'

There was a silence on the other end of the line.

'Steve? Steve, you still there?'

'Look, what do you want me to say?' asked Weathers. He sounded tired. 'You want me to guess at her motivations? Well, you're the psychologist, but OK, maybe she'd just had enough. Maybe she knew what to do, but just couldn't face carrying on the pretence. Maybe she'd had enough of carrying the can for that shit Hardcastle.'

Denison frowned. 'You don't seem too keen to pursue this.'

'Pursue what? Hardcastle had Amanda Montgomery's head in his bloody freezer, Matt. Olivia was already under lock and key in Coldhill when he moved into that flat. I mean, what exactly do you think I should be pursuing?'

'OK, OK,' Denison said, rubbing his forehead. 'Look, I'm not saying this changes anything. I just want to know why she let me catch her out. I need to talk to her. I need her number.'

'I'm afraid I can't help you,' Weathers said. 'Her parole

finished last month. She's had a nasty time of it, Matt. The papers have been trying to find her; any time anyone recognized her we had to move her to prevent the place she was staying being burned down. By the end of her parole she'd just had enough. She asked for a new identity and she took off. I've got a number I can give you if you want to leave a message, but I can't tell you where she is. I don't know myself.'

'You're telling me she's in the Witness Protection Programme?' asked Denison, surprised.

'Not any more she's not. She said we did such a lousy job of it that she'd be better off on her own. So she got a new passport, new National Insurance number, new birth certificate and *sayonara*.'

'But isn't anyone keeping an eye on her? Keeping track of her movements?'

'She's paid her debt to society,' said Weathers dryly. 'That's it. Done. We've got no reason to monitor her any more.'

'This is just ridiculous,' said Denison. 'She could be dead in a ditch somewhere, killed by some vigilante nutter and you lot wouldn't even know it!'

'It was her choice, Matt. She could have got protection from the state, but like I said, she told us she was better off on her own. Look, try not to take it personally. I know you liked her, but you can't blame her for not wanting to stay in touch with you.'

Denison ignored him. 'What about her friends, her family? Maybe one of them can tell me where she is?'

'Her dad's done a runner too. Could be she's still keeping in touch with her mum though.'

'What do you mean, her dad's done a runner?'

'He went AWOL a couple of days after his release. There's a warrant out on him since he's still got a month or so of his parole left to serve, but so far no joy.'

Denison was beginning to feel chilled despite the fact that the central heating was on full blast. He slipped a jacket on over his shirt. 'You don't think the two disappearances could be related?'

Weathers laughed, sounding strangely echoey on the phone line. 'What, those two, on the lam together? Doesn't seem too likely to me, mate.'

'No . . .' Denison picked up the photo of the school blazer badge. 'Hey, Steve, have you heard of the Rowe School?'

'Yeah – it was Hardcastle's secondary. Why?'

'No reason. Can I have that phone number?'

He listened to the ringing and then there was a crackling sound and a posh recorded voice told him to leave a message.

'This is Dr Matthew Denison,' he said. 'I'm trying to reach Olivia Corscadden. It's really quite important. Uh, let me give you my mobile number.' He dictated it twice for good measure. 'Right, thanks. Goodbye.'

He hung up and looked again at the photo. He knocked on his temples. 'Think, Matt, you arse. Rowe School . . . Rowe School . . .'

It made sense that the niggle he felt was due to a connection elsewhere in the Cambridge Butcher case. He jumped up and went to his filing cabinet, pulling out the six huge files of notes and the disks of audio files that related to the case. Radio 4 was unceremoniously switched off in favour of a CD recording of his sessions with Olivia.

'There's something you're not telling me,' he heard her voice say. It had been a few months since he'd last played one of the CDs. For a while, after she'd been taken away from Coldhill, he'd listened to them every day. Partly to try and convince himself that he couldn't have uncovered her malingering sooner, partly because he knew she still needed help and felt as though he'd somehow abandoned her and partly because – although he'd never admit it – he missed her and took some strange comfort in listening to their old conversations. And yet today something seemed to have changed. Today hearing her voice was like having some creature scratching at the base of his spine.

He sat down on his office chair and opened the first of the folders.

The third folder contained Olivia's school records. Olivia had gone to quite a rough comprehensive in Dalston; he doubted that it had a Latin motto, let alone a school blazer. But there in her school notes he found it.

The scholarship Olivia had applied for at the age of fourteen had been to the Rowe School.

He went through Nick's notes and found the year that Nick had been accepted as a scholarship student at Rowe – it was the same year.

So, Nick had taken Olivia's place. Olivia needed desperately to escape her family and going to a boarding school would have been a good way to do it. But a motive for murder? Would she not have been more likely to blame the people who had decided to award the scholarship to Nick rather than punish him in such an elaborate way?

He dug through the notes, but there was nothing that told him who'd made that decision. He remembered Sinead saying 'everything's on the Internet' and went back to the Rowe School's website. The school's past newsletters were archived as PDF files. He found one from the September when Nick would have spent his first term at the Rowe, and there was a photo of Nick – fourteen years old and a little bit goofy – smiling as he shook the hand of a tall man in a pinstripe suit. 'Mr George Spakes welcomes Nicholas Hardcastle, this year's recipient of the Rees-Hamer bursary. Mr Spakes, who oversees the bursary along with his wife Dolores and Mr Henry Wilcocks, the nephew of Peter Rees-Hamer whose generous endowment funds the bursary, says, "We had many impressive candidates this year, but thought Nicholas really stood out as the kind of young man we would be proud to have at the school."'

Denison opened a second browser window and went back to Google. He typed in 'George Spakes'. There were a number of hits, so he added 'Dolores' to the keywords. This time there were just three, one of which happened to be a link to another edition of the Rowe newsletter, published a year or so after the one he'd just opened: 'The school was greatly saddened to learn of the deaths last month of George and Dolores Spakes, two valued members of the Rowe School's governing body. The couple were involved in a traffic accident on the Rampton Road and sadly lost their lives in the incident. A memorial service will be held in the school chapel at 4 p.m. on 18 September; please let the school secretary know if you wish to attend.'

Denison was finding it hard to move the mouse, his hand was shaking so much. He went back to the page of search results and clicked on another link, this time to a local paper.

'Police found traces of another car's paint on the body-work of the Spakes' Nissan, and forensic tests have matched this to a blue Ford Focus that was discovered abandoned in a car park two days ago. The police confirm that they are now treating the death of the Spakes as vehicular manslaughter.'

He clicked the 'back' button and searched for 'Henry Wilcocks'. Again, there were several hits. He added the word 'death'.

'The identity of the man found stabbed to death in Huntsford Park on Thursday was confirmed this morning as being that of Henry Allan Wilcocks of Huntsford Drive, Caversham, who worked as a conveyancer for Danby & Sons solicitors. Police are keen to speak to anyone who was in the area at the time of the incident.'

Denison looked through Olivia's school notes for a copy of the higher education application form that would list the universities to which she'd applied.

There were just two: the University of Cambridge and Anglia Ruskin University. The latter, Olivia's second choice, was also located in Cambridge, just a few hundred yards from Parkside police station.

He went back to the first browser window and was confronted again with the Rowe School newsletter's photo of a young, smiling Nick Hardcastle. He looked at the happy eyes and thought he might throw up.

'Oh, Nick,' he said. 'I am so sorry.'

The phone rang and he nearly jumped out of his skin. He picked it up, hoping it was Weathers.

'Dr Matthew Denison,' he said.

'Hello, Matthew,' Olivia replied.

It was like someone had tipped a cup of iced water down his back. His stomach seemed to shrivel.

'Hello, Olivia,' he croaked. His mind was stuck; he needed to find a way to persuade her to come and see him and to make sure that there were about fifty armed police officers in his flat when she did. He willed his brain to think up a plan.

'The messages get passed on to me automatically,' she told him. 'Most of the time it's no one I want to ring back, but I'm glad you called. How are you?'

'Good, thanks,' he said. 'How about you?'

'Crap. Thanks for asking. I suppose if they gave you that phone number they've also told you that I've had to go into hiding? There's a hell of a lot of fucked-up people out there you know, thinking that they've been entrusted to clean the world up. You'd think I ate babies for breakfast, the hatred they have for me.'

'Olivia.' His mouth was so dry. 'Olivia, did you know your dad's on the run too?'

'On the run?' she said.

'Apparently he didn't want to finish up his parole. He's been missing since a day or two after they let him out.'

'Oh,' she said, without any note of surprise. 'Hey, doc?' He heard a smile in her voice. 'Did I ever tell you I have my father's eyes?'

'Really?' he said.

'Yes. I keep them in a jar under my bed.' She giggled and the suspicion that she was speaking literally made him feel like his ears ought to be bleeding at the sound of her laugh.

'Anyway, what did you need to speak to me about?' she asked. 'It sounded important.'

'Uh, I just wanted to know how you were getting on. Last time I saw you in prison you mentioned maybe getting together at some point once your parole was done.'

'That's right,' she said. 'I did. Unfortunately having a vigilante mob trying to track you down and kill you tends to put a dampener on your social schedule. I think I might have to ask for a raincheck on that. For the next ten years or so probably.'

He was silent, aware now that he wasn't going to be able to fool her into a trap. So what now? he thought. Could he trick her into admitting her guilt to him?

'So, when are you going to ask me?' she said.

'Ask you about what?'

'About the hypnotic logic tests. Yellow amethysts and numb spots.'

He fumbled the phone receiver, nearly dropping it. Had she tapped his phone?

'I assume that's why you called,' she said. 'I was so relieved that it didn't come up at the trial. That was a close call. But I read your book – bought it the day it came out actually – and I knew Sinead would read it too, the nosy cow, and get in touch with you. I was expecting your call.' She paused, then put on a little girl voice: 'Are you disappointed in me?'

'But, but . . . why?' was all Denison could think to ask.

'Why what? Why pretend I couldn't pass the logic tests? Well, because I wanted to get caught out, of course. Jesus, it took you long enough to get suspicious. I was getting to the stage where I thought I'd have to write "I am malingering" in black marker pen on my forehead.'

'So you faked it all?' he said. 'Even the catatonia?'

'Even that.'

'But you were out of it for four weeks!'

He could almost hear her shrugging down the phone line. 'It was pretty boring, I must admit. Though the drooling part was fun. What can I say, it's a gift. I might not have DID, but I'm pretty good at dissociating. Learned when I was a kid. There's nothing like being fucked up the arse by old men to teach you the trick of escaping into your head. I got some good thinking done during those four weeks. Think I might even have solved Fermat's Last Theorem in week three, at some point between dribbling at the television and being fed apple sauce on a plastic spoon.'

'Wouldn't it have been easier just to tell the police at the crime scene that you'd seen Nick kill June?'

'Of course. But easier isn't always best. It's often much more fun challenging yourself. I thought it would be better if the idea that I was sacrificing myself at the altar of Nick came from you. It took a while to get there. But I just contented myself with the thought of Nick dangling at the end of my strings, twitching, wondering what was going on, wondering what would happen to him.'

One of the folders was open, the contents spread across his desk. He saw the photo of Amanda Montgomery that he'd always liked best, the one of her in the paint-splattered jeans, playing with her baby brother.

'You killed them,' he said, 'didn't you?'

'I suppose I can finally admit that I did.'

'But why?'

'Well, at first I was just planning on killing Nick. But then I saw how much fun it would be to turn him into a

murderer. Sweet, down-to-earth, friendly Nick. Detested by
his friends. Spat at by strangers. And Lord knows what
they're doing to him in prison, a pretty boy like that. I
thought it was a more fitting punishment – now he's the one
getting fucked up the arse.'

'A fitting punishment? Is that what you call it? All he did
was win a scholarship that you'd applied for too!' Although
he knew psychopaths saw minor slights as major insults to
their ego, in the same way that stalkers saw declarations of
love in a stranger's smile, it was hard for him to comprehend
such a desire for retribution.

'It was meant to be mine,' she said, her voice hard and
sharp as a shattered china plate. 'My teacher told me. She
said she knew one of the members of the bursary committee
and that he'd tipped her the nod. I was nearly free. And then
Nicholas bloody Hardcastle submits a last-minute application and suddenly I've got my teacher apologizing for
speaking too soon, and my way out – my open door –
slammed shut in my face.'

'But I don't understand,' said Denison. 'If you hated him
so much how could you live with him for nearly three years?
How could you bear to sleep with him?'

That made her laugh out loud. 'Are you kidding? What
do you think I spent my childhood doing? I've had plenty of
practice at having sex with men I despise. It's only when you
equate sex with love that it's hard to fuck someone you
hate.'

'But why frame him for three murders? Wouldn't one
have been enough?'

'Multiple sexual or sadistic murders by under-21s carry
an automatic sentence of thirty years or more,' she said, as

though stating a well-known fact. 'There's a big difference between serving half a life sentence and being locked up knowing you're not ever going to get out.'

'True,' he said. 'But you're kidding yourself if you really think that's the reason.'

He could hear the smile in her words: 'Go on.'

'You killed them because you enjoyed it. Because that's what you are. A killer. You'd have murdered them anyway, whether you had to frame Nick for a crime or not. It's just what you do.'

She laughed. 'Someone's been doing his research. Come on then, what do you reckon my tally is? High enough to qualify to be a genuine serial killer?'

'I believe I know of at least six,' he said. 'But I've only just started looking.'

'You wouldn't find them all,' she said, sounding almost wistful. 'Some of them you wouldn't be able to link to me. They were just random. And some you couldn't find, full stop. I don't always leave them out on display.'

'Were the victims at Ariel random?'

'Noooooo,' she said. 'No, they all pissed me off one way or another. Paula was top of my list, but I knew if I killed the bitch I'd probably be the first person hauled in for interview, what with her being my "love rival" or whatever the fuck the tabloids would call it. Amanda was the next best option; she kept stirring things up between me and Nick, trying to make sure her darling Paula got what she wanted, and luckily Nick was no fan either. I was going to wait though, hold off till the second term, but then I overheard her spouting off to Sinead about how I wasn't smart enough to be there, how I was giving female students a bad name. I just lost it – I got into her room and was waiting for her when she got back from the party.'

He didn't want to picture what had happened next. 'And Eliza?'

'Eliza turned up her nose at my clothes, the little trust-funded, coke-headed tart, and told me I wasn't good enough for Nick. It was just a spur of the moment thing, to be honest. June was more premeditated – Nick didn't like her, so it was believable that she'd be one of his victims. And she slagged off my family. OK, so maybe she had a point. But I wasn't going to let anyone look down on me – not when they'd have crumbled and died if they'd had to go through what I'd survived.'

'They made you feel inferior.'

'I suppose so. It didn't last though. Only up to the point where I stuck the knife in. And then they knew which of us was the superior one.'

She was breathing quite hard, and he listened to her calm down.

'Explain it to me, Matthew,' she said. 'I've read the literature. I know that people with multiple personalities tend to have really awful childhoods. And I know that's often true of serial killers too. So why did I become one and not the other?'

'Some people . . . mostly women . . . internalize the pain they feel. Childhood abuse becomes depression in adulthood.' What he was saying was almost a recitation, a recycling of all the theories in all the research papers he'd read over the years, borne out by his patients at Coldhill. But if he could convince her that he understood her, maybe he could make her stop, even now. 'A much smaller minority, who are usually male rather than female, externalize the pain. They seek power over others in order to increase their sense of self-worth. Everyone else is just an object to them, something they can only perceive in relation to themselves. Other people aren't individuals with their own hopes and dreams, and with a right to their futures. They're just there to gratify the needs of the sociopath.'

'You've become much more eloquent than at the start of this conversation,' Olivia observed. 'I definitely prefer Dr Denison, psychiatrist extraordinaire, to the stuttering coward who answered the phone.'

'I don't think you do. I think you want me to be afraid of you.'

'You *are* afraid of me.'

'Isn't there anything else you want from people? Don't you want more than fear?'

'Fear's the brightest colour,' she said, sounding distant. 'My world is composed of faded shades of grey. It's all monochrome to me. Nothing stands out except for pain and anger and fear. I can listen to music that makes other people cry and to me it's just a sequence of notes. I have to watch others to work out how to behave. I have to parrot back their opinions on films and books. It's all guesswork. I'm just passing through and nothing can touch me. At least when I kill there's energy, there's adrenaline. I can feel something.'

'Perhaps there's something we could do,' he said. 'Some treatment we could come up with, to break through the numbness without someone having to die for it.'

'You want me to turn myself in?' she said.

'Yes. Come home. Let me look after you.'

'Fuck you,' she said. 'Do you really think that if I admitted to the murders they'd let me stay with you whilst you did a Henry Higgins number and taught me to be a normal human being? Don't be ridiculous. I'd be back in Holloway till the day I died. Fuck that. I'm happy here.'

'And where's here?'

'Closer than you think.' He felt something slice between his shoulder blades and cried out in panic, but there was no one there, just adrenaline firing off his nerve endings.

'Are you OK, Matthew?' she asked, sounding amused.

He covered the mouthpiece and got his breath back. 'I'm fine,' he said eventually.

'I didn't mean to scare you. I'm not sticking around for long – it's too bloody cold here. I fancy somewhere with palm trees and a nice sandy beach.'

He couldn't help himself. 'You're crazy,' he said.

She burst out laughing. 'Didn't you prove that wasn't the case?'

'Look, Olivia, it would be for the best if you just handed yourself in. Surely once the authorities start looking for you it won't be hard for them to find you.'

'But why would they come looking for me?' she asked. He couldn't tell if her bemusement was genuine or not.

'Well, once I tell them what you've said—'

'Don't be silly, Matthew, you're not going to tell them anything,' she said lightly. 'For a while you'll kid yourself that you will, that you'll do the right thing, but we both know there's too much at stake for you. You can write all you like about Nick's criminal past; he's convicted, he can't dispute it. But there's no way your publisher's legal team will let you get away with accusing a used and abused young woman of these crimes. So, your writing career, your tour around the bookshops of this country and beyond, your appearance on chat shows and interviews in the papers – all that goes out the window. Still, I suppose you could always try to get your old job back, return to Coldhill. Oh no, wait a minute – you told the court that a serial killer was nothing more than a woman suffering battered spouse syndrome, just a victim, and testified that poor old innocent Nick had the kind of anti-social personality disorder that would make him capable of the most horrific murders. Something tells me no one's going to be too impressed with your diagnostic skills, Matthew. Your psychiatric career would be dead in the water too.'

He thought the room was shrinking, that the walls were drawing in around him. He couldn't see a way out. 'You can't think I'd let him rot in prison,' he said, but his voice was weak and unconvincing. He could feel tears coming, felt his throat contracting.

'I think you might, Matthew,' she said. 'I really think you might. But let me give you a good excuse for not doing the right thing: if Nick ever wins an appeal I promise you he'll be dead within twenty-four hours of leaving the courtroom. So you wouldn't be saving him, not really. Feel better now? Does that help soothe your conscience?'

He tried to tell himself that she only thought that of him because she was incapable of understanding why someone would act against their own self-interest, but already his mind was focused on finding a way out of his predicament. If he could bring her back, if he could be the brilliant young psychiatrist that convinced a sociopath to confess and take responsibility for her crimes . . .

'Don't you want your story to be told?' he tried.

'I don't need understanding,' she said.

'But why then?' he asked, blinking hard. 'Why are you telling me these things?'

'I've missed our conversations,' she said sweetly. 'I always wanted you to know the truth. It's no fun winning games that no one else knows you've been playing.'

Epilogue

'For Christ's sake, where were you?' Nick yelled.

Olivia pulled a cigarette from her pack and snapped open her lighter. 'I'm sorry!' she said. 'You know what I'm like; I just forget.' She was careful to only play at fugues and forgetfulness in front of Nick. When the police eventually realized she was weaving them a story, it needed to look as though only Nick had corroborated her lies. She lit the cigarette and looked at him, trying not to let it show how much she enjoyed it when he got angry.

'Yeah, I know what you're like. But does it have to be *every single fucking time*?' He went into the bathroom, slamming the door behind him.

Olivia rolled up her sleeve, took a large drag on the cigarette so its end flared red and then pressed the tip against her inner arm. There was a faint sizzling sound, but she didn't even wince. She stubbed out the cigarette and pinched her cheeks until her eyes watered. Then she clutched her arm and ran noisily out of the room and down into the ground-floor bathroom, where she listened for the sound of June's feet on the stairs.

All the phones were in use. Olivia waited, needing one at the end of the row. She was careful not to catch anyone's eye.

The cons could go mental if they thought you were eavesdropping on their conversations, and though Olivia could
handle them easily enough she didn't want anything jeop-
ardizing her early release.

Finally the woman at the end of the row of payphones
hung up and ejected her phone card. Olivia took her place,
turning her back on the other women. This was as private as
she was going to get.

She dialled the number. In her hand she clutched an
address she'd obtained from a friend who had no idea of her
motives for requesting it.

A young girl answered the phone.

'Jodie, it's Cleo. Get Dad, quick.'

It was two minutes before he got on the line.

'What the fuck do you want?'

'Nice to hear your voice, too. Look, I need a favour.'

'You've got to be kidding.'

'No, Dad. No I'm not fucking kidding. And if you don't
want to end up inside on a kiddie rape charge, then I suggest
you pay attention. OK?'

There was a sulky silence on the line and then: 'OK.'

'Go to Kensall's Self Service Storage. It's in Southwark.
Go to lock-up 217. There's a keypad on the wall – the
entry code's 678901. Inside you'll find a freezer. Inside that
you'll find something that used to belong to a friend of
mine. I want you to take it and plant it in Nick Hardcastle's
flat.'

Her father coughed out a laugh. 'You're shitting me. Is
this item what I think it is?'

'Probably.'

He let out a low whistle. 'Well, they say an apple never

falls far from the tree. What's this item doing in Kensall's Self Service Storage though? Ain'tcha worried about a paper trail leading back to you?'

'I never dealt with anyone in person. And the lock-up's in Nick Hardcastle's name.'

'Clever girl. No wonder you got into Cambridge.'

'Someone with my grades had a one-in-three chance of getting a place at that college,' she said dismissively. 'Anyway, I'm apparently not clever enough: I thought someone at the lock-up company would have recognized his name by now and rung the police to let them know, but it looks like I'm going to have to speed things up if I don't want to stay here for the next ten years.'

Her dad chuckled. 'You know, you take after me in more ways than you realize, sunshine.'

'So will you do it?'

'It's a bit bloody risky. What if they catch me with it?'

'Pretend you didn't know what was in the bag. The alternative is that you end up inside with a nonce tag on your head. I might also consider telling the police about my childhood pal Christie and how one of your nastier film shoots ended up with her accidental suffocation. I've even got a copy of the tape. So don't think about trying to fuck me over, *sunshine*.'

There was no sound on the line except that of her father breathing hard through his nose, trying not to lose his temper. 'Give me your boyfriend's address,' he said.

Nick had gone into the bathroom to freshen up. Olivia waited until she heard him turn the latch, then quickly unzipped her ballgown so it fell to the floor. She picked up the knife she'd taken from the kitchen, the one they used to chop vegetables.

Adrenaline was blitzing through her arteries like lightning. It was neon in her veins. Her eyes were bright and pupils dilated. She looked transformed, a wild animal.

Stalking across the staircase to June's room she silently pushed open the door. June was getting undressed and was wearing just a slip. She had her back to Olivia and didn't see her come in. When Olivia closed the door behind her June heard the click and spun around.

Olivia was standing there, wearing nothing but knickers and a bra. The whiteness of her underwear looked very pale against Olivia's tanned brown skin. June saw the muscles taut underneath, saw Olivia's litheness and strength and understood what this meant even before she noticed the knife.

'Oh my God,' she said.

Olivia launched herself at her. June managed to push Olivia's hand away from its target – June's torso – and instead the knife dragged down her thigh. She began to scream, but Olivia's left hand was already covering her mouth. June smacked her hard in the face, splitting Olivia's lip. As the lip began to bleed Olivia stabbed at her again, having to push between June's fingers and this time she nicked a rib. She took her left hand away from June's mouth and used it to punch her hard in the gut. June lost all the breath in her lungs and stopped trying to scream.

Again and again Olivia lunged at her with the knife. June's hands batted at the blade and sometimes she succeeded in diverting it from its course, but more often than not the knife sunk into her flesh, or sliced through her skin. She kicked out at Olivia and the foot connected hard with Olivia's stomach, sending the girl spinning across the wooden floor. She never let go of her knife.

Olivia jumped to her feet and grinned at June through the blood on her teeth. She was in a crouching position, knees bent, ready to spring.

'No,' said June, palms up. 'No, Olivia, don't, please.' She was bleeding from a dozen different places, her slip soaked with the blood. Red was streaked across the cream-coloured walls.

Olivia leapt at her and June managed to elbow her on her cheekbone. The pain didn't seem even to register. Olivia pushed her back against the wall, forearm under her chin, pressed against her throat so she couldn't breathe. June's hands fluttered against Olivia's face, one of her rings bruising Olivia's brow. She was kicking at Olivia's legs, but the girl stood strong, feet planted on the floor, thigh muscles tensed.

Olivia gripped the knife harder and slid the blade into June's abdomen, just above her pelvic bone. It was buried so deep that the handle was touching the skin. June stopped moving and just stared into Olivia's eyes. Olivia repositioned her grip and, grunting with the effort, dragged the blade up through the front of the girl until it hit the bottom of her ribcage. There was a wet, slithering sound, and June's warm intestines slipped from her and splashed onto Olivia's feet.

Olivia stood back and watched as June, eyes now unfocused and unseeing, slowly slid down the wall and came to rest, askew, on the floor.

Olivia stood there for a moment, getting her breath back, readjusting, putting her mask back on. Then she knelt by June's body and pulled out the knife. She made herself breathe faster and faster until she was hyperventilating, and then she began to scream.

POCKET
BOOKS

Chris Ewan

The Good Thief's Guide to Paris

Flush with the success of his Paris book reading (not to mention
a few glasses of French wine), Charlie Howard – mystery writer
and professional thief – agrees to show a novice how to break
into an apartment on the Marais. Twenty-four hours later,
Charlie's fence hires him to steal an ordinary-looking
oil painting – from the same address.

Mere coincidence? Charlie reckons there's no harm in finding out –
until a dead body shows up in his living room.

Nobody ever said being a burglar was easy but things are getting
way out of control. And that's before Charlie's agent, Victoria,
finally decides they should meet face to face …

ISBN 978-1-84739-359-3
PRICE £6.99

POCKET
BOOKS

Chris Ewan

The Good Thief's Guide to Amsterdam

In Amsterdam working on his latest novel, Charlie is approached
by a mysterious American who asks him to steal two apparently
worthless monkey figurines from two separate addresses on the
same night. At first he says no. Then he changes his mind. Only
later, kidnapped and bound to a chair, the American very dead,
and a spell in police custody behind him, does Charlie begin
to realise how costly a mistake he might have made.

The police think he killed the American. Others think he knows
the whereabouts of the elusive third monkey. But for Charlie
only three things matter. Can he clear his name? Can he
get away with the haul of a lifetime? And can he solve
the gaping plot-hole in his latest novel?

'Intelligent and witty, with a lightness of tone more P. G.
Wodehouse than James Ellroy' *Sydney Morning Herald*

ISBN 978-1-84739-127-8
PRICE £6.99

**POCKET
BOOKS**

This book and other **Pocket Books** titles are available from
your local bookshop or can be ordered direct
from the publisher.

Free post and packing within the UK
Overseas customers please add £2 per paperback.
Telephone Simon & Schuster Cash Sales at Bookpost
on 01624 677237 with your credit or debit card number,
or send a cheque payable to Simon & Schuster Cash Sales to:
PO Box 29, Douglas, Isle of Man, IM99 1BQ
Fax: 01624 670923
Email: bookshop@enterprise.net
www.bookpost.co.uk

Please allow 14 days for delivery. Prices and availability
are subject to change without notice.